Sword of State

Nigel Tranter

coronet

CORONET BOOKS
Hodder & Stoughton

Copyright © 1999 by Nigel Tranter

The right of Nigel Tranter to be identified as the Author of
the Work has been asserted by him in accordance with the
Copyright, Designs and Patents Act 1988.

First published in Great Britain in 1999
by Hodder and Stoughton
First published in paperback in 1999
by Hodder and Stoughton
A division of Hodder Headline

A Coronet Paperback

10 9 8 7 6 5 4 3 2 1

A CIP catalogue record for this title is available
from the British Library

ISBN 0 340 69673 7

Printed and bound in Great Britain by
Mackays of Chatham, plc, Chatham, Kent.

Hodder and Stoughton
A division of Hodder Headline PLC
338 Euston Road
London NW1 3BH

SWORD OF STATE

Standing alone, Patrick bit his lip.

Then there was a surprise after all this. Suddenly the door was thrown open, and a youth came out to gaze, eyes alight, a slender, good-looking but urgent-seeming character, lips parted. And behind Patrick, everyone in the hall stood.

There was no doubt that this was the king himself, Alexander the Second.

"You are Cospatrick!" the youth jerked. "My kinsman!"

"Not Cospatrick, Sire – just Patrick." Not the ideal start perhaps, to correct the monarch. "Cospatrick is my father, the earl. Who sends his greeting and salutations."

Alexander waved that aside. "You are my late sister's son. And we have never met! This is good. I have ever wished to meet the Cospatricks. My father ..." He left the rest unsaid. "Where have you come from?"

"Dunbar, Sire. On the coast of Lothian."

"I have never been there. I have been to Haddington." He gripped Patrick's arm. "Why have we never met?"

That was a difficult question to answer, there and then, with all in the hall listening. "Our fathers, Your Grace ... disagreed! Latterly. As I understand it. But, now – he sends me with goodwill."

Principal Characters in order of appearance

Patrick, Master of Dunbar: Son and heir of the earl thereof, of ancient line.

Cospatrick, 5th Earl of Dunbar: Great Scots noble, of royal blood.

Alan Dorward, Earl of Atholl: High Justiciar.

Alexander the Second: Young King of Scots.

William, Bishop of St Andrews: Primate of the Scots Church.

Walter, High Steward: Seneschal, great officer of state.

William: Second son of Earl Cospatrick.

Farquhar Macantagart: Earl of Ross.

Lady Beatrix Stewart: Wife of the High Steward.

Euphemia Stewart: Daughter of above.

Christian Stewart: Younger daughter of above.

Walter de Gray, Archbishop of York: Metropolitan of the North.

Richard de Maresco, Prince-Bishop of Durham: Great English prelate.

Sir Hubert de Burgh: Great Chamberlain of England, later Earl of Ulster.

William, Earl of Pembroke: Lord Marshal of England.

Henry Plantagenet: King Henry the Third of England.

Ada: Daughter of the Earl Cospatrick.

Princess Joanna: Sister of Henry the Third.

Sir Duncan Campbell of Lochawe: Great Highland chieftain.

Ken Douglas: Scots wool merchant in Veere, the Netherlands.

Olaf Godfreyson, the Morsel: King of the Isle of Man.

Alan, Lord of Galloway: Great Scots noble.

John de Baliol: Lord of Barnard Castle, Durham.

Lady Devorgilla: Wife of above, daughter of Alan of Galloway.

Thomas the Bastard: Illegitimate brother of Devorgilla.

Walter Comyn, Earl of Menteith: Great Scots noble.

David de Bernham, Bishop of Dunkeld: Later Primate.

Deacon-Cardinal Otho: Papal legate.

Eleanor of Provence: Queen of Henry the Third.

Marie de Coucy: Second Queen of Alexander.

Ranald MacDonald of the Isles: Great-grandson of Somerled.

Walter Bisset, Lord of Aboyne: Northern noble.

Sir David de Lindsay: Grandson of Patrick of Dunbar, laird of Luffness.

Louis the Ninth: King of France, known as St Louis.

PART ONE

1

Patrick eyed his father doubtfully, as well he might. This all seemed to signify a notable change of tune on the older man's part – and *he*, it appeared, was to play the tune.

"You would have me to go to the dead Lion's den, and salute his cub?" he demanded. "You, sir, who ever preferred the Black Boar to the Red Lion! You are changing your colours?" Patrick was noted for his sense of humour; but this, perhaps, was taking a risk with it.

The earl tightened his lips for a moment, and then shrugged. "Lad, you will do as I say. *I* do not change, but circumstances may. I desire to know these circumstances. And you are the only one who will discover them for me, for *us*. To go myself would not serve. But I must know, and be sure."

"So! I am to be the pigeon to test the new young hawk!" Patrick was fond of his father, and they got on well normally; but he had been reared to speak his mind, like all of their ancient line.

Cospatrick diffused the incipient tension, smiling briefly. "Make up your mind, boy. Is it a lion's cub or a hawk that you go to?"

It was the son's turn to shrug. "Either way I am the bait, it seems. What shall I say? What excuse do I give? This Alexander, although only sixteen years, will know well enough of our challenge and claims. He is no fool, they say. And he will have his father's lords around him, advising."

"No doubt. But they, and he himself, will not wish to provoke us. Even that Dorward! Not at the start of the new reign. But to go myself would be unwise, I judge. As though seeming to yield in our claim. You they will not see thus."

"But they may see me as possible pawn, a sort of hostage! For *your* good behaviour."

"No. They will not wish to arouse me against them. See you, Patrick, here is a notable part which only you can play. Important it may be, for our line."

The son shrugged again and then nodded. "I see it, yes. But will our line ever hope to come into its own? Whatever we say or do?"

"If right and justice prevail, one day it may. I told William that, after he shamefully paid homage to English King John in London. Until then I had given him support against the English. After all, your mother, Ada, was his bastard daughter. But after that, in London, no more. William the Lion he may have called himself, but he was no lion! Now, as to his young son, we shall see."

None of all this, of course, was new to Patrick. Always the succession of Cospatricks, Earls of Dunbar, had cherished their right, on various grounds, to the throne of Scotland; and their wrath against Malcolm the Third, Canmore, Big Head. For Malcolm it was who had arrogantly, unlawfully, changed the line of succession to the crown after he married Margaret Atheling – if married was the word, for he already had a wife, Ingebiorg, the daughter of the Orkney Earl Thorfinn Raven Feeder, King MacBeth's half-brother. And he had had two sons by Ingebiorg, Duncan and Donald, legitimate. He got rid of Ingebiorg, and named his successors on the throne to be the sons of the new Margaret, a dire act. But the two older sons survived, escaped with the aid of loyal men over into Northumbria and Cumbria. And from there, in due course, after Malcolm's death, Duncan Ban had managed to seize his rightful crown, holding it for only one year as Duncan the Second. But the Margaretsons, all six of them, had put him down; and three of them, Edgar, Alexander and David, had reigned over Scotland in succession. And William the Lion, just dead after fifty years on the throne, was the grandson of David. These Margaretsons, two brothers, had left no competitors for the crown. But there had been a more lawful successor. The ancient Celtic royal house of Scotland had always been unique — save, it was said, for the Jewish realm of old — in that succession was matrilineal, that is the crown passing through the female heiress at each reign, not from father to son. MacBeth had not changed that, after Duncan's death, not his own son but his queen Gruoch's son, Lulach, succeeding. But Malcolm had done so. And there had been a more lawful candidate, Malcolm's own cousin on the female side, Maldred, also a grandson of the Princess Bethoc, daughter of Malcolm the Second. But Maldred had been passed over by Canmore when young; and his son was the first Cospatrick, Patrick-Comes, Patrick the Earl, given the earldom of Northumberland and Dunbar by way of compensation. This should have been the royal line. The fifth of that line stood there now, in Dunbar Castle.

All this complicated and infamous story had been instilled into Patrick since boyhood — for one day he would be Cospatrick the Sixth, God willing.

"So, when do I go to Roxburgh?" he asked.

"Forthwith, lad. Young Alexander should be made aware of our ongoing claim without delay. At but sixteen, and unwed, his hold on the throne is scarcely secure. He has no brother, only three sisters. If he dies or was slain . . . !"

"Do I put it to him? That *we* should succeed? Would that not seem a threat?"

"I do not think that you should put that in words. But . . . implied. Meantime we would hope to support him. It is his advisers that I fear."

"You send me on a hard task, sir."

"I know it. But I have reared you to use your wits, have I not?"

"Very well. Tomorrow . . ."

In the morning it was a forty-five-mile journey almost due southwards, to where Tweed and Teviot joined. Only

5

since King David's days had this been the favoured seat of the monarchy, not Dunfermline in Fife where his kin had dwelled, nor at the great fortress of Stirling, previously the royal base in the centre of the land. Roxburgh was anything but that, within a few miles of the borderline with England. That fluctuating frontier was partly David's concern in making his headquarters there, to emphasise his claims to Northumberland and Cumberland; but also to symbolise his good relationship with England, where he had spent many years as a kind of hostage for his brothers, and had married an English wife, Matilda.

Patrick rode through the Lammermuir Hills, a dozen miles, the greatest sheep-rearing lands in all Scotland and the property of his father, whence came their wealth; indeed much of the country he would traverse that day belonged to the earldom, the Merse as it was named, or the March, the shire of Berwick. By Ellemford and Duns he reached the limits of the territory to which he was heir, just beyond Home, and so passed into the royal lands of Edenham, or Ednam, where the religiously minded King David, in his efforts to promote the influence of Holy Church and limit the powers of his nobles, had established the first of the ecclesiastical parishes in Scotland, a most notable enterprise. From then on all the realm was divided into parishes, but this was the beginning of it all.

Soon thereafter he came to Kelso, or Kelshaugh, names becoming corrupted through time, where David had built one of his many great abbeys, a majestic towering building, another token of his godliness. If only the others of his line had been as excellent monarchs as David, Patrick thought, although his grandson, Malcolm the Fourth, the Maiden, unmarried, had sought to emulate him and had founded the first great hospital in the land, at Soutra in Lauderdale.

Just west of Kelso a mile the two great rivers of Teviot and Tweed joined, and on the arrowhead peninsula where they met soared the castle of Roxburgh, the royal residence, a great and elongated fortalice consisting of a series of towers in line, this positioning dictated by the narrow site above the two wide rivers. Above all these towers flapped the scarlet lion rampant on gold, adopted by the new king's father William the Lion as royal standard, he not having liked wild boars, for long centuries the standard of the Celtic monarchy. If it had been Patrick's father who had been riding here this day it would have been the black boar on silver that he flew. The son was perhaps a little less assertive, and carried no banner.

That may have been a mistake when it came to gaining admittance to the palace stronghold. One young man with only two attendants was not looked upon with any great respect by the royal guards at the gatehouse, despite announcing himself as the Master of Dunbar seeking the King's Grace. He was kept waiting for some considerable time before an individual, declaring that he was the Under-Doorward, loftily came to tell him to follow him within. Patrick did not look for respect from anyone using that style. The Dorward himself, one of the hereditary officers of court – not that he would ever demean himself by acting the conveyer – had the reputation of being one of the most arrogant nobles in the land, far from favoured by Earl Cospatrick. And he spelled his name with only one 0.

Led to the second of the free-standing towers within the outer walling, Patrick was left in an anteroom, his men in the courtyard outside, for a further quite lengthy interval. Then another official came to eye him assessingly and to enquire what was his reason for seeking the royal presence. Patrick curtly told him that that was between himself and the King's Grace. Although the other frowned at this, it was presumably a sufficient response, or the manner of it, to gain further ingress.

Patrick was taken out to still another tower, the largest, a tall keep, where he was conducted upstairs to the withdrawing-room of a vaulted hall, hung with tapestries, and again left alone. He had not realised that gaining young King Alexander's presence would be quite so protracted a process.

A burly man of middle years, richly dressed, anything but welcoming in attitude, arrived presently from the hall.

"You, I am told, are the Master of Dunbar, a Cospatrick," he said. "I am Dorward." Noticeably he did not say *Door*ward. "What, sir, is your business with the king?"

This, then, was the notorious noble from far Aberdeenshire, much decried by Patrick's father. He was Earl of Atholl, as well as being one of the officers of court, and married to one of the late monarch's bastard daughters. But the younger man was not going to concede him any undue deference, for he was of much lesser breeding than the Cospatricks, whatever his reputation.

"I come, my lord, on my father's business with His Grace. And *only* with His Grace." That was said quietly but firmly.

"Indeed! I could deny you audience with King Alexander, young man!"

"Could you? Coming in the name of Cospatrick? I think not." As well that Patrick had been brought up to behave, on occasion, like Cospatrick.

The other, unspeaking, turned abruptly on his heel and stalked back through the doorway, the visitor at his back.

The hall into which he was led was large and well filled with men, all notably well dressed, standing or sitting round a long table, many with flagons in their hands. Patrick did not see any faces he knew. They all eyed him and Dorward, but none did more than that. None was young enough to be the new king.

Dorward strode on to another door at the far end, knocked briefly and, opening it, entered without waiting, and quickly enough to shut it again in Patrick's face. None in the hall took any heed.

Standing alone, Patrick bit his lip.

Then there was a surprise after all this. Suddenly the door was thrown open, and a youth came out to gaze, eyes alight, a slender, good-looking but urgent-seeming character, lips parted. And behind Patrick, everyone in the hall stood.

There was no doubt that this was the king himself, Alexander the Second.

"You are Cospatrick!" the youth jerked. "My kinsman!"

"Not Cospatrick, Sire – just Patrick." Not the ideal start perhaps, to correct the monarch. "Cospatrick is my father, the earl. Who sends his greeting and salutations."

Alexander waved that aside. "You are my late sister's son. And we have never met! This is good. I have ever wished to meet the Cospatricks. My father . . ." He left the rest unsaid. "Where have you come from?"

"Dunbar, Sire. On the coast of Lothian."

"I have never been there. I have been to Haddington." He gripped Patrick's arm. "Why have we never met?"

That was a difficult question to answer, there and then, with all in the hall listening. "Our fathers, Your Grace . . . disagreed! Latterly. As I understand it. But, now – he sends me with goodwill."

"So! I am glad. But come you!" Still clutching Patrick's arm he turned to lead him into another withdrawing-room. "You have come from this Dunbar? Today? Long riding."

The smaller chamber seemed full of men also, perhaps ten of them, only Dorward of Atholl known to the visitor. All were eyeing the pair heedfully.

"Here is Cospatrick. Or just Patrick, he says. Kin to myself. Is it not strange? A sister's son. He has ridden far." Alexander did not introduce any of the company there, all fairly elderly men, the late monarch's officers and advisers.

"I am William, Bishop of St Andrews," a tall stooping man announced. "I know your father, Master of Dunbar. The Earl Cospatrick. As do others here." That was carefully said, as was not to be wondered at in the circumstances, the Cospatricks having long been not outlaws but uncooperative.

"It is, I hope, good to see you here, in His Grace's presence," another said, a good-looking, greying-haired individual. "I am Walter, the High Steward, Seneschal."

"My lords," Patrick said briefly, "I greet you all." That committed him to nothing.

Alexander nodded. "These are all the realm's great ones," he declared. "The High Chamberlain. The Knight Marischal. The Chancellor. The Justiciar. The Crowner. The, the . . ." His voice tailed away, as though he could not remember all the styles and titles.

Men inclined their heads, and for moments no one spoke.

Patrick recognised himself to be anything but welcome, save by the young monarch himself. He had known that this was going to be a difficult mission admittedly, but his various notions, on the way, had been of what he would say to the king, rather than to an array of distance-keeping magnates. But he had to say something.

"I come to wish His Grace well, on his accession to the throne. As does my father. I, I have matters to tell His Highness."

"Yes," Alexander said. "We must talk." He grinned. "I am your uncle, am I not?"

The High Steward it was who came to the rescue. "Sire, I think that we should leave you to speak with the Master of Dunbar alone," he suggested, glancing at his companions.

"That is best," Bishop William agreed. "Summon us when you require us, Sire." And he moved for the door.

The others, eyeing each other, began to follow him, some looking doubtful, especially Dorward. But the king's obvious approval of the move meant that none could refuse.

They filed out, closing the door behind them.

Alexander pointed after them. "They are all so *old*!" he declared.

Patrick nodded. "Your royal father's men. But I am five years older than Your Grace myself!"

"Are you? But that is different. They are so grave, so long of face! The Steward and the bishop are the best. But I find them . . . trying. All telling me what I should be doing. Do not do this. Do not do that. Is your father so? It

10

should be this way, not that. They are all wise, no doubt, but so heavy with it, so dull." Clearly Alexander was badly needing someone to confide in, to spill his youthful frustrations upon, someone nearer to his own age.

He went over to a table whereon were wine flagons and goblets and sweetmeats, he reaching for one of the last. "Take what you will," he invited. "There are wines and ales and these. Do I call you Patrick, then? Or Master? Not Cospatrick. Why this?"

That was as good an opening as any for what Patrick had to say. "Cospatrick, Sire, refers only to the one man, the head of the line. I know that we are called the Cospatricks, but only my father is that, meantime, the Earl Cospatrick. It is the ancient tradition. From the time, over one hundred and fifty years ago, when your forebear, and ours, changed the succession to the throne. Since then we have kept the style as a kind of token, a reminder." He could hardly say a claim to the throne.

"I have been told this of the succession. A strange matter. My father never mentioned it to me. But others have. Do you say that I am not truly the king? That you, or your father, should be?"

"No, Sire. You are the crowned and anointed monarch, King of Scots. We do not dispute it. Only that our ancient right is not forfeited, the descendants of the elder son. Of the same father, Malcolm the Third. I am here to assure you of my father's support. And mine. But to . . . remind you of all this."

"What would you have of me then, Patrick? Thus, Patrick, I call you? Yes? What is your other name? Patrick what? Dunbar?"

"No, Sire, just Patrick. We have no other name. Nor have you! You are just Alexander. Alexander the Second. Unless you name yourself Alexander mac William, after the ancient fashion. We have the same blood, of the old Celtic line of kings. No family name."

"I have it now. We are kin, then. In more than you being my sister's son. I never knew Ada. She was . . ."

11

"Yes. A bastard daughter of your father the king. One of not a few! She died fifteen years ago. I have a younger brother, William, whom she died giving birth to. And a sister, another Ada."

Alexander helped himself to another of the oatmeal cakes. "This is all good to know," he said, his mouth full. "I like you, Patrick!"

"Your Grace is kind . . ."

"This of Grace and Sire. Need you so call me, Patrick? Since we are kin." He smiled. "I would not have you call me Uncle! But when we are alone, Alexander will serve. Or Alex, as my sisters used to call me. I never see them now."

"As you will, Alex. But only when we are alone. And my brother and sister call me Pate!"

"Ha – Pate! I like that. Pate and Alex. I have three sisters, all much older. And all were married to Englishmen, and live in England. Why this, I know not."

"Your father, Sire – Alex – having made a compact with the English king, to pay him homage, chose to wed his daughters to English lords thus, part of the bond. This so that he could gain the return of Northumberland and Cumberland to Scotland. Our families' lands. Also why he wed your own mother as his second wife. This was when my father fell out with yours. For making such compact with the English. We, the Cospatricks, had held Northumberland and Cumberland since Malcolm Canmore's time. We were prepared to hold them by armed strength, not by paying fealty to the English king, as liege-lord. King William allowed himself to be brought into King Henry's presence, as prisoner, with his feet shackled beneath his horse's belly as sign of his homage. My father saw it, and returned to Scotland. Thereafter, William agreed with Henry, in the Treaty of Falaise, and he too returned to Scotland. That was before you were born, or myself. Since then, the Cospatricks have remained . . . aloof! Rightly or wrongly."

This was one part of what Patrick had come to say. Whether he had said it well or poorly he did not know. Had

12

he been somewhat unfair to the late William? But it was important that the new monarch should know the truth – if he had not known of it already.

"My father saw it all differently, I think. Not as *I* would, it may be. He saw peace as all-important. And would pay what price it demanded. And, and he reigned for longer than any other King of Scots!"

"That is true. But . . ." Patrick was doubtful indeed as to how to put the other vital matter that he had been sent to say, no easy task. "This of the succession," he went on, somewhat hesitantly. "We, the Cospatricks, support you on the throne, Alex. But after you? What then? It is . . . uncertain."

"After me? What mean you?"

"It is this of you being young. You have no close heir, no *male* heir. And Scotland has never had, nor desired, a queen-regnant. Only queens-consort. Your sisters, there-fore, would not serve if you were to die. And with English husbands. You are not yet wed. You may have sons, yes. Probably will. But, if not?"

"Die? You fear that I may die?"

"No. Not that. But we all could die. Or be slain, see you. Especially if there was to be war with England. And then?"

"Then you would wish to take the throne?"

"Mmm. Would it not be just? Our line sprung from the elder son of Canmore. Who *is* your nearest heir, Alex?"

"I know not. My great-grandsire, David, had but the one son, Henry of Huntingdon, who died before his father. Henry left two sons, Malcolm the Fourth, my uncle, and William, my father. Malcolm never wed. And I am my father's only son. Did David's brothers, who reigned before him, Edgar and Alexander, leave any sons? I have not heard of such."

"I think not."

"So you, or your father, could be my heir! I had not thought of that."

"It could be, yes. Let us hope, pray, that it would never come to that. That you would one day have your own son to succeed you. And you reign as long as your father. But . . ."

"We are more than just kin, then, Pate! We are closer than I knew. None has told me of this. If I have no son, you could be king one day."

"I am older than you, and could well die first. But if it was accepted, understood, that the Cospatrick line would then succeed, that would be just, fair. An ancient wrong righted."

"That is true. Good! We shall make it so, then. I will tell them all. Those old men!"

"Probably it will never come to that, Alex. You will wed and have sons. But the thing should be known. That was my father's message. In all loyalty to yourself."

"Yes. Then, you will be much at my court here? That will be good, Pate. We will be together much. I will like that. I get so weary of these men whom my father left to surround me. And I have no other younger friends. You will be my companion, no? You will do that? Come here to my side. And soon?"

"If so Your Grace commands."

"I do! I do!"

It was as simple as that, Patrick's task over, fulfilled, and satisfactorily. For he liked this royal youth, felt strangely close to him already. Somehow they seemed to match, to suit each other. And he, Patrick, could do with some getting away from Dunbar Castle, fond as he was of his family; a young man, now of full age, he often felt the need, as it were, to stretch his wings. This of attending on the king now and then would be an opportunity, a worthy one. And his father would see it so, undoubtedly.

"Are you an archer?" Alexander asked. "I much like archery. I am good at it. None of these others do it. I have to do it alone. I have many bows. I have a target-place down by the Tweed. But I shoot at hares, foxes, even roe-deer when I can. But these lords frown on it. They call it child's play."

"I have not done much at it," Patrick admitted. "I can use bow and arrow, but only now and then."

14

"I once shot a heron in flight! Tomorrow, Pate, will you come shooting with me?"

"If you wish it, yes. But I am not very good at it, see you."

"I will teach you . . ."

A tap at the door from the hall, and Dorward appeared. "Sire, the evening meal is prepared. They are laying the tables now in the dining-hall. If Your Grace is ready, we will move down to it." That sounded more like a summons than an intimation.

"Yes, Sir Alan, we will come. I am hungry. Are you, Pate? You have ridden far. Come."

Dorward led the way out, looking with no favour on Patrick. Few men were now in the hall, and none was of the great ones.

Downstairs in the vaulted lower hall, near the kitchens, most were already seated at the three tables, two lengthwise and one crosswise on the upraised dais at the far end. All stood, however, for the royal entry, with the High Seneschal announcing the King's Grace.

Patrick hesitated. The lower tables had benches for seating; but up at the dais there were chairs, nine of them, the central one and another at one end empty. Dorward strode on. Patrick hung back, looking for a seat at one of the lower tables.

But Alexander realised that behind him his new friend was no longer coming on at his heels. He turned. "Come you with me," he said. "Up there."

Decidedly doubtfully Patrick followed on again. There were only the two vacant seats up on the dais, the centre one obviously for the king, the other no doubt for Dorward. Officers of state and the like occupied the others. Where was he, Patrick, to go?

Alexander had no doubts. Climbing up the dais steps, he gestured to one of the servitors standing there on the platform's rear, waiting. "Another chair," he ordered, and pointed.

Dorward, conducting the king to his throne-like seat,

eyed Patrick less favourably than ever. Other eyebrows there rose also. But Alexander knew what he wanted. He went to his central chair, beckoning Patrick forward. Reaching it, he pushed it a little to one side, and, smiling to the man standing next to it on his right, Walter the High Steward, indicated that he should move his chair a little aside to make room for another. The Steward, with a slight shrug, edged his seat sufficiently. Alexander remained standing, awaiting the extra chair called for – and so long as the monarch stood, all must stand.

Fortunately the servitor was not long in coming with the extra seating, and under royal direction this was pushed in between the Steward's place and the throne. Alexander waved for Patrick to take it, and only then sat down, and all could do the same.

It was only a small and unspoken gesture, but a significant one, however many elderly lips were tightened.

Patrick sat on the king's right, next to the High Steward of Scotland.

The Seneschal, whom most were not yet used to thinking of as the Lyon King of Arms, called on William, Bishop of St Andrews, the Primate, on the monarch's other side, to say grace-before-meat.

Embarrassed by all this, Patrick, after the intercession, turned to the Steward. "I regret inconveniencing you, my lord," he said. He was thankful that it was the Steward, one of the only two who had acknowledged his first arrival with anything like welcome.

"His Grace is to be obeyed," the other said. "Your father, the earl – he is in good health?"

"Yes. He sent me, with his greetings, to His new Grace. With goodwill and support."

"That is well. We see little of him, these days."

Patrick was spared the answering of that by Alexander whispering in his ear. "The Steward is the best of them! I do not like that Dorward. Nor . . ." He left the rest unsaid.

The repast began to be served, a handsome one, to which

16

Patrick did full justice, as did his liege-lord. It was not any banquet, but with salmon, venison, swans' flesh and wild duck, all washed down with mead, wines and ale, it was the finest Patrick had partaken of for long. At the sweetmeats course, musicians struck up in the minstrels' gallery, and Alexander told his friend that if he had known that he was coming, he would have had dancers, jugglers, even the performing bear, to entertain them.

The music and dancing went on and on, and presently Patrick was smothering yawns, for he had left Dunbar at dawn for his lengthy ride through all the ranges of hills. Alexander saw it, and declared that he was ready for bed also. So they rose, as must all others, the instrumentalists halted their offerings meanwhile, and the Seneschal announced that His Grace would retire.

Everyone bowed, and Alexander was led to a door behind the dais, none but Patrick following him. This gave access to a turnpike stairway, which they climbed.

Upstairs two flights, above the upper hall they went, where they were ceremoniously handed over to two armed guards and two serving women who waited there with great jugs of hot water. It occurred to Patrick then that these were the first women he had seen, none in the dining-hall. These Alexander waved away, and taking Patrick's arm, ushered him into a chamber there, closing the door behind them.

It was a bedchamber, wherein were two great beds. But ignoring these, Patrick was led to another door beyond and a second room, this containing only the one bed, but a handsome canopied one, with a steaming tub of water beside it.

"You will share a bed with me, this night, Pate?" Alexander asked. "Then we can talk, before we sleep."

Somewhat taken aback, Patrick hesitated once more. This unexpected royal association was productive of much hesitation. He had never occupied a bed with another in his life, not even with his young brother William, nor with a female, although he was not entirely ignorant of lying

17

alongside a young woman or two, but this in a hay-shed or in a hidden woodland glade.

"If Your Grace so wishes," he said. "But . . . I may not stay awake. It has been a long day."

"You were to name me Alex, were you not? And we shall not talk for long. But in the morning . . ."

"Very well, Alex."

"Mine is a big bed! Room for us both. Better than going to one of those others there. I have never slept beside anyone. Have you?"

"No." Patrick was a little relieved at that last confidence. It sounded as though nothing unnatural was involved. This youth was just lonely. He had not realised how alone a young king could be, however many his elderly attendants.

"Do you wish to wash?" Alexander pointed at the steaming tub. "I will not trouble with that. And the garderobe is yonder." He gestured to a little recess, with drain, in the thickness of the walling.

Patrick was glad to use both the tub and the sanitary arrangements, elementary as they were. When he had finished, the king was already in bed.

"Tomorrow shall we shoot our arrows down at Tweed? Or go riding, with the bows, and hope for something to shoot at?" Alexander asked. "Or both. When I go a-horse, they always send men with me, guards. So foolish! For with a number of men, no game is like to be seen. The guards for my protection and dignity, they say! Who is going to assail me? But down at the riverside, where I can be watched from the castle here, I can be alone."

"Perhaps if I am with you, Alex, your lords will spare you the guard? But I might be the better of some trial at a target first." As Patrick was completing his undressing, the other was watching interestedly. "As I said, I seldom practise archery."

"Yes. Then we will do that first. Then go riding. But I fear they will send guards with us."

Getting into the wide bed and under the blankets,

naked, Patrick kept well to his own side. But his companion did not move closer, mind wholly on the kind of sport he favoured.

"For shooting at deer or hares the crossbow is best, although not so long in range, nor so fast with fresh arrows," he said.

"I am better with the crossbow, yes."

"The longbow in the morning. Crossbows later. There is a wood up Teviotdale where we often see deer. Not very far. Do you know these parts, Pate?"

"Not well, no."

"They are very different, Tweed and Teviot."

"Mmm." That was drowsy.

"I have been right to the head of Tweed, a very long river. One of the longest in the land, they say. And up on Tweedsmuir, Clyde and Annan also rise. Did you know that?"

No answer. Patrick was already asleep.

After an undisturbed night, in the morning the royal servants brought breakfast up to the king's anteroom when summoned, which spared Patrick the company of hostile-seeming magnates. Alexander said that the High Chamberlain, or more frequently his deputy, came to see him after breakfast; to say what was to be done that day, and if the royal presence was required for any important matter, affairs of state, receiving missions, and the endless signing of papers, deeds, charters and the like. How he hated all that, quills and ink and paper! He seemed to spend a lot of his life signing documents. Every sale of land all over the kingdom appeared to require his signature. Why others could not sign in his name he did not know, with the royal seal to cover it.

That led to Patrick mentioning the matter of regency. Was it not usual for a monarch, if under full age, to have a regent who could aid him, guide him, deputise for him? He had none, had he?

Alexander declared that this had been his father's wish

for him. No one regent, but a council of ministers. One of King William's last decisions. He had feared, it was thought, that there would be much rivalry for the position, leading to trouble in the realm, and had chosen thus, for which his son was grateful. For he might have had Dorward, who was also High Justiciar, as regent, or the Comyn Earl of Buchan.

They were selecting longbows and crossbows, and the different sorts and lengths of arrows to suit them when the High Chamberlain arrived at the royal suite on his routine daily call. He proved to be an old man and frail-seeming, Sir Philip de Valognes, who had been Chamberlain to King William for forty years, indeed then succeeding his own father, one of the English friends King David had brought north with him on his accession to the throne. He considered Patrick from rheumy ancient eyes, but showed no animosity. Alexander got in first, and announced that they were going down to Tweedside for archery and later would go hunting with crossbows. He would not require an escort, for the Master of Dunbar had two men with him who would serve for that. De Valognes did not counter this or comment, but said that there were a number of documents awaiting His Grace's signature in the hall below. If these could be dealt with first, it would be best. Making a face at Patrick, the king said that they would be down shortly, and the Chamberlain took his leave.

"Papers! Papers!" Alexander said. "Ever he is at me for signing. It is not his fault, I suppose. He is quite a worthy old man, better than most of them that I have to heed. But ancient!"

They went down presently, and there was indeed a deal of paper and parchment, with an inkhorn and spare quills, awaiting the royal hand, with de Valognes ready with lit candle, beeswax and the privy seal to confirm the signatures. Alexander did not read any of the writings presented to him by a clerk, Patrick noted.

Hurried through, it did not take so very long; and then, with bows and arrows, they went down to the courtyard,

20

hurrying lest the king got waylaid by other dignitaries, and out through the gatehouse arch. The Tweed flowed strongly on the north side of the castle's peninsula, with a strip of meadowland intervening. Down there a shed contained Alexander's targets, skin covered and padded life-size effigies of roe-deer and hares, the padding necessary to retain the arrows. They brought out one each of these, and set them up.

"Seventy yards," Alexander said, beginning to pace out the distance. "Or would you wish it one hundred? For the longbow?"

"I may be no better at seventy than one hundred. You choose."

"Seventy, then. Judging the arc of it is more difficult the longer the range."

"Yes. Unlike the crossbow, where you aim direct. Much simpler."

"But less powerful and lacking the range."

They took up their stance and tightened the strings of their bows, testing the tension, then fitting the arrows.

The king shot first, calculating the trajectory, for at that range, and further, it was not a case of aiming straight at the target but of allowing for the curving flight of the feathered arrow. And as his bow twanged, Alexander jerked a curse. "Too much to the right," he declared; and before that was out the arrow was projecting from the rump of the stuffed deer only just short of the tail. "Poor! Poor!"

Patrick lined up his bow, not very confidently, calculated the required height of the flight, and loosed off. The arrow soared, the line accurate enough but the height wrong. It disappeared well above the target.

"I told you that I was no longbowman!"

"Try again, Pate. Lower."

"After you, Alex."

The other's second shot hit the stuffed deer in mid-belly, which Patrick thought was good enough, but the youth pronounced poor again, for he had aimed for the heart, just behind the fore-shoulder.

21

Patrick's next arrow got the height right but the line wrong, missing the target once again.

"Let us try the hundred yards," the king suggested.

So they paced another thirty yards back, and shot again. This time Patrick's arrow hit the ground just in front of the objective, and Alexander's scored another hit, but not quite where he wanted it.

Patrick cast down his bow. "I am just wasting arrows," he declared. "*You* continue, Alex."

"It will come, if you keep on trying . . ."

There was little improvement on that man's part until, oddly enough, with his companion scoring well, Alexander decided to try the smaller target, the stuffed hare; and Patrick's first shot scored a hit, even though only just. Loud was the monarchial praise, even when Alexander himself did better still, and carried the hare some distance back.

But that was the height of Patrick's achievement. Thereafter he kept missing, and soon they had run out of arrows and had to go seeking to retrieve the missing shafts, which took some searching and time.

Then it commenced to rain, and they agreed that enough was enough. They returned to the castle.

With the rain continuing, and any hunt less than inviting, Patrick decided that he might as well head for home, cloaked against the weather, although against Alexander's wishes, who would have had him stay for another night at least. But the Earl Cospatrick would be expecting his son's return, and they ought to be able to make Dunbar before dark.

So after a meal, it was farewell meantime, with a promise to return to the royal presence, and soon.

It had been a strange and unexpected interlude, but as pleasing as it might be significant. Who knew what all this might lead to? Clearly Patrick would have to improve on his archery if he was to become some sort of courtier.

2

Earl Cospatrick stared at his son. "You are telling me that young Alexander is for making a *friend* of you! That you actually shared a bed with him last night! The Lion's cub! This is scarce believable."

"It is true, sir. He insists that I call him Alex when we are alone. And myself he names Pate. He is good company. And lonely. I had not realised how alone a king can be. Especially a young one. Being so cut off, as it were. Despite being surrounded all the time by lords, councillors, courtiers . . ."

"He is only sixteen years, yes. But you are now a full man."

"But five years between us. And he is, in many ways, old for his years. He has had only elderly company all his days. An aged father, and much older sisters, married off to Englishmen and away. Alexander is in need of closer company. And . . . I like him."

"This is extraordinary. The Cospatricks and the royal . . . usurper!"

"You, sir, married one of William's daughters, my mother."

"Illegitimate, yes. My father, your grandsire, deemed it wise. With William without a son then. We grew happy together. But it was a marriage of . . . expediency. Scarcely of my choosing." The earl waved that aside. "And he, Alexander, would have you to join his court?"

"Yes. At Roxburgh."

"And you? Would that be to your liking?"

"Yes and no. Not the company I would have to keep there. Save for the king's own. And, it may be, one or two

23

others. I found Walter the High Steward not unfriendly. And Bishop William, the Primate. And the Chamberlain, old as he is. They are *all* old, or elderly."

"It comes to us all! And the succession? You spoke of that to Alexander?"

"I did, yes. And he saw it in our way. There is none nearer, indeed, to succeed him, if he has no son, think you, sir? He accepted that without dispute. That is what you wished, is it not? What you sent me there for? I judged that you would be well pleased."

His father nodded. "I am, yes. It is good. I am only surprised at this of friendship. That youth desiring your presence with him. A Cospatrick! We have so long been distant from the throne. But, so be it. If you are content. It should serve our cause. And you will not be with him all the time. I require you here, see you, son. I will miss you." It was not often that the father spoke thus.

"Roxburgh is but five hours of riding, sir. I can be home here often. I, too, will miss Dunbar. And Roxburgh is so different, so enclosed-seeming . . ." And Patrick glanced out through the window.

Certainly Dunbar Castle could not be called enclosed. It was one of the most extraordinarily placed strongholds in the land. Although its gatehouse and entrance tower rose from a cliff-top above the harbour of the quite sizeable town, the rest of the fortalice stretched seawards, this made possible by a series of rock-stacks rising out of the waves, three of them bearing their own towers and all linked by covered bridges of stone. Roxburgh Castle was elongated, but nothing like this one, the total length nearly three hundred yards, this dictated by the distance apart of the tall columns of rock. It was all but impregnable even against cannon, for only the gatehouse tower could be assailed from the land, and even that so placed that the barrels of artillery could not be raised at a sufficient angle to batter it effectively. And attack by sea would be equally unproductive. The Cospatricks had known what they were at when they constructed this curious fortress.

Father and son were presently in the first and largest of the stack towers, which formed the principal living quarters for the family, with the best accommodation. But Patrick's own chosen roost and bedchamber was in the outermost tower, skied amongst the wheeling, screaming seabirds, its walls and windows often drenched with foam and spray from the crashing seas, a challenging eyrie indeed for a young man. And not only was this a building that seemed to shake its fist in the face of the Norse Sea, but it also posed another and more profitable challenge, this to the fisherfolk of Dunbar. For the gap between this tower and the next landwards was, because of the long and curving pier and breakwater of the harbour, this itself specially constructed for the purpose as well as for sheltering the haven and anchorage, the only access from the sea; so that every fishing-boat had to pass under that last bridge on leaving or returning. This was important for the earl, for part of his dues as superior of the town and its trade was that he received one-tenth of the fishermen's catches, lobsters and crabs as well as fish; and having to pass below that bridge, from which a sort of gate could be lowered, like a portcullis, if this tribute was withheld, was a very effective way of ensuring payment.

Patrick's father, wanting to hear when these new duties with the king were to commence, and being told that it was to be as soon as was convenient, said that he had a task for his son before he departed again for Roxburgh. There was friction, squabbling, between the Abbots of Kelso and Melrose over sheep-grazing rights in the Lammermuir Hills, part of the Dunbar earldom. Cospatrick's father had granted such rights, over a south-westerly portion of the great hill area, to Kelso Abbey when his son had married William the Lion's illegitimate daughter, Patrick's mother, this at the king's behest. But a cousin and close friend of Cospatrick's own, Hugh, had become Abbot of Melrose, a rival establishment, and he had been allotted an adjoining area as a kindly gesture and in order that prayers should be said in perpetuity for his soul in Melrose Abbey;

after all, the earl could afford this, for the Lammermuirs were the greatest sheep-rearing tract in all Scotland, two hundred and fifty miles square, if very rounded, the wool therefrom the most valuable of the realm's exports. Now argument had developed between the two abbots as to the boundaries of their respective areas, or at least between the lay-brother shepherds, with appeals made to the earl for support and favour. Clerics could be just as contentious about their rights as other men. So Patrick was to go and survey the terrain in question, and decide upon a fair solution to the dispute. And it would be best, on this occasion, if he was to take his brother William with him, now aged fifteen; for if Patrick was to be spending much of his time hereafter in the king's company and court, young William would have to begin to take a greater and more useful part in the administration of the earldom.

The next day, then, the two brothers and Patrick's usual pair of attendants set off again for the hills, almost due westwards. William was a cheerful, lively, indeed ebullient youth, all high spirits and noise. Although barely a year younger than King Alexander, Patrick decided that he seemed much more than that, junior as to maturity and responsibility. But he would learn – he would have to. Their sister Ada was, on the other hand, a rather solemn and very serious girl, not beautiful but reliable.

They rode by the villages of Beil, Stenton and Garvald into the grassy and heathery slopes, these positively littered with sheep, the earldom's wealth. As far back as the fifth and sixth centuries these hills had been the source of prosperity, even Loth, who gave his name to Lothian, King of the Southern Picts, having relied on the sheep for his kingdom's main sustenance; indeed despatching his own daughter, Thanea, the mother of St Mungo, to be a shepherdess in these hills in 517, this to teach her to obey her stern father. It was amongst these sheep-strewn slopes that St Mungo had been conceived, he who was to found Glasgow.

Presently the brothers and their escort were passing the

very farmery at Johnscleuch where Thanea had done her shepherding, and allegedly had quite enjoyed it, before she had been raped by a Galloway princeling, whence came her child. Patrick told this story to Will as they rode, the youth demanding details as to the physical aspects of the incident.

Here they were nearing the southern flanks of the range, facing on to the Merse, or March, the heights giving dramatic views of the far Cheviots, the border with Northumbria. These Lammermuirs were not high as Scotland's hills and mountains went, few rising above fifteen hundred feet; but they were very extensive, averaging fully a dozen miles from north to south and twenty-five from east to west.

They reached the headwaters of the Whiteadder, which in due course would become a major river, and there, south-westwards, they were approaching the area under dispute, the hill slopes around the somewhat isolated summits of the two Dirrington Laws, Great and Lesser, this admittedly the furthest away from Dunbar and the harbours for exporting the wool to the Low Countries, which may have had something to do with the two Cospatricks giving to Holy Church. Onward, south and west of these, all the way to Lauderdale, was the land conceded to the churchmen, not given, for it was still the earldom's property, some thirty square miles.

Patrick was making for the farmery of Kilpallet, where the Melrose chief shepherd was said to be based, amongst a welter of minor, grassy hills, little of heather on these south-facing slopes. They found the man at his midday meal, a lay brother named Gavin, with one of his associates. Offering the visitors heather ale and oatcakes, he informed them as to the cause of the altercation between the abbots. It all was concerned with the matter of water boundaries, the headwaters of the Rivers Blackadder and Whiteadder. The Dye Water, a tributary of the latter, was the line separating the two grazing areas. This was no problem where it ran east and west for most of its course.

27

But around the southern side of the quite major hill of Meikle Law, it turned abruptly northwards, or at least two of its main feeding burns did, one on either side of the Law, the Sheil Burn on the west and that of Kersoncleuch on the east, two miles apart. Each abbey was claiming the intervening area as their own, and grazing sheep thereon, the respective shepherds even on occasion coming to blows over it all, with quite a large and worthy grazing involved, their sheep of course becoming hopelessly mixed, and this creating further trouble and complaints. Each side claimed that their grant from the Earl Cospatrick was in their favour, the wording of the charters stating that the Dye Water's main headstream constituted the boundary. The controversy was over which of these two burns was the main headstream. Patrick's grandfather had apparently not given the burn an actual name in his grant to Kelso.

Brother Gavin did not own a horse, so they mounted him behind one of the escorts, and rode on westwards over the slopes. In something over two miles they came to the first of the burns, the Kersoncleuch, which they duly examined for width and flow, a sizeable stream, Meikle Law rising high behind and ahead. Then over the flanks of this hill they proceeded, crossing sundry other lesser burns on the way, Patrick considering all the surroundings heedfully. Will pointed out the mixture of blue and scarlet stains on the animals' haunches, mixed as they were, the marks of the two abbeys' ownership.

On the far side of the hill they reached the Sheil Burn, with Brother Gavin strongly asserting that it was the larger, deeper than the Kersoncleuch, although Patrick would have been hard put to it to say which was indeed the greater, the other insisting that it was so, and that therefore this was the boundary of the Melrose holding. Making no definite decision, they rode on to near the other side's views, the lay brother muttering.

They had almost still another two miles to go to reach a scatter of cothouses and sheds which formed the base of the Kelso herders, the sheep that they passed now all bearing the blue colours. The lay brother in charge here, one John, scowled at Gavin but had to be civil to the Master of Dunbar. He was voluble in his assertion that the Kersoncleuch Burn was larger than the Sheil, and therefore that his grazings went eastwards right to that; and when vehemently challenged by his rival, declared that it had a three-mile-long burn feeding it from the Kilpallet Heights, whereas the Sheil Burn had nothing such. At which Gavin proclaimed that the Sheil was itself much the longer, rising on Willie's Law of the Hope Hills, fully two miles north-west, and therefore must be the greater.

The argument was prolonged and anything but clerical in tone.

Faced with this, and Will all but egging the arguers on, Patrick had to end the unsuitable dispute and come to a decision.

"I see no means by which we can declare one stream larger than another," he said. "They both looked very similar to me. But I noted, as we came round the side of Meikle Law, that we crossed, amongst many small streams, one quite large. Indeed at first I assumed that to be the Sheil Burn, but was told that it was not. I would say that it was more or less midway between the other two. So, since *I* have to make the decision, in my father's name, I say that this one should be the boundary between your two holdings. Which is fair to you both. What is its name?"

Gavin looked sour. "It is not important, my lord. It has not got a name."

"A mere trickle, my lord," John declared. "Not worthy of a name."

"Nevertheless, my friends, that will be the march between your two holdings. This is my decision. We shall call it the Betwixt Burn! This side of it will be Kelso's grazing, beyond it Melrose's. The Betwixt Burn!"

Silence from the lay brothers.

"So be it. Tell your abbots, in due course. A fair division. Your sheep will still mingle, since there are no walls or fences. If this troubles you overmuch, you can use your shepherds to build a long wall, or dig a deep dyke or ditch. That is your decision. You have mine." Playing the earl's son and heir, Patrick waved a hand. "We will return to Dunbar." Will grinned and made a face.

They went back to the horses, Brothers Gavin and John not exchanging fare-thee-wells.

One day Patrick would presumably succeed his father as Justiciar of Lothian. He had made his first judicial pronouncement.

That evening Cospatrick applauded his son's decision, declaring that although it was a small matter it could have its significance. The abbots could scarcely contest it, and it might bring peace between them, which was surely worth the doing?

3

A week later, then, Patrick set off for Roxburgh, for an indefinite stay, assuring his father that he could be back at Dunbar, if need be, at a day's notice. Cospatrick suggested that he called in at Melrose Abbey on his way, to assure his friend Abbot Hugh of his good wishes, and to tell him that if he felt so inclined his shepherds could use a stretch of land east of their present boundary in compensation for the loss of grazing on Meikle Law – but not to reveal this offer to Kelso.

The call at Melrose, under the three Eildon summits, involved some slight diversion westwards from the most direct route to Roxburgh, but not sufficient to delay Patrick greatly. He found his far-out kinsman Hugh there amiable enough and registering no complaints, but glad to avail himself of the extra ground eastwards of Kilpallet. For the further east his sheep could graze, of course, the shorter the distance for their wool to be transported to the harbours of Dunbar itself, Eyemouth and Berwick, for profitable export.

But that evening, at Roxburgh Castle, the matter of sheep walks and bickering abbots was swiftly driven from Patrick's thoughts by a vastly more serious development nationally. This was revolt in the realm, in the north-east Highlands. Donald Ban mac William mac Kenneth mac Heth mac Malcolm had raised Moray and Nairn and Badenoch against the young king, claiming that *he* was the rightful occupant of the throne, and calling for a general uprising to support him, especially from the High-land chiefs. Alexander's reign had thus hardly begun before he was faced with challenge and civil war.

Patrick was much concerned, and not only for his young monarch, but because this Duncan was seeking to undermine the Cospatricks' own rightful claim of succession. He was indeed a very distant kin of their own, descended from Ethelred, third of the Margaretsons, who had rejected his mother's Roman Catholic faith and returned to his father's ancient Celtic Church, and been banned from the succession therefore, in favour of his younger brothers, Edgar, Alexander and David. His son, settled in the Highlands, had taken the name of MacEth or Heth. So in fact this Duncan was senior in line to the present royal family, but less senior than the Cospatricks, who stemmed from Malcolm Canmore's earlier sons by Ingebiorg.

Alexander was very much put about, as were his advisers. He told Patrick that he wanted to muster an army and lead it himself against these insolent Highlandmen. But his lords would not hear of it. He was much too young to become involved in war and battle. He had a sufficiency of others whose place it was to deal with such treachery, the High Justiciar, the Knight Marischal, even the High Steward. In fighting these Highlandmen in their own difficult country, where ambushes and mountain passes and lochs had to be coped with, it was best to have one of their own kind leading, guiding. It was suggested that Farquhar, Earl of Ross, known as Mac-in-t'-Sagairt, the Son of the Priest, was the man to use in this, believed to be loyal to the crown, which could not be said of many of the Highland chiefs with any confidence. So, a deputation to go up to Dingwall, in Ross, and rather than seek to muster and lead a Lowland army which could well be at a distinct disadvantage in those Highland fastnesses, try to enrol this Farquhar.

When they were alone, Alexander said, "Pate, I am thankful that you have come, and now. They will not have me to go up to Ross. Will you go for me? To see that all is well done, that there is no ill to come out of it between these lords and the Highlandmen. I do not trust all of these old men whom my father has left me with. This Earl of

Ross, with the strange name – I know him not. He, or even some of my lords here, might think that this Duncan could make a better king. Older, better for their own interests. Will you go, Pate?"

"If you wish it, Alex, yes. But surely you can trust some, the Steward, the Marischal. And others?"

"The Steward, yes. But not all of them. Some do not like me, that I know well. They mislike having to serve one whom they still look on as a child. That Dorward of Atholl. And Comyn, Earl of Buchan."

"Very well. When do we go?"

"They say not yet. It is still late winter, and the Highland passes are blocked with snow at this time. This Duncan will not be able to raise his fullest strength till later because of it. We would wish our strength, or at least the Earl of Ross's, to be mustered first, yes. But, with the passes not yet open, and horses unable to win through . . ."

"If you, or your lords, are sending no army north, Alex, only a few to speak with Ross, give him your royal commands, why go by land, on horse? Go by sea," Patrick suggested. "Once in those Highlands, most travel will be done afoot, besides. Sail up to Ross by boat. Much more speedy and no trouble with snow. Sail to Inverness. Or this Dingwall."

Alexander stared. "A ship! Pate, yes! A large ship. Could we find the like? Then *I* could sail with you, in a ship. We could reach this Highland earl that way. And I could tell him what I wanted myself. Not depend on others. Why has none thought of this?"

"These lords are used to doing all by land, a-horse. The sea never for them. But we Cospatricks live by the sea, at Dunbar. My father has two good ships. We could go in one of them. Our castle reaches out into the waves itself. We *use* the sea."

"This is good. We will do that. Not wait for the Highland snows to melt. You are clever, Pate!" He faltered. 'But they may not all like it well, these old men."

"Does that signify? You are the king. If it is a royal

33

command, they must abide by it, obey. See you, Alex, tell the Steward first. He is the best of them. Leave him to tell the others. Not that many of them need go, no? So long as your royal self, and the Marischal and myself are with you. And the Steward . . ."

They went in search of Walter, the High Steward and Seneschal.

They found him with Bishop William, the Primate, and Bruce of Annandale, in one of the lesser towers. Alexander burst out with the ship suggestion and its benefits with much enthusiasm. At first the older men looked doubtful, but when Patrick joined in, more coherently, they began to look more favourable. When they were assured that one of the Dunbar vessels could have them up at Inverness or wherever the Earl of Ross abode in two days' time, if they were spared head winds, they saw the point and became convinced. And when Alexander made it clear that was his royal decision, they agreed to inform the others of the council. And they accepted that the sooner the move was made, the better. Much cheered, the king left them.

Patrick said that if their move north was to be made shortly, then he ought to return to Dunbar almost forthwith to ensure that a ship and its crew were available and ready for the voyage. So far as he knew, neither of his father's large vessels was away elsewhere at this time; they were most often used to send to the Low Countries with the earldom's wool, returning with cloth and lace, pottery and roof tiles, but this was not the time of year for woolshearing. And the shipmasters and crews were local, and it all should not take long to make ready.

It was agreed that he would be off next day, and the royal party would not be long in following him.

That night Patrick spent in the king's bed again, and only slept after much talk.

Back at Dunbar, Cospatrick had no objections to one of his ships being used, and declared it all a worthy action of his son's, and in fact declared that he himself would accompany this mission to Macantagart, this to emphasise that the Cospatrick succession was senior to that of Duncan Ban; and besides, an earl's presence would not come amiss in support of the monarch. He would order the *Falcon* to be prepared for sea, and have as comfortable berths as was possible made for the distinguished travellers.

All was ready when, six days later, the royal party arrived, amidst flurries of snow, which emphasised the problems of Highland travel, but also might indicate northerly winds, which could delay the ship's progress.

Alexander was much intrigued with Dunbar Castle's dramatic and unique positioning, and although he did not share Patrick's bed that night, he did choose to sleep in the outermost tower, despite the noise of the waves and seafowl. At first he showed himself as somewhat in awe of the Earl Cospatrick, whom he had been reared to think of as something of a threat to the crown; but that man sought to dispel any such impression; and the fact that he was electing to come north with them helped to quell any doubts. Included in the company were Sir Philip Keith, Great Marischal, Sir David Hay and Sir William Bruce of Annandale, together with the High Steward, all amongst the least elderly of the officers of state.

The *Falcon* was a typical trading ship, of a fair size, single-masted with a large square sail. She was not made for carrying passengers but wool, and the oily smell of the fleeces permeated all. But every effort had been made to improvise reasonable accommodation for these especial voyagers, and the bunks and blankets offered modest comfort. It was hoped that they would not have to be occupied for more than a couple of nights. No complaints were voiced, for none there expected fine quarters, sea travel all but unknown to them. The king was excited by it all, and eager to be off.

The shipmaster, one Rob Meldrum, was somewhat put about by the company he was to transport, needless to say, but under Alexander's questioning and exclamatory interest he soon got used to the royal presence, more so than he did to the lords. The crew, all fishermen, kept their heads down.

They sailed next forenoon, relieved that the wind was from the south-east and that the snow had ceased, cold as it still was. And the breeze helped not only to fill the sail but to dispel the wool smell. The vessel heaved and dipped rhythmically into the Norse Sea swell, but no admissions of seasickness were voiced.

Heading due north, they soon were passing the mighty Craig of Bass, with its myriad of swooping and diving gannets or solan geese, greatly impressing not only Alexander. Then they were crossing the mouth of the Scotwater, or Firth of Forth, fourteen miles across, and sailing close to another very different but famous island, the May, cliff-girt and a mile in length, where six centuries before the Celtic St Ethernan had established the first warning beacon for shipping in all Scotland, to aid mariners to avoid wreck on the rocks and skerries, a most notable accomplishment, since the wood for the beacon fires had to be brought by barge from the Fife shore six miles away, no trees growing on the isle. Cospatrick pointed out that the very fact that this had been considered a necessary objective of Christian charity indicated that sea-going had been much undertaken even in those far-off days.

They then skirted the extreme easterly point of Fife, the territory of the MacDuff earls, one of whom had slain King Macbeth at the behest of the odious Malcolm Canmore. By mid-afternoon they were off a second great estuary, that of Tay, at the mouth of the longest river in the land, many more miles than even Tweed.

Darkness saw them off the Angus coast, near Aberbrothack, they were informed. They ate an evening meal of cold meats washed down with ale, but the movement of the ship tended to limit appetites, and it was not long before bunks were sought. There could be no discrimination between royal, lordly and lesser accommodation here, and they all bedded, without any undressing, where they would, Alexander and Patrick one above the other.

It seemed strange to most to be sailing, asleep, through the darkness, leaving all to God and the presumably wakeful shipmen.

Daylight and more cold meat, fish and oatmeal porridge saw them off what they were told was the north Aberdeen-shire seaboard, the south-east breeze having favoured them. If it continued thus they could be well into the vast Moray Firth by mid-afternoon. After that, it was decided, they would have to proceed more warily. The shipmaster, Meldrum, was not very well acquainted with the coasts as far north as this, but he knew enough to be aware that they could not sail in darkness beyond this Moray Firth, aiming for the Ross earldom's seat of Dingwall, careful navigation very necessary. Had it not been for this of Duncan Ban's raising of Moray against the king, he would have suggested putting into the haven of Inverness for the night; but that town might well be occupied by the enemy. So what was to be looked for was a sheltered anchorage somewhere remote from populous country, where they could lie up safely until daylight. Then on to Dingwall in the morning.

His passengers, used to travel by horseback, were astonished at the speed with which they had reached this far, and said so.

In the late afternoon, the great Spey Bay formed an unmistakeable landmark, and their skipper drew close inshore to seek out a suitable anchorage thereabouts. The mouth of the River Spey itself was not advisable, communities on the fertile land there. But only three or four miles west of it they found a small headland, flanked by tall sand-dunes and no villages in sight; this Meldrum said should serve. Inland, far behind the dunes, they could see snowy mountains.

So the second night was spent, undisturbed, in calm conditions.

By this time the travellers had developed a fairly close companionship inevitably; and fortunately all got on well with each other, Cospatrick more or less assuming the lead, not only because they were in his ship, and he was the only earl present, but because of a kind of inborn authority. Not that he made any display of this, but the potency was there, and somehow accepted. Alexander and Patrick were very much left together, as the younglings, and enjoyed their association the more. They at least, however, would be glad to get ashore and stretch their legs.

At dawn they were on their way again, slightly north by west now, crossing the mouth of the inner firth. The River Ness, entering this, represented the boundary between Moray and Ross, and just north of this lay the great peninsula of Cromarty, a score of miles by eight, with its own firth separating it from Ross proper. Ross, Easter and Wester, was one of the largest provinces in all Scotland, even greater than Moray, and Dingwall its capital at the extreme south-east tip of it all, at the head of the Cromarty Firth, perhaps a strange location for it, dictated by the fact that the province had been dominated by the Norsemen and, very much shipmen, they required a sheltered port for their base, and this at the head of its firth suited them; in fact, Dingwall got its name from the Norse *thing*, meaning council or capital-place.

When the *Falcon* did reach the tip of the Cromarty peninsula, they saw at once why this had been chosen by the Vikings. For the firth had the narrowest entrance of any in the land, a gap of a mere seven furlongs between the Cromarty shore and another peninsula, that of Nigg, although it broadened out into a six-mile width in a twenty-mile estuary thereafter. So it was readily defendable, and as their ship passed through the narrows, all could see stone forts on either side. Today, however, these outposts did not seem to be manned.

With high white mountains ahead, soon they found the firth narrowing again, and twisting as it did so, all providing excellent defence from attack by sea; presumably those mountains and their passes would be equally effective protection by land. The Earl of Ross could not be easily assailed.

When at length they reached the head of the firth, where

the River Conon entered it, there was quite a large township, with quays at the shore, many boats moored there. But none was of the size of the *Falcon*: fishing-craft, small galleys and old-style longships, rather. The arrival of this large trading vessel would undoubtedly cause some stir amongst the inhabitants, especially with the royal lion rampant flying from the masthead.

A castle, not large by Roxburgh and Dunbar standards, rose on an eminence a little way from the town, presumably Farquhar Macantagart's seat. None of the present company had ever met him, great chief as he was, possibly the most powerful man in the Highlands after the Lord of the Isles, to whom he was related. He was only the second earl, but of an ancient line, their style prior to the grant of the earldom being, strangely enough, Hereditary Abbot of Applecross, a Celtic dignity dating from Pictish times, a title of which Farquhar was alleged to be much more proud than that of earl. Applecross was far distant, nearly one hundred difficult, mountainous miles, on the seaboard of Wester Ross facing Skye and the Hebrides, emphasising links with the Lordship of the Isles.

The visitors' arrival was not long in being acknowledged, welcome or otherwise. There was no convenient gap at the quayside for a vessel of the *Falcon*'s size to tie up so Meldrum manoeuvred his ship close to the craft already moored there, as his passengers perceived a party issuing from the castle and coming along the shoreline. This would be their reception. They waited.

When the castle group reached the quay nearby, now backed by many townsfolk watching, the problem of communication presented itself. A voice did hail them from the shore, but unintelligible, thin and in the Gaelic. Meldrum bellowed back that here was the King of Scots come to visit the Earl of Ross. But whether this was heard or understood by the others at over one hundred yards was doubtful.

There was a pause, and then movement. Three of the shore party clambered down from the pier and into a small rowing-boat, and two of them taking the oars, the other casting off, came rowing out. The big man standing in the stern shouted something, again in Gaelic, and then changed it to the visitors' own tongue.

"I am Ranald, steward to Farquhar, Abbot of Applecross and Earl of Ross. Who comes here, flying that banner?"

"Alexander, King of Scots does," he was answered. "I am Walter, High Steward of Scotland. We come to see your earl."

That produced some consultation in the boat, and the oarsmen pulled closer, to lie alongside the *Falcon*'s timbers.

"Come you, then," the big man called.

Cospatrick, frowning, shrugged. "A ladder, Rob. For him to come up," he ordered. "Enough of this shouting."

Meldrum was already having crewmen put a rope-ladder over the side. The man in the boat reached out for it, but did not start to climb.

"Come you," he repeated.

The Lowlanders looked at each other questioningly, all men of rank and standing, not used to climbing down swaying ladders at the behest of a Highlandman.

"This is unsuitable!" Cospatrick declared. "A buffoon! Descending that ladder – it is not for us."

"*I* will do it," Alexander announced. "I can climb down that."

"Sire, no! It is not for you. Lacking all . . . esteem."

"Your Grace should not," added the Steward.

But the king was already moving to the head of the ladder. "I *will*! It is nothing." Undoubtedly the young monarch was eager to show these old men that he was better at something than were they.

Patrick went after him.

Alexander was not to be stopped. Getting over the side and on to the upper rungs of the ladder was the worst of it, with the wood against the ship's timbers; but he managed it effectively enough, while the watchers held their breaths.

40

Then down he went agilely, adjusting to the sway of the vessel which swung the ladder's ropes in and out, to and fro. Before he had reached the fishing-boat, Patrick was following him down, in duty bound.

The Ross steward, after handing Alexander and then Patrick inboard, was gazing up at the ship still, ignoring these two, clearly waiting for more senior men to descend.

"Steward Ranald," Patrick said. "Pay heed, I charge you. This is your liege-lord, King Alexander himself."

The other stared. "The king!" He added something in the Gaelic.

"Yes. His Grace's self."

Alexander, looking up and seeing no sign of any of his lords coming down, grinned. "They are afraid of the ladder!" he asserted. "Take us ashore, Master Steward."

Wagging his head, the big man changed that to a nod, and gestured to his rowers to ply their oars. The boat swung out and headed for the quay, amidst cries from above.

In this strange fashion did Alexander the Second of Scotland come to set foot, for the first time, on his Highland soil.

On the stones of the pier the rest of the castle party waited. And if the steward had seemed large, much more so was the central figure of the group, an enormous man of middle years, clad in a saffron kilted tunic, bare of knees, and with a tartan plaid over his shoulder.

"I am Farquhar Macantagart," he declared, looking at Patrick. "Who are you, at all?"

"Who I am, my lord, is not important," he was told. "But this is the king himself. Come to visit you. However odd the reception!"

"The king? Alastair mac William mac Henry mac David! The Ard Righ," he exclaimed, giving him the Gaelic style. He hooted a great laugh. "Here is a wonder!" And he made a sort of semi-mocking bow. "Welcome to Ross, Sire!"

"You are the earl?" Alexander said. "We have come far

to see you. This is the Master of Dunbar, son of the Earl Cospatrick. *He* is on the ship still."

"Indeed and indeed? And he lets you to come ashore alone, Your young Grace?"

"They are all afraid of the ladder, I think." He added, "I was not."

"Can you arrange for the ship to be suitably berthed, my lord?" Patrick put in. "That they may come ashore with more dignity."

The Earl Farquhar hooted again. He was clearly a man of humour. "Dignity, eh? But not for this one?" And he waved at the king. "But, yes. We will clear some of these boats so that your vessel may reach this quay." He signalled to his steward to see to it. "So you are Dunbar's son. I have heard of the Cospatricks. Kin to this Donald Ban who makes claims to the throne?"

"Very far distant, my lord. And *senior*!"

"Ah, yes. He is a difficult man is Donald. I frequently have trouble with him, whatever."

"That is what we have come to see you about," Alexander said.

"Ha! Indeed and indeed! Well, we shall see." He chuckled. "But come you, Sire. To my poor house. All yours, whatever, while you are in Ross. Your people can be brought on by Ranald Dubh when your ship is moored."

So they were led along to the castle, Alexander pointing at the mountains inland and declaring that he would wish to go visit them; he had never seen such high hills. One in especial towered majestically. That was Ben Wyvis, he was told.

Dingwall Castle proved to be unlike any of the Lowland strongholds they knew, diverse as these could be. It was, in effect, a separate village set within a high stone wall topped by a parapet and wall-walk, this of irregular outline following the lines and contours of the mound which it crowned, with no keep nor towers. Through the gatehouse arch they were into all but streets of cottages, sheds and outhouses, even a forge and an oxen mill, all thatched-roofed and timber-built, ranged around a large hallhouse with tall central block and wings. To this the pair were conducted, the king declaring that he had never seen the like, Farquhar asserting that he had a better house at Applecross, but that this hold was best for winter residence. Within they were presented to the Countess Seona, a smiling little woman who seemed tiny beside her huge husband. Their sons, William and Malcolm, they were told, were presently away in the north, by boat, visiting Edderton, where the earl was founding an abbey. This information came with further hoots of laughter, as though it were a source of great amusement.

The two visitors were plied with food and drink. When their companions arrived and were duly introduced, the two earls in especial eyed each other assessingly.

It was not long before they got down to the object of the visit. They were glad to obtain a receptive hearing, Farquhar asserting that he did not love Donald Ban mac William, and that the man was a scoundrel and always causing trouble along the borders of Moray and Ross. He knew of the present uprising against the king, indeed declaring that this claim to the throne had largely been occasioned by Donald's resentment that the late King William had made his, Farquhar's, father an earl and not himself likewise.

When it was put to him that they wished him to lead a Highland army against Donald, the earl showed no signs of surprise, saying that he had guessed as much, and was quite prepared to do so. Indeed Patrick got the impression that he was quite glad to have the opportunity to do so with royal approval, the chance to teach his troublesome neighbour a lesson, an excuse to settle old scores. Yes, he would do it.

Getting down to details, over more provender and mead, Farquhar declared that, given one week, he could assemble five thousand men in arms; two weeks, three times that number. This, he asserted, was more than Donald Ban could do in the time, for the Easter Ross and Cromarty area had a much more populous coastal plain, to the north, than Moray could boast. He had heard that Donald was assembling his force near to his main seat of Lochindorb, in the Findhorn uplands; but his major support would come from further afield, Badenoch and Speyside to the south and the glens of Lossie, Avon, Livet and Deveron. These were presently largely cut off by the snow in the passes, so he would not be able to muster in full strength until a month or even six weeks yet.

How many, then, would Donald have at this Lochindorb at present? Cospatrick asked.

It was hard to say, he was told. But not more than three or four thousand probably. But later he could raise twenty thousand for his move south.

As they pondered this, Farquhar added that Donald could probably pick up some thousands more from the Highland areas he would have to pass through, and from Buchan and perhaps Atholl and Strathtay. The clans were always spoiling for a fight after the winter and the booty they could collect, especially from Lowland sources; it could be that, rather than who wore the crown which would be apt to concern these. Clearly the matter of the throne was of scant importance to most in the Highlands.

Equally clear to most present was the recognition that any move against Donald should be made at the soonest, before he could muster his full manpower. They all looked at Farquhar.

That man made no bones about it. He was quite prepared to act, and at once, if it was the king's command. And if there was some modest reward for so doing!

Alexander enthusiastically declared that there would be, others wondering what. Details were not discussed that far, there and then.

What, then? Farquhar would send out his summons to arms that very evening. Much of it could be carried by boat up the Easter Ross coast, and there were sixty miles of this, to the borders of Caithness and its Southernland. He would send word to his sons up there. A week, as he had said, and he would have a sufficiency of men to cross into Moray and make for Lochindorb. Donald would not be expecting assault from the north, and they ought to be able to deliver their message to good effect!

After much hospitality, including the typical Highland gesture of offering female company for the night for those so inclined, it was bed-going. With his father present, Patrick could hardly share a bed with Alex, but at least they occupied the same room, all pleased with progress.

In the morning, Farquhar said that he would personally go round Cromarty summoning his chieftains and their folk; and when offered the use of the *Falcon* for this, he accepted. The king, the Steward, Patrick and his father went with him, and they spent an interesting day sailing from one side of the Cromarty Firth to the other, calling at hallhouses and communities, then turning back again to reach the narrow mouth between the two forts, and thereafter to head down the southern side of the peninsula to the very edge of Moray land at Beauly, calling in at Rosemarkie, Avoch, Munlochy and Kessock, a very full day. The earl seemed pleased with the reaction aroused.

Next day Farquhar took his guests, at Alexander's request, inland by Strathpeffer and Loch Garve to the mountains. They did not use horses for travel much in the Highlands, but the earl did have a number of garrons, shaggy, stocky, short-legged ponies, for pack-carrying peats and the like, and, his guests being but little used to walking, mounted them on these, using plaids instead of saddles. Not able to ride fast, they headed westwards up the Peffer to Fodderty and then northwards into the empty hills, soon into snow. Ben Wyvis, the giant, of course was Alexander's target, some nine miles north by west, its vast bulk beckoning them on. Farquhar claimed it as the highest summit on the north-east side of Scotland after Cairngorm and the Monadh Ruadh, at well over three thousand feet.

Not able to ride direct, any more than fast, and over wild country, it took them two hours to reach the lower slopes of the mountain, amidst ever deepening snow. They would take the garrons as far as they could go, Farquhar said, which was probably about halfway up, but by no means could they reach the summit in these conditions. Apart from the king, none expressed disappointment at this; in fact there were mutterings about it being time to turn back. But at least they got on to a lofty shoulder of the mountain, a steep escarpment ahead, from which they gained magnificent views far and wide, and Alexander had to be satisfied. Their ponies were all but up to their bellies in the snow here. At least, without going higher, it all demonstrated the virtual impossibility of conducting any large-scale warfare in the Highlands in winter.

The following forenoon the first of the clansmen began to arrive at Dingwall for the Moray invasion, armed with broadswords, battle-axes and dirks, a fierce-looking lot. Farquhar's two sons were recruiting effectively. Their father said that not all his force would come to Dingwall. Those from inland, westwards, Strathglass, Strathgarve, Strathconon and Glen Orrin, would come to near Beauly, which was on the way that Farquhar would lead his array, to enter Moray in the most secret way possible so that Donald was not warned: that is, up the Beauly River as far as Kilmorack, and then eastwards to cross the River Ness at the furthest possible point from Inverness itself, near the foot of long Loch Ness. Then still east across the hills to Strathdearn, with Lochindorb beyond that. This way, they would have no high passes to thread.

Alexander and Patrick spent that day on garrons exploring the coastal area to the north as far as Kilfearn, accompanied by four of the earl's running-gillies to ensure their safety. They were astonished at the seemingly untiring ability of these men to keep pace with the garrons in their steady loping jog-trot.

The next day was Sunday, and after a brief service in the Dingwall church for prayer and petition, the earl took his visitors, using a galley, to visit Edderton, on the Dornoch Firth further north, to see the abbey he was building, this while more men came to the assembly point. Next morning they would be off.

They all admired the quite large building, which was being erected by the sandy shore of a wide bay in the firth, and were told that the burgh of Tain was not far to the east, second only to Dingwall in size in the earldom. They duly commended Farquhar on his piety in doing this, to his usual laughter. It all seemed a strange interlude before battle.

Fully three thousand men were ready to march on the Monday morning, Farquhar and his sons afoot with them, although the Lowlanders rode their garrons. With pipers at intervals in the long column to liven the march, they headed south to Beauly, quite a large community, where they found at least another two thousand assembled. Then they followed the Beauly River up another five miles to Kilmorack, where they crossed it to head for the River Ness, this through snow-patched hills, but not hindering them greatly. This of the Ness crossing was the most vital matter of their march. They halted for the night in a shallow valley, devoid of snow, where they wrapped themselves in their plaids, after a meal of cold venison and oatcakes, and slept, the visitors having to do the same however unused to passing a night thus. Alexander at least found it all an adventure to his taste, even though sleet fell on them at intervals.

In the morning, after more cold feeding, they soon reached the great river, great in width if not in length, the part of the journey Farquhar was most concerned about. There was only the one available crossing, by an underwater stone causeway near Dochfour, this about a mile from the river's issuing from Loch Ness; and inevitably a small community had been established there for long, some six miles from Inverness. There was no avoiding this; and indubitably, once the army had crossed, the local folk would send word of the fact down to the town. The question was, of course, would the townsfolk there, or their leaders, despatch messengers forthwith to inform

Donald Ban? Probably they would. But would such be able to reach Lochindorb before the Ross host? Possibly not, for Inverness was slightly further away therefrom than this Dochfour, and the news had to be got to the town first. So the chances were probably in their favour.

Beyond the Ness six miles they had to cross the River Nairn, less of a problem this. These Highlanders did not seem to find crossing fords any hardship, even all but waist-deep ones, merely hitching up their kilts and striding through, usually with laughter and comments, however chilly the water. The garrons, of course, splashed over readily enough.

They were into higher, rougher country now with quite lofty mountains, but fortunately no real passes had to be got over. Once over Findhorn they would have only another ten miles to their goal, fairly empty territory. They would camp for another night therein, so that their host would be reasonably rested and fresh for battle, after the few further miles. No piping was now allowed, no campfires, nothing to draw attention to their presence and progress.

Alexander's excitement was intense. Battle, real battle! How would it go? What would be the plans, the strategy? What would *he* do? Patrick was unable to inform him adequately, he himself never having been in a battle, although he had once or twice been involved in tussles with Border mosstroopers.

Farquhar, with the dusk, had sent scouts ahead to spy out conditions. Such had gone before the army all the way, but these were to creep as close to the enemy assembly as possible, to learn positions and strength. After all, if any were seen by foemen, there was nothing to distinguish them as Rossmen in the darkness.

By dawn all were awake and ready. The scouts' reports were that the enemy camp, on the west shore of the loch, scattered and extensive, appeared to be unwarned, no sign of alarm, campfires burning, no guards actually patrolling. How many there were assembled it was impossible to ascertain, but probably considerably fewer than the Ross force.

Farquhar briefed his chieftains and leaders, not consulting the Lowland lords, even the Knight Marischal. These could take what part they chose. But he did declare, and the others agreed with him, that the young monarch was not to be involved in the fighting in any way, and Patrick was to see that he kept his distance from the fray. And if by any mischance the day went against them, Alexander was to be got away swiftly and safely, back to Dingwall and the ship. Cospatrick also emphasised this to his son, however protesting the king. On this occasion, royal commands were of no avail.

The advance began, while still it was not much more than half-light, the army in a wide, crescent-shaped formation, pacing slowly, all on foot, the garrons left behind, scouts ahead again. This entire area was a fairly lofty grass and heather plateau, the loch in the middle almost two miles long and fish-shaped, its castle-island, an artificial crannog, it was said, near the eastern side, midway. There was a series of ridges in the moorland, with one to the west somewhat higher than the rest; and it was on to the slope of this that Patrick and the High Steward took Alexander, to seek to view the engagement as far as that was possible.

No comprehensive prospect was provided, owing to the uneven nature of the ground and the scatter of wind-blown pine trees intervening; but they were able, tensely, to follow the general advance. There was perhaps two-thirds of a mile to cover. No awareness of danger was evident beyond, from the area where presumably was the enemy encampment, although in the poor light this was not clearly in view. It seemed strange to the anxious watchers that this Ross approach, in such numbers, should still be undetected by the Moray men; but Donald Ban's people would not be expecting any assault at this stage here in their own Highlands, and their present camp no more than a preliminary assembly place, not any armed and defensive fortress.

The minutes passed, almost breathlessly.

Then suddenly there was reaction. First a single horn blew, high and distant but continuing. Then noise began to erupt, noise in clamorous variety, shouts and yells, screams and the clash of arms, produced by the alarmed enemy but also, no doubt, by the advancing Rossmen.

Quickly now the din grew, a confusion of sound, but the high shrieking the most evident, a pandemonium that sent shivers down Patrick's back, whatever his companions' reaction, men in agony and terror.

And it went on and on. Gazing and listening, the watchers exclaimed and stamped and fretted. To stand idle, useless, while direst clash, endeavour and struggle were going on none so far ahead was a trial indeed, all but intolerable for men of any spirit. Alexander cried that they must go, must hurry forward, do something; but the others restrained him, however exercised themselves. There was nothing that they could do to any effect, no advantage to be gained, only danger for the monarch, for the crown, for the realm that he represented. The battle would be won or lost irrespective of whether they stood here or plunged recklessly into the seeming chaos.

For how long they waited there was no knowing, unaware of time in the stress and tension. The sun was well risen now, full daylight, if with slanting shadows; but details ahead were little less difficult to distinguish. The dark masses of men at this distance seemed to stretch wide and far. They could see the castle walls on its islet amidst the glistening waters of the loch, but that was no help.

Patrick did begin to imagine that the din and clamour ahead was lessening somewhat, by no means dying away but reduced in intensity and volume. He did not say so, but Alexander soon announced a similar impression. The battle – was it nearing an end? The fighting lessening? Was it victory, or defeat? This waiting, watching, was insupportable. They knew nothing . . .

Then, presently, the Steward pointed. Three figures

could be seen making for their position, hurrying, part running. The trio, with the garrons and their few attendants, would be easily seen on their hillside. News, then?

When they drew near, it was to be seen that these were two running-gillies with William, Master of Ross, if that was what he called himself, Farquhar's elder son. Panting, he hailed them as he came up.

"All is well!" he cried. "They are swept away, whatever! Defeated. All over, just."

Exclaiming their relief, the trio hurried down to meet him.

"We had them by surprise. Asleep. The first of them, just. Och, they ran, those that could, at all. We slew most." Breathlessly this William went on, "Those that fled ran into the others beyond. Awakened but not knowing what was to do, at all. Some fought us, but more fled further. A long line of them along the lochside. No real array to attack. We just swept them up, whatever! Still they are at it . . ."

"It is victory, then?" the Steward demanded. "All over, save for the stragglers?"

"Good! Good!" Alexander actually clapped his hands. "Indeed and indeed!"

"No great losses amongst our people? Or yours?" Patrick asked.

"Och, no. Scarce any, at all. Come, you. You shall see . . ."

As they began to move downhill, the Steward asked further. "What of Donald Ban? Is he safe in yonder castle?"

"No, thanks be! He is down. Dead! At the least, he died like a chief should, the man. He was in his castle, but when the fighting began he was after coming ashore in a boat with some of his friends to take command. Foolish, belike. For he could have remained secure in his island hold. But he was too late. He was struck down. My father finished him, whatever, with his own dirk! He and his are no more."

"Donald Ban dead!" Alexander said, wagging his head. "Here is a wonder! No more of his threat."

"Had he a son?" Patrick wondered.

"Aye, but he fell also. Seumas Odhar. Moray is down, just."

They hurried on through the heather and scattered pines, and presently they were amongst fallen bodies, most still but some twitching, stirring, groaning. Alexander bit his lip, his first experience of a battlefield. He paused beside one whimpering man, and then moved on with the others unhappily.

They were led through the multitude of the fallen to the lochside opposite the castle, where a group was assembled, the Earl of Ross's huge figure prominent. Patrick's father came to them, clearly unhurt.

"Sire," he said, "all is well. The enemy defeated, dispersed. And with little loss to us. Donald of Moray dead. Your Grace has the victory."

"I have done nothing!" Alexander cried. "Nothing. Others doing all."

"You are the king, Sire. Not for you to wield the sword. Only the sceptre!"

Seeing them, Farquhar came over. "Alastair mac William," he exclaimed, "here is an end to this stramash, whatever! All over. And I have a gift for Your Highness!" He hooted one of his great laughs. "A notable gift, just." And he waved to some of the group he had left.

Four men came forward, carrying a plaid between them, a weighted plaid. And when they reached the earl and Alexander, at the earl's gesture they lowered their burden. At a further wave, they opened up the folds. And therein were about a dozen severed heads of men, hacked off at the necks, hair and beards all matted with blood. Stirring his grisly offering with his foot, Farquhar bent and picked up one of the open-mouthed, glazed-eyed trophies by the hair, and showed it to Alexander.

"Donald Ban of Moray!" he said.

The young monarch tried to swallow, could not, and

turning hastily away was violently sick, laughter behind him. Patrick felt none so sure of his own stomach either.

Cospatrick pointed towards the plaidful, and made a covering gesture. Farquhar tossed back the head he held, and the symbols of defeat were enfolded again and carried off.

Patrick led his gulping liege-lord a little way aside, to where he could partly recover his composure. "Be not so upset, Alex," he urged. "It is offensive, uncouth! But Donald and the others would not have felt it, suffered. They would all be dead first. In war, this can be the way of it, men's passions hot. Donald could have done the same to this Farquhar had *he* won the day!"

Alexander, wiping his mouth, nodded. "I did not know . . . I, I could not help it, Pate. I will try . . ."

Much hanging about followed for the Lowland group as the aftermath of battle was dealt with, bodies gathered in piles, weapons and booty collected, wounded given some attention. Who would bury all these corpses was uncertain, for it seemed that they were going to be left in their heaps. The king shook his head over this, for, after all, they had all been his subjects; but there was nothing he could do about it, it seemed.

He did confer with Patrick not only on this, however. He had more or less agreed to reward Farquhar Macantagart for his aid if he could defeat Donald Ban. He had done so. What was to be done about it? What to give the man? He was an earl already; he could not raise him higher. And as for land, he already had hundreds of miles of it up here. He probably would not want a Lowland property. What . . . ?

Patrick could think of only the one thing that the youth might confer: knighthood. To be knighted on the field of battle was a recognised honour. The monarch could do it. Would that not serve?

"I have never done it. Never knighted anyone, Pate. I have seen my father doing it. But . . ."

"It is simple enough, Alex. Just tell him to kneel. Take a sword and lay it on each of his shoulders. Then tell him to be a good and true knight until his life's end. Then say, 'Arise, Sir Farquhar!' That is all. But enough."

"Yes. I could do that. Would you think that he will judge it sufficient?"

"Your first knighting! Yes, I think that he will esteem it. And I do not see what else you can do."

"A sword, then . . ."

"My father's will do."

So, when all seemed to be ready for a departure, Alexander, Patrick at his side, went over to Farquhar and announced, a little hesitantly, that he had his own gift to offer to the victor of the battle, the other raising eyebrows enquiringly.

"Will you kneel, my lord of Ross?" he was asked.

"Kneel? You say kneel! For why, at all?"

"For your own weal." That was Patrick.

"I have never knelt to any man!" the earl declared.

"This kneeling will not displease you, I think. One knee will serve."

"Do it, my lord. No humbling is intended. The, the reverse." That from the king.

Staring doubtfully, the other sank on one knee.

Alexander took the heavy sword and, after balancing its weight, brought it down on Farquhar's right shoulder. "I hereby knight you," he got out. "Knight. You, Farquhar Macantagart, Earl of Ross." He got the sword over the man's head, only just high enough to avoid the bonnet, to the other shoulder, plaid-hung. "Be a, a good knight. Until you die. Until your life's end." He glanced at Patrick, who nodded. "Arise, Sir Farquhar. Arise!"

The earl got up, his ruddy face a study. Then he barked one of his laughs, gazing around him for all to see. "*Sir* Farquhar! A knight, whatever! God save us, a knight!"

"Yes, my lord. My first. My first knighting."

Patrick was reaching for the sword to hand it back to his father, but Alexander shook his head. He pointed to the ground. "Kneel, Pate," he said. "You also."

Astonished, Patrick shook his head. But at the other's

54

continued pointing he sank down obediently, glancing over towards Cospatrick and Farquhar almost apologetically.

The king managed more efficiently this time, tapping the shoulders less clumsily.

"Arise, Sir Patrick. Be you a good knight also." Then he remembered. "Until your life's end."

So, to the stares of all present, his friend stood, and bowed. "My, my thanks, Sire!" he got out.

Alexander grinned. "Good!" he said. "I am glad. You are *Sir* Pate now! My knight."

"I am not worthy. To deserve this . . ."

"You are my friend," Alexander said simply. And handed him back the sword.

When Patrick gave the weapon to his father, Cospatrick eyed him almost grimly. "There will be no living with this son of mine after this!" he said.

A move was made then, with columns of the Rossmen already beginning to march westwards. Soon they reached the garrons on the hill, and the Lowlanders were able to mount, to their relief. It was still only early forenoon.

Their return journey was a deal easier, and shorter, than their coming, for now they could go back by Inverness, with no need for secrecy nor fear of opposition, themselves the victors. But it was still twenty-five miles to the town. They camped for the night by the River Nairn, with fires now and ample food and drink from the enemy camp. Alexander was in buoyant mood now, telling Farquhar that he would be welcome at his court if he cared to venture south.

They reached Inverness next day before noon, and found no difficulty in passing through the town, probably the word of their victory having preceded them. After that it was only some ten miles to Beauly and another ten to Dingwall. Twenty miles in a day, afoot, did not seem to worry these Highlanders.

So the visitors were able to spend a night in beds again. And there would be no lingering thereafter.

Next day, then, it was farewells, thanks for Farquhar's efforts, and his and his wife's hospitality, assurances of esteem. They were piped aboard the *Falcon*, and to that skirling music, if such it could be called, sail was hoisted and they were for Dunbar. It had been a most notable and successful enterprise, and King Alexander, not to mention Sir Patrick, had learned a lot.

4

Patrick did not stay at Dunbar but went with Alexander to Roxburgh, on royal urging, this in especial because they were informed that there had been trouble on the border and involving Cospatrick's land of the Merse or March, as well as areas near to Roxburgh. There had been quite a major raid over Tweed, from Norham, by the barons of Northumberland, with much devastation and damage, considerable loot taken. It seemed that military matters were by no means over. So while Cospatrick raised a force of his own to head south and help to deal with this, Alexander wanted Patrick at his side to assist him in coping with this unexpected development.

It all was alarming and most disappointing, for peace with England was the policy, and had been fairly well maintained for some years. This affair could, of course, represent only some local initiative by the Northumbrians, aggressive border barons, and not denote any intention by King John; but the fact that it was said to stem from Norham, the prince-bishop of Durham's castle, seemed to be significant. At any rate, something had to be done about it. And Alexander, so fresh from his northern triumph, was in sufficiently martial mood to see to it in person, not leave it all to the Earl of Dunbar.

No time was to be lost, for the raid had taken place ten days previously. Acting in concert with Cospatrick, whose lands had suffered the most damage, around Ladykirk, Swinton and Kimmerghame, an armed move must be made against Norham itself, it was decided. But at the same time, representations should be made to the English King John, on the assumption that this trouble was not his royal policy, despite the prince-bishop's castle being used as a base. That churchman, like his predecessors, was very much a royal-appointed power in the north of England, all but a viceroy indeed; and if he was involved, the matter was the more serious. So, a mission to go south, first to Durham itself, and if no satisfaction was gained there, on to London and King John, Bishop William of St Andrews, the Primate, to lead this. Meantime, Alexander himself would take force against Norham, to demonstrate that raids of this sort were not to be countenanced. It was not possible, at short notice, to raise any large army at Roxburgh, nor to equip it with bombards, battering-rams and the like for a siege; but a few hundred could be mustered, Kerrs, Turnbulls, Elliots and the like, mos-strooping Borderers; and these, in co-operation with Co-spatrick's people, ought to be able to make due impact at Norham. Alexander would lead in person. Patrick's duty was to act as link between his father and the royal force. But first he was to go up Teviotdale and summon companies of men, in the king's name.

He started with Kerr of Ferniehirst, near to Jedburgh, chief of that powerful if unruly clan, which could, allegedly, raise four hundred men at one day's notice. He found that laird glad enough to become involved, he concerned over the English raiding, which could so easily spread westwards to his own lands. Then on to the secondary branch of the Kerrs, Cessford. Here was an older man who was less helpful, but thought that he could contribute one hundred. The Turnbulls of Bedrule and Fatlips, the Elliots of Minto and the Baliols of Cavers, still further west, were nothing loth, and, with the others, promised a total of about nine hundred. Patrick returned to Roxburgh, Alexander well pleased.

The former was off next day to try to contact his father, who might be anywhere between Dunbar in Lothian and Tweed, depending on how long it had taken him to muster a sufficiency of men from the mixture of coastal and hill areas. Bishop William and his fellow envoys were already gone south for Durham, by Carter Bar and Redesdale.

Reckoning that since Norham had been the source of the trouble, his father would be aiming for the Tweed in that vicinity, Patrick headed eastwards in that direction first, to turn northwards somewhere in the Ladykirk vicinity, to seek to make contact. At least this travel, unlike that in the Highlands, was done on a good horse and speedily.

By the time that he got as far down Tweed as Birgham and Coldstream and Lennel, he was seeing the signs of devastation and ruin, villages and farms burned, stack-yards demolished, crops trampled and trees hanging with corpses. This had been no typical small-scale border raiding, but a major incursion. Why? What was behind it? It looked like a deliberate demonstration of hostility, not some booty-gathering sally. Perhaps Bishop William would learn what was behind it.

Just before devastated Ladykirk, even the ancient church burned, he turned northwards for Whitsome. This was all his father's territory of the March, one day to be his own, and the sight of it all made his blood boil. This must be avenged. But vengeance could result in full-scale war with England. In which case the March could be much further endangered. That had to be considered well. Not that *his* decision would be in any way important in this, save in that he might influence Alexander.

Actually Patrick had not very far to ride northwards before he gained information, from a shepherd in the low hills of the Hutton and Eddington area, that a large force of men, no doubt the Earl Cospatrick's, had been seen crossing White-adder near Foulden that very morning. So Patrick had to turn right-handed, east by south now, to try to intercept. A single horseman on a good beast such as his could travel a deal faster than any host, which must go at the pace of the slowest, so he ought to be able to catch up before long. It proved, at least, that his father had wasted no time in making a move.

In fact he came up with his people at West Fishwick, well within the devastated territory, where he found his father and his lairds and men fuming at all the traces of ruin and savagery. On his arrival, with the news of the widespread extent of the damage westwards received with further cursings, he was also able to tell of the king's plans and intentions, and the numbers of men likely to be in the royal force; but how long it would be before they would appear he did not know. He did understand that Norham Castle was the objective.

Cospatrick, despite the urgings of some of his lieutenants that they should get across Tweed at once and start ransacking the Northumbrian lands forthwith in response to all this depredation, decided to wait and align his activities with those of the king, as Patrick had been instructed to advise. They would wait in the Horndean area, not too near Tweed and Norham, so as not to warn the enemy of their approach.

They settled down in that ruined village, then, and men set to burying the dead, seeking to comfort and aid some of the local folk who had fled and escaped and had now come back to their ravaged homes. Patrick departed once more, to go and seek out the royal presence.

He again did not have far to go up Tweed, meeting the king and some fifteen hundred men near Birgham. Recognising that the ford at Norham itself might well be guarded, Alexander was aiming to cross the river beforehand, at Coldstream, this less likely to be held against them. They would wait at that ford for Cospatrick then, and make a joint assault on Norham. So back to Horndean with Sir Patrick, the courier.

The link-up of the two forces was accomplished without difficulty or opposition, and the combined array, quite an impressive host although scarcely an army, crossed into Northumberland and headed eastwards down Tweed. Alexander had been shocked by what he had seen on the Scots side; and he and Cospatrick had forcefully had to restrain the Dunbar men from wreaking their vengeance on the English communities they passed. Such would only delay them and give warning to Norham.

Patrick now rode with the king, beside the Knight Marischal, the High Steward and Bruce of Annandale.

Whether Norham Castle was indeed warned of their approach there was no knowing. They reached it after about seven miles' riding and suffered no intervention nor sign of enemy presence. The castle was some distance from the township which lay inland at a great bend of the river, the stronghold on the riverbank itself, guarding the ford, on a fairly lofty bluff, a major fortalice. Flags flew from its towers and smoke rose from its chimneys, but no man-power was in evidence outside.

It did not take long for the newcomers to recognise that this would be a very difficult place to take, on its mound-top, the walls sheer and high and using all the levelish space to the edges of steep drops. There was nowhere that any real assault could be made, and rams or bombards based – not that they presently had any such anyway. A night-time attempt to climb up in large numbers and to scale the walls would be all but impossible, with a guarded parapet-walk. There were towers at all angles and, within, a great donjon keep.

Gazing up at all this, even the least well informed as to castle assault perceived that siege was the only option here, no storming possible. And siege implied time, days, possibly weeks, all depending on how well stocked with food and drink was the stronghold; that, and the size of the garrison that required feeding. And, of course, during the period of waiting, rescuers could possibly arrive, and these might outnumber the besiegers.

A council deliberated. Just to retire over Tweed again was unthinkable. But for two thousand men to sit idly around this castle, waiting to starve out its occupants, was likewise scarcely to be considered. All discipline and morale would suffer. It was decided that groups of their men should go off in turns to harass the Northumbrian countryside, far and wide, returning to take their turns at the siegery. Whatever was behind the English raiding, whether on the prince-bishop's authority or his king's, it certainly had been carried out by the Northumberland barons, lords and squires. So, punish these and their people while waiting for Norham to surrender through starvation.

This, to be sure, much pleased the rank and file of the Scots force, the sort of thing that they could enjoy, doing vengeance, and loot to be gained. Oddly enough, however, two of the king's advisers were somewhat doubtful about this, the Earl of Dunbar and his son. The fact was that the Cospatricks had been Earls of Northumbria before ever they were allotted Dunbar and the Merse; and they did not relish the province being savaged, still having some feeling for it. To see it devastated, however deservedly, would give them no joy. But they could not deny that this was the obvious course to take. Retribution was called for, and without it there could well be further incursions into Scotland.

So the policy was put into effect. It was judged that only perhaps three hundred men were required to encircle and threaten the castle at any one time: the garrison therein was unlikely to be more than one hundred at most. So the great majority of the Scots force could go mosstrooping, as most called it, in bands of about two hundred. Northumberland was a huge territory and provided ample scope for punishment, many hundreds of square miles of it, between the Cheviots and the sea.

Meanwhile, Alexander and his magnates would take over the village of Norham, half a mile from the castle, a quite attractive little township offering a degree of comfort, so no burning and harrying there.

Cospatrick and his son had little difficulty in persuading the young king to command that the roving bands exercised some restraint, no unnecessary slaughter, no raping of women, no deliberate cruelty. How much attention would be paid to that royal instruction, of course, was another matter.

The siege of Norham, then, commenced. It was not the first such, for Alexander's great-grandsire, King David, had done the same once, and gained the day. But its bishops had strengthened the place since then.

Siegery is the most boring of all military efforts, especially when no battering of the walls or scaling attempts are possible; and Alexander and his lords were no more proof against the boredom than were other men. As the days passed they had to devise ways of filling in the time, if not pleasurably at least more to their taste, sport of a sort, hunting, fishing in the Tweed, even going out with the raiding bands. The king did not engage in the last, judging that he had to be present if and when the castle yielded, to accept the surrender. He did exercise his fondness for archery, although only with crosshows, since no longbows had been brought on their expedition. He asked the raiders to try to collect falcons for him from any castle or hallhouse they might sack, so that these could be used for hawking along the riverside for wild duck and heron.

Patrick remained with the king as companion, although once or twice he went out with his father on sightseeing rides, not always relishing what they saw in country now almost as devastated as that of the southern Merse.

The days extended into weeks, still with no sign of capitulation from the castle, no signs of any sort indeed. Apart from the smoke rising from two or three chimneys, the place might have seemed unoccupied. Patrick wondered how the folk therein were passing their time.

Alexander held his seventeenth birthday while they waited, and Patrick organised a celebratory feast of sorts, the villagers of Norham pressed in to help. Some of the young women thereof were not entirely averse to providing their own cheer.

But with no surrender from the stronghold, all but starving as its inmates must be, as time went on Alexander and his advisers began to get worried. After all, there was a whole realm to rule back over Tweed, and its monarch and councillors could not be absent overlong without trouble arising, the Scots being the sort of people they were. This could not go on. Another few days and they would have to leave the siege to lesser men.

This decision taken, the very next day there was a development. Bishop William and his colleagues arrived at Norham. And their news was good, reassuring. The raid on Scotland had not been on the prince-bishop's orders, nor yet King John's. It must have been purely a Northumbrian venture, for what reason, other than sheer hostility and the collection of booty, was not known. Perhaps the barons there imagined that so young and new a monarch would present them with an opportunity, his hand uncertain on the helm of the ship of state. At any rate, the situation was clarified. There was no longer any need to besiege the bishop's castle. Northumberland had been taught a lesson. A return could be made to Roxburgh.

But first, it was felt that Alexander must make some demonstration, not just seem to go off home as it were with little achieved, his siege abandoned. It was Cospatrick who suggested an advantageous display. All the lords and landholders of Northumberland who could be rounded up in the present state of the province should be brought into the presence of the king and there forced to bow their heads before the monarch whose realm they had injured, and ordered to swear an oath never again to repeat such behaviour. This would enable Alexander to retire with dignity and authority intact.

It was agreed by all, and since it was Cospatrick's idea, and he was probably the most knowledgeable of the Scots magnates as to Northumberland, he was allotted the task of arranging it. With a couple of hundred supporters, he set off on this project. He was to assemble these English barons at some suitable place, fairly deep into the province, not bring them to Norham, so that the Scots monarch could be seen to be master of it all meantime, riding over it in victory, a telling indication.

Two days later he returned, with only a few of his party. He had achieved his objective and apprehended some thirty of the landholders, this at Felton, between Alnwick and Morpeth, some thirty miles away, due south. He had left them under guard there. He did not think that any rescue would be attempted in the circumstances, for the land was now thoroughly subdued.

Next morning, then, Alexander and most of his lords, with a fair-sized escort, set off on the quite lengthy ride, down parallel with the coast, the lion rampant standard flying, by Duddo and Lowick, Doddington and Falloden and Alnwick, signs of the Scots' punishing activities evident all the way. Three hours' riding and they reached Felton, four miles inland from the coast, a village chosen because it had two large hallhouses for installing the representatives of the Northumberland lords and squires. These were not exactly captives or hostages, having been persuaded to come there by Cospatrick to offer token to King Alexander of their remorse for the invasion of his kingdom and the evil done, with promises of nothing more of the sort, this in the name of all the province, on the understanding that there would be no further Scots hurt visited upon their countryside.

So, in Felton church, they were brought before the king, a distinguished but wary-eyed company, Delavals, Percys, Charltons, Greys, Forsters, Collingwoods, Radcliffes, Ogles, the cream of Northumberland. How many of them had been involved in the Scots raid was not disclosed, but some certainly had, and all looked apprehensive, if not guilty.

Alexander, flanked by Earl Cospatrick, the Steward, the Marischal, Bishop William and Patrick, eyed them all from the chancel steps, himself a little uncertain.

Cospatrick spoke first. "His Grace of Scotland greatly deplores your attack on his realm and people," he said. "And this resultant but necessary affray of retribution. That, and the danger of fullest warfare with England, as a consequence. But, if His Highness is assured of the regrets and contrition of all present and those whom you represent, and the promise of no further such hostile acts, he is

65

prepared to return to his own land and leave you in peace. Is it agreed, promised, vowed?''

There were murmurs, mutterings, assertions and noddings from the Englishmen, no voice raised to the contrary.

Bishop William spoke then. "I have been to visit the Lord Bishop of Durham, your master in God, but also your liege-lord John's representative. He assures me that the invasion of the Scots March was done without his sanction or permission. He condemns it. You are in default therefore, before God and both monarchs. I, Bishop of St Andrews, require your confessed guilt and penitence.''

More murmurs.

The bishop turned to the king, who drew a deep breath. "I, Alexander, do condemn what you have done,'' he said, not very forcefully. "I have witnessed your deeds but also your. repentance. I accept it. I hereby . . . receive you. Receive you into my peace. And, and bid you to keep it.'' He glanced at Patrick, to see if he had missed out anything that they had rehearsed on their way here.

His friend nodded reassuringly.

There were moments of silence. No spokesman for the Northumbrians raised voice.

"Is it understood?'' Cospatrick demanded.

There was then much exclamation of agreement, noddings and bowings.

"Very well,'' The earl turned to the bishop.

That man raised his hand high. "Then, let peace prevail, as the Almighty requires of men,'' he intoned. "In the name of God the Father, God the Son and God the Holy Spirit, I bless all present. Go in peace. Amen.''

Amidst shuffling of feet and questioning glances, Cospatrick bowed to the king, who, looking relieved, turned to depart, making for the vestry door, followed by his party. The Northumbrians were left to mull over the proceedings.

It was back, then, for the border for the Scots, the entire episode over and, it was judged, successfully. They had made their presence felt in this England, and at practically no cost to themselves, however much they had paid in advance, and however boring they had found siege-making. It was to be hoped that there would be no need for any further demonstration in the foreseeable future.

5

The return to Roxburgh had quite notable consequences for Patrick. For they discovered that, in the interim, Philip de Valognes, or Vallance, had fallen suddenly ill and died, an old and ailing man. So the office of High Chamberlain, held by him for just over thirty years, was now vacant. And nothing would do but that Patrick should fill it, however much he declared that he was unworthy and too young for the rank and duties of one of the principal officers of state, for the position carried with it much more than just the close attendance on the monarch, many ceremonial and other duties, acting as royal representative on occasion, superintending the royal palaces and collecting the king's revenues. But Alexander was insistent. Pate was his friend, his only *real* friend. He had wished him into this office almost since they had known each other. He had felt unable to demote the venerable de Valognes, but had to confess that he had almost wished that he would die, or at least become incapable of the duties. Now the way was cleared. It was something that he could do himself, without consulting the Privy Council. So – no more objections to be permitted or heeded: Patrick was to be High Chamberlain.

There was another deed that the king could perform without consulting his councillors – and only the king could do it. This was to create an earl. That was the highest rank of the realm's nobility, and there were only a very limited number of such. He, Alexander, realised that there could well be a few of the highly placed lords who might covet the position of Chamberlain. One of the earls might desire it, and might resent a mere heir to an earldom, such as the Master of Dunbar, winning it. But if *he* was an earl himself, that would not apply. So, how would it be if he was made earl now? Earl of the Merse, say? Or March?

Patrick was very much in doubt, appreciative of course, but in doubt. At his age. And with no notable achievements to warrant it. Many would see it askance. His own father perhaps. To see his son raised as high as himself, higher almost, since *he* was not an officer of state. Others. The Steward – he was not an earl. Nor Keith, the Knight Marischal. Nor Hay, the Constable. Alexander would risk the resentment of these if he did this, as well as making him Chamberlain.

The king shook his head. "I care not, Pate! I can make whom I wish to be earl, a lord or a knight. And you are closer to me than any. All know that one day you will be the Earl Cospatrick of Dunbar. Why not Earl of March now?"

"No, Alex – no! It is kind of you, yes. But kinder not to do it. Not yet. Later, perhaps. Others of your court would look on me with enmity. As it is, as Chamberlain, some will see me as a young interloper. But as a new earl! How many earls are there? A dozen? Less? Atholl, Angus, Caithness, Buchan, Carrick, Ross, Fife, Dunbar, Lennox, Mar, Strathearn? Many of the blood-royal."

"Your own mother was of royal blood."

"Illegitimate. I beg you, no. You have already knighted me."

Alexander shrugged. "As you will. But at least you will be ever close as High Chamberlain. After Vallance is buried, I will announce it."

They left it at that.

The burial was not to be delayed, the Chamberlain having already been dead five days. And for one in that position it was expected that the monarch should attend the interment. So two days later, all present at court, led by Alexander, joined the funeral procession, riding the dozen miles to Melrose Abbey where, with due ceremony, the aged man was solemnly laid to rest, Patrick's distant kinsman the Abbot Hugh officiating.

Thereafter, at a meal in the refectory, the king declared that he had an announcement to make.

"After due consideration," he said, "I have decided to appoint Sir Patrick, Master of Dunbar, in place of our late friend Philip de Valognes. He will take up his duties as an officer of state forthwith. All heed it. High Chamberlain. It is my royal will." And he turned to Patrick nearby.

That reluctant nominee stood and bowed. "All unworthy," he said briefly, and sat.

There were mutters throughout the refectory, but it was the High Steward who rose, and bowed. "His Grace's choice is to be commended," he declared. "The Master of Dunbar has proved himself deserving of the esteem of all, despite his years. May he remain Chamberlain for as long as did his predecessor!"

No cheers greeted that, but nor was there any contrary comment voiced, although Dorward of Atholl glowered.

"Sir Patrick will require some instruction as to all the Chamberlain's duties," the king went on. "I appoint the High Steward Walter to guide him in this, out of his long experience. He knows it all, I judge." All this had been decided on as they rode here from Roxburgh. The Steward was to be relied upon.

The situation was accepted, no one being in a position to controvert it, however many may have had their doubts.

A return was made to Roxburgh.

They were barely back before news of trouble in the west reached them. It came in a protest to the King of Scots sent by the O'Donnel, Earl of Tyrconnel, in Ulster. He declared that a son of the Scots Earl of Lennox had invaded his land and slain Fergus of Donegal, a kinsman, and many of his people, with great slaughter. He demanded retribution.

This produced much upset, inevitably. Trouble with the Irish was to be avoided at all costs. The princelings there, always being threatened by the English kings, in especial the present John, relied on the Scots as allies, and

this suited Alexander and his advisers very well, the said
John being unreliable and treacherous as well as ambitious,
ever a possible menace. So no raiding by Scots over into
Ireland was to be countenanced. And that it should be
done by a son, unnamed, of the Earl of Lennox was the
more unfortunate. Why? Lennox, from his great castle of
Dumbarton, controlled all the Clyde area and right up to
Kintyre and Argyll, the nearest part of Scotland to Ireland,
a mere fourteen miles from Ballycastle in Antrim. Trouble
from there was serious.

Walter the Steward advised prompt action, as well he
might, for his own lands of Renfrew and Paisley neigh-
boured those of Lennox; moreover, his own daughter,
Beatrix, was married to a son of Lennox. He was for
Dumbarton at once and advised that the king should go
with him, to impose the royal authority.

This was agreed. Next morning a small party, including
Patrick, set off with Alexander and the Steward for the
west, little-known territory for most of them. They rode
up Tweed as far as Broughton, where it swung southwards, and then over the hills to the upper Clyde, covering
over sixty miles that day, to halt overnight at the priory of
St Kentigern at Lanark, fair going.

Next day, passing through Glasgow but not delaying
there, they followed the widening Clyde along its south
bank, coming to Paisley and its abbey, founded as a priory
by the first High Steward, Walter's grandfather. Beyond
lay Renfrew, where the Black Cart river joined Clyde; and
nearby, on a sort of island created by a meander of the
Marline Water joining Clyde, rose the Steward's castle.

This was a fine place indeed, all but a palace, one of the
finest in the land, even though it could be but seldom
occupied by its lord, whose duties kept him always close in
proximity to the monarch, so that his family were apt to see
but little of him. His wife Beatrix, a daughter of the late
Gilchrist, Earl of Angus, called herself all but a widow in
this; but at least she had had the company of four sons and
four daughters.

The Steward's concern with the earldom of Lennox, as well as through the marriage of his daughter, another Beatrix, with Earl Alwyn's son Malduin, was emphasised by the fact that across the Clyde, now developing into an estuary, only ten miles away, soared the great castle-crowned Rock of Dumbarton, seat of the earldom.

The visitors found the Lady Beatrix, a large and hearty woman, welcoming and not at all over-awed by the arrival of the King of Scots. She genially informed them all that she hardly knew her husband! Of her eight children only four were at home: Alexander, the eldest son and heir; Walter, the third son; Euphemia, the second daughter; and Christian, the youngest daughter. Margaret, the other daughter, was married to the Earl of Carrick. Patrick had difficulty in memorising the identities of all these young people.

He had no difficulty, however, in establishing in his mind the daughter Euphemia. At twenty years Phemia, as they called her, was a well-built but not large young woman, fair of hair and feature, with deep dimples in her cheeks when she smiled, which was often, and most lively eyes. Patrick found her to his taste, as indeed did Alexander, and both tended to pay more attention to her than to the others, even to her mother's relevant comments on the Lennox-Irish situation.

"It will be that Havel," she declared. "He is the black sheep of the family – and quite a family they are, Eva of Menteith even more productive than was I!" This with a laugh. "She and Alwyn have nine of offspring, only one a daughter. They are none so ill, Malduin the eldest wed to my daughter Beatrix, a worthy young man, if over-fond of spearing fish in the sandy shallows of Clyde, which daughter Bea finds a dull way of passing the time!" Another laugh. "But this Havel, or Hamelyn as it should be, is the wild one, ever the plague to his sire."

"He is too good-looking," Phemia said, smiling. "He sees himself as superior. Irresistible to women. None to say him nay!"

72

"Save my daughter!" her mother observed. "But this of the Irish trouble. I know not what took him over to Ulster. But he has been misbehaving nearer home for long, making raids on the isles, Islay in especial. Causing upset with the Lord of the Isles, which his father has to try to smooth over."

"Can Alwyn not control him?" her husband demanded.

"Evidently not. He has a band of ruffians and runagates, all but outcasts, it seems. And he does with them what he will. Alwyn is getting old and seeks a quiet life. And Malduin, our goodson, is no warrior either, preferring to spear salmon and flukies than men!"

"Havel has his own place at Rosneath, near the mouth of the Gare Loch," Phemia put in. "Earl Alwyn must regret ever giving him that. For it is quite a strength, on the site of an ancient fort, they say, and he is not to be ousted from it. It is said that he keeps a clutch of foolish captured women there, some quite high born, who have fallen for his good looks. That is Havel mac Alwyn!"

"We shall go over to Dumbarton tomorrow," her father told the king grimly. "I shall have a boat made ready."

That evening was pleasantly spent in good company and comfort, especially the feminine side of it, the feeding excellent. Patrick and Alexander managed to sit, usually, near Phemia, who obviously took after her mother in her ability to hold the attention and amuse. The Steward had never spoken of his womenfolk, although he appeared to appreciate them now well enough. Alexander, unused to the company of young women, of any women at all other than serving-wenches, was clearly much intrigued.

Although they were allotted different bedrooms in that commodious establishment, the king came to Patrick's chamber, near his own, before sleeping that night.

"She is good, that Phemia. Very good," he declared. "I like her. She smiles a lot, does she not? I did not know of her. The Steward has not spoken of her. Nor of her mother indeed. Of any of them here."

"No. I think that he keeps his two lives very separate, his

73

life at your court and his life here at home. You should have more women at your court, Alex – women like this Phemia. And the Lady Beatrix, indeed. Over-many men, old men."

"Yes. But how could I do that, Pate?"

"Some of the wives and daughters of your other lords might well be glad to come, on occasion. Not all the time, but now and again. The younger ones. I could bring my own sister Ada. She is young yet, but has spirit. Not so much as this one, perhaps, this Phemia. But good company."

"That would be good. We must do that. My father never seemed to have women about him. He was old, of course."

"Yes. You were born to him late, by his second wife. And his brother whom he succeeded, King Malcolm, never married. So for long the court life has lacked women, no?"

"She is friendly. And, and warm! And her body, her shape, is very . . . becoming. When she smiles her face, her cheeks . . ."

"Dimples, yes. I did not fail to note that!" Patrick eyed his royal friend, one eyebrow raised. "You will have to learn about women, Alex. There is much to learn, I think. Myself also, perhaps!"

"You? You have known about them? Been close to some? Not only to your sister?"

"Not really close, no. I have gone with girls at times. Dallied, just. Farm girls and the like. Had . . . play with them. But never anything of meaning. Nor of my own kind."

"I have never known any. I have seen serving ones. Seen them when they bend down. Their, their chests. The shape of them. But that is all. I have never touched one."

"It may be time that you learned, Alex!"

With much to think on, the King of Scots retired to his own room.

Renfrew did not have any fishing-haven, the Clyde there still too far from real salt water; but the castle owned rowing-boats beached nearby, and one larger craft, oared, but with a sail to hoist. In this, next morning, with six servitors at the oars, the Steward took the royal party down the river the ten miles to Dumbarton, passing Kilpatrick and Langbank. The former, their host pointed out, lay just opposite where St Patrick was born, whom so many thought of as Irish because he was the patron saint thereof; but he had been born here by the Clyde, only going to Ireland as a young man, captured by raiders.

The estuary was over a mile wide by the time they reached Dumbarton Rock, a dramatically pyramidal hill rising from the very shore, the Lennox castle crowning its summit, and quite a large township lying to landward. There was a sizeable harbour here, and their craft tied up amongst many boats.

The visitors were faced with a steep climb up hundreds of steps to the castle, which must have held its inconveniences for the occupants, since all horses had to be left in stabling at the foot. But there was no doubting the security of the stronghold, however constricting the site on top. Two guarded gatehouses had to be negotiated on the way up, but the Steward was known to the men, even if they did not recognise his youngest companion.

At the summit, they perceived that there was more space than appeared from below, the hold's towers based on different projections of the rock, and quite an area to walk around, stony necessarily, but airy and lessening the feeling of constraint, offering magnificent views.

Their arrival had not gone unnoticed, of course, and great was the stir when the identity of the visitors was learned. Malduin, Master of Lennox, was first to greet them, a man in his late twenties, friendly and unassuming however surprised to meet his liege-lord, and eyeing his father-in-law speculatively. He led them to his mother, the Countess Eva, a tall, gaunt woman of somewhat forbidding aspect but proving to be amiable enough in a stiffish way. Another son, Gilchrist, appeared, studious-seeming and quiet, and then the Steward's daughter Bea, very obviously pregnant, not unlike Euphemia but less fair and lacking those dimples. She was clearly glad to see her father.

The whole company was led across to another tower where they found the Earl Alwyn at a table strewn with books and parchments, a greying, stooping man most evidently short-sighted, who peered at them from amongst his papers, and rose distinctly stiff-limbed when Alexander was announced. It was apparent where Gilchrist got his studious nature from, and to Patrick at least, understandable that here was a father who might be unable to control a difficult son, of whatever the mother might be capable.

When the Steward said that he had brought His Grace here to discuss the Earl of Tyrconnel's complaint about a Scots assault in Ulster, Alwyn looked unhappy, raised both hands in a helpless gesture, and glanced over to his son Malduin.

That young man nodded. "It is bad, Sire," he said. "Grievous. My brother Havel is responsible. We all much deplore it. He is difficult, hard to control. A law unto himself. He holds that certain lands over there in Ulster should be ours. They belonged to our forebears. Have been taken over by the Fergus family. He claims that they should be returned to us, to him. *We* do not, Sire. But Havel does. And, and . . ." He did not raise his hands as his father had done but spread them, eloquently enough of his inability to persuade his brother.

"He killed men. This Trad mac Fergus. And raped women, we were told," Alexander said.

"Yes. It is . . . unfortunate."

"It is more than that," the Steward declared. "It is an offence against His Grace's realm, endangering our good relations with the Irish. And that is important. Apart from a sin, the sin of murder."

"I know it," the Earl Alwyn said. "But what can we do?"

76

"You can take steps to show your displeasure. You have a sufficiency of men in your Lennox to teach that young man a lesson. Send them to this Rosneath which he holds and enforce it. And send your regrets to Tyrconnel, with some token of restitution for harm done. You can do that, Alwyn."

Again the earl looked at Malduin. "If it must be . . ."

"It must. His Grace will inform the Irish lords of his regrets and displeasure at it all. Declare that there will be retribution on the perpetrators. I say that you should use your strength to take Havel's house, this Rosneath, strong as it may be. Bring him here and imprison him for some time. He will be secure enough up in this hold. And if you cannot bring yourself to constrain your own son, hand him over to His Grace's officers. Do that, my friend." But it was at Malduin that the Steward looked.

His son-in-law inclined his head. "I will do what I can, yes."

"You could raise a thousand men and more in Lennox, if you so chose, no?"

"Perhaps. But . . ."

The Steward looked at Alexander, who took his cue.

"It is my royal command," he said.

"I will do my best, Your Highness."

"So be it," the Steward declared. "We shall not delay you longer."

"You will not bide here for the night?" Malduin asked.

"No, lad. We must be gone." The Steward glanced at Alexander. "His Grace cannot be away from Roxburgh for any longer than is necessary. So much demands his presence. Back to Renfrew with us, and in the morn we will be on our way south again."

The king nodded. He was almost certainly as well pleased, as was Patrick, at this. It meant more time with Phemia.

So, after some refreshment, they left Dumbarton Castle, unable to do more on the Irish matter meantime, Malduin and Gilchrist conducting them down to their boat, and promising due action, however uneasily. Then down Clyde again.

At Renfrew Castle the two young men were not long in approaching Phemia on the subject of attending at court, Patrick raising the matter as soon as they could be alone with her, Alexander enthusiastically supporting. On the way they had agreed that it was hardly suitable to make it a royal command, so persuasion was necessary. The girl looked from one to the other wonderingly but by no means unfavourably.

"At court? What would we do there?" she asked. "At your Roxburgh, Sire? I have never thought of this."

"There is very much that you could do, Phemia," Alexander said, but did not elaborate. "Much that would please us. And do not call me Sire when we are alone. Pate calls me Alex, just."

She raised brows at that. "Dare I? You, the king!"

"There is much that you could do at Roxburgh," Patrick said. "And your mother, to be sure. And . . . others. The court is all lacking in women. You could much improve it, cheer it, enliven it. For Alex. For us all. There are too many elderly men. If you came, others would, no doubt."

"Would my father approve?"

"If the king said that he wished it, I do not see that he could refuse. Alex *is* liege-lord of us all."

"Your mother . . . ?" the king asked.

"Oh, I think that my mother would not mislike it. She is ever fond of company, of visiting and meeting others. Let us go ask her." It was evident that Phemia was by no means averse to the proposal.

They went through to the Lady Beatrix's withdrawing-room off the hall. But she was not alone, her husband with her. This had Alexander and Patrick looking at each other; but the young woman was nowise inhibited.

"The King's Highness would wish us to attend his court, Mother," she announced right away. "At his Roxburgh. He says that they lack womenkind there. That would be good, would it not?"

"At court? Visit it you mean?"

"Not just one visit, I think," Phemia looked at Alexander. "Attend it, he said."

"Why, that would be . . . interesting, yes." Mother looked at father. "Here is something new, Wattie."

The younger men had never heard the Steward referred to as Wattie before.

"I have not heard of this," he said. "I do not know . . ."

"I would like it, wish it," Alexander said in a rush. "I would. Very much so. It would be good."

"I would like it also," the daughter declared. "A change from this Renfrew."

Lady Beatrix laughed. "I see! A change, yes. What would we do at court, Your Grace? Simple women like ourselves."

"You would make it better. More kindly. Good company. I say that we need the like."

Patrick added his voice. "The court lacks what women can give it, my lady. It is long since His Grace's mother died. And there has been little of lightness and warmth, such as women can give, I think."

"You are of a discerning mind, young man! We are flattered! How say you, Husband?"

"There could be something in it, perhaps. If there were others also."

"Yes," the king assured. "We would have other women to come. Wives and daughters of the lords. Some more younger men also, no?"

"If it is your royal wish."

"It is, it is. I have long felt that something was needed. This could be it."

"Then who am I to say no?" He looked at his wife. "If you, my dear, would have it so?"

"I think we should try it, at the least. We might have something to contribute, yes. And I would see more of *you*, my heart!" That was with another laugh.

"Very well. I think that the new High Chamberlain has had something to do with this!" He raised his brows enquiringly. "When is it to be, Sire?"

"So soon as is possible, my lord. And Pate, my Chamberlain, deems it good."

Phemia, gurgling, led king and Chamberlain out. "We will leave you to make the arrangements, good parents!"

"Will my brothers come also?" she asked, back in her own anteroom off her bedchamber. "I do not know whether they would wish to. Alexander very much lords it here in Father's absence. And Walter spends much time up in Angus. While William is young . . ."

"They can come if they wish," Alexander said, but less than eagerly. It was evident whom he saw as the favoured courtier.

A thought occurred to Patrick. "Is there accommodation for all at Roxburgh Castle, Alex? If we have others coming. With all the lords of your court there."

"Oh, yes. There is one tower but little used. Next to the gatehouse. And there are good houses in Roxburgh town. Some of the lords lodge in these, not in the castle. It is no distance off."

"I have never been in those parts," Phemia said. "Near to the border with England, is it not? I know little of that south land. The Highlands and Isles, yes. We go up to the Loch Lomond much. And to Arran and Bute in our boat. And to my mother's Angus. But not the south. I have heard of the Borderland, so different from here."

"We will show it to you. My Dunbar also, I hope. With its great cliffs and coves and dizzy heights." And Patrick risked squeezing her arm, to reassure her that she would be well looked after.

Her dimples reappeared, and she patted his hand.

They made a congenial evening of it.

In the morning it was farewells and to horse again, but with declarations that it would not be long before there was a reunion.

6

Concern for the coming of women to the royal court, unfortunately, had to be delayed. Quickly after the return to Roxburgh, crisis over relations with England developed, and the Scots were faced with serious challenge. King John, the unpopular and unpredictable monarch, resorted to arms, this despite having been forced by his lords to concede the great charter of freedom for Church and state, the Magna Carta, only six months before. Now he violated its clauses. A strange man indeed, he had succeeded his crusading and heroic brother, Richard the Lion Heart, in 1199, a more different pair of sons of Henry the Second being hard to imagine.

Now, he used that meeting of the Northumbrian barons with Alexander, at Felton, as his excuse for warfare. He claimed that there they had paid homage to the King of Scots, accepting *him* as their liege-lord, and were therefore guilty of traitorous rebellion, and must be crushed. Not only that, but that Alexander was thus seeking to incorporate Northumberland and Cumberland in the Scottish realm. Gathering an army, he marched on South Yorkshire and Northumberland with fire and sword, and proclaimed his intention of invading Scotland. Fleeing before him, some of his northern England lords had arrived at Melrose to plead for Alexander's aid against their own monarch.

This extraordinary situation demanded immediate and positive reaction, especially when another deputation arrived, this from Carlisle, from the barons of Cumberland, declaring that they were to be next on their wicked king's campaign of devastation, and urging an invasion of their shire by Alexander as a pre-emptive stroke.

In all haste, then, a Scots army must be assembled, all agreed. But that would take time. The king had no standing force, only his royal guard. And John would move fast. He had reached Morpeth in Northumberland, and burned it. Then Alnwick and Mitford, and advanced swiftly north to the Tweed, sacking the township of Wark just across from the Coldstream area, and no more than ten miles from Roxburgh.

With the aggressive enemy so near, Alexander was advised to leave Roxburgh forthwith. Besides, it was no suitable place to muster an army, in the wedge-shaped peninsula between the two great rivers. Space and grazing for all the horses were needed. But the normal rallying-place for armies, the Burgh Muir of Edinburgh, was much too far off. Somewhere in the Merse would serve better. Patrick suggested the Home area, where his father would be able to raise a large number quickly; and it was reasonably accessible for others from north and west.

So a hasty move was made to Home Castle on its steep ridge amongst the grassy levels, and the summons to arms sent out far and wide.

Strategy had to be decided upon. With King John's army so close, and a head-on clash, in the circumstances, inadvisable, some diversionary move was indicated, until the full Scots strength could be assembled, much of it having to come great distances. The Marischal suggested that they should do as the Cumbrian lords had pleaded, make a swift assault over the border there, to Carlisle and beyond, where they might be welcomed and reinforced. This could well bring John hastening westwards and give time for the main Scots army to assemble at Home and move over Tweed behind him, thus threatening him on two fronts.

It seemed excellent tactics, and was agreed.

Patrick hurried north to Dunbar to have Cospatrick gather as many mounted men as possible in shortest time, himself raising the Middle Merse. He reckoned that they could probably muster fifteen hundred in two or three days.

When father and son joined the king at Home Castle, it was to find over one thousand men assembled, from Tweeddale, Lauderdale and the Gala Water areas. So, leaving the Steward and the Justiciar to lead the larger hoped-for force on across Tweed and if possible behind King John, Alexander, the Marischal and Cospatrick headed westwards by south, over the masses of the Southern Uplands for Nithsdale, Annandale, Dumfries and the West March, picking up reinforcements as they went.

They got as far as Tweedsmuir where that great river rose, to camp for the first night, and had only just left next morning when hurrying messengers caught up with them to announce that the English army had not only crossed into Scotland but had attacked Roxburgh itself. The castle there was too strongly placed to be taken without siegery, but the enemy had burned the town.

Much upset, Alexander was for turning back and going to the rescue of his folk there, but was persuaded to carry on for Carlisle, their chosen strategy, assured that many of the Roxburgh people would have taken refuge in its castle.

They reached the Solway shore at Gretna the following late afternoon, and crossed the Sark and Esk into Cumberland. The Marchmen, of course, had not failed to learn of their approach, and mustered, and hastened to inform the city of Carlisle. But instead of the normal reaction of alarm and hasty marshalling against invasion, the Scots were received with acclaim by the bishop thereof and many of the local magnates, Musgraves, Metcalves, Forsters, Dacres and the like, all loud in their enmity to King John. Alexander told them that this was not his main army, which would be seeking to turn back the English invasion of their land. So the advised tactics were to advance eastwards into Northumberland, devastated as it was, to threaten John's rear, while the Steward and the Justiciar were now seeking to counter his front.

This was accepted; but the Cumbrians would require a

few days to gather their full armed strength. And meanwhile there was a problem, in that the governor of the castle was refusing to welcome the Scots, remaining loyal to his monarch, this somewhat inhibiting eagerness to start an advance eastwards, for Carlisle Castle was a strong fortress. So Alexander and his lords were installed in the bishop's palace to wait, distinctly impatient.

Three days kicking their heels and there were developments, as the Cumbrian levies assembled. The castle garrison rebelled against the governor and yielded it up. And a courier arrived from the Steward to announce that King John had changed his assault, headed back to Berwick-upon-Tweed, sacked that town, torturing many of the inhabitants and then marched northwards, burning the priory and town of Coldinghame, had assailed Dunbar, failed to take the castle but ravaged its town, and gone on as far as Haddington which he had also attacked. The Scots army was hastening northwards also, not south, to seek to counter the dire challenge, and save Edinburgh, presumably the main target.

Needless to say Alexander and his leaders were grievously worried by this news. Here they were idling at Carlisle while their land was being savaged. They would wait no longer for the Cumbrian fullest force. They would head eastwards with what they had at once, and then turn north to hope to come on John's rear.

But not Cospatrick and his son. Shaken by the word of Dunbar being devastated, they were for home forthwith, to do what they could for their people. Taking about half of the Merse force with them, they said farewell to Alexander and set off immediately north by east, the king declaring his sorrow and sympathy.

Riding fast they went back to the Esk, up its dale, and then over to Ewesdale and so up to the heights of Mosspaul. Then down to Hawick and the Teviot, anxiety driving them. No halting was considered even though they all but killed their mounts. By Selkirk and the Gala Water they crossed into Lauderdale, riding through the night. By dawn, through the Lammermuirs, they began to smell the reek of burning, stale but very evident.

Exhausted, men and beasts, they came down to the coast in the morning. Had anyone ever ridden non-stop from Carlisle to Dunbar before? Over one hundred miles. They found their little town devastated, the thatches of some roofs still smouldering. There were few people to be seen, only some burying dead around the church, itself roofless and ransacked. These told them that most of the folk had escaped, warned of the English approach by the sacking of Coldinghame. Some had fled to take refuge in the hills, some in the castle, many sailed off in boats from the harbour, probably for refuge on the Fife coast, even on the Isle of May.

At the castle, overcrowded as it now was, they were relieved to find the remainder of their family safe, however distracted. The English had made an attempt against the gatehouse tower but had failed to achieve anything in the face of its inaccessible position on the cliff, the further towers on the stacks in the sea of course being quite impossible to approach.

Weary as they were, after the briefest rest the earl and his men set about improving the situation as best they might, comforting the folk and seeing what could be done to make habitable such of the shattered township as was possible at this stage. Most of the houses had been thatch-roofed, not tiled, and although this had been easily set ablaze, and the burning debris falling into and destroying the interiors beneath, it left the stone walling intact. The reed thatching could be fairly readily replaced, timbering taking longer to cut and fashion. But the community could be restored. The people who had fled into the hills could be left there meantime.

But Patrick was not concerned in this labour and care. His task was to ride off again, on a fresh horse, with two of his men, to discover where the main Scots army, under the Steward, was now. And where were the English? Would the invaders be likely to go on further, or to return this way? It was obviously vitally important to know.

Patrick rode first along the coast northwards to the Earl MacDuff of Fife's castle of Tantallon near to his ferry town of North Berwick, a dozen miles. This, it turned out, had escaped the enemy assault, King John having turned inland, westwards, to take the more direct route to Haddington, the shire town, which he was known to have sacked. The keeper of Tantallon was able to give some information. After Haddington, the English had headed on westwards, presumably making for Edinburgh, another seventeen miles. But not far beyond, John had evidently changed his plans, and turned southwards, no doubt to face the Steward's army. He could tell Patrick no more than that.

West of Haddington was the Gleds' Muir, a lengthy barren area before Tranent was reached. If John had turned south there it would be to cross the upper Tyne river at one of its fords, at Samuelston or Herdmanston, with the western Lammermuirs still ahead and Lauderdale well beyond. Would the Steward have come north that way? It seemed probable. There were few routes for any army through those hills. And his scouts learning of it, John turned south to meet them?

Patrick required to know the situation.

He swung off south-westwards then, to reach the foothills, by Traprain Law and Morham and Gifford, avoiding Haddington. This vicinity had obviously not been assailed. But a few miles further he came to burned cottages and ravished farmsteads, in the Gilchriston and Humbie area, indicative of the invaders' passage. It looked as though they were heading for the Soutra Pass over into Lauderdale; indeed they had little option if they sought to enter the Merse. Where was the Steward?

He went on, by Fala, to climb up to Soutra, and passed the great hospital founded by Alexander's uncle, Malcolm the Maiden, the first such in all Scotland. Some of the buildings close to the road had obviously been raided, but these were hospices and shelters for travellers; the great majority of the extensive establishment's many departments, for the sick, those with infectious diseases, the wounded and the aged, were inland on a sort of heathery plateau, these remaining apparently unassailed, for which the monks who administered it all would thank God.

Presently Patrick was riding down into Lauderdale, watchfully. There was no sign of ravishment now, although every indication that a large force had passed this way. The English would be concerned not to herald their coming if they anticipated armed opposition ahead.

Down the long dale he got to the town of Lauder itself before he gained the information he sought. Here he learned from the townsfolk unexpected tidings. There had been no battle, only a mere skirmish. The Scots army had been coming up the wide branch valley of the Allan Water, northwards, only some three miles from Lauder, when they had encountered an outriding party of the English, watching their flanks. There had been a brief affray before the surprised enemy got away. But one of their wounded, left behind, questioned, had revealed the situation. King John was not now looking for battle. He had received word that King Alexander, with a large host of Cumbrians, Northumbrians and Yorkshiremen, was assembled and threatening to cut him off from his home-land territory in the south, and he was now heading thither with all speed, and anxious to avoid the delay of dealing with this array, with grievous news from further south. So now the Steward's force was following the English and hoping to trap them between the two forces. Just what the grievous word from southern England was none knew.

It was a complicated situation, militarily; but at least Patrick now had what he had wanted to know: further threat to Dunbar, or otherwise, meantime over. Alexander's advised strategy had worked out to good effect. Now it was return to Dunbar, and thankfully.

Thereafter it was all activity at Dunbar, repairing, rebuilding, cutting reeds, felling timber, reassuring distressed folk and welcoming back those who had fled, by land or sea.

Patrick wondered whether he ought to head off southwards to try to rejoin the king, but his father declared that, High Chamberlain as he might be, his first duty was to his own people here; anyway, chamberlains were not expected to be warriors – the monarch had marischals, constables, admirals and the like for that.

When news did reach them as to the overall situation, it was surprising again. There had been no great battle. King John had deliberately avoided it by heading on southwards along the English coastline where he was not expected to be – and for very good reason. His lords in middle and southern England apparently were just as dissatisfied with their present monarch as were those in the north. Led by the Earl of Salisbury, John's half-brother, they had actually invited Prince Louis of France, son of King Philip, to come over and take the English throne. And Louis had indeed come, whether eager for a crown other than France's was not known. He had landed at Thanet, taken Winchester, then Dover Castle, and besieged Windsor Castle itself. John had reason to hurry homewards.

Just what was Alexander's reaction to all this was unclear. Probably he was waiting at Carlisle or elsewhere to see what transpired. Certainly he had not returned to Home or Roxburgh.

When they did get news of their young liege-lord it was as extraordinary as all else. John was now said to be a sick man, whether as a result of all the hostilities or merely from personal physical disability was not known. But he had seemingly retired to some remote area of the Welsh marches, apparently with most of his army deserting him, seeing his cause in all but ruin. And Alexander, because of the Scots-French alliance, had elected to journey south, with a strong escort, but sending his main army home, this to confer with the Earl of Salisbury and Prince Louis.

The entire situation, thus, was in a state of chaos and uncertainty, what would happen next anybody's guess.

That summer had certainly been one of confusion. What would autumn bring?

October, in fact, brought tidings that changed all, more or less settled all. King John had died, apparently from natural causes. He had left a nine-year-old son, Henry. And Salisbury, his uncle, seeing the opportunity to rule England in the boy's name, abandoned his support for Louis and, with the majority of the barons' and magnates' agreement, had the youngster crowned King of England as Henry the Third. Louis returned to France, disappointed or otherwise, and Alexander to Scotland.

The prospects of peace suddenly became good, relief general in the two kingdoms, not least at Dunbar.

Patrick set off for Home Castle hopefully.

7

That year's experiences had much aided Alexander towards maturity, as Patrick discovered when, finding no royal presence at Home, he went on to Roxburgh. The castle-palace there having survived intact, the king and his advisers were doing what the Cospatricks had done at Dunbar, restoring the adjacent township to order as far as possible, and seeking to return court life to normal. And, delighted to see Patrick again, and not in the least critical of his friend's absence from his side for those months, Alexander promptly declared that the said normalcy should be bettered by their projected feminine presence. The Steward and Patrick were in fact despatched without delay to Renfrew to initiate the process.

Back on the Clyde they found the Lady Beatrix well pleased to comply, her daughters far from objecting. In the three days that it took to prepare the ladies and their female attendants for the removal, Patrick enjoyed and made the most of his opportunities to establish good relations with Phemia, not displeased that Alexander was elsewhere, so that his attentions were not shared, the monarch having been almost as appreciative towards that young woman. Phemia's sister Christian was apt to be present, the youngest of the family, at sixteen years; and she found considerable interest in the visitor, and did not seek to hide it, which had its drawbacks, to Phemia's obvious amusement. But Patrick nevertheless did judge that he was making some progress.

The word from Dumbarton was that Malduin and his brothers had managed to deal with Havel, and had dispersed his unruly following. Presently he was imprisoned in Dumbarton tolbooth. How long they would keep him there was not known. But at least the Irish princelings could be informed that action had been taken.

The late October evenings by the fireside in the hall's withdrawing-room of Renfrew Castle were spent with Patrick managing to sit between the two sisters in fairly close contact usually; and sometimes he perceived the Steward's speculative eye upon the three of them from across the hearth where he sat with his wife. Both sisters chose to accompany the guest to his bedchamber door each night, which at least presented him with the opportunity, by embracing and kissing Christian first, of doing the same, or not quite the same, to Phemia, without his attentions appearing over-forward, or so he judged. The fact that the pair came again on the second and third nights probably bore out his assessment.

At any rate, when all was ready for departure, and farewells were said to the two brothers, who were being left to look after the castle and its properties, all were on easy and friendly terms – a little too easy perhaps, since ease was not exactly what Patrick sought.

They made quite a train of it, with seven women, the Steward's escort, and a string of packhorses laden with female clothing and gear. Inevitably they went fairly slowly. They got as far as Lanark the first night, where they put up at St Kentigern's Priory again. And there, unfortunately, the monks saw to it that the women were quartered well apart from the men, so that evening and night-time associations were impossible, even their feeding separate, Patrick for one wondering at some branches of Holy Church's attitude to the other sex, despite their adoration of the Virgin Mary.

However, the next day's travel got them to Peebles, on the Tweed, where the monkish hospice was less strict than at Lanark, and they were at least permitted to eat together and sit thereafter at tables until bed-going. Patrick had quite enjoyed riding in feminine company. With a little care he was able frequently to manoeuvre his mount so that

91

he was alongside the young women; and since the tracks they covered were usually very narrow, permitting only two to ride abreast, he saw to it that most often he rode next to Phemia, sometimes close enough to touch. He was able to point out items of interest on the way, for the young women had never been in these parts. Phemia proved to be of an enquiring mind, particularly interested in Pictish stone circles, forts and cairns.

They reached Roxburgh to find Alexander supervising the restoration of the ravished community in person, however unsuitable some of his lords considered this to be for the monarch. But he promptly abandoned this when the Steward's party arrived, and nothing would do but that he still more personally should conduct the ladies to their quarters, which he had especially prepared for them in his own tower, paying particular attention to the young women's bedchamber which he had arranged should be next door to the room he shared with Patrick. He was clearly going to be an attentive host. Since the Steward, and now his wife, occupied a different tower, this arrangement offered distinct possibilities.

The girls seemed well pleased with their reception and all that they saw of the palace and its amenities and surroundings, exclaiming over the River Tweed which ran swiftly directly under their bedchamber window. Also the company they were to keep, or some of it, although they did remark on the number of old men in the royal entourage, Alexander sympathising.

Patrick was not entirely sure as to all his duties as High Chamberlain; he had had little opportunity to learn of them since his appointment. But presumably the very term indicated that he had some responsibility for the rooming, comfort and entertainment of all at court, especially guests? At any rate, he would make it his business to seek to please, although the king himself seemed to be similarly concerned.

It was Patrick's hope that Alexander would find young Christian still more to his taste than was Phemia, being nearer to his own age but although he got on well with the younger sister he still evidently preferred the elder. And with Christian herself clearly smitten with Patrick, the situation was not entirely as the High Chamberlain would have planned it. However, the royal court was much improved, he felt, at least for some of its members.

The Steward was one of these, needless to say. But he did keep an eye on his daughters, especially in their close companionship with the young monarch, this sufficiently for him to observe to Patrick, after a day or two, that he should seek to ensure that Alexander did not get too fond of his daughters, too close to them in all this. After all, as king, he would in due course, possibly fairly soon, have to find some suitable young princess or other to wed, to ensure advisable alliance and the required royal succession; and he, Walter, was not prepared for his daughters, either of them, to become mere mistresses. Patrick saw the point of this, and agreed to use what influence he had; but at the same time he wondered whether the Steward was hinting that he also should watch his step with his daughter.

Another aspect of it all was the bringing in of other women to the court; it had never been intended that it should be only the Steward's family that was to come. Who else, then? Most of the officers of state and advisers whom Alexander had inherited from his father were too old to change their ways, in this as in other respects, and were not interested in bringing their families to Roxburgh from their various estates and properties. One or two might consider it, but their wives would be apt to be elderly also and less than eager to take up new ways and living conditions, leaving their homes. Moreover, Alexander was determined to replace these oldsters as soon as was decently possible; and the bringing in of new blood could perhaps be linked with the women-introduction process. They would have to consider well the possibilities as to the suitable nominees for office, their wives and families not unimportant in the choice. Patrick wondered whether ever before there had been such a preoccupation in the selection of a royal council and regime.

The pair of them discussed the possibilities. Patrick said that since the Steward had led the way, it might be wise to start by inviting more of his kin and friends, who would tend to be influenced by him. An obvious choice was Malduin, Master of Lennox, his father Alwyn unlikely to object although not come himself. Then there was Neil, Earl of Carrick, of the Galloway line, who was wed to Phemia's and Christian's sister Margaret. These two might be offered minor duties at court. Some others of the younger earls and lords might be glad to come; Randolph, Earl of Moray and his Juliana, known to the Cospatricks; Malcolm MacDuff, Earl of Fife and his wife Matilda, a daughter of the old Earl of Strathearn. Another possibility Patrick knew was a supporter of his father, Sir David de Lindsay, of Luffness and Crawford, Deputy Justiciar of Lothian, not married but with a pleasant sister. Alexander, on his excursion to Carlisle, had met and involved Sir John Maxwell of Caerlaverock, on the Solway; his wife had entertained the royal party kindly.

So there was a selection, to start with. The king had been told that the monarchy frequently had courtiers who were given honorary offices such as Royal Falconer, the Butler, the Standard-Bearer, the Cup-Bearer, the Armour-Bearer, the Dapifer, the Paniter and the like. These positions could be offered to those invited to give them some standing; most would come under the authority of the High Chamberlain anyway. The older and senior officers of state could not dispute it.

The Steward, apprised of all this, was agreeable, the Lady Beatrix even more so, happy to have much of her family around her here.

Phemia and Christian were not left out of these deliberations, and had their own suggestions to make. Neil of Carrick was keen on hawking, and would probably like to be Falconer. And was there a position which was linked to the sport of fishing? This for Malduin, with his love of spearing flukies. With these rivers so close! This was asked with laughter.

The young women, although a little over-awed at first by all the king's stern-looking and grey-bearded advisers, quickly learned how to keep their distance from these. Alexander now having his own tower in the castle, this was not difficult; and although they usually ate with the Steward and Lady Beatrix, and only occasionally in the main keep's great hall with all the court, the young people managed to be alone together not infrequently.

Their friendship ripened, which was good. But for Patrick there was frustration in it also. For he admitted to himself that he now wanted Phemia for himself, wanted it urgently, all of her and all of him, his heart and mind and his body. This ease and proximity was all very well, but it did produce its stresses for him. Four of them always, when he wished so often that it was only two. Especially with Alexander competing with him for Phemia's smiles and dimples, and Christian over-affectionate. If only he could see Phemia alone was his frequent longing. But it never seemed to be possible, save for the odd moment or two. And having her sleeping in the next room of a night was no great help to a man becoming very much in love.

He wondered, of course, what Phemia's feelings for him might be. Her goodwill and friendliness were evident; but deeper than that? She allowed him his gestures and tributes of admiration and esteem, his touchings and pattings and goodnight kisses at the bedroom door; but then she permitted that to Alexander also. Did she realise how much she had come to mean to him? He did not know, he just did not know.

It was a full week after their arrival at Roxburgh that he got, or contrived, his opportunity. The king had to attend one of his frequent and to him boring signing sessions of documents, charters and the like, and invited the two sisters to come and help him with the business of appending the privy seal to the signed papers, which demanded much handling of lighted candles, tapers and coloured wax, the work of clerks; but Alexander saw it as something at which the young women could assist, and better company than the monkish assistants. The girls were quite happy to co-operate, and Patrick accompanied them over to the document-room in the main keep. And there, after a while, with Christian taking her turn with taper and wax and Alexander handling the seal, Phemia watching, having done her stint, it came to Patrick that here was a chance, with many more papers to seal. He touched Phemia's arm.

"This could go on for some time, and it does not take four of us," he said, pointing to the pile of parchments. "Come, you, I will show you how they net the salmon you eat, from the Tweed. So that you can tell your good-brother Malduin, if and when he comes to court."

She nodded agreeably.

The king looked up. "I will join you, Pate, when I have finished this."

Christian, lit taper in one hand, red sealing-wax stick in the other and held over the required space below the signature, could not but continue with her task. Patrick led her sister to the door and out.

"You have had a sufficiency of sealing?" he asked.

"Oh, yes. Chris seems quite to enjoy it. Where do we go for this of the salmon, Patrick?" She never called him Pate.

"We have boats down at the riverside. On the Tweed, not the Teviot. The fish seem to prefer the larger river. It runs less fast, save in spates."

They went out through the gatehouse arch and down the hill on the north side, and a little way along towards the township, to where a little wooden jetty was built, with three small rowing-boats tied thereto. Patrick pointed to one of these.

"You are happy enough in a boat, Phemia? We could go and see how the nets are set and handled. It is quite an art that I had not known before I came here."

"Yes, I am used to boats. On the Clyde, we have some. But not to net salmon."

He took her arm to help her down into one of the craft,

taking great care of her, and approving as she hoisted up her skirts to step over the side. Once therein she promptly sat down on the central thwart, not on the stern seat as he would have expected. She reached for one of the two oars lying there.

"I will row," he declared, stepping in after untying the rope. "No need for you to do it."

"Two rowers are better than one. I often use the oar."

Nothing loth, he pushed the boat off and sat down beside her on the thwart. It was only a small craft, and there was not much room for two on that cross-bench, which meant, of course, that they were close together, indeed in contact, and such contact was very pleasant, stirring indeed, stirring in more ways than one.

They rowed upstream some four hundred yards, Patrick very much aware of his companion's oar-work, anything but critical, especially its effect on her breathing and bosom movement. He had to explain that this salmon-catching for the castle tables required the use of nets, two sorts of nets, drag-nets and bag-nets, the former weighted down and drawn along the bed of the river to reach the sleeping or idling fish; the other, a wide-mouthed sacklike contrivance, its front held open by a fixed bent sapling-rod, to be trawled along behind the boat to net swimming fish. In theory this could be done anywhere on the river, but in practice the chances could be improved by using a permanent under-water barrier, part stone, part wood, which had the effect of narrowing the river and forming a channel into which the moving salmon were forced. It was to this that they were heading now. The barrier, he informed, had to be constantly renewed, liable to be damaged by spates.

Whether the young woman was very interested in all this was to be doubted, but it served as an excuse for his purposes.

He indicated as much. "I never see you alone, Phemia," he told her presently. "Always Alexander or your sister are with us, or both. I like them well, but . . . it is *you* I would be with. On occasion. Alone."

"I guessed as much," she said simply.

"You did?"

"To be sure. I am not stupid, Patrick!"

"No. Oh, no, I did not think that. But have I made it so evident?"

"Frequently, yes. Should I be flattered?"

"Not flattered, no. But not, not displeased?"

Unfortunately just at this stage they came to the place on the river where was the underwater barrier, marked by posts on each bank, and Patrick could scarcely go on without pointing this out. Not that there was anything much to see. He explained that the construction could be glimpsed by peering down into the water. It could not come up to close to the surface, of course, or boats would strike it.

Phemia duly looked down over the side, said that she could see nothing to effect, and turned to eye him quizzically.

"What now?" she asked. Did a quizzical brow raised make that something like a challenge?

"We need not turn back. Not yet," he said. "We can row on a little further to the township before we turn. If you do not mislike the rowing?"

"Very well."

"I do like it. With you so close. Sharing it with you."

"I can feel that!" She moved her leg a little way apart, where their thighs had been touching. But she said it with a little laugh.

"You are not displeased?" That brought them back again to where they had reached before in this exchange.

"Would I be here if I was?" And she allowed her knee to return to its former position against his own.

Encouraged, he took a breath. "I am fond of you, Phemia." That came out with a jerk. "Very fond. More than fond."

"Are you? I guessed as much. But what does fond mean to you, Patrick?"

The rowing had faltered somewhat, for them both.

"It means, it means much. All. It means that I love you, need you, ache for you, lass! Can you understand?"

"Oh, I can, yes. Well understand."

"And, understanding, you, you do not . . . object?"

"Why should I? When I am fond of you also!"

He swallowed. "You are? Fond . . . or, or more!"

She looked at him, wagging her fair head, wordless. But her eyes said it all.

Patrick all but tossed away that wretched oar he held, encumbrance as it now was for what was called for, demanded of a man – and he was all man indeed at that moment. But at least he could free an arm. Around her he flung it, to draw her still closer; and now it was her oar which got in the way, coming between them, getting pressed between her breasts.

But, twisting, he did manage to kiss her, first her hair, then her ear, her cheek and, as she turned her head, her lips. And they opened slightly under his own.

The boat swung round with the current.

He found no words for a space, neither of them did, however active and eloquent their lips. But his oar, slipping from his now feeble grasp and all but falling over the side, had the man turning back, grabbing for it, lessening grip on soft femininity for hard wood.

She took the opportunity to ease her oar-shaft out from her bosom, with a murmured incoherence, one hand still holding him.

Their boat was now drifting quite swiftly downstream, sideways on.

"My love, my love!" Patrick gasped. "My very dear heart! My precious one! You could love me also?"

"Could and do, foolish one! I have felt for you, wanted your favour, wished you mine almost from the beginning, when first we began to know each other. Did you not perceive it?"

"I knew that we could be friends, but . . . oh, Phemia, woman! Here is heaven on earth!" He reached for her again, his oar shipped now.

"Or on *water*!" she gurgled. "Dear man, you choose a strange place to, to . . ." She got no further, mouth and tongue otherwise engaged.

Holding each other, and one oar, heedless of their drifting craft, they were despoiled from immediate bliss by a hail, a royal hail. The river's current had carried their boat back to near the jetty, and there were Alexander and Christian gazing and waving.

Patrick did not exactly curse but muttered, and released his companion, to reach for his own oar. "I suppose . . ." he got out, and shrugged.

They righted their craft as well as themselves, and headed for the jetty.

"What were you at?" Alexander demanded. "Was it the fishing? You aiding Phemia, that way?" He peered down into the boat, but saw no catch.

"We but went to look at the netting-place. Then, then one of the oars was all but lost. And we drifted . . ." That was the best that Patrick could do, however feeble.

"Phemia is good at the rowing," Christian all but accused.

"The river runs quite fast. The boat difficult to handle," her sister contributed as they clambered ashore, the monarch aiding her up.

"Shall we try the archery?" he suggested. "We have not done it for long."

"If you wish . . ."

They moved along the riverside to the fairly narrow stretch of meadow where the shed in which the bows, arrows and targets were kept, Christian now clinging to Patrick's arm and eyeing her sister sidelong.

At the butts the men set up the targets and paced out the distances. Neither of the girls was proficient at this sport, and there was much opportunity for male guidance and physical support and demonstration. In the circumstances Patrick paid rather more attention to the younger sister's instruction, however little accuracy resulted. There was much competition and laughter, easy association returning.

That night, at bed-going, it was Phemia who did the contriving. Heading up for their bedroom doors and good-night kisses, suddenly somehow one of her slippers fell off and went rolling down the winding turnpike stairway. Exclaiming, she went after it, leaving the others – but of course quickly had Patrick following her down.

That stair descended a long way, for two storeys, and strangely the footwear kept on falling. At hall level however there was a wide landing, and even that rogue slipper could not proceed further. But probably that would be enough. Phemia, smiling, turned and held out her arms to Patrick, and he swept her up off her feet, delighted, proud of her. Clearly she had initiative to add to her other qualities.

They could not remain down there overlong, to be sure, without investigation from above arriving. But they made good use of the time available, although mirth in some measure limited their appreciative explorations. Added to Patrick's recognition that this young woman could display swift and positive reaction to opportunity was perception and satisfaction that she could participate and enjoy the physical as well as the mental and emotional aspects of being in love.

Slipper replaced, they went upstairs again, hand in hand.

At their doors, both still open, they eyed each other with an understanding and assurance and promise, before a final brief embrace. Christian appeared, brows raised questioningly. Phemia smiled to her, entered, and closed that door behind them.

Long after Alexander's chatter was stilled that night, Patrick lay awake.

8

Thereafter, strangely perhaps, the man was less concerned to be alone with Phemia, glad as he was when such opportunity arose. Assured now of her love and attachment, possibly even desire, he could wait, in the certainty of fulfilment; not wait overlong, he hoped, needless to say. Frequent eye contact and little gestures served now to seal the promise between them. He was even less concerned over Alexander's continued and so evident admiration for the young woman, and more patient with Christian's little advances.

The so necessary togetherness and its advancement was, of course, much on Patrick's mind. When might that be achieved? The least possible delay. She was just under full age, and her father's permission had to be sought; it would have been, anyway. But he did not think that there would be refusal. He got on well with the Steward. And Lady Beatrix was always friendly. Moreover, he might be looked upon as a reasonable match. He was, after all, High Chamberlain, and would one day be an earl.

It occurred to him that before putting the matter to the Steward he should perhaps inform Alexander of his intention. Not that he could object; but their strange friendship called for it.

So, two nights after their boating venture, he broached the subject in their bedroom.

After, that is, a royal disquisition on the unfortunate requirement that he, the King of Scots, would have to go south to pay homage to the new child monarch of England, Henry the Third, for the lands held there. It all seemed wrong, absurd, that one monarch should have to pay

102

homage to another, and of independent realms; but it seemed that there was no way out of it. His great-grand-sire, David, had married one of the richest heiresses in England, and with her gained the county of Huntingdon and much else, the revenues from which were great, too valuable to lose. To retain them, according to English law, this gesture of homage had to be paid, it seemed. It would not be so bad if the English monarch held some land in Scotland, when Henry would have to do the same; but he did not. He, Alex, would have to go soon, for the royal coffers were all but empty, and no great input likely from his own lands. The Kings of Scots had never been rich, save in that, lands.

Patrick was well aware of all this, for as Chamberlain the king's personal finances came under his supervision. His sympathy with the other's reluctance to pay fealty to the child King of England was undoubted, but he recognised that the funds produced were very important to the royal treasury. So long as it was understood by all that the homage paid was *only* for such English estates, and implied no sort of subservience as to the monarchy, it could be accepted.

Alexander declared that he would make that very clear.

This dealt with, Patrick came out with his announcement. "I intend to marry, Alex," he declared.

The other, to *his* surprise, showed none. "I wondered when it would come to that, Pate," he said. "I know that you find Phemia to your taste. As indeed do I! Only *I* cannot seek to marry the likes of her, it seems. Only some foreign princess or other. Who would be a king! But I will be sorry when we will be unable to share a bedchamber, as now. When you are wed. I have liked this."

"Yes. As have I. But you also will be having to wed soon, no? When this would have to end. We shall still be near, in close friendship, Alex."

"No doubt. But it will not be the same. How does Walter the Steward see you as goodson?"

"I have not asked him yet. I have not even asked Phemia

if she will be my wife! But I judge that she will not be too unhappy."

"I think not! You will wish to ask her first? Before the Steward?"

"I had better do so, yes." Patrick took his opportunity. "If I can be alone with her. Christian is ever with her. Could you contrive it, Alex? Soon. Take her off somewhere?"

"There are always charters to sign. And seal. She is good at that. I will take her to the document-room in the morning."

"Good. Tomorrow, then . . ."

At breakfast with the Steward and his wife, the talk was about court improvement. Malduin of Lennox had agreed to come, with his Beatrix, and would arrive shortly. They had not heard from Carrick and Margaret yet, but were fairly sure that the couple would agree. Keith the Marischal had sent for his wife and daughters. And MacDuff, Earl of Fife, the Crowner, was likely to bring his wife Matilda.

The meal over and the young people leaving for their own tower, Alexander announced that he had papers to sign and that Christian should come and aid with the sealing. Patrick took Phemia's arm to hold her back.

"We may join you later," he said, and turned in the other direction from the gatehouse tower, the young woman nothing loth. Arm-in-arm they went.

"I did not think that you would mind missing the wax and candle activity," he told her.

"I can think of better things to do," she answered, squeezing his wrist.

"Yes indeed, my love. Where shall we go?"

"Somewhere quiet! And not where we may concern our good and busy servitors!"

"I very much agree." He grinned. "You may think, lass, that I am over-much concerned with fish and fishing. But in this castle, so hemmed in by the two rivers, it is not to be wondered at. I have more than once tried angling with a rod on that Teviot side. There is a little track down the steep slope, to a sort of ledge just above the water." He pointed forward. "Could you venture down there? I will hold you safe."

"I am sure that you will! So I will trust you."

"Trust me in what degree?"

"To keep me . . . safeguarded. Down there."

"Ah! Safeguarded! I must not fail you, then."

They went along towards the further, eastern end of that wedge-shaped peninsula, to where there was a little postern gate in the high walling. Through this they found themselves on a narrow track topping the sheer drop to the Teviot, dizzy-making for anyone concerned with heights. Pacing on this a short distance, at a brief lessening of the steepness a branch track led slantwise down the rocky slope. Patrick pointed, and taking his companion's hand instead of her arm, glanced at her enquiringly. She nodded.

Picking his way slowly, carefully, testing for secure footholds, he having necessarily to move sideways-on, he led his companion a cautious way down, Phemia heedfully watching where she placed each step, eyeing the track not the water below. Zigzagging, the path, after a drop of perhaps twenty-five feet, reached the ledge just above the swirling river, this littered with debris brought down by spates, but about a yard in average width. Along this they went, to where there was a recess in the bank, with a broken rock which offered a seat. Here Patrick released his tight grip of the girl's hand, and they sat down.

"No very easy place for fishing," she declared. "How could you wield your rod from here? And play a fish if you hooked one?"

"It was difficult, yes, but just possible. I have caught a trout or two here. Never a salmon. You are well enough? Not afraid?"

"Afraid of what, High Chamberlain? This roost? The water? Or yourself!"

His arm around her now drew her closer. "Thus far you are safe, no?"

"I hold my breath!" she said.

"You do?" He reached over with his free arm, to cup her breast. "Your, your breathing seems to me normal!" he judged.

She did not seek to free herself, indeed she turned towards him. "I am in no position to repulse you, I think!"

"My dearest! My love! Woman of my heart!" he got out. "And you are mine, yes? All mine?"

"Here, Patrick, I dare not disagree with you!"

They kissed then, and went on kissing, with murmurs and brief endearments.

Presently that right hand, very much aware of the more pronounced heaving of the bosom it held, the man's fingers began to probe, to explore. Phemia did not protest, but she did find more coherent words amidst the kissing.

"You are . . . seeking something?" she asked. "My person? In, in advance?"

Patrick disciplined both his lips and fingers, then with the latter reached down to grasp her hand and spoke, words coming more clearly, urgently.

"I seek . . . this hand . . . in marriage, my love! That is what I seek. Will you take me? Take me for your husband, woman dear? Will you wed me?"

She drew back a little, to gaze into his eyes. "Need you ask?" she said simply.

He drew a deep breath. "I ask. To be made one with you. And for always. You and myself, joined. Man and wife. No longer two but one. Will you have it so, my dear?"

"So long as I remain my own woman . . . to others!" she said, smiling. "But your woman, yes, Patrick. You would not have me half a man!"

"That you could never be! But together, as one. My dear, my dear!"

They kissed again. That hand returned to her bosom. But now the man was otherwise concerned, action demanded and not just the fondling. "Your father. And mother," he declared. "We must go to them. Tell them, ask them. They will not . . . ? He will give you to me? Has not other plans for you?"

She shook her head. "I think not. And they both know of my fondness for you. They will scarcely be surprised, I judge."

"Then, lass – let us up and go to them. Have this, our union, made sure, affirmed."

"Is that not for the priest to do, my so eager man? In due course. You are over-hasty, I think."

"Do *you* not seek haste? The least of waiting? Our bliss to be fulfilled. Come, you, then." He rose, and aided her up.

They mounted that precarious ascent, still cautiously but more swiftly than they had come down, and on back through the postern, to make for the main keep. Patrick hoped that they would be spared the company of Alexander and Christian.

They found the Lady Beatrix alone in their quarters, her husband having gone to settle some dispute amongst the guards of gate and walls.

"We have come back, Mother, to tell you," Phemia said at once. "Patrick has asked me to marry him!"

"Ah! We wondered how long it would take him to make up his mind!"

The man all but choked. "I, I have wanted it. All but from the first. I but delayed until, until I judged her ready, perhaps. Ready to hear it. My mind, lady, has been set on it for long."

"And now you think that she is ready to accept you?"

"Oh, I am!" the younger woman exclaimed. "I . . . we love each other."

"We could have told you both that some time ago!" her mother said. "We have all but become impatient!"

"Then, you will agree to it? Your husband and yourself, my lady?"

"If it is our daughter's wish, yes, to be sure. So long as we are assured also that you will make a good husband, Patrick."

"Oh, I shall, I shall. I swear that Phemia will find me so. I realise how blessed I am in this. And will remain so. Be assured."

The younger woman pressed his arm.

Her mother looked from one to the other and, rising from her seat, came to embrace her daughter. Then turned and did the same for Patrick.

Much moved, he could only murmur his joy.

But this happy scene was abruptly interrupted. The Steward came in, looking concerned. If he realised that his wife was showing affection and approval towards Patrick, he did not comment on it.

"Where is the king?" he demanded. "He is not in his tower. Here is a to-do! I must see him."

"Walter, here is Phemia and Patrick with word for us . . ."

"Ah! But that can wait. The king must be told of this. Word has come from England. Where is he?"

"He is in the document-room," Patrick said. "Signing papers. Your daughter Christian with him."

"I must see him. You had better come with me, Patrick. It is important."

The younger pair eyed each other. They thought that *their* news was important. But . . .

"Very well." The High Chamberlain had his duties. He followed the Steward out.

"What is this word from England" he asked. "It is ill?"

"Ill, perhaps; and not so ill, I think. It is from Salisbury, the regent. In the name of Henry. He wants all Scots claims to Cumbria yielded up. Alexander to withdraw his people from Carlisle. He is sending up the Archbishop of York and the Bishop of Durham to Berwick to receive the submission. And on gaining it, the Archbishop will lift the excommunication from Scotland."

"That folly!"

"Folly, yes. But with its drawbacks, trammels. The churchmen here are much upset over it."

This matter of excommunication, not only of Alexander

but of the whole realm of Scotland, was an astonishment indeed, few in the land, save for the senior clerics, taking it seriously. The new Pope, Honorius the Third, had foolishly imposed it a year before, all part of the Vatican's present ongoing feud with France. Because of Prince Louis's attempt to win the English throne, with Salisbury's support against King John, Honorius had put the papal anathema on him, on Salisbury and all who aided them. And on account of Alexander's alliance with France and with Salisbury against the late unlamented John, he too, and his kingdom, had been more or less automatically included in the sentence of denunciation, this by the Cardinal Gualo of St Martin, papal envoy. It was all so indirect and ridiculous that most considered it ineffective, invalid, if they considered it at all. But it did mean that the bishops of the Scottish Church were unable to have papal authority for their actions, and could make no new senior appointments. The Bishop of Caithness had died, and not been replaced. Likewise the Abbot of Cumbuskenneth. And since bishops and mitred abbots held seats in the Scottish parliament, this had its effect on more than Church affairs.

The two officers of state found the king and Christian, finished their signing and sealing, poring over a large dossier of old paintings which Alexander had discovered in his great-grandsire's archives, these evidently done by monks in the Low Countries, the pair interested especially in pictures which dealt with Adam and Eve, these in a state of nudity and variously employed. Those monks had obviously researched their subject thoroughly. The monarch looked somewhat guilty, although his companion did not.

"Sire, an envoy, Sir John de Lacy, Constable of Chester, has arrived from the Earl of Salisbury with tidings, strange tidings," the Steward informed. "Before you see him, I judged that you should be warned." And he began to explain the situation over Cumbria, Carlisle, the proposed Berwick meeting and the excommunication.

109

Alexander shook his head in some bewilderment. "But this of the excommunication is of no real moment, is it? Scarcely worth paying the price for, of Cumbria."

"But if Salisbury seeks it, and he speaks for young Henry, then peace and harmony with England would be the prize, Sire. Especially with this of the homage for Huntingdon coming up."

"Mmm."

"And this of Cumbria and Carlisle? Have you any true intention of seeking to win these back to Scotland? It would demand great effort and much struggle, I fear."

"No. I have not considered it seriously. It would be good, to be sure, to recover them. Northumberland also. But I fear that it would be scarcely likely to succeed. And we have other tasks ahead of us the more vital."

Patrick listened interestedly to all this, for he had his own concern for these two counties. After all, they had once belonged to his own forebears. King Stephen of England, grandson of William the Conqueror, had ceded them to Scotland, to King David, about a century before, and they had been handed over, as earldoms, to the two brothers whom the Margaretsons had displaced as Kings of Scots, as a gesture of, as it were, contrition. His own direct ancestor, the first Cospatrick, had been Earl of Northumbria, and his brother Earl of Cumbria. So Patrick's concern was there. Not that he was going to think of war with England to seek to repossess them.

"This of the Berwick meeting," the king was saying. "Think you, should I go to it myself to meet these English clerics? Or send Bishop William, perhaps? One churchman to another."

"I would think go yourself, Sire," the Steward advised. "They come in King Henry's name. And with Your Grace's going down for this homage-giving for your English lands, it would be wise to risk no offence. Until you have that matter secure."

"I do not wish to seem to go begging! Cap in hand to

110

these bishops. Or to the young Plantagenet. Or to Salisbury."

"No. But those revenues from Huntingdon and the others are of much importance, Sire. Your treasury needs these. Your crown lands here bring in insufficient. Until you gain from parliament better royal moneys from taxes, dues and the like, the English gold is all but vital."

"Very well. I will go to Berwick. And thereafter go south to wherever I can find Henry. You will come with me? And you also, Pate. I shall need you both."

"Yes, Sire. Now, will Your Grace come and see this envoy, de Lacy? Give him audience."

Patrick saw no need for him, as Chamberlain, to attend at this interview with the Englishman, with Phemia awaiting him, and the watching and listening Christian to conduct back to her mother and sister.

They parted then, and only part listening to the girl's chatter, it was a little while before the man realised that he had not actually sought, or gained, the Steward's agreement for his marriage – although perhaps it had been implied?

He would let Phemia tell of it all to Christian herself.

9

It turned out that the king's visit to Berwick, and onwards, was not to be long delayed, word reaching Roxburgh that the archbishop and prince-bishop were already there, waiting. So it was all preparations for the journey down through England, and marriage plans rather in abeyance. Both young people concerned desired no long wait, although Phemia did indicate that wedding arrangements, for the bride at least, could not be rushed, just what to arrange not specified. It seemed to be taken for granted that the Steward was agreeable; indeed he announced that the small property of Dargavel, near Paisley, was to be his daughter's dowery.

Alexander desired an impressive train to accompany him down to King Henry's court, so there was much assembling of lords and officials, all to be clad in their best. Sir John de Lacy, the English envoy, was still at Roxburgh, so he would complete his mission by coming with them, first to Berwick and then onwards, his authority perhaps proving useful on the journey through England.

It was parting then, meantime, between Patrick and his love, a frustration for them both at this stage of their relationship. At least Phemia could use the interval to plan some of those arrangements for the wedding.

They rode down Tweed for Berwick. Cospatrick joined them at Coldstream. He was interested to hear of his son's betrothal to the Steward's daughter, a suitable match, he agreed.

Berwick Castle, high above the quite large town, was already thronged with the trains of Archbishop Walter de Gray of York and Richard de Maresco, Prince-Bishop of

112

Durham; so there was little room for the Scots party, and most returned to the town. The two clerics were both haughty and all but condescending towards Alexander, indeed paying more respect to de Lacy than to the King of Scots, and all but dismissing the person of Bishop William of St Andrews, head of the Scottish Church. Whether this attitude was policy or just their own arrogance was uncertain; but the Earl Cospatrick, for one, was not prepared to put up with it, and made that very clear to them.

For his part, Alexander declared that he had no intention of claiming Cumberland or Northumberland for the Scottish realm and, on the lifting of the papal excommunication, he would withdraw his forces from Carlisle. Also that he was on his way down to see King Henry regarding his lands in England. Whereupon, without more ado, the archbishop, raising a hand, announced almost curtly that, in the name of the papal nuncio, the Cardinal Gualo of St Martin, he lifted the sentence of excommunication upon Alexander of Scotland and his people, Bishop Maresco adding Amen. They both turned away.

Astonished, the Scots eyed one another. Apparently that was it, no further proceedings seemingly called for. The entire interview had not taken ten minutes.

All but at a loss, Alexander stared from the two clerics and their monkish supporters to de Lacy and others of his own people. Most, including Patrick, were equally surprised that those few brief and all but casual words could have such significance as to releasing a monarch and nation from the pronunciation of God's curse, and to allow Holy Church in Scotland to resume its full spiritual authority to operate, to promote bishops and abbots and to minister fully to a worshipping people. Did Almighty God, the loving Creator, work in this fashion? Surely not. Was not this just folly, the invention of prideful and power-hungry men?

Cospatrick it was who took the lead. "Sire," he said, "shall we return to Berwick town? Leave these clerks to whatever may be their further devices? If Your Grace so wills."

Murmurs of agreement from others of the Scots, including the Steward, heartened the young monarch, and he nodded.

"I bid you good-day!" he called to the Englishmen. "I will speak of you to King Henry." And he started to lead the way out.

"*I* go to Carlisle," Archbishop de Gray declared. "To ensure that all is in order there."

"His Grace's commands will be obeyed," Bishop William said, his first and only contribution to the proceedings.

It was parting, de Lacy still with the Scots.

It was just past noontide and there was no point in lingering at Berwick when they could be on their way, hundreds of miles ahead of them. Exchanging comments on the ways of men, especially Englishmen, the party did not delay, and headed southwards. The Steward told them that the Berwick governor had said that King Henry was presently at Nottingham, not London nor Windsor.

They rode inland by the most direct route to the English Midlands, all wondering what sort of reception would await them at Nottingham. That was not where they had anticipated that they would meet Henry and Salisbury; but de Lacy, a quite amiable character, said that there was a royal palace-castle there, offering better sport for the English court, in the great Sherwood Forest. It was a popular resort, especially in the festive season, and they were now into December.

They were glad to avoid the Durham lands, and headed westwards by Wooler and Otterburn for the North Tyne valley, getting as far as Rothbury only before the winter darkness fell, and they found a monastery to offer them shelter. These short days of December would much limit their progress and lengthen the time taken to reach Nottingham, which de Lacy estimated would be some two hundred and fifty miles from Berwick. How many miles a day, then? Seventy at the most, probably. So another three days.

Through the hilly country of West Northumberland they passed Hexham-on-Tyne, with its great priory of St Andrew's, fine as any abbey. Still keeping west of the so-called principality of Durham they headed for the Yorkshire dales, to cross Tees and lesser rivers, to reach Richmond on the Swale, where they found a Franciscan priory, more modest than Hexham's but adequate for the night's lodging. Then more dales to cross in West Yorkshire, Ure and Nidd and Wharfe, pleasing country, rich as Lothian. Darkness found them at Doncaster which, de Lacy explained, although now very much part of Yorkshire, had once held a palace of the ancient Kings of Northumbria, for, as that name implied, it was the territory north of the Humber. There, on the Roman road, they found no priory or large monastery but had to divide up to sleep at hospices and hostelries. However Nottingham, they learned, was now only some thirty-five miles away.

They arrived at their goal shortly after midday, having been not a little impressed by the quality of the countryside they had traversed, less scenic and spectacular than that of most of Scotland but richer and much more populous, with much woodland, good country for riding through. It was more than just woodland around Nottingham, with the great forests of Bulwell and Sherwood.

De Lacy suggested that he should go on ahead to warn his young liege-lord of the approach of another monarch, as was suitable; and Patrick agreed to go with him. He got on well with this Englishman.

He found Nottingham a major city, as large as Edinburgh, with a cathedral, seat of a bishop, the town thronged with people; although the citizenry would be added to by the many retinues of the lords of the royal court presently visiting. Its fortress-palace could not rival Edinburgh's but it was a worthy hold and quite dramatically sited nevertheless, crowning a steep rock, with many towers, bartisans, parapets and defensive features, all flying banners with the three golden lions passant-guardant on red of Plantagenet. Up the winding ascent the pair rode, and had no difficulty in gaining entry at the gatehouse, de Lacy, who was of course well known at court, calling out that here was the Constable of Chester to see His Majesty, with the High Chamberlain of Scotland.

The captain of the guard took them to see Sir Hubert de Burgh, who proved to be Patrick's opposite number, the Great Chamberlain of England, a portly man of fine presence who eyed Patrick assessingly. He told them that the young king was presently out hunting in the Bulwell Forest, but would no doubt be back with the dusk. Informed that the King of Scots was approaching, de Burgh asked how large a train he had with him, for castle and town were already crowded. Assured that the Scots party only amounted to some two score, he said that he would do what he could to accommodate them, but only Alexander and perhaps six others would be able to lodge in the castle. The bishop's palace would probably take the rest.

So Patrick rode back whence he had come to acquaint Alexander and the others of the situation.

In the event the two monarchs arrived together at the foot of the climb up to the castle. It seemed that in chasing a wounded deer in the forest young Henry had ridden under a bent tree and been swept out of his saddle by an overhanging branch and, falling, had bruised forehead and cheek, and so was returning early. As a consequence there was something of a mix-up at the rock-foot, anything but a ceremonial meeting between two kings. The nine-year-old boy was preoccupied with his not very serious injury, and Alexander, almost nine years older, sympathetic. Not all the huntsmen had come back with their liege-lord, but Salisbury the regent had, and he sought to sort out the situation in some measure. He had met Alexander before, at Dover with Prince Louis, and, scarcely an affable man, was reasonably civil and respectful towards the King of Scots, de Lacy helpful in it all.

Leaving most of his company in the town to seek out the bishop's palace, a small group, including Patrick, his father and the Steward, ascended to the castle, the two monarchs riding side by side with Salisbury and another magnate who turned out to be Sir William de Brotherton, Earl of Pembroke the Lord Marshal, Henry dabbing at his bloody cheek with his glove and showing the red result to Alexander in some alarm. At least there was no stiffness nor distancing about the meeting.

De Burgh, the Chamberlain, had found quarters for the Scots in one of the lesser towers, giving Alexander a room to himself but Patrick sharing one with his father and the Steward. They all wondered how the homage-giving would go, when and where? Would they have to travel to Huntingdon itself which, according to de Lacy, was some sixty miles to the south-east?

Not being invited otherwise, they stayed in their tower, with light refreshment being brought by servants. It all made an odd reception for a visiting monarch.

However, after almost two hours de Burgh arrived to conduct them to the main tower of the palace for a repast; he did not name it a banquet. At the great hall, Alexander was taken, alone, to a side anteroom behind the dais platform, and the others left to find places at tables where they could, Cospatrick for one declaring this unsuitable. But barely were they seated in quite lowly position when de Lacy appeared, to wave towards the dais where additional chairs were being brought and a rearrangement going on. He declared that King Alexander required the company of his Chamberlain, Steward and Earl Cospatrick up there, and King Henry had agreed. So the three were led up on to the platform, the magnates already seated there having frowningly to change their positions. Patrick and the others found themselves ushered to seats at a much smaller board, just erected, immediately behind the centre of the main dais table, de Lacy with them. There they sat, eyeing each other.

Presently the door behind them was flung open and de

Burgh led in the two monarchs, with Salisbury and the Marshal, all others standing now. Alexander approvingly nodded at de Lacy and his friends, indeed pressing Patrick's shoulder as he passed them. The English did not appear to go in for a High Sennachie, Seneschal or the like, to announce the monarch's entry.

Henry looked more cheerful, his brow and cheek gleaming with some sort of ointment which had stopped the bleeding. Clearly it was no very grievous hurt.

The kings seated, they all could sit. Minstrels struck up from the gallery at the back of the hall with music.

Close as they were to the two royal backs, Patrick could hear almost all that was said. Henry Plantagenet appeared to be something of a chatterer, and was detailing at length to Alexander all about the hunt and how he had used his crossbow to hit a stag but only wounded it, and how the animal had bolted and got clean away under the wretched tree which had knocked him off his horse.

After much of this they heard Alexander ask about the homage-giving for Huntingdon.

"Where do we go?" he wondered.

"Go? Do we have to go somewhere?"

"That is what I want to know. In Scotland when fealty is done for lands it is done at Scone Abbey, near to Perth, the coronation-place. It is thought right that winning the royal approval for the possession of land should be done on that land itself. But, to be sure, if this was done it would require the king to travel to every piece of land in his realm. So it is arranged that the fealty-seeker brings a handful of the soil of his land to this Scone Abbey, and there spreads it for the king to put his foot on, while the other gives his oath – a most notable saving! The lords and barons take their oath of homage to a new monarch in the same way at his coronation. Aye, and over the years quite a tall mound of this earth has grown there, known as the Moot Hill. You do not do the like in England?"

"Just handfuls of earth?" Henry grinned, then grimaced as his cheek hurt. "To stand on! Here is a strange device."

Salisbury, at Henry's other side, had been listening also. "We do not engage in such child's-play here," he said scoffingly. "Wherever the King's Majesty is, there can the homage be done. Here and now indeed, Highness. All that is required is for the homage-yielder to kneel before His Majesty, take the royal hand, and swear fealty. The king accepts, and the matter is done with. That is all."

"Kneel?" Alexander said.

From behind the royal backs it was Cospatrick, who had been listening also, who spoke then. "It is not meet that the king of one realm should kneel to another, my lord. That would imply allegiance. No kneeling!"

"No," Alexander agreed. "I can do it standing."

Salisbury shrugged. "As Your Highness wills. It can be performed now. And be done with it."

"Now?"

"As well now as later. Before all. That the matter may be known, seen to be done."

"What do *I* do?" That was Henry.

"Your Majesty stands. Takes His Highness's hand between both your own, and he makes his vow. That is all."

The boy jumped up then, and because the monarch had arisen all must do the same, surprised as they might be in the middle of a meal. Alexander, looking round at Patrick and his father questioningly, was given a nod, and he rose also.

Henry, looking distinctly doubtful, said, "Here? At table? What, what . . . ?"

"Hold out both hands, Sire," his regent instructed. "His Highness will put his hand between those of Your Majesty's." It was noticeable that Salisbury called Alexander Highness and not Majesty. Cospatrick certainly noticed it, and spoke again, and used the Scottish usage.

"Your Grace, if this is required, can say the words. It all seems . . . less than imposing, worthy. But . . ."

Henry held out his arms, well apart. And smiling at the boy, Alexander waved them together, and then put his right hand between the two palms. He bowed slightly.

119

"I, Alexander, do pay homage to you for my lands in your kingdom of England, those of Huntingdon and others, held by my father and forebears," he said. "This to continue to hold of Your Highness."

Still clutching the other's hand, Henry looked round. "Is that all?" he asked.

"Yes, Your Majesty, that is all." Salisbury gestured towards the chairs.

Thankfully the boy sat down, and all others could resume their seats, amongst murmurings and comments.

Patrick muttered to his father, "Here is a wonder! Hollow! A mere gesture! To have come all this way for *that*!"

Alexander looked round at them and shrugged.

The musicians, who had halted their playing at their king's rising, resumed, if somewhat raggedly. The repast continued.

Obviously relieved to have done with this, Henry was soon chattering again, asking about this earth-carrying to the coronation abbey and saying that he had never heard the like. At *his* coronation at Westminster it was all prayers, archbishops, blessing oil and holding the crown over him. They could not put it on his head because it was too big for him. He made a face.

Henry had become entirely at ease with Alexander, whatever his regent's attitude.

The eating over but the drinking continuing, Henry was soon yawning. Alexander sympathised. It had been a long day for the visitors also.

"Bed?" he asked.

"Yes. We started the hunting early. Before sun-up. I do not think that I will go hunting tomorrow."

So, presently, the two monarchs stood, again to much rising all over the hall, and another halt to the music. Alexander turned to his trio and de Lacy.

"No need for you all to come away yet," he said.

The Steward, glancing at the others, nodded. "We shall all be the better of our beds, Sire."

So, leaving de Lacy with Salisbury and the other English magnates, the Scots filed out behind Henry through the anteroom behind the dais, where they said goodnight to the boy and took their way to their own tower.

Discussing the evening there, it was Patrick who mentioned the lack of any women, apparently, at the English court. *They* had decided to improve the Scots one in this matter; seemingly their neighbours in the south required to do likewise.

"This is scarcely the seat of the court," the Steward said. "That is at Windsor, I think. Or Whitehall in London. This only a hunting interlude. Perhaps the women remain behind, not huntresses."

"Yet Christmastide is almost upon us, and them."

"Aye, *we* must get home for that," Alexander said.

In the morning, breakfast brought to them in their own quarters, they were still at it when they had a visitor, young King Henry himself. He came, announcing that he was feeling stiff and aching from his fall, and lying abed had become uncomfortable. He was not going hunting today, but they could go if they so desired.

"I think not," Alexander told him. "Since we do not have to go to Huntingdon, it is best that we return forthwith to Scotland for Yuletide. There are the celebrations. If we go now, we can be at Roxburgh in three days' riding, we have discovered."

Henry looked disappointed that they were not staying.

"Do *you* not go back to your family for the festive season?" he was asked. "You have a family, have you not?"

"Oh, yes. There is my mother, the queen. And I have two sisters, Joanna and Eleanor. We all go to Windsor in a few days' time."

"They do not come here with you? They mislike hunting?"

"No. It is my lord of Salisbury and the others who prefer the hunting without the women."

"And the queen does not object?"

121

"She does not like riding in winter. She enjoys the comforts of Windsor."

"But you do have women at court?"

"Oh, yes. Many women. Over-many, perhaps! I find them tiresome, at times. I like other matters from them. And I have few friends of my age."

Alexander exchanged glances with Patrick. There was a familiar ring to that.

"What is your Scotland like?" Henry went on. "I have heard that it is very wild, with mountains. And is wet and cold. The people strange. Talking a strange language."

"That is scarcely true. We have many hills and mountains, yes. But also much good land for tillage and pasture. Fewer large towns and cities. The folk do not all speak the Gaelic. You should come and visit us, Henry. You would be very welcome."

"That would be good. I would like that. I will come if I am permitted."

"You are the king!"

"Yes. But my lord of Salisbury is very strict. And my mother favours him. My father was different, difficult, you see. So I am much held. Even now they will be wondering where I am." The boy looked uneasy. "But tell me more about Scotland, Alexander. It is almost as large as this England, they say. But many fewer people?"

"We have Lowlands and Highlands, very different people . . ." Alexander went on to give some description of his kingdom and its diversities, lengthy history, the most ancient royal line in all Christendom, but also the problems and difficulties of ruling, the boy much interested. But presently Henry became restless, clearly concerned about being sought by his regent and all-but-governor. They let him go, but said that they would be bidding farewell shortly.

They did not delay, all now eager to be back home as soon as possible, especially Patrick. They took leave of Henry much more ceremoniously than they had met him, less congratulatory towards Salisbury and the nobles, although some were apparently already away to the hunt. De Lacy accompanied them down to the town to collect their escorting party from the bishop's palace. Their good-byes to him were very appreciative, with hopes expressed that when next King Henry required an envoy to Scotland it would be himself.

Then onwards, northwards. They hoped that they would get beyond Doncaster before they must halt for the night, Yuletide ahead of them. And Phemia.

10

Although they reached Roxburgh four days before Christmas, to find two groups already arrived to improve the court, the Earl and Countess of Carrick and Sir David de Lindsay and his sister, all were in fact in favour of going back to their own homes for the Yuletide festivities, this very much a family occasion, the Steward and Lady Beatrix themselves so inclined. But Patrick and Phemia were not eager to be parted again so soon, and it was decided that she would accompany him and his father to Dunbar; and Alexander, not desirous of being left more or less alone at Roxburgh, would go with them. It was not perhaps the best time of year for a visit to that sea-girt stronghold, but the welcome would be warm enough.

So the court more or less dispersed until the Epiphany, Twelfth Night, the joint Christian and pagan celebration of the Scots Church.

Alexander was intrigued to be invited to the seat of the line which he had been reared to think of as rivals for his throne, the first monarch to have visited it. At least it was sufficiently spectacular on its rock-stacks thrusting out into the waves for the king and Phemia to approach, all but shrouded in spray as the outermost towers were in a blustery wind and a turbulent sea, the young woman declaring that she had never seen anything like this on their inner Clyde coast.

Cospatrick's daughter Ada, young as she was, made a good hostess, however surprised she might be to find herself entertaining the monarch and her brother's betrothed. When it came to accommodation, Patrick made it clear that he wanted his two guests to share his own furthest tower, weather conditions notwithstanding. So fires out there had to be lit immediately and all made as comfortable as possible at short notice. The trio looked upon it all as something of a challenge, in more ways than one, Cospatrick shaking his head over them.

Out on the dizzy rock-top amidst the salt spindrift, the screaming seafowl and the crash of waves, the visitors were all but spellbound by the sheer wild drama of it in the dusk, the very tower seeming to shake with the impact of the breakers, far below as they were, and the battering of the wind and splatter of water on the windows' glass and shutters. Excited, Phemia clutched Patrick, shaking her fair head, at a loss to express her reaction. Alexander declared that he had never experienced the like, and wondered how many men had died in building this sea-eagle's nest of a hold.

The young woman was shown her room, wondering whether she would be able to sleep with all that noise and the rattling of the window shutters. Patrick would have liked to offer to aid her in the matter, with comforting arms around her, but could hardly suggest it. He and the king would share the chamber above. That crackling log fire would have to serve.

They went back over the covered-in bridges to the main tower for the evening meal.

As ever, Patrick was concerned with getting Phemia alone, but only managed to snatch momentary opportunities, with the family and Alexander seemingly ever present. He did sit beside her in the great hall's fireplace ingleneuk, pressed close necessarily with three to fit in at each side. Alexander, who clearly liked women also, did what he could with Ada, Cospatrick's presence inhibiting.

But it was very pleasant round that well-doing fire after their long riding, and soon beds beckoned.

Returning over the bridges, as it were into the Norse Sea, the three of them hurried, no friendly warmth there. Nor was the stone stairway up in their tower, with its open shot-holes for defence – although who could be repulsed out there? – any less chilly. But when they paused outside Phemia's room, Alexander, after giving her a goodnight kiss, had the tact to go on ahead further. So Patrick did have the young woman alone for however brief a spell; and the whistling wind gave him excuse to accompany her into her chamber, to ensure that the fire was burning well and the warm-water tub for washing reasonably hot.

At the fireside, Phemia it was who turned, to throw her arms around him, gulping endearments. Holding her close, he all but shook her in his need.

"So hard! So trying!" he got out, between urgent kisses. "Never alone. Always others watching. Wanting you, my dear heart! You, my beloved, to be my wife. Near, and yet ever apart. When I would, would . . ." He left the rest unsaid.

"How, think you, *I* feel?" she exclaimed. "You away in England all those days and nights. Endless. When, when . . ."

"You missed me? You wanted me? As I wanted you? *Want* you, woman!"

"Yes. Oh, yes. Do you deem me cold? Unfeeling? I am not that sort! Oh, Patrick – the waiting!"

"Bless you, my dear, bless you! Your need also?" His hands were busy now about her rounded person.

"Thought you otherwise? See you!" She pulled open her bodice at the neck, and taking one of those active hands carried it to her warm bosom. "Yours, to be. A, a foretaste!"

He needed no encouragement, no guiding, his fingers stroking and pressing and seeking, he rejoicing at all that he touched and felt, the smooth delight, the curving weight, the response, the motion, the promise. Nothing would do now, of course, but that he left off kissing her lips to uplift out one of her breasts, to bend over it and kiss that instead. Then the other, not to be neglected, she rubbing her cheek on the top of his head, wordless now.

Then, as it was Phemia who had initiated this very physical appreciation, she it was who concluded it by moving back a little and gently raising his head. She patted his cheek.

"Enough, perhaps, for this present, my dear," she said. "Alex will be coming down to see what has happened to you! Forby, we may be in danger of becoming over-impatient, over-ardent! No? Before we are made man and wife!"

He began to protest, and then shrugged, although still holding her. "Is that so important? Ah, well. And when is that to be, the wedding? How much longer to wait?"

"Not so long, I think. How about St Kentigern's Day, Mungo's? That would be suitable. Mungo it was who came from Fife to our Clyde, to found Glasgow, and perhaps Paisley also. And Paisley Abbey is where we shall be wed."

"When? When is that? St Kentigern's Day?"

"None so far distant. The thirteenth day of January. Three weeks. And the day before my twentieth birthday. Then I will be my own woman, as well as yours!"

"Three weeks yet!"

"But worth the waiting for?" She was rearranging her bodice, stepping further back, and shaking her head over him.

"Mmm. Well, yes. But . . ."

"I promise you that it *will* be, my demanding one! Now, go you up to your liege-lord's chamber, Chamberlain! And allow me to calm, aye, calm myself! And sleep. If the waves and the wind and the spray will permit it. Apart from all else!"

Reluctantly he left her.

They all spent a pleasant Christmastide; and with some improvement in the weather, Patrick was able to take his visitors to see some of the nearby countryside, the sheep-populated Lammermuirs, main source of the earldom's wealth, with their hidden valleys, heathery heights and Pictish forts and stone circles, naming the hills for them: Eweslaw, Wedder Law, Tuplaw, Hogrigg, Wool Hill,

Rammerscales, Lamb Hill, Wedderlie, Sheeppath, Lammerlaw itself. Also he took them along the coastline southwards, so very different, exciting indeed, the cliffs soaring to dwarf even Dunbar's, the tracks such as to daunt their horses, so beetling and overhanging, to St Ebba's Head, where that Northumbrian princess had immured herself and her nuns to avoid the Viking ravishers, where they marvelled at the plunging drops and jagged buttresses and pinnacles, and heard the singing of the seals amongst the skirling of the kittiwakes, guillemots, petrels, fulmars and gulls, and the crashing seas.

Patrick did contrive some all-too-brief goodnight interludes in Phemia's room, to be sure, she restraining him, and herself, however understandingly, will triumphing over desire, she pointing out how every day brought them nearer to fulfilment.

The bringing in of the Yule log and its setting alight was duly performed on Christmas Eve, with the gathering of mistletoe and holly, pagan as this might be in origin, in an open-air and bonfire-lit feast for the townsfolk, held in the fishmarket beside the harbour, this undoubtedly the first here that a King of Scots had attended, a drizzle of rain not allowed to dampen the occasion nor the spirits of all concerned, oxen and sheep roasted whole and ale and mead flowing freely.

They attended mass not so long afterwards in the ancient Celtic church on Christmas morning, Phemia whispering that soon it would be another altar that they knelt before, at Paisley Abbey. And more feasting thereafter, more private this, having the men all but falling asleep during the evening's entertainment by the two young women with lyre and lute and song, Patrick perhaps somewhat less urgent that night.

They saw in the new year, 1217, again in traditional fashion, with late-night salutations, dancing and gaiety, all but exhausted by the ongoings.

A day to recover, and then it was back to Roxburgh, Ada coming with them for a short appearance at court, telling

Will that he could look after himself for a couple of weeks, no doubt with some small help from village girls.

Only twelve more days and nights to wait, Patrick counted.

11

It thus happened that the arrival at Roxburgh of the new and female courtiers more or less coincided with the wedding and the departures for Paisley; and with the king declaring that he was not going to miss this ceremony, and of course the Steward's family also going, some of the new arrivals decided to attend also. So it was quite a company which set out on the journey to the Clyde estuary, Phemia and her mother, father and sisters having gone on two days before to see to all the necessary preparations.

It was fully one hundred miles to Paisley and Renfrew, following the Tweed up as far as Broughton and then crossing the high ground to the upper Clyde valley; and present company was not such as could travel at great speed, however impatient the bridegroom was to get to his destination. But they did win as far as St Kentigern's Priory at Lanark for the night, more than halfway, and so were able to reach Renfrew by early afternoon, the castle's accommodation stretched to the utmost to hold them all. Patrick saw little of Phemia, and never alone, that day and evening; and in the morning, of course, he was not supposed to see her at all.

He, dressed in his best, rode off to Paisley with Alexander, who was going to act groomsman. St Mirren's Abbey, named after one of the female Celtic colleagues of St Bride or Bridget, was a handsome shrine, built by the Steward's grandfather, another Walter. They were there much too early, to be sure, and the Abbot Mark, who was to conduct the ceremony, was in something of a stir to entertain the monarch as well as see to all the necessary arrangements for the service, the choir and musicians, the seating and so on. The king had never attended a wedding before, and was much interested, Patrick less so, only eager to get it all over and done with. Supplied with wine in the monastic quarters, they just had to wait.

At length the tuneful clangour of the abbey bells indicated readiness, and the prior came to conduct the pair to their place. They found the nave full to overflowing and the choristers chanting. There was some confusion amongst those with seating, the minority necessarily, at the entrance of the monarch, most rising, with Alexander waving them down, as he and the groom were taken to stand at the chancel steps, there to wait, a new experience for the king, backs to the congregation, Patrick again making sure that Alexander had the ring ready.

They did not have long to wait now. The musicians struck up a new and resounding air, the choir joining in, and Abbot Mark and his supporting clergy and acolytes paced in from a transept door to take their stances before the altar, all the company standing now. Then, at the ululation of a single horn, high above the rest of the music, the bridal train came in from the main west door, Patrick refraining from turning to watch, his groomsman less restrained.

On the Steward's arm, Phemia came forward looking loveliness itself, flushed with excitement, eyes lively, dimples very much in evidence, dressed in white satin and gold, a pearl-edged coif adorning her fair head. At her back came Christian, as bridesmaid, suitably gowned and looking much more nervous than her sister.

They came up to join the two at the chancel steps, Patrick turning now to eye his bride, all but to devour her with his eyes, she reaching out to touch his arm briefly, smiling.

The music ceased, and the abbot stepped forward, bowed to the monarch, and commenced the celebration by calling on all present to heed God's presence. Then he delivered a brief address on the sanctity and importance of marriage, this symbolising the union of Christ and His Church.

A pause, and then he asked Patrick if he would have this woman to wife. On the emphatic affirmative, however seeming unnecessary the question, he put the same demand to Phemia. She assured him that she would have that man as husband.

"Who gives this woman in holy matrimony?" was then asked. The Steward nodded, wordless.

The celebrant then directed the groom to take the bride's right hand in his, and to declare that he would love and cherish her for all the days of his life until death did them part, thus plighting their troth. Phemia was required to say the same.

The king was then requested, with another bow, to produce the ring, over which the sign of the cross was made. Then Patrick was told to repeat after him the words, "With this ring I thee wed. With my body I honour thee. And all my worldly goods with thee I share."

Patrick took the ring from Alexander, one long in the possession of the Cospatrick family, and slipped it on the fourth finger of the bride's left hand, she in turn giving him a squeeze.

"I declare you man and wife," the abbot asserted. "In the Name of the Father, the Son and the Holy Spirit. Amen. Kneel."

"Patrick and Euphemia – these two whom God hath joined together, let no man put asunder. Rise!"

They turned to gaze at each other.

There followed a reading, from the Gospel of St John, on the marriage at Cana in Galilee which Christ had attended and blessed with his first recorded miracle.

Abbot Mark then raised his hand in a general benediction, bowed to the king rather than to the new man and wife, and turned away.

The choir sang a hallelujah chorus. Alexander gripped Patrick's shoulder and shook it, then kissed Phemia warmly. The couple faced the congregation, the man shaking his head in something like disbelief that this was all, that these words and gestures by one not very impressive man could have made him one with his beloved, fulfilled all his urgent desire, or some of it with the assurance of the rest. What Phemia was thinking he did not know, but she looked radiant.

They paced down the aisle to the far door, to the waves and congratulations of the company, the king and the Steward close behind, the Earl Cospatrick with the Lady Beatrix coming next.

But just outside the actual doorway, where Patrick paused to hug and kiss his wife for the first time, Alexander tapped his back, and waved him to forbear meantime.

As people came flocking out behind them, the monarch went forward and turned to face all.

"My people and lieges all," he called. "To celebrate this most happy event, it is my pleasure and satisfaction to show my regard for my friend and Chamberlain. And, to be sure, for his wife." He delved within his doublet and produced a folded paper. "Here is the deed and charter, duly signed and sealed, which creates Sir Patrick, Master of Dunbar, Earl of March. Come, Patrick!"

Gazing at Phemia, speechless, he left her to move forward to the king, who held out his two hands for the token of fealty. Sinking on one knee, as he had done for his knighting, Patrick placed his own hand between the two royal palms, head bowed.

"Since your father, the Earl Cospatrick of Dunbar, already owns the March I need give you no earth therefrom," Alexander said, glancing over at Cospatrick. "But I can, and do, make you one of the earls of my realm. Arise, Earl of March!"

Getting to his feet, Patrick was handed the piece of paper bearing the red seal. The king gripped him around the shoulders in a gesture of affection and esteem. The new earl could find no words, merely searched the royal smiling face.

Alexander continued to grin, looking over at Phemia. "My greetings, Countess!" he said.

There were more congratulations, but also some jealous looks from older officers. Cospatrick eyed his son and the king assessingly. Phemia did not appear to be greatly impressed by her change of status, much more preoccupied with the fact that Patrick was now her husband, at last, than by his becoming an earl.

A move was made by all back to Renfrew Castle for the wedding banquet. Riding together, the happy couple did some planning, however excited and all but bemused over their situation, and their union. They were united also in one aspect of it all: they were both determined to avoid any bedding ceremony. This was a frequently held activity at a marriage, whereby the bride and groom were conducted to their nuptial chamber by the wedding guests, and there actually put into bed by the company, the men undressing the bride and the women the groom, this with inevitable hilarity and much advice as to ongoing procedure, an ordeal which the couple could certainly do without. So the device was for Phemia to slip away at some stage in the feasting, change hurriedly out of her wedding dress into travelling clothes, Patrick following after a short interval, joining her, and then both hastening downstairs to the courtyard and their horses, hoping that none would suspect their flight. Then off to Blackhall, a small Steward property and tower-house about four miles to the south-east, dark as the ride would be. There they would pass their wedding night. Phemia would order her personal attendant to go there beforehand and arrange for the keeper and his wife to have a room ready. They ought to get away with it undetected; after all, diners were always leaving the tables temporarily, for natural functions. Lady Beatrix and the king would be informed.

The feasting was very fine and of lengthy duration, with entertainment and music, the bride's health and future joy and well-being toasted, and speeches made, the entire process going on for hours, so that the couple were far from the only one going out, on occasion, to relieve themselves. Phemia's eventual departure occasioned no comment or raised eyebrows. And Patrick was left debating with himself how long it would be before suspicions might begin to be aroused that she was not coming back, and how swiftly he could follow her, a delicate balance.

It was Alexander who helped his friend in this, after only four or five minutes, rising from his seat, and waving others down who thought dutifully to rise with him, and beckoning Patrick to his side, to lead him out through the dais doorway. None could seem to question the monarch.

Outside, he patted the other on the shoulder and wished him well, before returning to the hall.

Patrick ran upstairs to Phemia's room, where he found her all but ready for him, her handsome bridal gown lying on the floor. Much as he would have liked to help, or perhaps hinder, her changing of apparel, he recognised that this was no time for that. Grabbing a riding-cloak, she draped it round her, and together they hastened down a private stairway, passing a maid servant coming up with a steaming ewer. In the yard below, Phemia's attendant had the horses saddled and waiting. Mounting thankfully, they rode for the gatehouse and out. How long it would be before the guests might begin to seek bride and groom they did not know.

There was no difficulty in finding their way to Blackhall in the darkness. Phemia knew the road well. She chattered in lively fashion for the first mile or so, and then fell unaccustomedly silent.

At Blackhall Tower they were greeted by the keeper and his good lady, offered refreshment which they refused, and were escorted upstairs to a bedchamber which Phemia often used, for this was a sort of hunting-seat, favoured for hawking and angling along the White Cart Water. Thankfully they were left alone. At last!

Over to the fire they went to stand, hand in hand, Patrick

135

as silent now as she had been, telling himself that the time for haste and tension and question was now over. Although the urge was to take his woman to himself at once, he restrained himself, partly that he could savour it all the more fully and enjoyably, but also to give Phemia the time that a woman might need to prepare herself for what, after all, must be one of the most incisive and challenging experiences of her life. He gazed down into the flames, disciplining himself.

The woman it was, however, who made the move, and with a little laugh.

"I am glad of this fire," she declared. "For I am but scantily clad! And that was cold riding. Kentigern must have been a chilly saint!" She drew back a little, and let her riding-cloak fall to the floor.

"I am sorry," he said, looking at her questioningly.

"But . . . *you* will warm me, I think?"

He reached over to her now, to take her to him, but she held him off with one hand outstretched. "Wait, you!" she said.

She undid a topmost button of the samite gown she was wearing, and, with a twist and shrug, it all fell away from her to join the cloak on the floor. And she stood completely naked there in the firelight.

Patrick drew a great quivering breath as he gazed, wordless.

"Think you . . . think you that I am over-bold?" she asked, breathless herself. "Shameless? Oh, Patrick, I have wanted to do this for long, long. To give myself to you. And, and to receive you to myself. Is, is that . . . wanton?"

Gulping back inadequate, unnecessary words, he reached out, to take her into his arms, all of her, all the delicious, smooth, rounded and warm loveliness of her, whatever she said about being cold, she clinging to him, clasping him to her, all offering, all giving and all desiring, her breathing deep, her bosom heaving, her open lips seeking his.

The man held her so for long moments, trying to control himself still, speech, emotion, yearning all in a whirl, one hand running down her back to the swelling cleft delight of her bottom, this while they kissed deeply.

Then, almost abruptly, he pushed her from him, to stand back and stare, eyes and senses devouring her beauty. And she was very beautiful, from her long and graceful neck, her moulded shoulders, the thrusting fullness of her breasts, the dark triangle at her groin below the slender torso, and then the lengthy and shapely legs. Oddly enough, her knee-length riding-boots, which she had not yet removed, somehow added to the attraction and enticement of it all.

She let him feast his eyes for a sufficiency of time, head on one side, smiling. Then she turned her back on him, to bend and take off those boots. Patrick could not resist that, and went, to bend in turn, to kiss her rounded buttocks, finding it best to kneel. In that position he turned her round, and so started a more comprehensive kissing from the knees upwards, lingering, savouring. Presently she had to lean over to aid him in this to reach her breasts; then, at his urgency, thought fit to kneel beside him there. Clutching each other thus, before the fire, Phemia was not long in raising his nuzzling head and busy lips, in order to remove the kerchief at his neck, indication of her opinion that it was time to acknowledge that he was over-clad for the circumstances.

He needed no further reminding. Jumping up, Patrick began to tear off his clothing, she helping him at it while he kicked off his own boots. Then, laughing and rising, she ran over to the great bed. On to this she climbed, not to sit or lie, but to stand, arms out towards him, all allure and invitation.

Naked as was she, he now came to her, his masculinity very evident, to leap up beside her and lift her up off her feet. That bed was not made for such as this, and shifted under them so that they collapsed on to the blankets in a flurry of waving limbs and contortions, with clutchings and gasps and laughter.

Disentangling themselves, the man was no more to be content with admiring and fondling. Now male dominance took over in all its emphatic requirement, as he turned her on her back and bestrode her, demanding entry.

Whether she was as ready for him, physically as she obviously was in will and desire, was doubtful, for she gave a little gasping cry, nails digging into his back. But Patrick was loving as well as needing, and did not fail to recognise her need. Holding himself back, he sought to be gentle, patient, but at the same time to try to stimulate her arousal, with lips and hands and endearments. And her yearning was sufficiently strong, as she had demonstrated, so that she was able to respond in ever increasing degree to his persuasions. He felt her breathing deepening, her body stirring, her growing excitement. Unfortunately, perhaps, this affected his own reactions, so that he had to seek to control himself the more, difficult as this was. But at last, with another cry, different this time, panting, glad and of longer duration, he felt her convulse beneath him in an ecstasy of fulfilment.

He could let himself go, then, and knew a satisfaction of body and mind both such as he had never before experienced.

After a few moments, activity over, he sank down and rolled off her. She reached out for his hand, and fingers entwined, they lay there, silent, too rapt and wrought for any words.

Presently Phemia murmured into his ear that perhaps they should get *into* the bed rather than just lie on it, and he nodded. And somehow, this very different activity of rising, folding back the blankets, and climbing up again and under them, together, had an effect on the man other than sleep-inducing. Whether it did on the woman also, he did not know, but soon he was kissing comprehensively, hands busy. She did not repulse him, and quickly it was union again.

This time the urgency was modified and the pleasure

prolonged, with Phemia becoming more in concert, enough so to climax, to his renewed satisfaction.

Thereafter, the Earl and Countess of March lay still in each other's arms, and let sleep enfold them.

12

The couple did not linger long at Blackhall, guessing that it might well be assumed by all at Renfrew Castle that they would be there, and visitors perhaps coming, particularly a royal one. Fond as he was of his liege-lord, Patrick wanted to be alone with his bride for more than one night. So the further they got away from the Renfrew vicinity the better.

They would go to Dunbar, where they could achieve some privacy. There was much along that dramatic seaboard, inland also, which Phemia ought to see. Admittedly she had not brought any of her clothing and gear, other than what she wore, from her home, coming deliberately under-clad, but Patrick's sister could supply a certain amount of women's wear in the interim – they were none so different as to build – and her own required belongings could be sent for.

They rode eastwards by the shortest route, through Glasgow and on by Airdrie and Caldercruix, and then over the moors to Armadale in Lothian, to reach Torphichen Priory for the night, some forty miles. So the second night of marriage was spent apart, for the monks maintained separate quarters for men and women, grimaces at the parting.

Then on past Edinburgh and Musselburgh and by the great Aberlady Bay to North Berwick. They discussed setting up house together, of course. One day Dunbar Castle would be Patrick's, to be sure; but that could be many years hence. The earldom had many subsidiary houses and properties, other than the seats of its vassal lairds; but as High Chamberlain, Patrick would inevitably have to spend a great deal of his time with the king at

Roxburgh. So somewhere near there was called for, where the pair of them could be together, but available when not actually at court. Home Castle, almost at the edge of the Merse and near to the royal lands of Edenmouth and Ednam, seemed to meet the requirements. Something smaller would have been preferable, less dominantly sited on its ridge-top perhaps; but it at least looked a suitable dwelling for an earl and his countess, and was very much of the March. Patrick reckoned that they could make it, or parts of it, sufficiently comfortable.

Brother Will welcomed them to Dunbar gladly enough, even though mildly embarrassed by them finding him sharing his premises with a young woman from the township, in the absence of his father and sister at Renfrew; not that Patrick and Phemia had any objections, so long as they had the furthermost tower to themselves. Phemia collected a few lesser garments from Ada's wardrobe.

That night they made up for their separation at Torphichen, in most exemplary fashion, the young woman proving a most rewarding partner in marital bliss, and with her own initiatives. They decided that they were well suited.

On the morrow, Patrick, as a change from long riding, took Phemia to indulge in a different kind of positive activity. She had much admired the isolated hill of North Berwick Law just behind the little town of that name, and he had told her that there had been a Pictish fortlet on the lofty top of it. So they went to climb the steep green ascent, all six hundred-odd feet of it, she wearing an old smock-like dress of Ada's, and caring nothing for her appearance once she discarded her riding-cloak. If any of the locals saw this short-skirted, long-legged female climbing the up-thrusting cone of the law, in their round-about progress – it was too steep for direct ascent – they would not have imagined that it could be a countess, however newly so.

The grass-grown ramparts and ditches of the fort were pointed out, but the young woman, breathless as she was, could scarcely heed these for exclaiming at the tremendous vistas which now challenged the eye. Far and wide she viewed, and that wonderingly, for far meant far indeed in almost every direction. Westwards to Edinburgh's lion-like Arthur's Seat, but so many miles beyond, possibly sixty, to the blue summits of the Highland Line itself; northwards across the mouth of the Forth estuary, past the mighty towering cliffs of the Craig of Bass and the further Isle of May, to all the coasts of Fife and its hills beyond, to the next estuary, that of Tay; eastwards only the limitless reaches of the Norse Sea; and southwards, behind another isolated hill, Traprain Law, the entire extent of the Lammermuirs merging into the Morthwaites and then into the central spine of Lowland Scotland. Never had Phemia seen the like. Patrick explained that this prospect was why the Southern Picts had built an outpost hereon, as a sentinel for King Loth's capital at Traprain, not because it could ever be attacked but for the commanding field of view in all directions which could warn of any enemy invasion by land or sea.

Phemia said that she would like to climb that Traprain Law itself one day. It seemed a strange place for a Pictish kingdom's capital.

It was windy and cold up there on the summit amongst the wild goats, and they did not delay overlong.

When they got back to Dunbar it was to find Cospatrick and Ada returned, and not surprised to find the newly-weds there. They brought a request, not exactly a royal command, from Alexander, to come to Roxburgh as soon as might be, important developments having arisen.

Less than eager as he was to go back to his duties at court so soon, Patrick felt that he could not delay. His father did not know just what was behind it all, but said that an envoy from England, some sort of lofty cleric, had arrived at Renfrew, so it could be connected with relations between the two realms, or just religious affairs.

Phemia agreed that they should go to Roxburgh in the next day or two.

On the matter of Home Castle, Cospatrick was quite

142

happy about Patrick having it, indeed he had been going to suggest it as a suitable seat for his heir now that he was married and created an earl himself. It would be convenient for its proximity to Roxburgh, yes, but also useful to have his son in residence in that far-out area of the earldom, to keep an eye on the ever lawless Border mosstroopers.

So next day the couple rode off to Home, to let Phemia examine it, before going on to Roxburgh. It lay some thirty miles to the south, and the young woman remarked on the fact that it was interesting that the Dunbars could travel on their own land so far; the Stewards had no such great domains. Patrick declared that it was probably a sense of guilt, on the part of King David, over the Cospatricks' claims to the throne which made him give so great an area with the earldom.

In the fertile and fairly level spread of the Merse the Home ridge stood out in lengthy whaleback fashion, an abrupt rocky escarpment at the north end but sinking to grassy and gentler slopes to the south, its castle at the northern and most defensive end. It was a large, rectangular building within a high, parapet-topped enclosing wall of great thickness, with towers at the south-east and south-west angles where the need for defence was greatest.

They made their ascent by a zigzag track for horses, nothing like that up North Berwick Law to be sure but offering its own extensive views, of the Eildon and Earlston Hills westwards, the far barrier of the Cheviots southwards and the dale of Tweed and all the Merse lands right to Berwick-upon-Tweed eastwards. Phemia, who took pleasure in scenic vistas and the feeling of space and freedom engendered thereby, declared that this place would suit her very well as a residence, whatever the conditions within.

There was a keeper on the premises with his family, but Patrick had no intention of demanding their removal, there being plenty of accommodation in the extensive fortalice for these to occupy their own quarters and still leave ample room and privacy for themselves, this at the southern end with its two towers.

Examining the accommodation available, Phemia asserted that it had obviously been more or less unoccupied for long, but it was quite capable of being improved and made comfortable, certainly enough for their foreseeable heeds. She would enjoy making a home of it, and pointed out to her husband various possibilities and opportunities.

They spent the night in one of the upper rooms of the south-east tower, hurriedly made ready for them by the keeper's two daughters, with no complaints.

On to Roxburgh in the morning, only another ten miles. There they found Alexander glad to see them and in a state of some uncertainty and question. He declared that he was going to require Patrick's help and guidance in more respects than one, especially, it seemed, in the matter of handling a marriage and a wife! For that was what was proposed. Henry of England, or at least presumably Pembroke, who had become regent in Salisbury's place, was suggesting that the peace between the two kingdoms could and should be strengthened and sealed by him, Alexander, marrying Joanna Plantagenet, Henry's sister, and was offering large dowery lands in England as inducement. He was requesting a conference at York to consider and settle the matter, and soon.

Patrick had always said that as king he must find some suitable princess to marry. But now he expressed surprise. He had understood that the Princess Joanna was betrothed already, to Count Hugh de Lusignan, in France.

This comment produced an extraordinary story. The count had reneged on his commitment, and had actually married Joanna's own mother, Isabella of Angoulême, widow of the late King John. So the princess was free to wed elsewhere. What did Pate think of that?

Astonished, his friend shook his head. It looked like second choice, making the best of a difficult situation. But it could be none so ill a match nevertheless. Joanna was but a slip of a girl yet. But this might well be the best solution to the inevitable royal problem, which had to be faced sooner or later. Suitable and available princesses were seldom thick on the ground, and this one would at least bring major benefits with her for the realm as well as this of the dowery. And at this stage it would only be a betrothal, presumably, with possible repudiation if such became advisable.

Alexander, although less than delighted over the prospects, seemed to be of much the same mind. And, as he pointed out, he could do with that dowery, or what it represented in moneys. For the other matter which the envoy, actually a papal legate, one Jacobus of St Victor, had come about was a Vatican demand for what was known as Peter's Pence, that is, a papal contribution from all the princes of Christendom. This was to help pay for another venture to recapture the city-fortress of Damietta in Egypt recently lost to the infidels by the crusaders. A large sum was being required to equip a mighty army and, as usual, the royal treasury was practically empty. This proffered English provision would greatly help.

Patrick wondered about the necessity of complying with this demand by the Pope, but Alexander said that he had consulted Bishop William of St Andrews and Bishop Walter of Glasgow, the High Treasurer, and they declared that the Peter's Pence was a duty required of all Christian monarchs as part of their support of Holy Church, with excommunication possible if not met. Moreover, Scotland had not provided a contingent for that last crusade, as had been requested, and any failure to pay up now would result in grievous papal punishment.

So it seemed that the royal betrothal must go ahead, and the so-important dowery be obtained at the earliest. Alexander would send Legate Jacobus back south with agreement to meet Henry and Pembroke and presumably young Joanna, at York in due course, and with promise of payment of the papal dues without undue delay. Meanwhile, he would seek to raise what extra revenues he could here at home. Had Pate any suggestions as to possible sources, apart from fresh demands on the Churchmen?

Patrick admitted that he and his father had more than once spoken of the inequity of the Low Countries demanding cess or tax on the entry of Scots wool and other goods sent there in trade at their ports; yet nothing such was required from Flemish and other imports of cloth, blankets, pottery, leather goods and the like coming into Scottish harbours, their own Lammermuir wool situation in especial concerning them. If some such duty could be imposed, and collected by the local provosts, justiciars and lords, who could retain some small part of the receipts for their trouble, the treasury could greatly benefit.

Alexander thought this a splendid notion, and declared that he would give it his royal sanction, and have it confirmed at the next parliament.

They discussed what sort of amounts should be charged for the entry of various commodities, Patrick saying that he would consult his father, who would know best what was suitable and practical.

So the papal legate was sent on his way. Roxburgh Castle duly filled up with the new courtiers and their womenfolk, to the great improvement of conditions and general felicity. Alexander was gradually getting rid of most of the elderly men he had inherited from King William.

Patrick and Phemia were able to get away to Home for a night or two quite frequently that spring, to that castle's much improvement in comfort, only an hour's ride away after all, Alexander sometimes accompanying them. Cospatrick drew up a proposed list of charges on imports for consideration by parliament, to general approval.

Then, in May, another envoy arrived from England, Sir Stephen de Segrave, announcing that King Henry, his regent Pembroke and the Princess Joanna would be happy to meet the King of Scots at York on 16th June to discuss marriage and other matters. He brought letters of safe-conduct, and notice of orders given for the Scots entourage to be kindly entertained on their journey south.

For better or worse, Alexander expressed his agreement.

13

A suitably impressive cavalcade in due course set off for
York with the king, including Patrick and his father, the
High Steward and Bishops William of St Andrews and
Walter of Glasgow, with sundry other earls and magnates,
this of a possible queen for Scotland seen as important by
all. They went by Coldstream, Wark and Wooler and on to
Alnwick for the first night, assured by the safe-conduct
and Henry's instructions that they could request hospitality even from such as the Percy Lord of Northumberland at his castle there. Actually they found the Lord
Henry Percy already himself gone to York, where apparently a major assembly of the English great ones was being
staged. Cospatrick and his son felt distinctly strange at
being entertained by the Lady Percy and her son, for of
course their own ancestors had been Earls of Northumbria,
before Dunbar, although Bamborough Castle, not Alnwick had been their main seat.

They got as far as Newcastle the next day, where there
was ample accommodation for even their large company,
the citizens however apt to eye them somewhat askance,
Scots being in their eyes associated with raiding and
reiving.

Alexander was not desirous of calling on the Prince-
Bishop of Durham, that haughty prelate, although he
almost certainly would be present at York, so they by-
passed Durham city to the west, by Brancepeth and on to
Auckland, which admittedly was still episcopal property,
indeed often called Bishop's Auckland, but they were
unlikely to find the man there, and there was a large priory
to house them overnight.

Into the Yorkshire dales thereafter, and they were able to reach the abbey of Rievaulx for their fourth night, this being extended and made very fine by the Archbishop of York, and so prepared to welcome them. Patrick and Alexander were fretting by this time; they could have ridden so much faster and further each day; but with this large company and the elderly clerics to consider they had to hold themselves and their horses in.

It was less than thirty miles, by Brandsby and down-river past Strensall, to York.

They found the city full to overflowing, and large as the archepiscopal palace was, there was insufficient room for all the Scots party to lodge therein. But, of course, Alexander and his closest associates were allotted fine quarters. They were welcomed by Pembroke, a tall, stooping but masterful man who eyed the visitors critically, and by the Archbishop Walter de Gray, more genial, although he considered Bishop William less than favourably, for these two were inevitably at loggerheads, the archbishop claiming, as the most northerly based metropolitan, to be the ecclesiastical superior of the Scottish Church, and the Bishop of St Andrews maintaining that it was totally independent, and recognised to be so by the Vatican, and he its Primate and head. Actually the same claim was made by that other metropolitan, the Archbishop of Trondheim, based further north still; and the Scots had used these two's rivalry to their advantage for long.

Alexander was informed that he would be presented to King Henry in due course, and he and his conducted to their chambers, and refreshment provided. Quarters would be found for the less important of the Scots company in the town.

Patrick and his father shared a room with the Steward, next to the king's apartment, with the two bishops on the other side. This of waiting to be presented to Henry Plantagenet had raised their eyebrows, but it was not something that it would be suitable to make protest about. They were all glad enough to relax after their long riding.

At length Hubert de Burgh, the Great Chamberlain, came to lead them to the principal hall of the palace, he greeting Patrick amiably enough.

They found the hall filled with the pride of England, noble and clerical. Up on the dais platform at the far end young Henry, now aged ten, sat on a throne-like chair, flanked by Pembroke and other officers of state, and the archbishop with de Maresco, Prince-Bishop of Durham. There was no sign of Princess Joanna, nor indeed of any women.

This of the dais platform was unfortunate, as had been the delay, possibly intentionally so, for it meant that the King of Scots had to walk thereto and then climb up to the seated Henry. Cospatrick it was, as they were led forward, who murmured to Alexander that he should halt just short of the steps and there wait, to indicate his equality with the other, as a monarch, and the climbing approach, like the postponement of meeting, unsuitable. Alexander nodded.

So, as all watched, the King of Scots, a pace or two ahead of his supporters, strode forward almost to the dais and there stopped and stood, looking up at the boy-king and inclining his head in something less than a bow. For moments there was complete silence in that great apartment.

Henry looked up at Pembroke on his right enquiringly. That man stared down at the Scots but made no move. Henry turned his head to look for guidance at the archbishop, but that man, blinking, only smoothed a hand over mouth and chin. The silence maintained.

Henry made his own decision. He jumped up from his chair and came hurrying to the dais steps and down them, hand out to his fellow monarch. Patrick, for one, sighed with relief.

Exclaiming that it was good to see him again, the boy, ever chattersome, asked if they had had a good journey down, and how long it was since they had last met.

Alexander responded in friendly fashion, and took the lead in nodding towards the dais steps and taking Henry's arm. So the two kings climbed side by side on to the platform, followed up by the other Scots, Cospatrick looking at Pembroke and grimly smiling.

There was another pause, uncertainty about what to do next evident. Only the one chair was on the dais, and after this interlude Henry could hardly sit and leave Alexander standing, however much Pembroke and his colleagues might have so advised. All stood there, then, at something of a loss, until de Burgh, the Chamberlain, bowing twice, suggested that Their Majesties might wish to retire to the privacy of the anteroom which opened off the rear of the dais. Thankfully Henry nodded, and led the way to the door, all but at a run, Alexander following.

Faced with this situation, Pembroke and the others had no option but to go likewise, ushering in the Scots group.

The anteroom was quite large, furnished with a long table on which were wine flagons and goblets, and there was a sufficiency of chairs and benches. Henry sat down, with Alexander beside him being offered wine.

Seeking to recover his authority, the regent, or governor as he preferred to be called, spoke up. He declared that Their Majesties had come together for important business of state, important to both kingdoms, for the peace between them, and to arrange and negotiate the marriage-betrothal of King Alexander of Scotland to the Princess Joanna, now free to wed, and the settlement involved therefore, this for the better furtherance of the desired peace between the realms. Also to decide on the attitude of both nations to Pope Honorius's requirement that large contributions should be made to the Vatican, in moneys and men, towards the retaking of the crusaders' base of Damietta from the infidels, this demanded of all Christian princes. It would be wise and beneficial if an agreed decision was made to this.

Heads were nodded at this announcement, and Archbishop Walter added that His Holiness saw the saving of Christ's birthplace and earthly homeland as vital for all of them on the road towards the heavenly one.

Pembroke went on. "As to the dowery for Princess Joanna, His Majesty offers the lands and barony of Wenlock, in Shropshire, of large extent, adjacent to the Cluniac Convent, with the revenues thereof. Also the lordship of Towton in Wharfedale, in this shire of York, with its pertinents and pendicles. Also the lands of Aberglashen in the shire of Carnaervon of Wales. All these to be held directly of His Majesty King Henry. Is it agreed?"

Alexander looked at Patrick, his father and the Steward. It all sounded well, even generous. But without an inspection of the said properties and their revenue-raising capacities, effective evaluation was impossible.

The Steward spoke. "His Grace of Scotland will take it that these lands are . . . of adequate worth, to fit the occasion. Or His Majesty Henry would not propose them for his sister's dowery. But perhaps he might visit one of them? This of Wharfedale, in this county? Towton was it? Wharfedale I have heard of, and judge it none so far off our road back to Scotland?"

Pembroke frowned, and shrugged.

Henry spoke. "It is not far away, is it? We crossed the river, that Wharfe, on the way here, did we not?"

"It is some dozen miles from here, Sire. south by west." That was the archbishop. "Towton adjoins my own lands."

"Then we could go there. See it. Only a few miles."

Pembroke frowned still more. "It is not necessary that Your Majesty should so trouble yourself. If King Alexander wishes so to do . . ."

"But I would like to," the boy declared. "We could go now. A ride would be good."

"There is much to discuss yet, Sire. This of the Peter's Pence, the Vatican's demand."

"Oh, well. That first, then."

Patrick nudged Alexander's arm. "What of the princess? To *see* her, at least," he murmured.

"Yes." Alexander raised his voice. "Sire, may we meet the Princess Joanna? Who it is proposed should be my wife! In due course."

"Yes, yes. To be sure. She is somewhere in this place. In the far wing. We shall go see her. Pleasing, my sister is. Younger than me, but good enough company."

"This of Pope Honorius's demands, Your Majesty. It was deemed that a joint message to Rome from the two kingdoms would be wise," Pembroke insisted. "If both spoke, as it were, with one voice, it would be helpful. This of the crusading is costly. The late King Richard, your royal uncle, cost the nation much, in moneys and men. And his absence. And paid for it with his life. The recapture of this Damietta is not so necessary to Christendom's well-being that the realms should have to tax themselves greatly. I have written to King Louis of France on this. He favours the crusading, yes, but not at present. After a major defeat. So, a united address to the Vatican." The governor looked over at the archbishop warningly, who might be expected to take a different view of the papal directive. "If England, France and Scotland make their views known, His Holiness may well see fit to ease his demands."

Alexander glanced over at his own two bishops, and then at the Steward and Cospatrick. The last it was who spoke.

"We in Scotland do not wish to seem to refuse the Pope's wishes," he observed. "But nor would we impoverish our realm greatly in this matter, Sire. To send men to fight and die for what appears meanwhile to be a lost cause. As Your Grace has conceded."

The Steward nodded.

"Holy Church will not fail His Holiness," Bishop William declared. "But the treasury of the realm need not be greatly the poorer." And he turned to Bishop Walter, the High Treasurer, who waved a confirmatory hand.

"So say we," Archbishop Walter put in. "*Our* contribution will be . . . adequate." Prince-Bishop de Maresco inclined his head.

"That is well. But we send no crusading army," Pembroke added.

Henry, less than interested, was fiddling with a loose doublet button.

Alexander assented. "Let it be so, then. Our treasury, and yours, to make only modest additions to the Churches' contributions. And send no men. It is agreed." He turned to Henry, hoping that was an end to the debate.

The boy clearly was of the same mind, and promptly jumped up. "Let us go and see Joanna," he said. "And then go riding to this Towton." All had to rise.

Henry, taking Alexander's arm, led him off to another door, and out, the Scots group uncertain whether or not to follow, their English counterparts clearly not going to do so. It was only Patrick who actually went after the two monarchs.

They went along many fine corridors and tapestry-hung passages, and up a wide flight of stairs. At an upper landing they heard high feminine voices and laughter. Opening a door, they entered a room where three girls, or very young women, were throwing little hoops, trying to hang them on a pegged board. These stopped, to gaze at the newcomers.

The gazing was mutual, Alexander and Patrick looking from one of them to another. Which was Joanna? Allegedly she was only of nine years.

One, by her figure, looked older than that, fair-headed and with long, thinnish features. One was plump and stocky, with very rounded cheeks. The third was taller, big-eyed and dark of hair. None was in any way beautiful, but the last bore herself best, and had perhaps some promise of quite good looks to come. And there was something of Henry himself about her appearance.

"Joanna, here is King Alexander of Scotland," he announced.

That last girl looked at Patrick interestedly and dipped a little curtsy.

"No, no, that is the Earl of March. *This* is the king," her brother said.

"Oh!" A giggle. Then another curtsy. "Your Majesty. I greet you, greet you kindly."

154

"And you, Princess." Alexander was quite frankly sizing her up, as was only to be expected. "We have heard much of you." That was not really true, but he had to say something.

She giggled again, but her smile was pleasing, and neither nervous nor forced.

"This of marriage," the proposed husband thought fit to put to her, difficult as it was to find words to fit the circumstances. "How see you it?"

She shook her dark head. "I, I do not know. I know little about marriage."

"That I can understand, Princess."

Into the silence that followed, Henry said, "These are the ladies Isabel and Martha." He did not indicate which was which.

Another pause in an uneasy interview, and Henry spoke again. "We are going riding, now. To Towton. In Wharfedale. To see a dowery property."

"Riding? Can I come also, Hal?" Joanna asked quickly. "I like riding. It is very dull here."

The other girls joined in the request.

Henry looked at his two companions, and shrugged. "If you wish." He added, to the others, "Joanna is quite good in the saddle. At Windsor she rides a lot."

"To be sure," Alexander agreed. "It will add to the occasion. A dozen miles, it was said? Just over an hour's riding."

They had to wait down at the horses while the girls changed into riding-gear, and the Captain of the Royal Guard assembled an escort, which apparently was demanded when the King of England went even for a short distance. While waiting they saw the archbishop and other prelates getting to horse and trotting off. Henry explained that this castle in the city, above the Ouse, was the old episcopal seat, but that a great newer palace was now the main residence, situated some three miles to the south. That is where the churchmen would be going.

155

Alexander and Patrick felt that they had to make some comment to Henry as to his sister.

"The princess seems . . . amiable," the king said. "She smiles much. A girl of some, some character."

"She could grow into quite a comely young woman, I judge," Patrick added, this for his friend's benefit.

"Oh, she is well enough," her royal brother acceded. "When think you to wed her?"

Alexander glanced at Patrick. "That will have to be decided," he temporised. "Much to be considered, you will understand."

Fortunately he was spared more by the arrival of the girls, now in a very vocal state. There was much helping up on to horses, and the marshalling of the so unnecessary escort.

They rode off into the streets and out of the Micklegate Bar – the city's gateways were called bars, it seemed – and turned south by west, Alexander tactfully making a point of trotting beside his proposed bride-to-be, Patrick with Henry.

They soon were crossing higher ground, cattle-dotted, between this dale of the Ouse and its tributary streams, excellent farming country. After a few miles of this they had to descend again, into Wharfedale, where they presently came to the small town of Tadcaster, modest as to size but of notable Roman fame. Here they learned that Towton village was some two more miles ahead, with its royal residence just beyond. Royal it might be in name, but Henry had never before seen it.

The village proved to be quite sizeable, with three mills, a brewhouse and a tannery, which Alexander noted as indicative of industry and rural prosperity and therefore productive of revenues. And half a mile further they came to the fortified manor-house within its moat, an extensive establishment with many outbuildings and a farmery, all prosperous-seeming. It looked as though the King of Scots was not going to be fobbed off with any second-rate property, here at any rate.

This impression was further strengthened when they met the keeper of the so-called lordship – why this style was not explained – who was somewhat overcome by being called upon unexpectedly by two monarchs. He conducted them over the premises but, of more importance, informed them that the lands he was responsible for extended southwards and westwards, out of the dale on to higher ground again, for fully two thousand acres of good tillable ground and fine pasture. He offered to take the party over some of all this, but Alexander declared himself well satisfied with what he had seen and been told of. If the two other properties involved were up to this standard, then the dowery offered was entirely adequate. Princess Joanna showed no concern over the matter, no doubt seeing it all as really nothing to do with herself. But she did now chatter to the visitors quite freely; the late King John may not have been a very eloquent man, but his offspring were notably voluble.

They all rode back to York in quite cheerful fashion.

That evening there was a much reduced company for the repast in the great hall, although Joanna and her two companions graced the dais table, for the archbishop and the prince-bishop and other clerics were not present, and some of the noble magnates had evidently departed also. Pembroke, his aims achieved, was less assertive and critical, and Henry more at ease, he and Alexander getting on very well together. It all made quite a pleasant occasion.

In the morning it was farewells, Joanna present and smiling, Henry urging a return visit soon and Alexander not exactly committing himself but clearly thinking better of the entire situation than when they had arrived, his advisers likewise.

Then it was the long ride home to Scotland.

14

Back at Home Castle, Patrick it was who was glad of the news from Phemia. She was pregnant, she was sure, their love fulfilled indeed. She calculated that the birth would be in April. As yet she showed no physical signs of her condition however joyful her reactions. Her husband took her to him the more dearly.

During his absence she had been busy improving their quarters in the castle as to convenience and appearance, Patrick duly admiring. With a family to house, he declared, they must have their home suitably comfortable, this to her laughter, with the suggestion that he was somewhat previous in this thinking. She pointed out that it would be into years before this token of their oneness within her would be in any state to appreciate his surroundings. He quickly took her up on that: *his* surroundings! Did she believe that the child would be a boy? Phemia admitted that it had scarcely occurred to her that it would be otherwise.

One aspect of it all did concern her, however. This was that with a baby to tend and look after she would not see so much of her spouse, his duties at court apt to take him away from them for much of the time. He declared that he was sure that Alexander would welcome mother and child at Roxburgh when he was there, never fear.

She was interested to hear of what had transpired at York, especially of Princess Joanna. Questioning him about the girl, she said that she thought that the king should go ahead with the marriage, and fairly soon. Girls of that age, just about to develop into young womanhood, were very impressionable to influences bearing upon them, the conditions and the company they kept. Alexander could exert a good and favourable effect on her well before ever he sought to take her to his bed, she hoped. Patrick was uncertain about his liege-lord's attitudes in this regard; but he did not think that he would be likely to force himself on one who was still only a child, married or not. He would pass on Phemia's views to him.

It was not long before opportunity to do so developed, for only a few days later the king sent for him. They both went to Roxburgh.

Another extraordinary situation was reported, they discovered, which could have its effect on relations with England and otherwise. It concerned a woman whom Patrick had only occasionally heard of and never seen, a half-sister of Alexander, an illegitimate daughter of the late King William, much older than Alexander, indeed married off as a child to Sir Eustace de Vesci, a Northumbrian notable, as far back as 1193, five years before her legitimate brother was born. This Margaret had been widowed when de Vesci had been killed in battle in 1216, and had then been wooed and wed to Matthew, Count of Boulogne, in France, she something of a beauty. Now this count had also died, and Hubert de Burgh, Henry's Great Chamberlain, and acknowledged as the coming man in England to succeed Pembroke, was eager to marry her. And since she was half-sister of the King of Scots, his royal permission had to be granted. Alexander had nothing against de Burgh, although he had the name of being something of a womaniser; but some of his advisers thought that a still better match could be arranged for one of the reputedly most beauteous and attractive females in Christendom, certain royal princes being mentioned, and she still of under forty years. How thought Patrick? It was rumoured that even Prince Louis of France was interested in her.

His friend, never having seen the lady, indeed Alexander himself seemingly having met her only once or twice years before, felt that he was scarcely the one to ask. But his feelings were that ties with England were more important to Scotland than any other factors, at present, and de Burgh clearly was highly important in this respect, very close to Henry, more so, he judged, than any continental prince, even the future King of France, widower as he might be. If Alex refused de Burgh, and his influence on young Henry likely to be great for years to come, it might well have unfortunate consequences.

The king said that he felt that way himself. The Countess of Boulogne might refuse de Burgh herself, of course. She had the reputation of being a woman who knew her own mind, as well as being a magnet for men. But if she did so, that would be different, no blame attaching to Alexander.

Phemia was much diverted over this debate amongst her menfolk. Let Countess Margaret make her own decisions. At her age and in her position was she not entitled to it?

As well as sending this request to the King of Scots, de Burgh, now it seemed made Earl of Ulster, had revealed information regarding the Peter's Pence matter, which was, he declared, shocking, and could well affect the nations' reaction to the papal demand. It was now known that Pope Honorius, in his preoccupation with the crusading situation, had ordained a new Bishop of Damietta, even though that fortress-city was presently lost, and endowed him, the new prelate, with no less than one thousand silver talents, a vast sum; that, and entitled him to appoint no fewer than forty canons, of various nationalities, each with a yearly revenue of one hundred talents, each talent worth almost 5,200 pounds of English money. The Vatican must have run mad. What good these clerical appointments would do towards the recovering of the fortress and the furtherance of Christendom's advance on the Holy Land was difficult to see. If most of the nations thought the same as did England, as was likely, then all could agree to scale down their contributions to the Peter's Pence to a mere gesture, without, surely, any fears of excommunication.

This line of thought, to be sure, commended itself to Alexander, as it did to his advisers, Patrick included.

So the courier from de Burgh was sent back with the word that the King of Scots agreed that Sir Hubert should wed the Countess Margaret of Boulogne, if she was so minded; and that the reduction of the Vatican levy would be welcome indeed, he to be kept informed of the parallel English payment. That the government of a kingdom was apt to be an involved and selective business became ever more evident.

This recognition was reinforced shortly thereafter by news reaching Roxburgh from a very different quarter, namely the Highland north-west. This, sent by Duncan Campbell of Lochawe in Argyll, informed that Reginald or Ranald, Lord of the Isles, who was calling himself King thereof and of Man, was now raiding into Argyll, this nothing new, but he was now claiming that this mainland Highland province, with Kintyre, was his by right. He looked set to invade and take it by force. Moreover he was known to have approached the King of England, or at least the Earl of Pembroke, and paid homage for the Isle of Man. That great island was of course nearer to the English coasts than the Scottish. This was strange but ominous, and must represent some intention that could only be contrary to Scotland's interests; quite possibly that he, Reginald, need have no fear of attack from Ireland, at his rear, if indeed he made the attack on Argyll, the English presence in Ireland being strong.

These tidings worried Alexander, needless to say. He was far from anxious to get involved in warfare with the Islesmen, an all but independent lordship of largely Norse background and strong in warships where he was not. But if they invaded this mainland area with any intention of taking it over, he, the king, would have to act. Such threat had largely been kept in bounds by the Irish princes, who favoured the Scots rather than the aggressive Norsemen. But if Reginald had made some sort of pact with England it could be awkward; and apparently de Burgh had just been

161

created Earl of Ulster. Was this significant? It all did not seem to match up with the recent accord with Henry and England.

After counsel with his advisers, Alexander decided to send to Campbell of Lochawe assuring him of support if there should be any large-scale invasion. And to send to Henry, informing him, or Pembroke and de Burgh, of his concern over this development, and hoping that no encouragement would be given to Reginald of the Isles. Also adding, by way of persuasion, that he had decided to confirm the marriage with Joanna, and indeed make the wedding reasonably soon, within the year.

It was to be hoped that this reaction would have the desired effect, somewhat contorted politics as it undoubtedly was. The rumour was that there was friction between Pembroke and de Burgh. If they could exploit that to Scotland's advantage, so much the better.

So the court at Roxburgh, now much enhanced by womenfolk, became still more female-concerned, with the prospect of a young queen arriving before long, and all that this would mean. Phemia's own pregnancy, which soon became known by all, fitted into this preoccupation quite naturally, Alexander taking an ongoing interest in her state.

A by-product of all this was the king's increased interest in the other sex. Hitherto he had not been greatly concerned with feminine attention, friendly as he had been with Phemia and her sister Christian. But all this talk of his half-sister the Countess Margaret and her many admirers, and the prospects of his own marriage, was not without effect on him, and he began to look at women with a more speculative eye. Indeed, one night, before going to their now respective bedchambers, Alexander actually broached the subject to Patrick.

"This of my marriage," he said. "I am unsure about it all, Pate. What is expected of me. It will be a marriage in name only, will it not? Joanna will be only of ten years. How, how soon will it . . . ? When will she be . . . ready? It

162

is difficult. I would not wish to be too hasty. To distress the girl. For she will be still only that. I do not know about girls of such age. Indeed, I do not know much of older ones either. In, in these matters . . ."

"I understand your situation, Alex, and sympathise," Patrick said. "It is all very difficult, yes. Myself, I am not too knowledgeable about young girls either. I mean, at what age they become, shall we say, interested in men, bedable! Without becoming upset, fearful, distressed. I think, you know, that you should have a word with Phemia on this. She will probably be able to help you. Would you find that awkward? She is fond of you and will know what to advise. Guide you in this matter."

"I think, yes. I think that I could talk to Phemia. I like her well. Always have done."

"She would be very understanding, I am sure. Delicate as the subject is." He paused. "But you yourself, Alex? You are in an awkward position in this of women. You will be wed to a child. But you are a man! With a man's . . . needs. It could be a matter of years before this Joanna is ready for you. And meanwhile . . . !"

"Yes. Think you that I do not know it! With so many women now here at court I am not unaware of them! Of Christian in especial. But others also. Being the king, I am hindered, limited. Women may see me as different from other men. I would not wish to seem to command, use my position to persuade . . ."

"No, I see that. But, to be sure, there are pleasures for a man to have with women without taking them altogether to himself. Kindnesses of friendship and person, short of full giving and taking. This can be very pleasing. You must have felt that, Alex? Men and women, I judge, were made to please each other, to give enjoyment, not only on a bed!"

The king looked interested, but did not comment.

"See you, why not come with me now to our chamber? See Phemia. She has just retired there. She will not be abed yet. I will go tell her that you come. She is a woman of understanding. And very frank of nature. She would advise you in all this, I am sure.''

"If you think it suitable. If I do not offend?"

Patrick went upstairs, and found Phemia just finished her bathing, beginning to dry herself. Never failing to admire her body, he did not omit to kiss her on more than the lips, somewhat damp as she still was. Then he told her.

"Alex is concerned about this of marriage to a mere girl. Having her as wife, and not taking her before she is woman enough. Also his man's needs meantime. He is scarcely wise in such matters yet. His has been a strange coming to manhood. I told him that you might help him, guide him somewhat. Will you, Phemia?"

"Me? A strange task, Patrick. For any woman."

"Only a woman can tell him what he needs to know, I think, as to this young queen-to-be. And other matters relating to womankind."

"Mmm. If he needs it, I suppose that I could do it as well as any other. Without over-much embarrassment. When will this be?"

"Now, lass. He waits downstairs. I did not think that you would refuse."

"Now! When I am unclothed!"

"You can wear your bed-robe. We have just been talking of it all. He is ready for guidance. It is not a subject which can be spoken on just at any time or place. Will you do it, my love?"

"If you deem it right, suitable."

"Bless you! He needs it. I will bring him up."

Alexander, led upstairs, was distinctly doubtful, more so than had been Phemia indeed. He was very silent.

They found his instructress sitting on the great bed in her robe in the half-dark, some of the candles doused. The king eyed her, moistening his lips.

Patrick sought to ease tension. "Alex requires advice, lass," he said, "as to this of wedding a girl of but ten years. A woman's guidance. I say that you can give it. He is unsure of how he should . . . behave."

"If I can help, I will," she agreed.

The king cleared his throat, but did not speak, standing there looking wary.

Patrick had to go on. "He does not want to cause the princess any distress. She *may* be prepared for some intimacy. But what should be his attitude? His behaviour towards her at first? And for possibly years!"

"Yes," Alexander jerked briefly.

The young woman, understanding his discomfort, smiled, moved a little aside on the bed, and patted the blanketing beside her. "Come. Sit here, beside me. You too, Patrick. We can talk the better, so."

Alexander did as he was bidden, and relaxed somewhat, finding it easier to gaze away rather than at her.

"It is her age," he said.

"Yes. But often princesses are wed very young. Your royal half-sister, was she older than this Joanna when she was married to Eustace de Vesci? She will expect some small attentions, even at that age, having been schooled, almost certainly. But only minor attentions, I would say. For some time."

"When?" That was still abrupt.

"Well, girls reach an age of, shall we say, some interest in men at differing years. Some as young as twelve years. Others up to fifteen it may be. Their bodies begin to develop towards womanhood. That will be apparent, unmistakeable. But the rounding out of them does not necessarily mean that they are yet prepared for taking a man to themselves with any satisfaction. That can vary also. At such stage they can be emotional, difficult, even seeking to avoid men. You will learn of it, Alex, sensing Joanna's state."

"I have been friendly, close, to only you and Christian, Phemia. And not over-close!" That was hurriedly amended. "So I need the guidance."

"To be sure. And if I may, I will seek to guide you, in time coming. The princess, or new queen, may be fifteen perhaps before you can treat her as a wife in that respect."

"And in the meantime . . . ?" Patrick joined in. "Alex is tied to little more than a child. Yet is himself almost of full age, and needful of women's kindnesses, no?"

"I recognise that. Kings and princes have been seeking female company, other than their wives', since kings were. After all, they have so often had to wed for reasons of state, not out of love or esteem or desire – as has been *our* bliss, Patrick. So Alex will have to find kindnesses elsewhere in the interval."

"Kindnesses?" the monarch wondered. "What means that? *How* kind? Me, the king. Without, without . . ." He left the rest unsaid.

"Women can grant kindnesses in varying degrees," she said. "You will discover it. Some may offer much, all even. Others but fondlings and kissings. Others again but smiles and whispers and promises. We are not all alike. But you will perceive how far you may go without giving offence. And without giving any royal commands!"

"I would never do that. To any woman."

"No." Again she patted him. "But you may not require to! You are an attractive man, as well as liege-lord of us all."

Alexander was now clearly very much aware of the warm and lovely womanhood so close to him. Smiling in turn, Patrick rose to his feet.

"There you have it, Alex," he declared. "Your guidance given. Very much so. You will know now where you stand, in all this." And he emphasised the word stand.

The other took the hint, and rose and, all but stumbling, the King of Scots was led to the door by Patrick, a man in something of a daze.

15

Whether as a result of this discussion, or because Alexander had been moving in this direction anyway, the opposite sex began to feature ever more prominently in his life. Not that he became any sort of womaniser, but the appreciation was there and made itself very evident. The ladies at court were not long in discerning it, in especial Christian, Phemia's sister. She had always been friendly with him, but now they became closer. The Steward and Lady Beatrix observed it, of course, whether or not they spoke to their daughter on the matter.

Patrick and Phemia looked on interestedly, all but amusedly.

That proved to be a fairly trouble-free autumn and winter for Scotland. Ranald of the Isles did not invade, however much casual raiding there was along the Argyll coasts. No problems developed with England, either governmentally or otherwise, although the Border' folk were always unruly, on both sides. They heard that Pembroke was a sick man, which meant that de Burgh, or Ulster as they now should style him, would in effect be ruling for Henry. At Yuletide they learned that he had wed Margaret of Boulogne.

A carefree Christmas was passed at Roxburgh, although not a few at court went to their own homes for the festive season, these including the Steward and his wife, although it was noteworthy that Christian stayed on. More than once Patrick or Phemia came on her and Alexander in each other's arms, and made no comment, or smilingly left them to it. How far this closeness went they did not know and were not informed. And the Yule celebrations, amidst much feasting, jollity as well as more worshipful activities, provided much opportunity for togetherness and intimate association.

Patrick and Phemia did manage to spend brief spells at Home Castle, to their satisfaction. With her delivery expected in April, she was now begining to show her condition, and her husband was all solicitude and care, although she announced that she was quite able to behave normally, to ride to and from Roxburgh, and still act the wife.

A concern which was now preoccupying the king otherwise was the matter of Princess Joanna's jointure. This was a sort of dowery to be provided by the husband on marriage, so that should the woman become a widow she would be left suitably endowed. When such lady was to be a queen, the provision had to be substantial, with adequate sustenance and housing. It was long since such had been required in Scotland, with King William's prolonged widowerhood, and there was much debate on the subject. Alexander had inherited properties in various parts of the realm, but most of these had been largely neglected for years, his father's old age seldom taking him away from Roxburgh. The great royal citadels of Stirling, Edinburgh, Dumbarton, Dundee and Inverness were not to be considered, fortified strongholds, something less military required. Eventually Linlithgow was decided upon. This was a more modest castle, rising above a loch in the ancient royal demesne in the west of Lothian, halfway between Edinburgh and Stirling, in a community possibly of Roman origin near the east end of the Antonine Wall, and where a Columban chapel had been founded, dedicated to St Ninian, although this had been superseded by a very fine church erected after Queen Margaret's putting down of the old Celtic Church, St Michael's. All this would offer a worthy jointure for the princess, not to be looked down upon by the proud English as inadequate compared with their handsome dowery.

Then in February the papal legate, Jacobus of St Victor,

arrived again in Scotland. Pope Honorius was grievously disappointed over the very modest sums sent as Peter's Pence, and was showing his displeasure thus. The legate summoned all the bishops, abbots and priors of the land to meet him at Perth for a general council. This was to express papal disapproval and to arrange for the appointment of a direct and continuing representative of the Pope in Scotland, to be termed the Conservator, who would be something less than a metropolitan archbishop but who would be more responsible for the good behaviour of the Scottish Church than was the present leader thereof, Bishop William of St Andrews, more active in collecting the necessary revenues to be submitted to the Vatican, especially in view of the poor responses of the King of Scots and other kings to the crusading Damietta appeal.

So all the churchmen had to assemble at Perth, and for four days were given their orders and mandates, also an official order of precedence under this new Conservator who was, in fact, to be the Bishop William, at least to start with, although this might be altered if the Pope so decided; something of a warning, undoubtedly.

All this was not lost on Alexander. He wondered whether similar cautions and admonitions were being delivered to the churchmen of England and France. Getting on the wrong side of Rome was clearly not to be considered lightly.

Patrick was perhaps less concerned over all this than he should have been as High Chamberlain, his preoccupation with Phemia's approaching maternity being urgent, however little fuss she made of it, indeed she chiding him that it was almost as though *he* were having the baby, not herself! Fortunately all seemed to be going normally, satisfactorily, and the midwife predicted no problems.

Home Castle became in a stir, and the king had to do without his Chamberlain for a number of days that month, although he himself visited there on two occasions, displaying his interest and fondness.

On the Eve of St Serf, the nineteenth day of April,

Phemia was brought to bed, this date being considered a good augury in view of his help in the birth of the blessed St Mungo.

It was quite lengthy travail, Patrick at the bedside hour after hour; but in the early morning the thing was accomplished and, sure enough, another Patrick was born, one more to add to the long line of Cospatricks of Dunbar, in good order and looking interested. His father's sighs of relief were more profound than the mother's, the midwife bustlingly cheerful despite the hour.

After that, pride was almost sufficient to warrant a downfall, that baby shown off to great and small as though quite unique.

But the parading suffered an interruption when a messenger arrived a few days later from Campbell of Lochawe to announce that the feared invasion of Argyll by Ranald of the Isles had indeed begun, and in large numbers, fleets of longships landing the Islesmen in Kintyre, Knapdale, Cowal and up Loch Fyne-side.

Alexander had to act, little as he felt inclined, with the arranged date for his wedding barely six weeks away. The areas being assailed were apparently quite widespread, and there was no time to assemble any large army to try to deal with them all. Where would Ranald himself be apt to do his leading? Probably up Loch Fyne, the lengthy sea inlet which led deep into the heart of Argyll. So, gather as many ships as could be obtained quickly at Dumbarton, fill them with men, and sail up the inner West Highland coast past the Isle of Bute, Kintyre and Knapdale and into Loch Fyne.

Contingents were demanded from lords and magnates not too far off, speed being of the essence. Patrick went through the Merse to Dunbar, and managed to raise some six hundred men at short notice, even though it was still late lambing time in the hills. He led these to Renfrew, where they joined the Steward's force. Alexander was already over at Dumbarton, seeking to assemble a sufficiency of shipping for his host.

170

Even ferrying this joint muster across Clyde took time, in small craft. Then all had to be transferred into larger vessels at Dumbarton, the main Clyde port. Quite a considerable army had now assembled, over three thousand, and packing all these into the ships that had been gathered from the Clyde, Bute, North Ayrshire and Arran havens was itself a major problem, for unfortunately few really large craft had been found ready and crews available at this time of year when long voyages overseas had recently begun for trading, after the winter's storms were hopefully past.

On the eighth day of May the assorted fleet set sail, most of the leaders and men being distinctly doubtful about the entire project, for they were all used to doing their fighting on horseback, and their mounts had to be left behind at Renfrew or Dumbarton; anyway, in the Isles and amongst the Highland mountains and sea lochs only foot warfare was effective, indeed possible.

But in fact such fighting was to be the least of their difficulties, for the shipmen were all muttering about bad weather looming and unseasonable gales possible. Rounding Garroch Head, at the southern tip of Bute, and turning northwards up that sound, these fears were proved far from groundless, as strong gusting north-westerly winds developed, and even in these narrow waters the seas began to rise. Overladen as nearly all the vessels were, this became not only unpleasant but dangerous. Soon Alexander's skippers were advising the king to put into havens such as the Kyles of Bute offered, in the hope that the winds and seas would abate.

This was agreed, although the small harbours and coves available were insufficient for convenient shelter for so many craft. Evening and night were spent in these constricted Kyles channels – the name merely a corruption of the Gaelic *caol* meaning narrow. In the morning the winds still blew, and the shipmen were unhappy about proceeding; but Alexander and his lords, with insufficient supplies for their thousands, were concerned to be on their way.

They had not mustered all these men just to sit idly in open boats in squally rain. Let them try to proceed.

So it was south again down the sound to round Ardlamont Point and turn up what was really the mouth of long Loch Fyne. And it was soon thereafter, opposite Knapdale of Kintyre, that actual storm hit them as it swept down the channel of Loch Gilp from the north-west, waves rising alarmingly, ships heeling and slewing and being blown off course. Soon they were no longer a fleet but a mere scatter of ships, each for itself, passengers cowering, huddling together, many seasick.

The king saw that this was of no use, vessels and men dispersed, demoralisation setting in, possibly some smaller craft already capsized, folk drowned. Such shipmasters as he could contact all urged turning around, back down the sound, the wind behind them, going with the seas not against them. Reluctantly he acceded. They swung around, and quickly other shipmen saw it and were glad to do the same. A ragged string of craft, they returned whence they had come, concerned only to keep afloat.

Alexander was distressed, all but humiliated. To be fleeing like this with never a blow struck was grievous, deplorable, somehow worthy of scorn, mockery. But he saw no way of mending matters so long as this untimely wretched gale maintained, and it was increasing rather than lessening. Not only Patrick agreed that in these circumstances they had no real choice but to effect their return to Dumbarton and Renfrew. And once they got there, with the men exhausted, gravelled, to wait until the conditions improved and then to try again would be folly, impracticable, especially with time running short and the so important royal wedding ahead. First things first, then. Argyll and Ranald must and could wait. After all, the threat was only to a very limited and remote area of the kingdom, they told themselves.

It all made a sorry episode nevertheless.

16

The preparations for the marriage were prolonged, various, all but multitudinous, in a way absurdly so considering that the bride was a ten-year-old, and there was no love involved, nor passion to be anticipated. But of course it was much more than a wedding, representing peace and hoped-for harmony between two kingdoms which were all too apt to be at war with each other, a linking of the two nations. And this to be celebrated and exhibited in more than formal nuptials, with something of rivalry between the two, with the larger, more populous and richer realm conditioned to look down upon the other as comparatively poverty-stricken, outlandish, almost barbarous. So the English had to be shown otherwise in no uncertain fashion, and the preparations and display consequently the more important and elaborate. All the royal entourage were to take their finest clothing, even though these could not be worn on the long ride down; gifts were to be taken for their English hosts, even falconry selected to present, the Scots long proud of their hawks; escorting men-at-arms carefully chosen, and instructed as to how to behave.

Patrick was unhappy over leaving his little son so soon for what inevitably must be quite a lengthy period. Needless to say he was also disappointed not to be able to have Phemia with him, for a few women were accompanying the men, including the Lady Beatrix and Christian; but it could not be, in the circumstances.

The resplendent company set out in great style, however concerned Alexander and his advisers might be over leaving the Islesmen on the rampage in Argyll. In these numbers, and with the women, they could not cover so many miles in a day as they would have liked, so the journey would take some time. They were thankful that Henry and Ulster had decided to hold the ceremony at York, not at Canterbury or Windsor, as they might have done, which would have doubled the distance. Suitable accommodation for the travellers *en route* had been ensured, which was a blessing, the English lords and prelates vying with each other in providing hospitality, by royal command. It felt strange for such as Cospatrick and others of middle years to be entertained by those whom they were more used to look upon as potential enemies to be fought.

The weather and conditions kind, they made it to York in four days, and to a worthy and notable reception, Church and state uniting to mark the occasion memorably. However important the marriage of princess and king might be in itself, the implied peace and friendship between the realms were the more so. Oddly enough, the disapproval of Pope Honorius over the Peter's Pence had the effect of bringing the two kingdoms the closer, for Henry informed that England also had been allotted such punishment as the Vatican might prescribe, which was not minor, in that here too the Church produced most of the nation's wealth, and penalties on the prelates and clerics could seriously affect not only the king's treasury but also the conditions of the nobility and of the ordinary people. Walter, Archbishop of York, could not openly criticise the Pontiff but he made it clear that he resented these impositions, and the present papal concern with crusades which lay behind it all. Patrick, and indeed Alexander, like so many others, agreed with this attitude; after all, he contended, if Almighty God was so anxious that the former Holy Land should be purged of the infidels, surely He could order it so that this was achieved without impoverishing Christendom? Was this heresy? they asked of Bishop William, who was cautious in his reply, however benevolent his expression.

At least this mutual preoccupation over papal demands had the effect of preventing any voicing of archepiscopal claims of metropolitan superiority over the Church in Scotland meantime.

There was a great exchange of gifts, and the Scots dowery-house and lands duly announced and described.

The Princess Joanna made her appearance at a great banquet in the palace that first evening, looking with renewed interest at her husband-to-be, her youthfulness very evident to all, seated on her brother's left hand while Alexander sat on his right.

Entertainment and drinking went on far into the night, long after Joanna and most of the women had retired.

The next day, while the final arrangements for the wedding were being made, Henry and his lords and guests tried out the Scots hawks on the water meadows and reaches of the River Foss, and were well pleased with results, Henry and Alexander, as before, getting on well together. Cospatrick struck up some rapport with Ulster, now Earl of Kent also; and the Countess Margaret confided in him that, in her judgment, experienced as she was, young Joanna would develop into a personable and worthy wife and queen.

That evening there was dancing, and the princess proved that, whatever else, she was light on her feet, indeed sprightly, losing her diffidence in the exercise. Alexander went so far as to try to teach her some of the footwork, birlings and posturings in Scottish dance, different from her own.

Later, on their way to bed, Alexander confided in Patrick that he was unsure of what was expected of him on the following night. Did he have to share the same room, the same bed, with his juvenile bride? He had no desire to do so; but she might have been guided to look for it. And the others, Henry, Margaret and the rest, might consider it right. After all, allegedly in the sight of God, they would have been made one.

"Does it signify?" Patrick asked. "You, Alex, are the Lord's Anointed, the monarch. What *you* choose, ordain, must be. Expectations, customs here, assumptions, do not bind you. Do you as you feel best."

"Aye, but I do not want to offend. Seem to spurn her. Or to reject their ways, usages, Pate. What will she expect?"

"I know not. But if you do not wish to share a bed with her yet awhile, why not have two beds in the room? If there is only the one, have another brought in. Or make a couch for her on the floor, with blankets. So that she can be alone. Let her wash herself, then couch down before *you* undress and get into the greater bed."

"Ye-e-es. That will probably be best. Perhaps it will not be too difficult . . ."

They parted for the might.

In the morning, it was all arranging and preparing for the noonday nuptials in the great cathedral, the city full of guests, new arrivals pouring in. Patrick was distinctly doubtful about having to act the groomsman at a royal wedding, but Alexander would have it so; and, after all, he was now an earl himself as well as High Chamberlain, and of royal descent, he reminded himself, however distantly. Dressed at his best as he was, he could not compete with the English nobles; for that matter, neither could Alexander, although he could wear a gold circlet over hair and brow which none other than Henry Plantagenet might do.

Normally at a marriage the groom went up to the chancel steps of the church to await the bride's arrival; but when a king was involved, it was not considered to be suitable that he should seem to wait for anyone, even on this occasion. However, it was similarly unsuitable for Henry, who was to give his sister away, to do the waiting. So a careful arrangement had to be made that the two monarchs should simultaneously appear out of opposite transepts of the cathedral, at a given signal, to join and proceed up to the chancel side by side, with the bride and groomsman, dignity intact.

Alexander and Patrick were led to a vestry which opened off the east transept, and there left to fortify themselves with wine while awaiting the fanfare of trumpets which would summon them to the central aisle; as Patrick pointed out, still waiting, but in private. Quite a long wait, it seemed, too.

At length the trumpets sounded, and they moved out, Patrick a pace behind. In the doorway of the vestry they paused, and could see, across at the other side, Henry and Joanna appearing, the former grinning and raising a hand to them. There was to be no matron of honour.

So it was pacing out to meet in the central aisle, to bow to each other, and to turn to walk up, side by side, between the packed rows of standing folk, all in due order of precedence, while musicians played and choristers chanted.

Archbishop Walter de Gray awaited them at the steps, with the prince-bishop on his right and Bishop William on his left, other prelates behind, acolytes swinging incense burners, scores of tall candles ablaze around the altar.

As at Patrick's own wedding, the actual ceremony was comparatively brief, despite all the magnificence and arrangements. Once the music stopped and the arch-bishop took over, it was not so long before Patrick was producing the Ancient Celtic ring, much too large for Joanna's girlish hand, so that once she had it placed on her finger she had to clutch her fist to keep it from falling off. Throughout she had looked interested in all, nowise overawed, and now she giggled a little, by no means the blushing bride, indeed her brother the more concerned as to behaviour.

Presently, duly proclaimed man and wife, they knelt to receive nuptial mass; and then it was an arm-in-arm procession, to triumphant music and singing, the two monarchs still side by side, Patrick well in the rear, and the loftiest of the guests parading out after them from the front rows. There had been only standing for everyone, from the start, since the kings had not sat.

None of the normal congratulations followed at the cathedral entry, the royal party proceeding back to the archepiscopal palace between lines of guards.

Once therein bride and groom separated, and Alexander and Patrick went to their own quarters.

"As a union that all seemed very inadequate!" Alexander said. "I cannot say that I feel like a married man at all! How say you, Pate?"

"Does any man, after his wedding? That comes later!"

"With *me*, I think, much later! How deem you the girl feels?"

"No more wed than you do, Alex, I vow! She seemed to see it all as but play-acting. Yet she is now Queen of Scotland!"

"Guidsakes, so she is! A thought, that!"

The usual feasting followed and there was more dancing thereafter, which the new bride seemed to enjoy. She must have practised the Scottish steps and stances in the interim, for she had become quite good at this, sufficiently so for the royal pair to have the musicians play a tune and rhythm of approximately the same beat as a reel, and so to give a solo performance, in which they were presently joined by Patrick and Christian.

But, although Alexander at least was in no hurry about bed-going, it would have been noticeably strange if bride and groom had delayed their mutual retiring overlong, especially with a ten-year-old. They had to make quite a display of their departure, amidst well-wishing, sidelong looks and raised eyebrows. Fortunately no bedding ceremony was suitable for a king and queen. Henry alone accompanied them to their chamber door. The groom and Patrick had made a point of getting a small extra bed brought into the royal room beforehand, so . . .

Sharing a bedchamber with his father later, Patrick was probably not the only one who wondered that night as to how the newly-weds fared.

In the morning, it being Sunday and the Eve of St John the Baptist, it was incumbent upon the Scots party to attend divine worship before they set off on their journey homewards. So a special service was provided for them earlier than usual, before breakfast. Then it was only after prolonged farewells and much fuss that they got on their way. And since Joanna had to ride at Alexander's side, it was not until some distance had been covered and time elapsed that Patrick could have a quiet and private word with his royal friend.

"You passed a comfortable night?" he enquired.

"Yes, God be praised! Better than I feared. I showed her her bed, so soon as we got into the room and bade her brother goodnight, and she went to it seemingly content enough. Whether she had expected otherwise, I know not. But she made no enquiring looks at *my* bed. I judge that she had been told to leave all to me, to do as I told her."

"That was good. So there was no . . . explainings. That not necessary?"

"No. I left her to her washing and undressing while I busied myself with sorting my gear and papers. She displayed no reluctance about appearing naked at the washing-tub, and in drying herself. She has quite a pleasing young body, not womanly yet but well formed. She knelt to say a prayer before getting into bed, which I liked. So I went and kissed her goodnight. She seemed to take that naturally enough."

"She sounds admirable. In the circumstances."

"Indeed, yes. I think that I will grow to like her well. She watched me while *I* was undressing and washing, interestedly I would say, but only that. And when I called goodnight again, she announced that she liked Scottish dancing, and would learn more steps." Alexander glanced behind him from his saddle, to where Joanna now rode beside Lady Beatrix and her daughter. "I think that Christian will be interested to know something of all this, no? She was eyeing me last night."

"I dare say. This all may be somewhat trying for her?"

"I know it. But that is the way of life, it seems. We can continue to please each other, Pate."

"Surely. You must tell her so . . ."

"Lodging at the various houses, priories and castles as

179

we go north may be difficult in this also. In this of rooming, I fear."

"We will see to it well enough, Alex. You are the king."

That proved to be a fairly accurate assessment as they covered the long miles to Scotland. Joanna Plantagenet accepted all and in good spirits, interested in all that she saw. And Alexander managed to have brief periods alone with Christian now and again.

17

Unsuitable as it might be for a newly-wed monarch, they were not long back at Roxburgh when Alexander felt that he must be off again to try to deal with Ranald of the Isles. An armed force had to be mustered at Dumbarton and more shipping assembled – with prayers for better weather than the last time. It was July now and ought to be free of storms. Patrick had to say goodbye to Phemia and their son once more, with some anxiety this time, since he was going to battle presumably, not to attend a wedding. But at least she could go with the king's party as far as Renfrew, with her mother and sister and child, to wait there.

There was the inevitable delay on the Clyde estuary while troops gathered and the necessary vessels were sought, Alexander and Patrick spending most of the interval across the river at the Steward's house, in welcome female company.

They sailed on the day of St James the Great, which they hoped was a good augury, a larger fleet than the last time, the vessels not so overcrowded, heading for the Sound of Bute.

Word had been sent for Campbell of Lochawe to come and meet them, for guidance; and soon after the fleet turned Garroch Head of Bute and headed northwards, they saw a single many-oared longship approaching, its square sail bearing the black and gold gyrony-of-eight of the Campbells. Contact made, Duncan Campbell transferred to the king's ship, a saturnine, lean and hawklike personage in tartan garb, with a lilting, musical Highland voice which went but strangely with his appearance. He informed that Ranald of the Isles himself had gone back to

Islay with many of his clansmen to face trouble with Irish raiders, but had left Kintyre and Knapdale in the hands of his people. No doubt he would be coming back to try to complete and consolidate his occupation of Argyll and Cowal when he had dealt with the Irish. Apparently meantime there were no invaders further up Loch Fyne and into the Campbell country proper.

This was good news, since it meant that Alexander could limit his activity to only a portion of a vast area of mountain, sea lochs and islands for the present, even though Kintyre and Knapdale themselves formed a seventy-mile-long peninsula comprising some five hundred anything but square miles of wild country.

Loch Fyne, into which they had turned now, was one of the longest sea lochs in all Scotland, with a great right-angled bend in the middle, over forty miles from its mouth to its head, where it reached into far Breadalbane. This first half was flanked by Kintyre and Knapdale on the west and Cowal on the east.

Campbell's guidance was most valuable, advice welcome. He told them that the obvious strategy was to cut off Knapdale from Kintyre, and to deal with each separately. This could be done quite effectively, for it so happened that, although they together formed the long peninsula, there was a notable gap, or part-gap, all but dividing them. This was caused by two sea lochs named Tarbert, the eastern one short, little more than a mile long, but the western one over twelve times that, with land of only a mile between. So by holding that short, high pass, it was possible to cut off Knapdale from Kintyre, at least on the ground, although of course vessels could carry men from one to the other, and the Islesmen were naturally great sailors. Campbell's counsel, then, was for the king to land most of his force at this Tarbert, and so divide his foes, most of his men to deal with the greater area of Kintyre to the south, others to cope with Knapdale, but keeping a reserve at Tarbert itself to watch for sea assaults, and if necessary send his own ships up and down the coasts to aid in the task and threaten any sea activity.

Alexander was glad to have this guidance, and agreed to follow it. Loch Fyne averaged between two and three miles in width for most of its length, and they sailed up close to the Kintyre coast, rocky, with rugged hills rising almost from the water's edge, not high as mountains went but steep, craggy and forbidding. According to Campbell the western, seaward coast was less harsh, the hills in the main further back, with tillable and pasture land, MacAlister country, with a sprinkling of MacMillans and MacEacherans, small clans and no match for the aggressive Islesmen, the MacDonalds, Macleans, Macleods and the rest.

The fleet, then, had only about a dozen miles to go before they saw the half-mile-wide opening of East Loch Tarbert before them, very evident on this stern coast, the hills drawing back for a brief space. Into the entry they sailed, the loch narrowing and then widening again, with two islets in the middle, making it a sheltered anchorage. At its head was a small community.

Patrick for one, listened with interest as the Campbell informed that this Tarbert was quite famous to Highlanders. For here, in the year 1098, a notable feat had been achieved. King Magnus Barelegs of Norway, assailing in Ireland, Wales, Man and the Western Isles of Scotland from Orkney, had made a compact with King Malcolm Canmore of Scots. He would desist from further aggression against Scotland if he was granted overlordship in all the islands that he could sail his boat around. He coveted this lengthy peninsula of Kintyre, although it was no island. So he had his men fell many trees and cut them up into planking. Then, with this to base his longship's keel upon, he had it drawn out of the water of the West Loch and dragged over land uphill into the pass, and down the other side into the East Loch, he the while sitting in the stern, his hands on the rudder and the sail hoisted. So he claimed that he had sailed his boat around Kintyre, and that this now belonged to him under the agreement. Since then, local fishermen had been known to emulate this deed, drawing their smaller craft over the pass, and thus being able to fish in the wider waters of the Western Sea.

Disembarking most of their men at the haven and village, Alexander divided his force of some three thousand. The larger company, perhaps fifteen hundred, under Cospatrick and his son were to go southwards to seek to cleanse Kintyre of the invaders. Seven hundred and fifty were to deal with the smaller Knapdale to the north, led by the Steward, the residue to remain there at Tarbert with the king and Campbell to be available to aid where and when needed and to meet any emergency. Also to order their ships as the need arose. Alexander would have liked to play the more active part, but recognised his duty as overall commander was to direct and control.

They learned from the local folk, who confided in the Campbell rather than the monarch, that the Islesmen, always remaining near to their vessels, had been ravaging the fertile and wooded lands down the West Loch-side and round along the seaward coasts of Kintyre; similarly on and up the Knapdale shores. The word was that they were not penetrating far inland into the largely empty hills. But they had their watchers and scouts out and about always, appearing frequently here in Tarbert itself; so the likelihood was that their leaders would not be unaware of the arrival of the royal force and shipping.

Duncan Campbell led the king and his advisers up the fairly steep ascent from the village to what he called the beallach or high pass between the hillsides, no lengthy walk and climb; and they were interested to see the remains of Magnus Barelegs's wooden planking still in place there. At the summit they were able to look down the long reaches of the West Loch, this widening almost to a sound, with its islets and beaches and fairly level shores, the sinking sun making all seem fair and peaceful enough, with the Western Sea and the isles of Gigha and Islay and Arran in the distance, highly scenic.

Camping overnight at the village and in the ships, in the

morning it was departure for the majority. Patrick and his father took their long strung-out column up over the pass again, their men less than enamoured over this of doing their campaigning afoot. Cospatrick himself, a veteran at warfare as he was, had never done it other than on horseback, and was somewhat unsure as to procedure and tactics, especially with a cleansing and driving role to play rather than any likely full-scale battling.

Once they got down to the lower ground along the lochside, he spread out his troops in a line perhaps six hundred yards long, this from the waterside to the beginning of the rising ground, and so advanced, himself at the shore end, Patrick in the middle.

There were small communities of fisherfolk and cattleherders, these needless to say almost all at the coastal strip, their inhabitants looking at the trudging newcomers askance, probably seeing them as no more friendly than the Islesmen, and mainly hiding away in their cottages and shacks. But from one or two of the bolder ones they learned that the invaders had been there, stolen some cattle, raped women and burned some houses. But save for the odd small party keeping an eye on the overall scene, one of which had been there the day before, they had moved mainly southwards towards the mull of this Kintyre, where there was better and more populous land.

Their strange onward probing – it could scarcely be called a march – took the southerners about seven more miles that day, to halt at the hamlet of Kilchonaig, and that without seeing any sign of the enemy. It all seemed a somewhat pointless exercise, but at least they were ensuring that the ground they were covering was free of the Islesmen. Cospatrick sent back messengers to inform the king of the fact.

Next day, moving on, it was noon before they gained their first glimpse of what could be trouble, three columns of smoke rising high in the air a mile or two ahead, probably roof-thatching ablaze. But before they reached the burnings they saw four longships heading out from the shore westwards for the open sea. It seemed probable that these were the fire-raisers; and if so it looked as though they were hastily departing, leaving Kintyre, in the direction of their own Islay. That could be a good sign, indication that they knew of the royal force's advance and did not intend to try to combat it. If this was to be the reaction, however undramatic and heroic it might be, it was probably realistic from the invaders' point of view, and convenient enough for themselves in that no actual fighting was involved.

The burning houses proved to be at a haven called Portachollan, beyond a sort of low headland. Here the fisherfolk welcomed in more friendly fashion the newcomers, since obviously they had been responsible for the hurried decampment of the invaders. They were MacMillans here, with Campbell links, and confirmed that the majority of the Islesmen were further south, reportedly in the Killean and Kilchenzie areas.

Their second night was spent here, weary footmen thankful for the rest as well as some food provided by the local folk. Again word was sent back to Alexander as to progress. They wondered how the Steward and his people were faring in Knapdale.

Next day they saw more longships well ahead, making for the open sea beyond Gigha, which looked like further substantiation of their view that there was going to be no major confrontation with the king's forces in the absence of Ranald MacDonald. If this was the case, was there any point in carrying on with this weary tramping? Cospatrick decided that they would proceed with it for another day, and then send back to Alexander for instructions.

In the event, word came to them from the king that the Steward had discovered the same conditions in Knapdale, with the Islesmen sailing off before him and no real fighting taking place. Alexander suggested that Cospatrick's force should return to Tarbert, in these circumstances, rather than proceed on the long trail to the mull. Instead, they would all re-embark and sail back down

Loch Fyne to round the mull itself with the fleet, and assail such enemy as remained thereabouts from the sea.

This seemed wise strategy, and all were glad to turn back whence they had come, in column of march now, and in consequence less slowly.

Back at the ships they found the Knapdale force also returned, and Alexander well pleased with the situation, all but bloodless as it had been so far. As a warlike venture it was an oddity, certainly, but so long as it was effective that mattered not. Presumably Ranald MacDonald had told those he had left behind not to get involved in any serious fighting in his absence. Perhaps he would return later, but meantime they seemed to be clearing Argyll of its assailants, at minimum cost.

Before they set sail again the king declared that this strategic location, Tarbert, with its extraordinary access to the sea, should be safeguarded, in the realm's good. He would order a castle to be built here to seek to ensure that.

Down Fyne again they went then, right to Kilbrandon Sound, with the Isle of Arran now on their left, eventually to round the great clublike tip of the peninsula, the mull, with its cliffs and creeks, past the impressive castle of Dunaverty on its rock pinnacle, built by one of the Lords of the Isles and seeming to challenge all, although in fact no sign of life showed there that day. Then up the west and seaward side, the ships rolling now in the long Atlantic swell.

They were heading for the sheltered haven and anchorage which Campbell called Kilkerran, where their fleet could berth and the army land for a sweep northwards again. But well before they reached that area they again saw longships rowing and sailing off seawards, a continuing process, which confirmed their belief that this was Ranald's policy and there was to be no confrontation. After all, Islay, the Isles lordship's capital island, was only some sixteen miles from this Kintyre coast, and he could be in constant touch with his clansfolk here.

Duly landing at the quite large community of Kilkerran,

more than any village, the locals there told them that the invaders had known of the royal progress for days, and had been withdrawing to their ships and not indulging in their previous barbarities, no doubt not to arouse further hostility which could affect their departure. Alexander judged, therefore, that there was no need for them to go on northwards, the enemy leaving.

So the decision was taken to return to Dumbarton, duty done, purpose achieved, however modest as to action. No doubt the Kintyre population would be thankful to see them gone, even though Ranald might return hereafter, concerned that the royal army did not itself batten on their lands, as armies were so apt to do, even friendly ones.

One night at Kilkerran and they were on their way homewards, none now grumbling. Campbell was seen off in his own vessel back to his own areas.

But at Dumbarton next day Malduin, Master of Lennox, had more than congratulatory welcome for the king. There was news of a grievous happening, all but a calamity, up north again, but north-east this time and much further off, in Caithness. There had been some sort of revolt in those distant parts. Adam the bishop thereof had been cruelly slain, with his assistant, and other wicked deeds perpetrated. Holy Church was in a turmoil of anger and shock and was demanding redress and punishment.

Seeking details, the king was informed that apparently the prelate had been set upon by some of the people of the diocese while collecting tithes which were overdue and being withheld, these declaring that the demands were excessive; and they had stripped and whipped him, at a place called Halkirk, together with his assistant, the Deacon Serlo of Newbattle, tortured them and then slain them both, burning the bishop's body in the local church.

The king did not need to be reminded as to the almost certain reaction of the Vatican when this news reached Rome, especially when the Pope was already displeased with Scotland over matters financial. A bishop murdered and burned, and tithes withheld! There would be a mighty price to pay, anathema pronounced. This would have to be dealt with in no uncertain fashion, and swiftly, so far as was possible, that Honorius would know that the King of Scots was taking all due action. He, Alexander, would go himself, long as the journey would be. No army would be required for this, only a token force. And they could at least go on horseback.

So there was no return to Roxburgh and Home as yet, for Patrick volunteered to go with his liege-lord with a party of his Marchmen, although his father took the greater numbers back to Dunbar and the Merse.

Two nights at Renfrew, then, and it was farewell again, with a three-hundred-mile journey ahead, at least.

A company of some two hundred rode with the king northwards. They went up the River Leven flowing out of Loch Lomond, and so east to Drymen for the Trossachs area and Callander, and so up Strathyre for the first night, where there was a monastery and hospice. It was good to be mounted again. Then on northwards, ever northwards now, through eastern Breadalbane to Strathtay, and then over into Atholl, a lengthy day's ride indeed, eighty miles and more, to pass the next night at Blair.

Atholl was a mighty earldom, they learned, especially when they had to climb out of it by the high and gloomy pass of Drumochter and so down into Strathspey, another seventy miles, to Aviemore. They were not half way yet, their guides alleged.

Leaving the Spey, next day brought them another forty-five miles to Inverness, the capital of Moray, another great earldom. Here none of the company knew just how to proceed further, and they spent the night in the town seeking advice. There were another one hundred and fifty miles to go, it transpired, and directions being so involved, they managed to engage a local guide to accompany them onwards. Even Alexander had not realised quite how far his kingdom extended.

They were led across the base of what seemed to be

called the Black Isle, although it was a great peninsula, and no island, to Dingwall, into Ross now, with memories of Farquhar the earl. Then on to win round the head of the Dornoch Firth at Ardgay, to turn eastwards for the River Fleet and Strath Brora, where they camped. Now they returned to the Norse Sea coast, up which they turned, getting as far as Helmsdale. They were now into Sutherland, so called because, in the old days of the Vikings, who ruled from the Orkney Isles, this was indeed their southern land. Only another forty-five miles to go, they were told.

Leaving the coast at Latheron they crossed into Caithness at last, the most northerly earldom and diocese in the land. They rode over mostly low hills and high, bare, boggy moorland now, to come to the headwaters of the Thurso River, difficult going for their horses. What the late Adam had thought of being appointed bishop of this territory, after being Abbot of Melrose in the green Borderland, was anybody's guess.

Weary indeed they came to Halkirk, some eight miles south of Thurso town, the capital of Caithness and seat of the bishopric. It proved to be no large community, a wide scatter of cottages and farmeries, small black cattle and sheep the evident means of sustenance. The burned-out small church made the most prominent feature. Alexander decided to go on to Thurso for the night.

In that fair-sized town on its bay of the firth between Scotland and Orkney, the royal arrival was not greeted with any loyal enthusiasm, guilt fairly manifest. The bishop's house here – it was scarcely any palace – had been sacked. But there was a monastery some distance off, this presently being guarded almost like some small fortress. Here the monks received Alexander and his company thankfully, having been afraid for their lives.

They informed that although the atrocity had been committed at Halkirk, many of the perpetrators had come from Thurso, where opposition to Bishop Adam had been simmering for some time. They claimed that the tithe-gathering and cess-collecting had been too rigorous and severe, especially the fisherfolk, who declared that their catches, taken from dangerous waters, should be tax-free. After all, Christ's first disciples were fishermen, and He would never have taken much of their hazardous livings from them. The inland farm folk and fish-smokers and millers had followed their lead, and matters had come to a head at Halkirk when Bishop Adam was supporting the Deacon Serlo and another monk, who were responsible for the tithe-collecting.

It seemed that Serlo had been assaulted first, and when the bishop had protested and sought God's curse upon the assailants, the crowd ran mad, some three hundred of them allegedly, not a few from Thurso and around. They had been like wolves against their shepherd, knocked him down, stripped him of his vestments, stoned and slew him and then burned him in the church itself, Satan himself possessing them! Serlo and the other monk had been likewise murdered. So said the monks.

Alexander debated with Patrick how best to deal with this situation. First of all, who to punish? And how to punish them? Something drastic was called for. Three hundred, it was claimed, had taken part. And not all Halkirk men. These monks said that he should hang the malefactors. He could not hang three hundred. Even to hang any he would have to know who was mainly responsible. And discovering that might not be easy if it was mob madness.

Patrick thought that some sort of trial must be staged, and before the whole community. But here in Thurso, where the bishop's house had been sacked, presumably after the murders. Summon the Halkirk people to attend, all of them.

That was accepted. But the punishment?

"You sound as though you do not wish to hang them, Alex. I see that. I would not wish for hangings, slayings, either. But something very dire must be done, however grievous to yourself. The lesson taught. Others must learn that this is not to be repeated. Anywhere in the land. And the Vatican to be satisfied that you have taken adequate steps. Made example of the wrongdoers."

"I know it. But what? Imprisonment? That would be insufficient. And so many. Worse than that is required. I must not seem to show mercy. If the folk are not sufficiently punished others may try the same. Tithe and tax-paying are nowhere popular. There could be a plague of it."

"If not hanging, then mutilation? Less than death but a grievous penalty."

"Mutilation? Such as . . . ?"

"I have heard that in England they cut off noses and ears for some offences. Make the sinner to be laughed at."

"Mmm. Think you that Honorius and the churchmen would be satisfied with that?"

"Probably not. They will demand execution, I think. But something less, if that is your will, Alex, must be sufficiently harsh. Or it will be ineffective."

"A foot cut off? Or a hand? Or both?"

They gazed at each other, neither of them hard nor cruel men.

"The justiciars would undoubtedly hang them all. But *I* will not," the king asserted. "I will think more on this. But, meanwhile, we will order a trial here in Thurso. All the people ordered to appear, and to watch and heed. This we can have put in hand now."

So the royal commands went out. All the townsfolk of Thurso, men, women and children, were to assemble on the morrow before the bishop's house, where there was an open area. And one hundred of the Marchmen to see that they did so. The other hundred to go to Halkirk and its district and bring the people thereof to the town. And every effort to be made to discover who had taken the lead in the murders, the monks of this monastery set to that task.

Not only the local inhabitants were unhappy that night, the monarch and his friend by no means looking forward to the morrow.

The investigations as to responsibility for the outrage were not very successful. By midday, when the trial was due to start, only three names had been produced as ringleaders: one, a Rob Gunn being positively identified, this as the owner of a two-bladed axe which had been used to dismember parts of the victims' bodies. This axe was found and delivered to the king, who saw it as helpful in his predicament, whatever else.

Marshalled by the two hundred of the escort, the entire population was packed into the area at the bishop's house by noon, where a platform was erected for the monarch and Patrick and the prior of the monastery. It made an anxious-looking gathering.

To the beating of the monks' gong, all fell silent, and the prior instructed the crowd to heed His Grace Alexander, High King of Scots.

Far from comfortably, Alexander raised voice. He declared that he came to Caithness in royal wrath to punish the perpetrators of one of the most shameful deeds committed since he mounted the throne, an offence against the Most High, the laws of the land and against Holy Church. No punishment was too great for such wickedness and sacrilege. The entire community should pay the price. But it would be wrong for the totally innocent to suffer unduly. Therefore those guilty should come forward and confess their wrongdoing for the sake of their innocent neighbours. There were said to be some three hundred taking part in the slaying and burnings. Let these now admit it before all.

He paused.

There was shuffling and muttering and glancing amongst the crowd, but no stepping forward, no hand-raising, no calling out.

Alexander glanced at Patrick. "I say again, confess it, you who have sinned. Or I must punish at random, where I choose. Would you all still further sin for the punishment of your friends and neighbours, to be judged before Almighty God in due course?"

Silence. No coming forward.

"Very well. So be it! I have only the one sure name given to me: one Rob Gunn, whose axe was used upon the bishop and his assistants. Is the man Gunn here?"

There was a stir now, pointings and cries. A small but stocky man of middle years came pushing through the throng, looking defiant.

"Take him!" Alexander ordered his Marchmen. "Now, who else?"

None volunteered.

A royal glance at Patrick, who spoke up.

"Hear me, the High Chamberlain and Earl of March. His Grace could hang any and all for this dire crime. As is deserved. Do you wish that? The innocent as well as the guilty? Speak now, or . . ."

People eyed each other and there was some movement, some pushing and turning, but no actual confession.

"I do not esteem you, I say," the king went on. "I must and shall judge you, and punish as fairly as I may. On your own heads be it! I shall take fifty of you, from this Thurso and from Halkirk. Each of these shall lose one hand and one foot. Cut off with the same axe which sliced and cleft Bishop Adam and Deacon Serlo. You hear? Fifty. One hand and one foot from each. You shall not hang, no. But these shall bear testimony to their guilt, or the guilt of others for the remainder of their days. And you all shall share it. This is my judgment. All shall see it done, here and now."

There was a profound hush over all there.

"Fifty, then. Choose you them. *You* will know best who deserves it. If you do not, my lord's men here will take the fifty, as they please. I give you one hour of the clock to pick them. Then I come back. And will see the sentence carried out. All of you will remain here, under guard, while you choose."

Alexander stepped down from the platform to go into the bishop's damaged house. Patrick, following, noted that the royal hand was trembling. He told the prior to have wine brought to sustain the monarch.

194

"That was well done, Alex," he said, once within. "No easy task."

"The most difficult I have ever had to do," he was told. "Pray God that it was right, just, meeting the cause. Me, I would not have made a justiciar!"

"Nor I. But it had to be done. And the churchmen, and Rome, will see it so. And all the realm also. That of the axe, the guilty axe, was good. A notable thought."

The prior brought wine, and it was thankfully received.

"How goes the choosing?" Patrick asked. "Do all know who are the wrongdoers, think you?"

"There is much confusion, my lord," he was told. "Much blame, much denial. But most are known, I think. They will deliver them up. The women are loud in their blaming and judging."

"Yes. His Grace did well, I say, to make *them* do the judging, the choosing. Go you, Master Prior, and bring us word when the fifty are selected."

The cleric was sent off to have women prepared with bandaging, cords, ointments and spirits, to treat the bleeding stumps of limbs as best they might.

It did not take the full hour. Well before that the cleric was back. They went out to find Patrick's men guarding an apprehensive group of men, young and old, including Rob Gunn, and the crowd still arguing amongst themselves as to others who ought to be amongst these.

From the platform, when the gong had gained silence, Alexander made another announcement. "I have decided that it would be right and just if he who wielded the axe at Halkirk should wield it again! The man Gunn shall do the severing of hands and feet. Before his own are cut off."

That man scowled and muttered, and was slapped on the cheek by one of the guards. He was led forward to a stone near the platform, this to act as a chopping-block. There he was handed his own double-bladed axe.

"The first to be maimed," Alexander called.

A protesting, struggling individual was dragged out, while all fell silent.

Not Patrick however, who from the platform spoke up. "You, sinner, I advise that you submit quietly. This for your own good, that it can be a clean cut. Else you will suffer the more, cause the worse hacking and chopping from this Gunn. Heed me. And all others likewise."

The man at the stone glared at Gunn, shaking his head.

"Which first? Hand or foot?" Patrick demanded. "Right hand and left foot. Which?"

After a moment, the victim raised his left foot and placed it on the stone. Gunn, glancing up at the platform, shook his own head, and then stooping, positioned the leg and foot more suitably for an effective blow. He spat, for some reason, and lifting the axe, brought it down with a powerful swing, smashing it just above the ankle. There was a scream from the unfortunate, dying away as he fell into a dead faint.

"As well," Alexander jerked. He had been holding his breath. "Will not feel the next cut. And that foot – not, not fully . . . off!"

Gunn, with another blow, severed the remaining muscles and skin, amongst spouting blood, and then arranged the unconscious man's arm so that the right hand could be cut off with a single more expert blow, to the gasps of the crowd – and not only the crowd.

The casualty was then dragged away to be treated by the women with their salves and cloths, leaving a trail of blood. The next wretch was summoned.

Even more reluctantly this younger man was brought over, stumbling and protesting.

Again Patrick repeated his warning, and even Gunn went through his grim procedure with gruff and muttered advice. But this time the sufferer was less fortunate in not falling unconscious, the agony and throes in consequence being the worse. Guards had to hold him down. In his thrashing and heaving there was much more blood splattering.

Patrick, for one, all but groaned. Forty-eight more of this horror to face. Could they go on watching it? Could they? Alexander was looking away, set-faced. Justice being done? Did one horror justify another?

Be that as it might, the process went on. The pile of bleeding hands and feet grew and grew. Alexander, and therefore Patrick, made themselves stand and seem to eye it all, although in fact their gaze was elsewhere, inward, part of their concern that they did not actually vomit. The man Gunn, whatever his own basic reaction, did become more proficient with practice. The yelling and shrieking and moaning was now general, continuous. Patrick thought that hell must be like this.

How long it took to finish the punishment was not to be known nor calculated, time irrelevant. And even when the maiming was done for forty-nine of them, Gunn himself had to be mutilated. Who was to do it? So upset by it all, Alexander could not bring his mind to deciding this. Patrick called for a volunteer from the crowd, but none responded, all but hysteria reigning. In the end, one of the Marchmen, a hard one, was ordered to do the deed; and at least he had had sufficient demonstration and instruction. The last casualty himself, by this time, was in such a state of distraction as scarcely to know what he was doing nor what was to be done to him, although soon sheer, shocking pain took over as in swooning agony he too became a cripple.

Turning away, a man all but numbed with his own sense of guilt for ordering it, Alexander staggered off into the house behind, leaving Patrick to arrange the burying of the heap of hands and feet, justice done.

Later, back at the monastery, the king demanded of his friend, was *he* the greater sinner? Had he done the major sinning, causing suffering all but unimaginable? Should he have hanged them after all? Would that have been kinder in the end? But kindness was not the objective. Justice, punishment, retribution, there had lain his duties.

Patrick sought to support and sustain, himself unsure.

They were thankful, next day, to get away, to set off on the long road southwards. They hoped never to come to Caithness again.

18

Being back at Home Castle with Phemia and young Pate was bliss indeed after their dire judgment at Thurso, Phemia all sympathy and love. Not infrequently Patrick wondered whether he could possibly resign the high chamberlainship, in order to be able to live a sort of simple family life such as he and his wife longed for; but he was very fond of Alexander, as well as feeling that he had a duty to aid and support him. But somehow he must win more time at Home, even though Phemia could come to court at Roxburgh with the child, the king often urging it. Indeed Alexander had suggested that she came to act as a lady-in-waiting to the child-queen, who most certainly required help and guidance. To appoint Christian, her sister, to that position, as he would have liked, might seem just too obvious, in the circumstances.

The bliss of it, however, was somewhat diluted by word from Phemia herself. Her father-in-law, Cospatrick, had called at Home while Patrick was away in the north, and informed of trouble with the churchmen, of all things, this while the king was up in Caithness coping with other Church requirements. The monks of Melrose Abbey had been given by him years before the lands of Sourlessfield, in lower Lauderdale as a donation, which name they had changed to Sorrowlessfield in gratitude. But now they had begun to extend their cattle pasturing in a large way westwards into the area of Craigsford, part of the Dunbar barony of Ercildoune, this to the resentment of the tenant farmers and graziers thereof, and there had been clash and disorder, with the farm people driving off the intruding cattle back to Sorrowlessfield, and allegedly stealing some of them as compensation, and mishandling the monks when they objected. The new Abbot of Melrose had expressed his displeasure at this, and indeed had laid an anathema, a sort of curse, on the farmers; and extended this to Cospatrick himself when he supported his people, *he* pointing out that it was the monks who were in the wrong. So now the Earl of Dunbar was under the malediction of Holy Church, with all that this entailed; which was absurd, not only in its unfairness but in that Cospatrick had been exceedingly generous all his days towards the Church. He had founded a monastery for the Trinitarians, or Red Friars, at Dunbar in 1218, and well before that had granted the chapel and lands of Haliburton, or the Holy Burgh Town, to Kelso Abbey. And his late wife, Patrick's mother, the Countess Ada, had established a nunnery at St Bathans in the Lammermuirs. Admittedly the Church did produce most of the wealth of the land, but Patrick judged that it appeared to be falling into the sin of greed. Bishop Adam of Caithness himself, indeed, might still be alive had he not sought to impose excessive taxation and tithing on the folk there.

Patrick decided that he had better go and see his father. But first he had a call from Roxburgh to see the king again. And there he discovered that this was also connected with Church problems. There had, of course, to be a new Bishop of Caithness appointed, and although this was not exactly the king's responsibility, the monarch was always to be consulted in such matters. And in this case there were difficulties. The College of Bishops could not agree on an appointment. In fact, after what had happened to Bishop Adam, no candidate was eager for the office. Bishop William of St Andrews had come to Alexander for debate and royal guidance. So the king himself desired advice.

Patrick thought that whoever took on the diocese should be in a position to counter any large-scale opposition by those unruly Caithnessians. In other words, have armed force at his beck and call, other than calling upon the faraway crown for aid. Which implied someone from a powerful landed family, with many men available. Alexander said that he had been thinking along the same lines. Who, then? It had better be a northener, to be readily near at hand, and to be knowledgeable about conditions in those far parts. But there were none so many senior churchmen suitable to be bishops amongst such houses and families.

Patrick said that the only northern family he knew of having a member fairly prominent in the Church was that of the Moray earldom. He had met Gilbert de Moravia, Dean of Moray, more than once, brother of the present earl. Dornoch, where he was based, was not exactly near Caithness, as they had discovered, but at least it was in the right direction. Would that serve?

Alexander thought this a fair suggestion; he could not think of better, at least. He would propose it to Bishop William. It seemed that it would have to be the Church Militant!

The other ruefully pointed out that the Church was becoming militant enough much nearer home. He told of his father's troubles with the Melrose monks, and the malison laid upon him. This was worrying, to be sure, not only over the anathema and bad relations with the Melrose abbot, but when Alexander was endeavouring to improve Scotland's relations with the Pope, they could do without this sort of upset.

The king could not but agree. This must be settled as suitably and swiftly as possible. He would consult Bishop William on the matter; he was helping him on the issue of Caithness, so he could aid in this, surely.

Next day, Patrick and Phemia rode to Dunbar. Cospatrick was glad to see them, and to hear of the royal concern and desire to help. It was ridiculous that an Earl of Dunbar should be worried over the ill-will of a mere cleric, abbot or other; but the fact was that getting wrong with the Church could be serious in its consequences and inconveniences. And he had always been a religiously minded man. Not that the cause of this present trouble was anything to do with religion; but . . .

In the event, Alexander sent a message to suggest that the Earl Cospatrick should present himself at Selkirk two weeks hence, when there was to be a notable occasion celebrated there. Kelso Abbey was unique in Scotland in that its original foundation by King David, that excellent monarch, before he succeeded to his brothers' throne, had been at Selkirk, this in the year 1113. But it was removed from there over a score of miles eastwards some thirteen years later, to Kelso, this because of David's establishment of the royal castle at Roxburgh nearby, on becoming king, where it could serve as a convenient shrine for official occasions. This was now to be commemorated, a century later, by the establishment of a new priory on the site of the one-time abbey, and Alexander, great-grandson of David, had agreed to be present. All the Borders senior churchmen would be there. It would be a suitable opportunity to settle differences with the Abbot of Melrose. Bishop William, who would preside, suggested that Earl Cospatrick could ease the situation by making some small gesture, not relating to Sorrowlessfield but otherwise, which could allow the abbot to withdraw his malediction blandly.

The earl, while pointing out that *he* was the injured party in this squabble, agreed that this was probably the best way out of it all. He would add a few acres of pasture to the chapel lands of Haliburton, appendage of Kelso Abbey, not Melrose, as was suitable, to mark the occasion, and presumably the Melrose abbot would get the message.

Patrick said that he would accompany the king and his father.

A fortnight later, then, there was a great gathering at Selkirk, on the edge of the vast Forest of Ettrick, probably the largest wilderness area of southern Scotland, mainly of churchmen but with a few of the nobility accompanying the monarch. The town was situated on high ground above where the Rivers Ettrick and Yarrow joined before their waters reached Tweed and was divided into two parts, all but separate communities, Selkirk Abbatis and Selkirk Regis, the former around the ruins of the former abbey, the latter surrounding the royal castle, this now little used.

The company was entertained at the castle with refreshments after the twenty-mile ride, before a religious ceremony was held at the site of the priory-to-be; and here, with Bishop William at his side, Cospatrick announced his contribution to the occasion by donating those extra lands to the Abbey of Kelso as a gesture, with a sum in silver to aid in the new priory construction. This was received by Abbot Herbert of Kelso with suitable appreciation, no mention being made of malisons and curses; and thereafter Bishop William brought the Abbot of Melrose up, to declare his approval and goodwill, again with no reference to the anathema but with the understanding that all was now well between them. Presumably the curse was lifted, and the monks of Sorrowlessfield would be instructed to keep their cattle to their own territory.

Thus Holy Church displayed its benevolence.

Thereafter a move was made in procession round the town, with blessings on the population, and the prior named for the new establishment, a son of Uchtred Scott of Buccleuch, prominent amongst the Ettrick lairds.

Back at the castle for a meal before the return journey, at which Alexander addressed the company, informing all of the steps taken to punish the perpetrators of the Caithness assassinations, and the steps likewise taken to ensure that there would be no repetition of the acts of shame, the Vatican to be sent details, and papal goodwill towards Scotland thereby strengthened. Bishop William announced the appointment of Dean Gilbert de Moravia as Bishop of Caithness, with especial instructions to discipline the population there to God's service and purposes.

Then it was the slow ride back down Tweed, these clerics being apt to be less urgent horsemen than the nobility. Bishop William confided in the king that when word of all this was delivered to Pope Honorius, he might take it to Rome himself, and while there plead for the upraising of the Scottish Church to metropolitan status, this to put an end to the spurious claims of Archbishop Walter of York to be spiritual overlord. It was a good opportunity to request this, for there were growing reports of enmity between the archbishoprics of Canterbury and York over *English* superiority, the former demanding subservience from the latter and this being fiercely rejected. The Pope might well be concerned, and the more prepared to grant the Scots request. He, William, might just possibly come back an archbishop himself!

They all wished him well in this; but it hardly seemed an admirable issue for Christ's Body on Earth, the Church.

19

The Melrose monks were not the only source of concern for the Dunbar earldom that summer, and not only Cospatrick and his son involved, but the king also. It was the old problem of Northumberland, and to a lesser extent Cumberland also. These two counties, or earldoms, had long been a source of debate and uncertainty between the kingdoms. The ancient Anglo-Saxon realm of Bernicia had extended from the Firth of Forth southwards, down to the River Tees in Northumbria. But owing to the invasions of the Danes along the north-east coasts of England, as elsewhere, Athelric the Saxon king had managed to drive them out, and more or less annexed the southern half of this great territory to England. Needless to say, this much offended the Scots, and southern parts of Bernicia, beyond Tweed, became an area of contention, and remained so for centuries. Then King Stephen of England, in exchange for certain benefits, had ceded Northumbria and Cumbria to Scotland, and these two earldoms had been granted to Malcolm Canmore's elder sons by King David as a sort of compensation for the Margaretsons obtaining the throne. The Cospatricks had never formally relinquished their title to Northumberland, although they no longer called themselves earls thereof, and still looked upon it as rightfully theirs. And not a few of the local landholders there looked upon themselves as vassals of the Dunbar earldom, since that was much less demanding on their purses and responsibilities than was the de Vesci's English lordship of Alnwick. It all made a complicated situation, admittedly capable of producing friction.

And now some friction had developed. Certain landowners were refusing to pay cess and service to de Vesci, even though they were not actually paying it to Cospatrick either, and complaint had gone to King Henry, with the inevitable result. The peace between the two kingdoms, sealed by marriage, was not to be endangered, it was recognised.

It all made a rather difficult decision for Alexander. Patrick was his close friend, and Cospatrick one of his most reliable and powerful nobles. How to placate Henry and the English without offending the father and son? In the interests of harmony, the latter were prepared to give up actual claims to Northumberland; but this could affect more than themselves and those landowners, for it would imply making firm boundaries, which in turn meant drawing a line, a borderline, between England and Scotland, something hitherto left vague deliberately, often indeed termed the Debateable Land. The Borderers preferred it this way, on both sides, although their rulers might not, on occasion.

So now Henry Plantagenet, or his advisers, were involved and urging Alexander to come down to discuss the entire matter with them, indeed sending a safe-conduct missive, to Canterbury, for the Scots monarch. Alexander was less than happy about this, wondering why it should always be himself who was expected to go to England for interviews rather than Henry coming to Scotland? But Henry was much the younger, and his regent, Ulster, in failing health, they both now being kin by marriage. Alexander could have refused, of course, or even said that he would meet Henry at York, as before, halfway between the two capitals. But the very fact that the safe-conduct was to Canterbury was a determining factor, not at London nor Windsor. It looked as though Henry were supporting the archbishop thereof in his present rivalry with York; and this suited Scotland, in that it was York not Canterbury which laid claim to overlordship of the Scottish Church. So here was opportunity to make representations on that matter, to the realm's benefit. Also the full dowery-money for Joanna had not yet been paid, and this could be pressed for at the same time.

Another trip to England, then, Patrick and his father, being involved, to accompany their liege-lord.

On the subject of Queen Joanna, it seemed that her relationship with her husband was developing not uncomfortably. She was a cheerful youngster, easy to deal with, and ceasing to be shy with Alexander. While scarcely cohabiting, they could be alone together without embarrassment, and frequently slept in the same room, although in different beds. She was fond of outdoor activities and a good horsewoman, which pleased Alexander. And, importantly, she did not seem in the least inimical to Christian, although she must have been aware of that young woman's closeness to the king. He spoke of the situation more than once to Patrick, admitting that she would probably make quite a good wife. Just when they would start bedding together remained to be seen; but for his part, there was no hurry. He would know, he thought, when she was ready. *Then* there could be problems with Christian.

It was only a small party which duly set off for Canterbury, Alexander dispensing with any handsome retinue to impress the English, no longer concerned with this, and desirous of getting the visit over as quickly as possible. The smaller the escort the faster they could ride; so only the Steward and a dozen of the royal guard accompanied the monarch and Cospatrick and his son. They reckoned that eighty miles a day and perhaps more was reasonable, in fair weather conditions.

In fact, after the Cheviots were got through and their Northumbrian outliers they did rather better than that, reaching Weardale, and a monastery for the first night, and York for the second. Despite the royal safe-conduct, and what it implied as to hospitality, they avoided the archepiscopal palace, in the circumstances, bedding down at one of the abbey's farmeries, or granges as they called these in Scotland, a little way outside the town. So there was no embarrassment nor delay with Archbishop Walter de Gray.

With no difficult riding, they were at Newark the following night and Bedford the next, well pleased with progress. London was none so far ahead. They skirted that great city to the east, to cross Thames at Woolwich, to halt at the priory there. Canterbury was some fifty miles to the south-east, in Kent, amongst gentles slopes, scarcely hills by Scots standards, rich country indeed.

With their speedy travel, they arrived at Canterbury, within its lofty walls, before they were expected, King Henry not yet present, nor even the cardinal-archbishop. But they were adequately welcomed by the surprised dean, and found quarters in the handsome palace, word being sent to London as to their coming. In the meantime they were shown over the magnificent cathedral and told something of its story, how, although founded by St Augustine in the sixth century it had been twice burned and rebuilt. They saw, in the north transept, where Archbishop Thomas à Becket had been murdered by four of King Henry the Second's knights,; just why was not explained, tactfully, that being the present Henry's father.

That young monarch put in an appearance next day, having apparently come down the Thames estuary in a boat, to land at Whitstable and continue the few miles by horse. He was as friendly as ever towards Alexander despite this matter of Northumberland and Cumberland, and said that his Earl of Kent and Ulster would join them later, he being frail these days, and not able to travel fast. He asked after his sister Joanna, but when the dowery-money was mentioned by the Steward, he looked vague and said that was a matter for Earl Hubert.

That man, a mere shadow of his former self, arrived in the evening, with quite a large party, including the cardinal-archbishop. After a meal, no banquet this, the two sides got down to debate forthwith, Hubert de Burgh very much in charge despite his frailty, giving the impression that there was no time to waste, which well suited the Scots group. Nothing was said about the Canterbury-York tension.

The discussion that followed was mainly about Northumberland, the Cumberland position being less critical, for nobody was actually claiming that one-time earldom. De Burgh held that the two counties were rightfully part of the English realm, always had been since Athelric's time, and King Stephen's granting of them to Scotland a mistake and folly which he had no authority to do without his council's consent. Alexander countered that by declaring that it had not been formally contested at the time, and the transfer had been duly paid for by Scotland.

Henry said that it was all a long time ago and the conditions were different now. Clearly the two areas were part of his kingdom and should be recognised as such. He recited that as though he had been taught it as a lesson.

Alexander turned to Cospatrick. That man declared that his ancestors had been Earls of Northumbria for generations, a fact recognised by many of the most prominent of the landholders there; and the Lord of Alnwick's claims to their subservience contested. He held to the ancient privilege.

De Burgh said that such attitude was no longer tenable. The Earl Cospatrick of Dunbar was not a subject of King Henry, and as such would not be able to claim to be an English earl at the same time as a Scottish one. The case of Huntingdon was different. That had been an English earldom always, carried to the son of King David, Henry, by marriage to the heiress thereof, Joan Beaufort; and the present holder, although called John the Scot, was in fact an English citizen and paid no allegiance to King Alexander. The two situations were not comparable. However, His Majesty Henry did not wish to penalise and injure the Earl Cospatrick and his son. What was proposed was that Northumberland should be accepted as in the English kingdom; but that part of it, certain baronies and manors, should be handed over to the Earls of Dunbar in feudal tenure, the rents and dues thereof payable to them, but the overall superiority vested in the King of England, as in all other counties, earldoms and lands.

Cospatrick and his son exchanged glances. This was in fact more than they had expected, for it meant that, if accepted, they would be getting moneys from those land-holders lawfully, which had not been the case for long. Cospatrick nodded to Alexander, who kept a straight face, although he understood very well.

And Cumberland, he wondered?

That was different, he was told. There were no claims to the former earldom there. And, because of the Firth of Solway, it was clearly part of England, none suggesting that Carlisle was anything but an English city and bishopric. So a clear boundary would have to be drawn from the Solway north-eastwards along the lands of Northumberland, one side of it accepted as England, the other Scotland. Was it agreed?

Alexander accepted that in principle. But it would be a difficult task in the detail. For those Borderland lords and lairds and mosstroopers, on both sides, were apt to see themselves as all but independent, paying allegiance, if at all, to whichever kingdom suited them best at any time and occasion, all but a law unto themselves. Forming any firm and regular line would be difficult.

De Burgh acknowledged this, unsuitable as it was. It could be an awkward and lengthy process, but necessary. What was proposed was that a commission be appointed to consider, examine and decide, and then the boundary would be imposed. Say six commissioners on each side, and these make a recognisable and enduring borderline for all time coming. Was that agreed?

Alexander looked at his advisers, who all nodded. He accepted, then, with the proviso that the Earls of Dunbar and of March should be members of this commission, as best able to deal with the inevitable objections of both sides of the proposed line, as far as Northumberland was concerned. As to Cumberland, they would have to choose suitable nominees.

That was for the King of Scots to decide, they were told.

That concluded the business, to Henry's obvious relief, he indeed jumping up, and clapping Alexander on the shoulder. So they all must rise, the Scots well enough satisfied, their journey well worth the making. They adjourned for further refreshment.

They had the next day as guests of Cardinal-Archbishop Stephen Langton, who entertained them lavishly and provided a splendid feast in the evening, beyond all that the Scots had ever experienced. Alexander, on the prelate's left hand at table, took the opportunity to mention that he hoped that Walter of York would be discouraged from further assertions of his metropolitan claims over the Scots Church, the other raising eyebrows but inclining his head.

In the morning it was departure again, with de Burgh saying that the Scottish borderline commission ought to be appointed forthwith, as would be the English one, to meet together without delay. Alexander, taking leave of Henry, said that if another royal meeting became called for, he hoped that it would take place in Scotland, where the other would be a most welcome visitor, with much to see, his sister included. Henry looked across at de Burgh enquiringly, and did not commit himself.

Four hundred miles northwards for them, then.

20

Alexander decided on his four other members of the
boundary commission before ever they reached Scotland:
two from the Middle March, Adam de Rule from the Rule
Water in Teviotdale and Sir William Maitland of Thirl-
stane in Lauderdale; and two from the West March, Sir
John Macuswell or Maxwell, Baron of Caerlaverock on the
Solway and Sir Nigel de Herries, King's Forester for the
South, Patrick and his father representing the East March.
If de Burgh had his way, it probably would not be long
before they received word of their English counterparts,
and requests for their first meeting.

Phemia, for one, was glad to hear of this latest task laid
upon her husband, for the probability was that most of the
visitations and meetings would take place none so very far
from Home Castle, save for the furthest West March ones,
all within a day's ride at the most; so she could see more of
Patrick. She thought that she was pregnant again, so young
Pate might be having a rival.

The expected message came in due course. The English
commissioners would include two churchmen, the Bishop
of Carlisle himself and the Prior of Lanercost, these for the
West March; William de Acre, or Dacre, and Sir Henry de
Neketon, the Escheator, for the Middle; and William,
Prior of Durham, representing the prince-bishop, and
John de Bertram of Bothal, for the East. It was proposed
that they all met at Wark Castle, on Tweed, on the first day
of October for the initial survey.

This suited Patrick very well, for Wark lay no more than
a dozen miles from Home, south by east. He well knew
why this locality had been selected. The eastern stretch of

Tweed had been accepted as the border for long, west-wards of Berwick for twenty-five miles. But beyond Wark the river no longer served as boundary, the remainder of its course being all in Scotland, and the areas to the south of it could be called the beginning of the Debateable Land, although right to the Cheviot foothills the inhabitants looked upon themselves as Scots. Here would be an obvious place for the English to commence their negotiations. This destination would be less than convenient for the West March representatives.

October dawned. Cospatrick and his son joined Adam de Rule and Sir William Maitland at Kelso, and proceeded eastwards to Wark. Whether Maxwell and Herries from the West would appear remained to be seen.

At the castle, it transpired that the two clerics from Carlisle had not come either, presumably judging that this distant area had little to do with them, even though the entire border between the realms was the task to be accomplished. Dacre and de Neketon the Escheator – whatever that title meant – with Prior William and Bertram of Bothal, from Northumberland, were waiting.

This vicinity being just into the Middle March, Dacre knew it best, and led off by declaring that the borderline should rightfully start turning inland from Tweed just four miles to the west, this side of the Mill of Banff, where the Redden Burn joined the great river, and then run southwards through Sprouston parish, making for Softlaw and the Forest of Bowmont.

Adam de Rule immediately objected. That would include the small lairdships of Redden and Whitelaw in England, which would be ridiculous. These two lairds often attended the court at Roxburgh, a mere four miles away as the crow flew. King Alexander would never agree to that; Maitland supported him, and Patrick also.

Thus early did the dissension start, the English holding to their claim, obviously agreed on beforehand. Cospatrick, seeking to make a bargaining stance, proposed an alternative. The border should leave Tweed almost immediately west of this Wark, at Carham, and strike up by Holefield and the Pressan Burn, and so to the Bowmont Water at Shotton.

This raised indignation from Dacre and the Escheator – which apparently meant the official responsible for feudal dues where estates were forfeited to the crown or for lack of an heir – who asserted that it would give Scotland many square miles that undoubtedly were in England, and not to be considered. The Earl of Dunbar must know this.

Patrick, recognising his father's tactics, suggested that, as compromise, some line perhaps midway between these two proposals could be considered. Suppose that they made a start at the Birgham area, and headed across Tweed from there, by Hadden and Lempitlaw, so reaching the Bowmont Water by Wideopen Moor? Shotton, on the river, was certainly in Northumberland, but the approach thereto was undefined. Let them commence thus.

The prince-bishop's representative, Prior William, contended that this was getting them nowhere. Instead of discussing thus, the names of places, they go on together to inspect the ground itself. Thus a truer understanding would be gained. Let them begin at the first here suggested, at the Redden Burn and view the prospects. He was supported vehemently by his colleagues. The Scots shrugged, and declared that, by agreeing so to do, they were not by any means accepting that the line chosen should be so far westwards.

So it was to horse and on westwards up Tweed, five miles, to the entry of the Redden Burn, no major tributary however important it might be as a possible boundary mark.

This stream swung away south-westwards almost at once after the confluence, and led through level meadowlands for some four miles, to skirt the village of Sprouston. Not even these Englishmen contended that this should be included in Northumberland, however much they favoured the land immediately to the east. They rode on, due south now, over gradually rising ground, by Cockerlaw and Lurdenlaw and Gowdens, six miles. They thereby passed the small estate of Redden itself and Whitelaw and Hopriglaw, and de Rule did not fail to point out that these were typical Scots tower-houses, and not to be thought of as in England, to tight lips from the opposition.

And opposition it obviously had become already, not any boundary commission but two teams of antagonists.

After Gowdens, even the Englishmen did not pretend that they could continue due southwards into the valley of the Teviot tributaries of the Kale and Cessford, and they swung eastwards over the high ground to Graden Moor, where they were nearing the major valley of the Bowmont Water, part of which was recognised by all as in Northumberland. Here there was less disagreement, with the Scots agreeing to accept a line passing Hoselaw Loch and Wideopen Moor and so leading down to the Bowmont. But by this time the October sun was sinking, and enough was enough for one day. Not that any agreement was reached, both sides holding to their own contentions. Nor was there any suggestion that the Scots should share a night's accommodation at Wark Castle, with Kelso and indeed Home within easy riding distance. It was arranged to meet again in two days' time.

As they trotted Home-wards, the four Scots accepted that the task laid upon them was going to be difficult indeed, and probably lengthy, if they were going to obtain any equitable result for their efforts. And, even when a line was agreed by the commissioners, there was no certainty that the local folk would accept their findings, even if the monarchs did. Centuries of deliberately undefined areas and usages were not to be readily discarded. Fortunately, it would be a deal easier on the East March, with the Tweed itself making the boundary. But if this day's experience was anything to go by, the West March scarcely bore thinking about. Phemia, glad to welcome their visitors, sympathised.

Two days later it was back to Wark. There was still no sign of the West March representatives. This time the Scots insisted that they start at *their* proposed line, from Carham and on to Holefield and Pressan, the while pointing out suitable features for a common boundary, wasteland, burns, the edges of properties and the like, little of which met with any acceptance by the others. That is, until they got back up to Graden Moor and Wideopen, where there was no argument, and they all were able to slant down the quite steep descent, past the Pictish fort of Castle Law, and into the Bowmont valley, to reach that river opposite Shotton, accepted as part of Northumberland. That stretch at least was fixed.

This took barely until noontide, so it was agreed that they should ride back to Tweed, and follow thereafter along its course eastwards, this to mark the East March border, a mere token perambulation as the Scots pointed out, for the wide river had always represented where Scotland ended and England began, since Bernician days, a score of miles of it. Berwick itself was a large town, within walls, perhaps the busiest port in all Scotland, this of considerable concern to Cospatrick, for it was the main shipping centre for the export of the Lammermuir wool to the Low Countries, much greater than Dunbar and Eyemouth, with a better and larger harbour in the mouth of the Tweed. Much of its population was of Flemish descent, the huge wool trade bringing them over as merchants, just as many Scots followed the reverse course and settled in the Netherlands and Flanders.

It was here, where Tweed reached salt water, that Prior William produced controversy. He declared that the area on the *south* side of the river, really just a built-up extension of the town, and connected by a bridge, part of what was known as Berwick Bounds, was in fact and essence in England and should not be accepted as part of the Scots realm. The monastic hospice here which gave name to the area, the Spittal, was in effect an outpost of the prince-bishop's spiritual lordship of Durham. This must be acknowledged, and the English claim thereto established.

Cospatrick contested that strongly. It was an integral

part of Berwick-upon-Tweed, and as such part of his earldom. There was no other community of any size or importance in Northumberland for many miles. To separate it, in name and theory, from the rest of the town was absurd. Some of the ports wharves and piers were on that side. To seek to detach it was quite impracticable.

The Escheator backed the prior's claim, and so one more stumbling-block to agreement was erected.

The two groups separated here, their only consensus being that they met again in two weeks' time for the next stage of their survey, right to the Solway Firth. The parting was less than friendly.

When Patrick reported on all this to Alexander, the king was concerned. Peace and amity with England were all-important. It was tragic if this was to be jeopardised over a few acres of land here and there. They, his commissioners, might have to yield somewhat on occasion, not greatly to be sure, but on a very minor scale, for the sake of the harmony between the two realms. And they might be able to compensate somewhat, now and again, especially on the West March, with greater areas undefined, whole dales and valleys. Patrick said that he very much doubted that, indeed he foresaw greater troubles there than on the Middle March, so much debateable, and those mosstrooping Marchmen a law unto themselves. He was not looking forward to that assignment. Also he judged that to give in to the English even on small points would but encourage them to press for more.

However, they had two weeks of peace and lack of stress at court. The efforts to improve conditions there had proved very successful, the introduction of the female element notably rewarding, and most of the late monarch's elderly advisers having now departed, if not from life at least from the scene. Rather extraordinarily, the young Queen Joanna's presence had quite aided in this process, her lively and friendly nature and easy behaviour towards all helping to make for a congenial atmosphere at Roxburgh Castle. It had become a different place. Young Pate, Master of March to give him his due title, was now old enough to be taken there frequently, so his parents saw the more of each other.

Although the West March commissioners had not troubled to come to the Middle and East March surveys, Cospatrick and his son did not emulate, but decided to attend there, however disputatious they expected it all to be. The presence of two earls could just possibly aid Scotland's case in some small degree. Moreover the western end of this Middle March was still unvisited, and could well produce some friction also.

So de Rule and Maitland came to Roxburgh, and the four of them went south-westwards a score of miles to meet their counterparts at the Carter Bar in the Cheviots, south of Jedburgh, an obvious borderline point at all but a pass, with the land falling away on either side from its summit, the River Rede on the south side and the Jed Water's tributaries on the north. At least there was no argument about this. Nor did the land immediately east and west offer much reason for dispute, empty hillsides for miles, some sheep the only obvious denizens, although their shepherds must live somewhere; in hidden valleys presumably. The direction of flow of these Cheviot streams made the choice of borderline fairly evident, those flowing to the south clearly in England and to the north in Scotland. They would have cairns of stones erected on various ridges and summits to mark this line. It was good not to be arguing with the Englishmen – but for how long would that continue?

It lasted most of the day, in fact, for eastwards there was a succession of peaks and escarpments, with odd names, such as Ark's Edge, Leaphill, Hungry Law and Chew Green, these causing no debate. Chew Green was the site of a Roman camp. Thereafter the line proceeded along the famed Roman Road of Dere Street north-eastwards, heading for the Bowmont valley and Shotton. No problems there, for almost a score of windy miles. Then back westwards to Carter Bar again, and on, south-west now, still by heights and ridges for another ten miles or so until they came to Deadwater Moor and its flanking stream and valley. And here, although the obvious line was due south, the English wanted a diversion, in their favour, westwards for a mile or two, this on account of the lands of Kirshope Castle stretching across the Deadwater in that direction, this a Northumbrian squire's house. De Rule was taking exception, but Patrick, remembering the king's advice, intervened and declared that this triangular intrusion of mere moorland would do little damage to the Scots cause; and they might well be glad to have some similar exception in their favour further on. So no difficulty was made about this.

They marked the couple of square miles of intrusion, and continued on their way, south now, the great Northumberland area of Kielder on their left and the Scottish Sauchtree Fells on their right. This provided no real contentions. They called it a day when they reached the upper Tyne, with only a range separating them from Liddesdale. It had been a long day of riding, but little dispute.

De Rule, who knew the area best, said that there was a hospice at Bonchester, a dozen miles to the north beyond the Wauchope Forest, none nearer. They could pass the night there, for it was much too far to try to get back to Wark or Roxburgh or Home. And they would be well placed there to start on the West March in the morning, in Upper Liddesdale.

That was accepted.

The problem now was how to bring the western representatives into the survey. It was a long way to Caerlaverock and Carlisle to inform them. But it was decided that since the hospice at Bonchester was a monkish one, like almost all others, and the two English commissioners were churchmen, bishop and prior, one of the monks or lay brothers of the establishment could be asked to inform the clerics of the situation, and then proceed to Caerlaverock likewise, bidding all to come up to Liddesdale to join the group. Meantime the eight of them could commence the inspection, and hope that their findings would be acceptable to the newcomers.

Thankful that there had been so little disputation that day, they rode for Bonchester, on the Rule Water.

They did not have to pass the night in difficult company, at least, for the Scots monks, understanding the position, found alternative accommodation. And they provided two good horsemen to ride to Carlisle and Caerlaverock.

But in the morning trouble started as soon as they reached the head of Liddesdale and the Liddel Water's headstreams, disagreement voiced over which tributaries should mark the boundaries. By the time that they had gone even six miles it was apparent that this was getting them nowhere, five different locations contested. In the absence of the West March representatives, no decisions were possible. And it might be two or three days before these others put in an appearance. Another few miles, with continuing disagreement and growing hostility, and Cospatrick, the most senior of the Scots, declared that this was profitless, nothing being achieved. Let the West March commissioners make their own decisions for this area – if they could! Meanwhile, it was a return to base for them.

The English team appeared to be equally disenchanted, and made no protest at a retiral. So it was back whence they had come, and at Bonchester another two messengers were sent to inform their western colleagues of the situation, these to make their own arrangements. Then on eastwards, the two groups parting at Kelso, with little in the way of good wishes.

It had all been a trying and quite unproductive exercise, a waste of time.

When, in due course, they told Alexander of this, he could not but accept that there was little point in seeking to go on with the project. However valuable for the peace of the realms it might be, the fixing of an accepted borderline was apparently not to be, not yet at any rate. They had known that the West March would be the most difficult, but now they recognised any accord as all but impossible. The Debateable Land must remain as such. Alexander would let King Henry know it.

So much for diplomacy and goodwill between nations!

21

Almost inevitably, as a consequence of all this failed enterprise, Patrick, as High Chamberlain was asked by Alexander to go to England to inform Henry Plantagenet of the situation, and to declare that the non-success of it all was deeply regretted, and that every effort had been made on the Scots side to reach satisfactory conclusions and make compromises. Their opposite numbers would be telling a different story, of course; but at least the Scots regrets should be announced. Patrick could have done without this, but could not refuse.

It so happened that another task was laid upon him at this juncture, and one that could be undertaken more or less at the same time. His father was much concerned over a serious matter for the Dunbar earldom, and for others, which had suddenly blown up. This was the price being received from Scottish wool, the which represented the largest part of the earldom's income. It related to what was known as the Staple at Veere. This Veere was the port of the Netherlands, on the Walcheron peninsula, to which the wool was exported, there to be distributed throughout the Low Countries and Flanders, for weaving and cloth-making. And it so happened that the annual price paid for the said wool, which tended to vary somewhat year by year, was decided on by the burgomaster of Veere. Just why this individual had gained this privilege and authority was uncertain, but it had been so established for long. The variance probably depended upon the state and demand on the clothing industry. But this year the staple had dropped abruptly, an unprecedented fall which hit the Lammermuir wool-growers direly, to the distress of all farmers, shepherds and Cospatrick in especial. And when the latter had learned that the wool from the Cheviot Hills sheep flocks, exported from Alnwick and Newcastle-upon-Tyne, had suffered no such steep decline, he was the more troubled and angered. So he wanted Patrick to go on from London to the Netherlands, to enquire into the problem and seek to improve the situation. It ought to be easy to sail from the Thames in an English ship, and come home on one of their Scots craft.

So it was farewell to Phemia again all too soon, and, it was to be feared, for quite some time, her pregnant state concerning him. He would make it as brief a parting as was possible.

He rode, with only the one servitor, for London, unusual as it was for someone in his position, knowing that on his excellent horses they could cover the ground much faster than with the usual escort. Indeed he would have gone entirely on his own had it not been that he would not need, nor be able to take, a horse to the Netherlands, and the two mounts would have to be ridden back to Scotland by his man.

They made excellent time down through England, better than Patrick had ever done, averaging over one hundred miles per day, most of it of course over very different terrain than their more hilly Scotland. They had to spend only three nights on the way. However they found King Henry was presently at Windsor, and so had an extra score of miles to cover from London.

Patrick found the young monarch friendly, and was surprised to discover that he had not yet been given nor sent word of the non-success of the boundary survey. Possibly de Burgh had been notified, but he was not at Windsor, a sick man, his place being taken by his own son-in-law, Richard de Clare, Earl of Gloucester, a younger and less daunting man, with whom Henry seemed to be quite close.

Patrick was thus able to give them a first and first-hand report on the borderline problem and the failure to reach any agreement. He sought not to be over-critical of the English commissioners, but could not but indicate that most of the difficulties stemmed from that side. He did emphasise the difficulties involved, both on the ground and with the inhabitants thereof, with their ages-old traditions.

His hearers were not unduly critical, although they did question him in some detail, reserving judgment apparently. But there was no animosity, and Alexander's regrets accepted with understanding.

Henry was interested to hear, thereafter, of his sister's all but popularity at the Scots court, clearly pleased. He invited Patrick to stay on at Windsor for so long as he cared, with the hawking and the hunting good; but this was tactfully declined, on the grounds of the onward journey to the Low Countries, and his duty to be back at his liege-lord's side as soon as possible. Gloucester declared that there ought to be no problem in finding a vessel to take him over to the Continent from one of the Thames harbours, there being constant trade with Flanders in especial.

One night at Windsor Castle, then, and it was back to London and on to the recommended port of Tilbury where, with the king's commendation, he found a ship due to sail for the Schelde and Antwerp in two days' time, this able to call at Veere in the by-going without much of a detour. So another couple of nights in London, with his man seen off for Scotland with the horses, and he was able to board the *Thanet Star*, for the Low Countries.

Patrick had not realised that in fact fully one-third of his voyage would be spent sailing down the Thames estuary, some thirty miles, to between the Medway and Shoeburyness, passing innumerable other craft, great and small, and many towns on the way. He kept being struck by the large numbers of people in this England. He was well aware, of course, that there was fully ten times the population compared with Scotland, but seeing the proofs

of it was different. Were the Scots presumptuous to consider the realms of equal importance and status? Yet size
was not everything . . .

They were barely out of sight of land behind them
before they were seeing land in front of them, the Flanders
very level coastline. Sailing parallel with this, almost due
eastwards, and with a south-west wind, they made good
time; and ten hours after leaving Tilbury, at dawn, they
were tacking in towards the land, at dusk, this at what he
was assured was Walcheron. Rounding a low headland of
this, their ship swung into a half-mile-wide channel,
south-westwards now, which was apparently known as
the Veerse Meer. Some four miles up this, on the south
side, loomed in the half-dark a fair-sized town, with a long
succession of piers and jetties reaching out into the channel, with great storehouses behind: Veere. The *Thanet
Star* docked for the night at one of these, amongst the rows
of other vessels. Patrick, told that they would sail again at
sun-up and be at the Schelde and Antwerp by noon,
decided to pass the night on the ship, on the bunk he
had been allocated but had not used.

So, in the morning, with an early start, he found himself
on one of the quaysides of his destination, uncertain as to
his further moves. It occurred to him that there might well
be Scots vessels tied up at these wharves, and strolling
along it was not long before he spotted a quite large craft
bearing the name of *St Ebba*. The chances were that this
belonged either to Eyemouth or to Berwick-upon-Tweed,
St Ebba's Head being midway between these ports. So he
hailed two seamen busy on its deck dragging bales of cloth
to stow under canvas covers. He was answered in a good
Scots voice.

He called out that he was the Earl of March, and would
be glad of a word with the shipmaster, if he was aboard.

Staring, one of the men hurried off aft.

Soon he came back with a stocky, heavily bearded man
who came down the gangplank to greet him, declaring that
he was David Baillie, of Eyemouth. He was clearly much

225

impressed, as well as surprised, to see his overlord's son thus far from home.

Patrick explained the reasons for his visit and asked where he should go and whom to see? He spoke no Dutch nor Flemish and was uncertain as to how to go about his mission.

Baillie said that, being used to Scots shipmen and traders, most of the Veere folk could understand some English tongue. But it might be wise to see Ken Douglas. He was a prominent Scots resident here, a merchant trader who sorted and sold wool to Low Countries buyers. This before interviewing the burgomaster, one Molinaars. He would take my lord to the Douglas house.

So they walked through the narrow streets of tall tenements, behind the sheds and stores of the harbour, Patrick noting the high standard of buildings and houses, with their brightly painted and decorative shutters and doors, also the good and substantial clothing of the people. Clearly this was a prosperous place.

He was taken to premises, part hall, part dwelling, where they found the man Ken Douglas at his breakfast, with wife and children, a cheerful outgoing character who promptly offered hospitality, declaring that he had seen the Master of Dunbar on more than one occasion, for he came from Haddington in Lothian. He handled much wool coming from the Lammermuirs. He asked respectfully after the Earl Cospatrick.

Thus greeted, Patrick could launch forthwith into the reasons for his visit, the grievously low price of their wool for this season, lower than his father had ever known it. What was the cause, and what could be done about it?

The other shook his head. He was as concerned himself, for of course the drop in selling revenues affected his own living not a little. The cause of it was the switching of the Antwerp, Bruges, Eindhoven, Breda and Roermond washers, spinners, weavers, felters and tailors and their sellers to making and despatching finer cloth and materials, this for a trade which was expanding with areas to the south where not only did they use lighter and more decorative clothing but were increasing in prosperity, largely through the ever-growing trade in wines, olive-oil, paper, iron and marble, these such as Savoy and Piedmont, Aragon, Castile, Florence, Verona, Genoa and the like. They were fast becoming the favoured trading destinations, and finer wool than the Scots blackface sheep's was in demand.

Patrick said that this might be so; but was not the coarser wool as necessary as ever for normal northern clothing, serges and twills, for blankets, carpets, tapestries, these all needing thicker yarn? He had heard that Cheviot sheep's wool was not suffering a drop in price. Admittedly this was of a finer texture than their blackface, and might better suit this southern demand. But that should not result in any drop in the need for the longer-fibred, stronger and heavier wool, which had advantages in lustre and brushing and felting.

This was agreed. But Douglas said that the stocks in the warehouses were fairly substantial, and the buyers at present all tending to seek the finer fleeces. Probably it would be only a temporary setback, and the Scots trade recover. But meantime the Burgomaster Molinaars had fixed this reduced value, reflecting the market.

Patrick said that he would go and see him about this. Surely the sudden and grievous fall in price was as unjustified as it was unsuitable. If there was a temporary lull in demand it would quickly recover. Let them store the Lammermuir wool until it did.

Douglas declared that his own stores were already full. He agreed with what the earl said; but getting this Molinaars to see it so was another matter.

"You know the burgomaster, do you? Could you take me to speak with him?"

"Surely, my lord. I myself am a councillor of this Veere community, which elects the burgomeister. One of four Scots of the council."

So they went presently to the town-house and there met

a short, pot-bellied individual with a smile as wide as was the rest of him. He offered his visitors schnapps, despite the early hour.

"I am proud to meet a Schottishe count," he declared. But that was as far as his prodigality went, for when it came to the matter of the price of wool he was not forthcoming. He had no option, he said. The buyers would not pay more. Yes, it would probably be only a temporary drop, but until the demand returned again he must set such moneys as the Scottish wool would fetch.

"Wool will keep," Patrick insisted. "Store it meantime. It will not lose its value."

"My stores they are full. Also of the English wool which is wanted."

"Surely other warehouses are available? There is still more wool to come from our land."

"No. We have a sufficiency . . ."

Impasse reached, Patrick reluctantly came out with the only card he had to play. "The Earls of Dunbar and of March, and their dependants, largely rely on the Lammermuirs wool for support and means. We have hundreds of miles of sheep-grazing. We cannot afford to allow such great fall in moneys to hurt our people. When there are *other* ports in the Low Countries and Flanders than this Veere!"

The burgomaster drew a quick breath, smiles gone. He did not speak.

Douglas coughed.

"This has never happened before. I would be loth indeed to have to change. But many, and much, depends on this. Think on it, my friends." And as he turned away, he added, "And I am High Chamberlain to the King of Scots." He did not enjoy the saying of all this.

As they left to return to the Douglas house, that man remained very silent.

"Do you consider me as unjustified in making this move, this all but threat?" Patrick asked him. "That one seemed to give no ground. I would not wish to seem to harm Veere in any way, so long our partners in trade. But our case is serious."

"It would be bad, yes, if your Scots wool went other-where, my lord."

"Think you, then, that what I have said will have any effect on him, the setter of the price? Or is it the council, rather than that man himself, who sets it?"

"No. It has always been the burgomaster's decision. I know not whether he will think to make any change, now."

"It seems strange for that one man to have the decision. Is this one difficult?" A thought had occurred to him, and he voiced it. "You say that there are four Scots on this council. Are they all concerned with the wool trade? And men of some standing here?"

The other nodded.

"Then why not, on occasion, have one such stand as burgomaster? Such as yourself. With so much commerce with Scotland, this especial bond. And the Flemings so strong in Berwick and elsewhere in our land. Would the others not accept that? The Netherlanders?"

Douglas took moments to answer that. "It might be possible," he said, at length.

"Speak with the others, then. Consider it. Our wool is one of Scotland's greatest exports. Important to the realm, as well as to our earldoms. It is not only Lammermuir wool."

"Ye-e-s."

"For the good of Veere also, no? And meantime, tell me where is another port and town that I might consider, should Veere not improve the price. To send at least some of our wool. Somewhere that they might be glad to have our trade."

His companion, needless to say, was not eager to offer such advice. He shrugged. "If seek such you must, my lord, Bergen op Zoom might be possible. It is none so far off. And has many vessels which carry wool to places inland. By waterways. Much stone from Scotland comes to Bergen, for building. The Netherlands are short of stone. So they have many large barges at Bergen."

"Where is this, then?"

"It is some sixty kilometres, or forty miles. Round Beveland island, to the north, and up the Oosterschelde. None so far from Antwerp."

"Forty miles. Then I could get there quickly by boat?"

"Yes. If so you wish."

"My friend, it is not *my* wish so to do. But many at home are troubled over this matter. I must do what I can. Find me a vessel to take me to this Bergen. And meanwhile speak with your fellow Scots here on the council. And Burgomaster Molinaars himself."

There was no difficulty in finding a craft to take Patrick round the neighbouring island of Beveland and up the Oosterschelde channel, a sort of firth, past more of these detached portions of the Netherlands, for they were that rather than true islands, separated only by quite narrow waterways, the entire land seemingly a network of these, level and largely reclaimed from the sea, all protected by dykes and barriers from tides and storms. Bergen op Zoom, reached in five hours, proved to be a larger town and port than Veere, probably the nearest haven, for sea-going vessels, to Antwerp. Here much of the quite important trade in stone came, from Rosyth in Fife, for the Low Countries were founded on clay and sand rather than rock, these ships returning to Scotland with the red Dutch tiles so popular for roofing.

Patrick sought out the burgomaster here, the equivalent of a Scots provost or an English mayor; and with his quite resounding title of Earl of March had no difficulty in obtaining an interview. This man, lean and elderly but sharp-eyed and acute, listened to Patrick's account of the Veere wool situation with evident interest. Probably he knew the essence of it already, but he did not say so. When his visitor came to the point of declaring that he was considering the possibility of seeking an alternative entry port for at least some portion of the Scots wool, where a better price might be arranged, the other said that Bergen op Zoom was always ready to increase its commerce. It had always had excellent trade relations with Scotland, and would not be averse to further dealings and links. He did not comment on the present price of wools, however.

Emphasising the difference between the finer but shorter Cheviot and other southern wools and the longer-fibred and stronger blackface-sheep variety, Patrick declared that for the Netherlands and Flanders and the northern nations the latter was the more generally useful and valuable. This new preoccupation with the requirements of the southern states for lighter gear ought not to prejudice the ages-old trade with the Scots fleeces with their various uses. If Bergen could offer a better price than Veere, then this could be opportunity for commerce.

The burgomaster clearly saw the possibilities, and declared that he would debate the issue with his fellow councillors. He thought that there might well be co-operation.

Satisfied, Patrick took his leave, and returned to the dockside to seek passage back to Veere. This proved to be less simple than on the outward journey and, not wishing to linger here for any longer than was necessary, he chose to board another vessel making for Antwerp, laden with stone, this taking him up Schelde further, to drop him at Zandylie where there were narrows which caused the water traffic to pull into what was all but a canal. There he could find one of the Antwerp boats proceeding westward for the open sea to take him to Veere, this by Middelburg.

All proved accurate and convenient, and allowed him to view more of this water-girt land of windmills and dykes and polders, of tall-steepled churches and tight-clustered villages, of bridges and ditches and pools, with ducks and geese and swans everywhere despite the high population, even storks. He noted that despite all the major export of red pantiles, most of the houses and barns were in fact roofed with reed-thatch, reeds being very abundant in all that watery landscape.

At Veere he discovered that a Berwick ship was due to sail at the next tide, so he grasped the opportunity to get himself home as quickly as possible. He had only an hour or so to use to see Douglas and report on the probable interest of Bergen in the situation. For his part, that man said that he had spoken with his fellow Scots, who agreed with him that a Scots burgomaster would be an excellent development. They would sound out their Dutch colleagues to see if this could be a possibility; the main trade of Veere was with Scotland and the north of England, so there could in fact be some advantage in this for the town. They would pursue the notion. He had also had a word with Molinaars himself, stressing the earl's Bergen visit and proposals. And the burgomaster, troubled by this danger, had agreed to look into the possibility of increasing the price of blackface-sheep wool somewhat, to keep the threat to Veere at bay. Douglas imagined that there would be at least a slight improvement forthcoming.

All this was of satisfaction to Patrick, who urged that the sooner real progress was made on these issues the better for Veere as well as for the Scots. If all went reasonably well, he would have to try to arrange some trade of another kind than the wool for Bergen op Zoom, with which it would pay to be on good relations; this just a hint of warning, which Douglas undoubtedly would not fail to note.

Patrick sailed for Berwick-upon-Tweed thereafter, duty done as far as was possible.

22

Although Patrick had not been gone from Scotland for so very long, there had been significant developments in the interim, peace and quiet never of long duration in that northern realm. This time it was the Hebrides and Western Highlands again producing trouble, although not Ranald of the Isles's renewed invasion of Argyll. In a new situation Galloway was involved, together with the Isle of Man. Olaf Godfreyson, King of Man, known as the Morsel on account of his diminutive stature, of Norse extraction, had sought to extend his modest sway by adding the Hebrides, or at least the southern isles thereof, to his domains. These were already Norse-held in the main; but King Hakon of Norway was a long way off, and presently otherwise preoccupied. This would not greatly have concerned the Scots had Olaf's fleets confined themselves to the Outer Isles; but almost inevitably some of the invaders had assailed the Inner Isles, as it were in the by-going, and this had the great Somerled's son Ranald, and other kin, Lord of the Isles, involved in the upheavals. They claimed that not only their islands but parts of the West Highland mainland were being attacked, and of all things appealed to the King of Scots for aid in repelling the Manxmen, an extraordinary situation for those who themselves had been assailing the said area not so long before. Alexander might have ignored this plea had not Alan, Lord of Galloway, his domains lying only a score of miles from the Isle of Man, declared that the aggressive Morsel was a threat to his lands of Galloway also, and something had to be done about it. This Alan was something of a problem in the realm, unlike his late father, Roland, who had gone his own way but caused little trouble for King William the Lion. These Galloway lords thought of themselves as princes, paying only nominal allegiance to the Kings of Scots but acting as though more or less independent in their own great area, which included the shire of Ayr and some part of the West March. They were nominally earls of Scotland but they did not use that title, allowing their younger offspring to be earls, but not themselves, indication of their princely status. So they were called the Lords of Galloway in the rest of the kingdom, whatever they called themselves in the Land of the Southern Gael, which was the source of Galloway's name.

The king had sent the Steward's son-in-law, Malduin, Master of Lennox, with a small fleet of his father's ships, carrying Lennoxmen and some of the Steward's people also, nominally to assist Alan of Galloway pose a threat to Man, but in fact to see that this headstrong character did not overact, as he was apt to do. For although Alexander wanted Olaf Morsel to return to his own isle, he was aware and anxious of danger here. Any grievous assault on Man could have the effect of uniting the disputatious Norsemen of the Hebrides, Ireland, Orkney and Shetland and even perhaps King Hakon himself, in anger. War with the Vikings was anything but Alexander's desire.

That was the position when Patrick got home, some small concern. Himself, his concern was with Phemia's condition. Not that *she* seemed in any way anxious or preoccupied with it, save that she was beginning to find horse-mounting and riding less easy.

His father was pleased with Patrick's efforts in the Netherlands, and Alexander himself interested. Cospatrick thought that, in the event that they continued to trade with Veere, they might be able to develop the export of Lothian stone to this Bergen op Zoom; there was a superfluity of the product in their area, with quarries in the Lammermuirs and their solid rock cliff-girt coastline. A new trade could be valuable. There might also be a market for their salted mutton; presumably there would be no outlet for salted fish in that watery land.

Patrick's service as a sort of troubleshooter for his liege-lord was required rather sooner than either of them had anticipated. Word was sent by the Master of Lennox, from Man, that the Lord Alan was, as feared, interpreting his duties there considerably more assertively than he, Mal-duin, thought was called for or advisable, by no means confining himself to making warning gestures and demon-strations round the coasts, but was in fact landing his men and assailing the local population, slaughtering and burn-ing. This might indeed be effective in bringing Olaf home from the Hebrides, but it could also produce the feared trouble with the Norsemen in general. Perturbed, Alex-ander sent Patrick to go to Man in the royal name, to limit this Alan's activities. He could get a vessel at Dumbarton. It ought not to be a lengthy mission this time, it was hoped.

The ride to Dumbarton was accomplished in a day and a half, crossing Clyde from Renfrew. No very large craft was required for this hundred-and-fifty-mile sail through fairly sheltered waters. One was found for him without undue difficulty next forenoon. It was November now, but the weather conditions were reasonable, if grey.

The voyage down the Clyde estuary in fact constituted almost half the journey to Man, with that island's north-erly tip less than a score of miles from Galloway's mull. Once past the mighty rock-stack of Ailsa Craig, which reminded Patrick of the Bass at the mouth of the Forth, he was able to gaze forward soon to the quite lofty mountains of his destination. The shipmaster said that Man was only some thirty-odd miles long by a dozen wide. It seemed rather ridiculous to have a king when the Galloway earl-dom, so near, was fully five times as large, even their own Dunbar and the Merse much greater also.

They perceived smoke-clouds long before they reached the Point of Ayre at the isle's north, which at least ought to guide them to where the ravaging was going on. It was dusk when they passed this headland, and the skipper declared that it would be wise to lie up overnight in some sheltered cove under the cliffs. With the failing light, the smoke ahead had become tinged with red. That would be the town of Ramsey, it seemed, the second-largest community after Peel on the other, western coast.

It felt strange to lie there secure in their peaceful corner while savagery was being perpetrated so nearby and misery reigning.

In the morning they sailed on to opposite Ramsey. But they did not dock and land there, for it was obvious that this was no more than a smoking ruin, the attackers having moved on. There were now more and darker smokes rising to the south, which the shipmaster said would be the town of Laxey. Thither they headed.

At this Laxey there was a haven, with two large vessels docked. Pulling in, the acrid smell of burning thatch assailed their noses, and screams their ears. They tied up alongside one of the ships. Shouts came down from this to them, demanding in no friendly tones who they were and how they dared to come to this ill-favoured place.

Patrick called back that he was the Earl of March, High Chamberlain to Alexander, King of Scots. He sought Alan, Lord of Galloway, Thomas, Earl of Atholl, and the Master of Lennox.

That produced the information that the Lord Alan was not here, the other two not mentioned; he was further south at the next town, dealing with more of this den of evil Norsemen. Here was only MacLellan of Bombie, doing the good work.

So on down the coast they sailed, past two small smoking villages, until they reached a large bay wherein were many ships at anchor, and behind which was another town, seemingly larger than Ramsey and Laxey. They drew in again to one of these vessels, and were told, yes, the Lord Alan was ashore here, with the Earl of Atholl.

So Patrick landed and climbed up to the town, from which much noise emanated, shouts and shrieks and clashes of sundry sorts. He hoped that his dress and bearing would identify him as clearly no Norseman nor Manxman, and so not to be assailed.

He saw fleeing men, women and children. Presently, amongst the houses, there were bodies lying, some of naked women.

In a central market-place he found a group of better-clad men standing round a tall stone monolith, apparently waiting, idle. Approaching these he discovered that this was Malduin of Lennox's party. He told the Master, a man obviously much worried, that he had come at the behest of King Alexander.

The other was clearly glad to see him. This sacking of the island was uncalled for, infamous, he declared. But no heed was being paid to his remonstrations. If he had not been sent by His Grace to represent the crown here, he would have returned to Scotland ere this. Alan of Galloway was a man of fierce passions, headstrong, determined and ungovernable. He was intent on wreaking havoc here, his men slaying indiscriminately, ravishing and burning. His efforts to restrain him aroused only abuse. He much doubted whether Patrick would be any more successful.

That man declared that the king was much concerned. Where was this Alan?

Malduin led him through the devastated streets to a church, part demolished, where, in the kirkyard a crowd of men, Gallowegians presumably, were shouting and jeering as gallows were being improvised out of the church's roof timbers and erected, three of these already bearing twitching bodies. Superintending all was a tall, flaxen-haired, hot-eyed man, dressed in a saffron kilt and calfskin doublet, using a dagger to emphasise his directions.

As the newcomers approached, this character looked at them, glaring, but continued with his gesticulations.

"Lord Alan, here is the Earl of March, High Chamberlain, come from His Grace Alexander," he was told.

"Ha! To view the good work!" the other exclaimed. "The king should be well pleased!"

237

"Not so, my lord," Patrick said. He had to shout above the din. "His Grace is troubled at reports of the devastation here. He ordered this force to make a demonstration, a threat only, to fetch Olaf home from the Hebrides. Not to sack Man. He fears war may result, war with all the Norsemen, even with King Hakon. This is too much!"

"Folly, that! These Vikings are devils, the spawn of Satan! They raid my coasts. They must be punished, got rid of. I do Alexander a favour. Go tell him so."

"His Grace does not see it so, my lord. He sees it as a danger to his realm, the realm at large. He orders you to cease from it."

"Orders! I am Galloway! I take orders from no man. Even Alexander mac William, I say!"

"You are one of the earls of Scotland, sir, as am I. And your brother the Earl of Atholl. We are all subjects of the High King, paying allegiance to him. His decisions must be obeyed."

"Not if they are foolish, wrong, weak, sirrah! He sits in that Roxburgh, wed to an English wife. Friendly with the Plantagenet. What knows he of the Norsemen? If he dwelled in *my* land, he would be the wiser. My Galloway is but a score of miles from this Man and its demons."

"Are you refusing, then, to obey the royal commands?"

"I am doing what must be done. And shall continue to do so." As he spoke, he kicked an unfortunate who was being dragged past them to one of the gibbets. "If we have a fool on the throne, must we all act as fools?"

Patrick tried another tack. "Have you considered what Olaf may do when he returns and learns what you have done? Your Galloway may pay dearly."

"I can look after my own, see you."

"So be it. I will report to the king on your intransigence, my lord."

"Do so. It may teach him that not all in his realm are fools. Or cravens!"

Patrick turned away, nothing more to be said nor done here. Malduin of Lennox came with him.

"As I said, ungovernable!" he declared. "I am minded to leave here. Return home. I can do nothing with him. I but waste my time. To no gain."

"That is for you to decide," he was told. "I can well understand how you feel. I will tell the king. I fear that we are going to have more trouble with this Alan, and with Galloway. He may, however, think better of it, after this."

"I doubt it."

There was nothing to linger for on this unhappy Isle of Man. Patrick returned to his vessel, to sail north again.

Back at Roxburgh, Alexander was angry and perplexed. What could he do with this arrogant and unruly lord? Galloway had not been any real problem under Roland. But now it seemed as though it might well become a serious source of trouble in the kingdom, apart altogether from being the possible begetter of war, with a man like that in control of it. One of the largest provinces of the land, it had a strange character, all but detached from the rest, although not in physical fact, there in the south-west, a distinct people more akin to the Irish than to the southern Scots.

Patrick admitted that he did not see what could usefully be done. But also he did not see what major harm this Alan could do to the rest of the realm, apart from this of the Norsemen. He was not likely to cast covetous eyes on the main West March, with its fierce mosstroopers and dalesmen. And the Bruces of Annandale, the Maxwells and the Douglases would not allow any filching of their territories.

The king could not refute that. But he was still concerned. Meantime, over this of the Norse, what should he do? Probably the best course would be to send an envoy to King Hakon of Norway expressing friendship and emphasising that this attack on Man was not of his devising, indeed contrary to his will. It remained to be seen what Olaf might do on his return. He might also, of course, suffer a setback in the Hebrides, and be inclined to lick his wounds for a while at Man.

This was to be hoped for, Patrick agreed. He also hoped, although he did not say so, that he would not be chosen to act that envoy to Norway. He had had a sufficiency of travel and mission of late. He was almost glad of his non-success in this last.

Home to Home Castle he found all well. There was a message from his father declaring that he had had reasonably good news from the Netherlands. The burgomaster of Veere had agreed to increase the payment for the wool somewhat; not to its normal price but at least an improvement. The man Douglas there had sent word that he thought that he might well be the next burgomaster, which would be a help for the future. Meantime they must see what could be done about a new trade with this Bergen op Zoom, in stone and possibly mutton, which could be a valuable asset for their folk's prosperity, and their own. He urged his son to come and see him soon, to discuss it all.

So that was satisfactory. Now, some welcome family life, with the anticipation of an addition to the family, hopefully soon and without complications and undue sufferings for Phemia.

23

A daughter was born, with less upset than had been their son's delivery, to Patrick's relief, on 8th December, Conception Day in the Calendar for the Virgin Mary. So they named her Elizabeth Mary, as suitable, amidst much rejoicing. She was a healthy, burbling infant, with the king acting as her godfather.

So a happy Christmastide was passed at Home.

At Roxburgh also no immediate troubles loomed. Olaf had indeed returned to his Man, the Hebridean venture less than successful; and Alan of Galloway had not waited to challenge him there, returning to his own lands prepared, Malduin of Lennox reported, to repel any revenge attacks. Such had not so far developed apparently, the Morsel presumably having a sufficiency on his mind for the moment, with much restoration and revival of his island kingdom to see to, as well as the threat of retaliatory action from Reginald, so-called King of the Hebrides, his own kinsman. If it was scarcely a season of peace and goodwill, at least no major strife was taking place meantime. Alexander had sent Robert Bruce of Annandale, the fifth of that line and a far kinsman of his own through David of Huntingdon, to King Hakon, as envoy, and as yet he had not returned from Norway.

There was news from the south. John the Scot, Earl of Huntingdon, son of the said David, who had succeeded to the earldom, had wed a daughter of Llewellyn, Prince of Wales, an interesting link between that principality, England and Scotland; for until Alexander had a son, this John was a close heir to the throne. If *he* now produced a son, Alexander would be the more apt to hasten to do likewise with his Joanna. That lively youngster was developing fast, and making her own mark on the court at Roxburgh, her urgings for the Yuletide celebrations quite clamorous.

At Dunbar, Cospatrick was more concerned with trade and the well-being of his earldom than with festivities. This of the stone export, something that he had never thought of previously, was to be pursued, quarrying, hewing and shaping encouraged amongst his people. Shipping the resultant heavy supplies over the sea was a problem; but shipmen said that the answer was large barges to be towed behind sea-going vessels, possibly hoisting square sails to assist. It all seemed distinctly strange to the folk there, who could scarcely visualise a land anywhere without stone, and having to rely for their buildings on bricks made of baked clay, an expensive and lengthy process both in the making and the laying and constructing. There was clearly wealth to be made from this new trade, however unused Cospatrick's people were to much quarrying and stonework. His father would have liked Patrick to go back again to the Netherlands as his representative to arrange this export, but was convinced to send his second son, William, instead. It was time that that young man learned that the lands which he had been granted at Haliburton and Fogo had to be paid for. He was also to prospect any possible demand for salted mutton while he was at Bergen.

So the new year began, and this ushered in with a spate of deaths, these with their own significance for the nation. Firstly Pope Honorius passed on, to be succeeded by a Cardinal of Ostia who took the style of Pope Gregory the Ninth; whether he would be more kind to the Scottish Church remained to be seen, none underestimating the importance of this appointment. It was hoped that the vexed matter of the Peter's Pence would be forgotten. Then Richard de Maresco, Prince-Bishop of Durham died, and was by no means mourned in Scotland, having long been an adversary. He was replaced by another Richard, Bishop of Salisbury, and the probability was that he would be kinder. Stephen Langton, Archbishop of Canterbury was the next casualty; but his demise was not likely to affect Scotland greatly. What was of most impact was that the Earl Alwyn of Lennox departed this earthly life; so Malduin his son became earl, a useful supporter for Alexander. The fifth death was that of the aged Earl Dorward, the High Justiciar. The king promptly appointed Walter the Steward in his place, so *he* now became perhaps the second most important man in the kingdom, and with three sons-in-law earls.

This shake-up in the hierarchy prompted Alexander to wonder whether he might deprive Alan of Galloway of his hereditary office, that of High Constable of Scotland, unsuitable as he might be fot his position. It had been conferred on his great-great-grandfather, Fergus, more than a century before. But could the demotion be done lacking something more specific than his behaviour at Man and his insolent remarks to Patrick? Some sort of trial would be necessary presumably, with a conviction, and that was not really feasible at this stage. But he might well give due cause hereafter!

All this kept the court in a stir that winter and early spring. This was not the season for campaigning, of course, so none sought to prophesy that the comparative peace would continue.

Patrick's brother came back from the Netherlands with the desired good news. The burgomaster and council of Bergen op Zoom would pay good money for hewn stone and a still better price for cut and squared blocks. Even chippings and gravel would be welcome. In return, as well as silver or gold they could send goods, such as clothing, pottery, glassware and clocks. Cospatrick saw it all as excellent. His folk were going to be busy indeed, and prosperous. Quarrying, hewing, packhorse-carrying, barge-building were all but going to overtake shepherding and cattle-droving as major employment. Let those Fife folk of Rosyth look to their interests!

Patrick, Phemia and the children spent quite a deal of

time at Dunbar Castle, sometimes joined by the king, and once Joanna visited with him. She was now taking an interest in her new country.

What the Vikings called the hosting season duly began in April, and men's thoughts had to turn to preparedness for war, or at least conflict. Bruce had arrived back from Norway to announce that Hakon was in no mood to cross swords with the Scots. He was having much trouble with the Hanseatic League, that great trading empire based on Lübeck and Wisby, in Gothland, which was refusing to pay him the cess and dues that he considered were his right for lands and rights nominally his. The league was even threatening to persuade the new Pope Gregory to have the Archbishop of Trondheim lay the curse of excommunication upon the king if he persisted with his claims and his talk of military action. Hakon had deplored Olaf of Man's efforts to take over the Hebrides, and was prepared, in the circumstances, to overlook Alan of Galloway's excesses. So that was all to the good.

Nevertheless hostilities did break out along the western seaboard, Olaf by no means subdued yet, nor Alan either. The latter apparently had left his bailiffs on Man to demand and collect tribute, and these had not been able to get away in time before Olaf returned. The Morsel had caught them, and not only relieved them of their gains but hanged them and burned their ship. In fury, Alan sailed up to the Hebrides and made a pact with the equally angry Reginald, Norse monarch thereof, against Olaf. They together descended on Man, and there, at St Patrick's Isle near Peel on the western coast, surprised and captured most of the Manx fleet. Alan sailed these back to his Galloway, leaving Reginald to sink what was left. And while so doing, Olaf, thought to be in Ireland, had descended upon his kinsman and slain him. All a sorry story indeed, if fairly typical of these Viking sea-depredators. Whether Alan saw himself as a winner or a loser in this was questionable. But what was clear was that he was confirmed in this trouble-making and would have to be watched heedfully.

Of more immediate concern to Patrick, as to others, was an accident to the king himself. Out boar-hunting in the Cheviot foothills, his horse had taken fright when charged by a tusker, and thrown Alexander. His companions had managed to divert the creature from attacking the fallen monarch on the ground, and slain it; but the monarch had been badly shaken, his shoulder dislocated and bruised. This mishap had shaken more than the king, and was productive of results constitutional as well as physical. For it concentrated the recognition by his advisers, nobles, prelates and officers of state on the fact that their liege-lord had no obvious heir. If that boar had in fact reached and killed him, Scotland would have been left without a monarch.

So a meeting of the nation's council was called, Alexander presiding, to consider the succession to the throne in the grievous event of it being left empty. There were no close male kin, William the Lion having only had Alexander, and this late in life, and his brother Malcolm the Maiden no offspring. These monarchs' father, King David's son Henry of Huntingdon, had died before his sire; but he had left another son, named David, who had succeeded him in the English earldom of his mother, this earl having John the Scot, as he was known, the present nearest representative. Unless the Cospatricks' ancient claims were revived, this seemed to be the only choice. Patrick and his father, at that table, eyed each other.

Grave doubts were promptly expressed by many about this John. Although he was called, in England, John the Scot, he was to all intents an Englishman, had spent his whole life in that realm and sat in their council of state. What sort of a King of Scots would he make, even if he agreed to the appointment?

Alexander himself was in a somewhat difficult position in this matter. While much aware, and sympathising, with the Cospatrick situation and claim, he knew well that the great majority of the nobility, and probably the senior clergy, were likely to be otherwise minded. Most of them, or at least their immediate ancestors owed their status, lands and titles to the Margaretsons' line, or to David's introduction of young Norman supporters after his long stay as a sort of hostage in England. These would not wish to revert to the pre-Margaret family, when there were so many of their number who could claim far-out royal blood from Malcolm Canmore's second wife. He hoped, of course, that all this discussion was merely a precautionary move, and that he himself would in due course produce the required son and undoubted heir. But meantime he must carry the majority of the council with him.

As names were being put forward, none Cospatrick's, the king himself suggested his recent envoy to Norway, Robert Bruce of Annandale, as a suitable possibility. This, after some consideration, seemed to meet with general acceptance. He was the fifth Lord of Annandale, and his mother had been a granddaughter of Earl Henry of Huntingdon, King David's son. So he had royal blood. Admittedly others could make the same claim; but his position as one of the most powerful lords along that vague border with England, with vast lands on the West March and in the shires of Dumfries and Ayr, his son new-married to the Countess of Carrick in her own right, meant he could counter Alan of Galloway whose territory flanked his own, this a telling factor. And he was a reliable character and trusted by the king. Cospatrick and his son did not register protest, although neither voted when it came to the test, as reminding all that they had not relinquished their more ancient claim. The decision was made, and all but unanimously. Robert Bruce should be considered heir presumptive should Alexander produce no son. None there forgot that Alan of Galloway also included another granddaughter of Henry of Huntingdon as fore-bear; and he had two daughters.

Patrick and his father discussed the situation afterwards, as it affected themselves. They agreed that in the circumstances prevailing there was little point in making an issue of their theoretical right to the throne. Should Alexander not produce an heir they would get little support from the realm's magnates, with all the Huntingdon descendants probably jostling for the crown. They would let their hereditary right, as it were, lie dormant. Patrick's close friendship with the monarch, for his part, much influencing him in this decision. And the more he saw of kingship and the problems and responsibilities that went with it, the less he coveted that position. Had he been king he would not have been able to wed Phemia . . .

Surprising news reached them all not long thereafter. Alan of Galloway had sailed over to Ireland, with an impressive retinue, acting the prince indeed and there had wed Rohais, daughter of Hugh de Lacy, Lord of Meath. What did this signify? De Lacy was very powerful, with his close links with England. Alan had already had two wives, the first dying, and the second recently put away by papal decree as within the prohibited bounds of consanguinity. He must have known of this from the first, so there must be something behind this new marriage; and being the man he was, it was likely to be to his major advantage, which could mean to others' *dis*advantage.

It behoved the King of Scots to keep a wary eye on this subject of his.

24

It was Phemia who, woman-wise, claimed to notice a subtle change in Queen Joanna other than just normal and gradual physical development, soon thereafter. The girl had crossed some sort of watershed, she alleged, changed from that state into fuller femininity. She had become a young woman. Patrick had not noticed any difference, but accepted his beloved's perception. Joanna was acting more the wife, it seemed. Almost certainly, Alexander was now bedding her.

Patrick did not like to raise the subject with his royal friend; but it was not long before Alexander himself, at a masque in which Joanna quite confidently played the part of Artemis, remarked that she was proving to be quite a worthy spouse and helpmeet, despite her age. The way he said that struck Patrick as significant. This was probably a way of telling him of the new situation. Possibly the recent emphasis on the need for an heir had had some part in the development. Joanna was now of almost sixteen years. Whether the debate on appointing an heir presumptive to the throne had had anything to do with this was a matter for conjecture.

The Man and Hebridean situation continued to hold the attention of all at court. King Hakon had appointed one Uspak, son of Dungal son of Somerled, to be King of the Hebrides in place of the slain Reginald, and sent him, with the support of the Norse Earl Skuli and a force in eighty ships, to oust Olaf. The Morsel met this challenge by raising a still larger fleet, which encountered the Norse one at the Isle of Bute, near Arran, the unfortunate Uspak being slain by a catapulted stone early on. Olaf won the day, and promptly declared himself to be King of the Hebrides as well as Man. Alan of Galloway was still over in Ireland apparently. What his reaction to all this would be was the principal question at Roxburgh.

Patrick had a more personal concern. His father's health was giving cause for worry. He was not an old man yet but was beginning to seem so, and limiting his activities, at least as far as riding abroad, although he maintained his interest in the matter of trade links with the Low Countries, this becoming his main preoccupation, from Dunbar Castle. His son William in consequence spent much of his time sailing to and from Veere, Bergen and other Netherlands ports, acting as envoy and negotiator. And Patrick himself was pressed into service quite frequently, to superintend the quarrying, barge-building and mutton-salting activities of the earldom's available manpower, shepherding, to be sure, remaining the principal source of employment. It was as well that no major activities of state demanded his attention that summer; and Alexander was understanding and not calling for overmuch in the way of chamberlain's duties. The king in fact was himself much interested in this of trade advancement, for the chronically empty royal coffers benefited therefrom with harbour dues and import duties. Indeed he asked Patrick to explore other export possibilities, not only for the Dunbar and March earldoms.

So a fairly busy summer and autumn ensued for Patrick, which did not displease him, for this sort of activity allowed him to see much more of Phemia and the children.

It was late autumn when they heard that Thomas, Earl of Atholl, Alan of Galloway's brother, had been killed in a skirmish with Olaf's people, news which might well result in an escalation of trouble in the western seas. For although Alan had three daughters he had no son, save for an illegitimate one, and the late Thomas had been heir to Galloway. What would the repercussions be?

Repercussions there were, and not long delayed, strange

and significant ones. Alan thereafter married off his three daughters, and all to Englishmen: Devorgilla, the eldest, to John de Baliol, Lord of Barnard in Durham; Helen to Roger de Quincy, Earl of Winchester; and Christiana to William de Fortibus, Lord of Holderness. What could be the meaning behind this, since almost certainly it was all no mere coincidence? Galloway appeared to be specifically linking itself with England, not Scotland. Why? Alan's own mother Margaret had been one more of the daughters of Earl Henry of Huntingdon, so he had royal blood. Could it be that he was himself casting eyes on the throne, thinking to compete with Bruce of Annandale as heir presumptive, and seeking English backing? With that hot-headed and unscrupulous individual, it was a worrying thought.

Young Joanna gave no sign of being with child as the months passed, ever more mature as she seemed to be developing.

Alexander decided that a word with Henry Plantagenet was called for. He first thought of sending Patrick as his ambassador, then concluded that this was something best dealt with himself, in view of these powerful English nobles Alan had now allied himself to. A personal understanding between the two monarchs was probably what was required. But he could hardly just make an unheralded visit down to London, his status making that unsuitable. So, a more family-style meeting – after all, they were brothers-in-law – Joanna brought into it. How could that be contrived? An expressed wish to see her brother would scarcely be sufficient reason to such meeting without some specific cause.

It was Patrick who made the suggestion, very tentatively. Suppose it was thought that the queen might be pregnant? Was it not quite usual for a monarch to endow a sister's child with some token of favour and esteem, be it son or daughter? It might even be some nominal and dormant earldom merged in the crown, something suitable for the Queen of Scotland's offspring? The fact that, so far as they knew, she was not with child, was not really vital, so long as she and her husband thought that she *might* be. And she desiring to see her brother, after the years of separation.

Alexander considered that, and thought that indeed it might serve. Joanna presumably would not know much about pregnancy, although perhaps some of the women about court had discussed it with her. She could possibly be glad of the excuse. Christmastide would soon be upon them – the family festive season. A meeting, then.

A letter was sent south to Henry, proposing a Yuletide celebration; and while at it, Alexander would broach the subject of the three Galloway sisters new-wed to Englishmen, and his hopes that there would be no ill results for their two realms, not only for Scotland. After all, Henry would not want his sister to be displaced as queen there. So a compact suitable and acceptable to them both might be agreed.

In such ways were dynastic issues worked out, on occasion.

It was important, however, that the King of Scots should not have to go all the way to London or Windsor for the proposed meeting. Halfway for them both would be correct. So, York again? Meet at York, to celebrate Christmas.

The messenger was sent. And in due course the reply came, and in the affirmative. Joanna had no least objections to make.

The Scots royal party set out on the Eve of Ignatius, with a safe-conduct from Henry ensuring them a worthy hospitality on their way, Patrick included but not his father. They took their time, the winter days short, and Joanna having three of her ladies with her as appropriate for a queen, even though the slowed progress was somewhat tiresome for the younger men. One of their overnight stops was at Barnard Castle, in the principality of

Durham, where their host and hostess proved to be Sir John de Baliol and the Lady Devorgilla, eldest daughter of Alan of Galloway, a very good-looking young woman of amiable and gentle nature, very different from her father, but nevertheless giving the impression of strength of character.

They reached York two days before Christmas, to find Henry and his advisers already there, with the archbishop and the new Richard, Bishop of Durham, all very welcoming. The meeting between brother and sister was quite moving, each finding the other so changed in appearance and development over the years, but their evident fondness for each other nowise diminished. Henry Plantagenet was now almost of full age and looking so, scarcely handsome but of open features and an easy manner. He greeted Alexander in friendly fashion, and thereafter spared no efforts to make the visit a success, entertainment and bounty, all but prodigality, ongoing; although presumably it was the archbishop who was mainly responsible, as host, no doubt on royal urging.

So they all spent a pleasant four days, with much present-giving and feasting and jollification, but due worship also, Joanna demonstrating her ability as an actress in masques, and her fondness for dancing, indeed agility thereat, even if this was not exactly indicative of pregnancy.

What she told her brother about her marital affairs and present condition was of course private; but it did not seem to conflict with Alexander's confidences and suggestions, for the latter, although he did not have opportunity for any close conversation with Patrick, did indicate that all was going well in his association and relationship with Henry, the object of the exercise. Now that the Plantagenet was no longer a mere youth, he was less under the guidance of his advisers, which was advantageous.

At any rate, the visit was an enjoyable one, and hopefully good for the concord between the two nations.

Joanna was reluctant to leave two days after Christmas,

but since both monarchs were very much aware of their royal duties and responsibilities, and felt that they could not linger away from their centres of affairs, she had to accept the departure. She urged her brother to come up to Scotland to see her, and soon.

On the way home, Alexander did have opportunity for private speech with Patrick. He announced that that all had gone fairly well according to plan. Henry was concerned over the possibility of Alan of Galloway's ambitions, and his reasons for wedding his three daughters to English lords, and would keep that situation well in mind. He certainly did not want to see his sister displaced as queen, although if she was with child, and a son possible, that danger was the less likely. Surely this Alan would not aspire to assail Alexander himself and seek to grasp the throne? Alexander had revealed that he had then mentioned Alan's own recent marriage to Rohais de Lacy, daughter of the Lord of Meath, in Ireland. Was this wedding also of significance as far as Scotland was concerned? De Lacy was obviously a Norman name, not Irish, and he believed that there had been de Lacys in lofty positions in England. Could this possibly be an additional threat in some way? Henry had told him that this Hugh de Lacy's father had indeed been Earl of Ulster, before being forfeited for treason, and slain, with Hugo de Burgh given his earldom. So this family had to be watched, and not only by the Scots. Indeed, Henry had seemed more perturbed by this information than he had been by the word of the three daughters' marriages.

Patrick had shaken his head over it all, but recognised that with a man of Alan's character it all must be considered seriously.

As to some gesture towards Joanna if and when she became a mother, Henry had agreed that there should be some suitable provision made; that was as far as they had got meantime. But it was probably sufficient. Altogether their journey and device had been well worth while.

Let them trust that all went satisfactorily in Scotland.

This was not the season for Norse hosting nor military campaigning generally, so there ought not to have been any major upsets in their absence. But . . .

Amen to that, Patrick agreed.

25

His return home brought Patrick anxiety indeed, but personal. His father's health had taken a grievous turn for the worse four days after Christmas. The word from Dunbar sent to Home Castle was that he was in fact dying.

Phemia accompanied her husband to Dunbar without further delay, in very real distress, both praying that they were in time at least to see him alive. They found the castle in a state of hushed tension. Fortunately William was back from his latest visit to the Low Countries, and sister Ada and her husband were there from nearby Beil, she having been largely looking after her father these last months.

Ada, a motherly young woman, although as yet childless, was wed to a second cousin, another William, descended from the third Earl Cospatrick. She took them to the main tower and the earl's bedchamber.

He was lying, eyes open and gazing upwards, unblinking. When they stood beside and above him and he saw them, his lips moved slightly but he did not speak. Patrick stooped to touch a bare shoulder, himself wordless. He thought that there was recognition and acknowledgment and contemplation.

They waited by the bedside for some time, in what they hoped was a sort of silent communion. But Cospatrick never changed the direction of his regard, as though he were being held by something enthralling that he saw above him, and certainly not the canopy of his great bed. Was it the past that he was seeing? Or the future? Whatever it was, he did not seem in any sort of distress, or pain of mind or body.

In time Ada indicated that they should withdraw meantime, although they would make constant brief visits.

She told them, thereafter, that they had celebrated Christmas quietly but pleasantly, with her father up and about although clearly an ailing man. But the day after, he had, without seeming any the worse, summoned William and herself to his room, and informed them, quite factually, that he was about to proceed on a journey, a journey which would come to them all one day, and a momentous one. He would be on his way to rejoin the other Ada, their beloved mother, gone on ahead these many years. And others, indeed. But therefor he had preparations to make. They were to bring him a monk's habit, for that would be his garb in the going. William to fetch paper and quill and ink, to write down his requirements and instructions. It all had been very calmly said, orderly, without any discomposure.

He had announced then that all his life he had sought to worship God, however unworthily, and to thank Him for giving himself the position and possessions and responsibilities that had descended to him, and he had endeavoured to show this by certain small gestures, for instance the founding of the Trinitarian or Red Friars monastery here at Dunbar, to aid in the work of the crusades. Also building the chapel at Haliburton for Kelso Abbey, and giving the monks of Melrose those lands of Sorrowless field in Lauderdale. Now he desired, to speed his own way nearer to his creator, to donate to the Abbey of Dryburgh the lands of Elvinsley and half of Ercildoune. He wished his earthly body, no longer required, to be buried at Eccles, near to Home, already gifted to Holy Church, while his spiritual body and eternal soul was on its better way. To aid in which he wished the Abbot Waldeve of Melrose to come and give him the extreme unction, and this without delay, for the time was short. He had then dismissed them, much overcome as they were.

Ada told them all this, her voice choking on occasion. She said that Abbot Waldeve, a kinsman, had duly come

256

the next day and bestowed the unction with oil and blessing. And thereafter her father had almost immediately sunk into this strange trance-like state, almost as though he had begun part of his journey. His last words to them had been that their brother Patrick would continue with the earthly labours and duties that he passed on, worthily, he prayed, and would see that she and William were suitably provided for.

Patrick and Phemia were, needless to say, much moved by this account. He had known, of course, that his father was religiously minded, without making any great show of it. This final preparation demonstrated the depth of his commitment to his faith, and formed a challenge indeed for his son and successor to live up to. It was all something to ponder and mull over.

They went in to see Cospatrick a few times, all but on tiptoe, before retiring for the night, the five members of the family agreeing to take it in turns to keep watch and vigil, hour by hour, Ada taking the first period.

When she wakened Patrick for his turn, it was an extraordinary experience to sit there by the bedside in the candlelight, hearing the slow, gentle but nowise erratic breathing of his father, the eyes still open but gaze fixed elsewhere, somehow seeming neither awake nor asleep, near in body but evidently far away in spirit. Once or twice the son reached out to touch hand or arm, to no reaction, his own thoughts all but in limbo.

For how long he remained there he had no notion, but in time, finding himself nodding off to sleep, he thought it best to go and rouse his brother for *his* watch, before returning to the sleeping Phemia's side.

Again, for how long he slept there he knew not, when William came to shake his shoulder.

"I fear . . . I think . . . he has stopped breathing," his brother said. "Just stopped. I . . . I went close. Listened. But . . . I fear that he has . . . gone."

Phemia wakened at this talking, and they went together down, in bed-robes, to Cospatrick's chamber, lamps with

257

them to negotiate the twisting turnpike stairway. They found the earl, at first sight seemingly as before, eyes still open. But leaning over him they could detect no breathing.

Patrick and Phemia eyed each other over that still body while William went to fetch Ada. Where was Cospatrick's questing spirit now?

Round the bed they stood for some while, Ada quietly weeping, Phemia seeking to comfort her but her whispering itself broken, the men silent.

Presently they returned to their own beds, whether to sleep or not.

In the morning, after such preparation as they could make of the body for burial, with the help of the Dunbar leech and a midwife, it was time to take stock of the situation, for Patrick at least. He was now Cospatrick, sixth Earl of Dunbar as well as first of March, with all that this entailed, a great earldom to look after, govern, and act judge over for thousands of folk, to oversee, employ and protect, ports to control and trade and industry to nurture. Could he continue to act chamberlain to Alexander in these circumstances? He feared not. He hoped that he could still see much of his royal friend, and be able to assist in times of need; but attendance at court for much of his time would be impossible, even dwelling at Home Castle. This Dunbar must be his base now, his old home, along with sundry other castles, fortalices and houses, especially that of Berwick-upon-Tweed, that large and vital port, with all the wool trade and shepherding, the quarrying, the barge-building, the salting and the rest to supervise. It was a daunting thought.

At least he knew what he must do about his brother and sister, as his father had ordered and written. To William he would hand over Berwick Castle, with the immediate supervision of the port; this plus the personal lairdship and jurisdiction of Coldinghameshire, which would help in the superintendence of the eastern section of the March. And to Ada and her husband he would give Home Castle,

258

no longer to be his own and Phemia's dwelling, this central to the western Merse, these allocations advantageous for them and apposite, while lessening his own burden of responsibility. All sorts of lesser appointments and decisions he would have to make, but these were the most vital and important.

As to the chamberlainship, he could only visit the king, after the funeral at Eccles, and acquaint him with the position and seek release, reluctantly, from that office. It would be sad to give it up, but he hoped that he could still play some useful part at court, although, as it were, at a further distance. His father had, amongst other responsibilities, been Justiciar of Lothian. It might well be that Alexander would use him to fill that position.

Meantime, the interment. Eccles was a village and parish in mid-Merse, lying some six miles east of Home and eight north-east of Kelso, in typical fertile rolling grassland country. The late Cospatrick's grandfather had founded there a convent for Cistercian nuns in 1155, and this, St Mary's, had been a favoured establishment of the family. Now it was to be the burial-place of the fifth earl, as it had been of his two predecessors.

Abbot Waldeve of Melrose was sent for to conduct the service at St Mary's two days hence. It would be quite a lengthy funeral procession, for it was some thirty-five miles south of Dunbar, through the Lammermuirs, to the convent, and this not a parade to be rushed. They would set out early next morning and hope to reach their destination before dark; then have the burial ceremony conducted the following forenoon. All this arranging at least kept the grieving family busy.

Their spirits, at their early start next day, were not helped by the thin rain on a chill east wind coming off the Norse Sea. They rode, a quite lengthy file, with the corpse, wrapped in grave-clothes, drawn on a slype behind a garron – this a sort of stretcher or sled formed out of poles tipped with iron, of which only two ends reached the ground, the rest raised at an angle behind the animal, making a sloping litter, very effective for dragging over rough and uneven terrain. By the Beil Water they went up to Dunbar Common and into the Lammermuirs, making for the headwaters of the Whiteadder, a major stream, which led them southwards past its widening to all but a loch, and on by Cranshaws, hamlet of shepherds, to the small town of Duns, where they won out of the higher hills to reach the sister stream of the Blackadder, at Fogo. Now they were in the green and grassy Merse, after a wet journey with the burns running high, but only another seven miles to go to Eccles, the land sinking gradually towards Tweed, with the distant Cheviots ahead, although only dimly seen in the rainy dusk. Thankfully they reached the village, convent and church, their precious burden placed in the last, before the altar, for the night, while its weary escorts sought the nuns' care and hospitality. Abbot Waldeve was already there, and had informed the sisters.

So, after a restful night, with the men and women lodged in separate quarters, they went back to the church, in a more kindly morning with even a pale sun fitfully shining. There, with simple but heartfelt solemnity, the fifth Cospatrick was laid to rest in a crypt beneath the little chancel slabs, beside his forebears, although those close to him could not feel that he was truly there, but well on his way, his better way, to his so desired and desirable destination. The abbot assured them that this was no occasion for tears but rather quiet rejoicing and well-wishing.

The benediction given, and blessings for all, they went out to face a new dispensation.

Patrick and his wife left the others now, to head westwards, Phemia to Home and the children, looked after by trusted carers, her husband to make for Roxburgh Castle and the court.

He found Alexander very sympathetic over his father's death, and not a little concerned as to the consequences, the loss of a worthy and reliable supporter and the effect this would have on his son, realising that there would inevitably have to be changes in their association.

"How will this alter matters, Pate?" he asked. "You will now be one of my most notable and powerful earls, which is good. But . . . ?"

"Yes, Alex, it does alter my life and what I have to do," Patrick admitted. "Much now descends upon my shoulders, the care and direction of many, large lands to cherish and tend, much trading and labour to oversee. I fear that I can no longer serve here as chamberlain. Not to effect, not usefully . . ."

"I deemed it so. It grieves me, but I understand it. You will be at Dunbar in the main, not at Home? With all of the Merse and Lothian to see to. I shall see the less of you, to my regret."

"Mine also, Alex. But I shall come to you as often as I may. And be your leal servant still. With more men to aid in your causes when required. I will now be able to raise my thousands, at need."

"No doubt. But I am going to miss you here at court. Your Dunbar is almost a day's ride away. You must, to be sure, have some other office of state to hold. But that will not give me your good company and close accord, as has done the chamberlainship. I will have to think on this. I would make you High Constable in place of the wretched Alan of Galloway. But that would take time and some to-do."

"I need nothing more, Alex, so long as I still may have your friendship. That is what signifies."

"That remains, yes. Your father was Justiciar of Lothian, which you will now become. The pity that I have but recently made Comyn High Justiciar, after Dorward's death, or you could have been that. But we will think of something, never fear." The king spread his hands. "Joanna will miss your wife's good company and advising. She likes her well."

"It is mutual. She, the queen, is not . . . with child?"

"I think not. But it is early days yet."

They discussed affairs of state, particularly the Galloway and Hebrides situation, and what was likely to happen when the season for warfare, especially sea warfare, arrived. Trouble there would be, undoubtedly; but with Alan and Olaf at each other's throats, the possibility was that the rest of Scotland might not be greatly involved. Although in the event of one winning effectively, who could say what the result would be for the realm at large? They would have to be prepared. Patrick's thousands might well be required.

On that note they parted, and it was return to Home Castle. There would have to be much packing up and upheaval there, and as much and more at Dunbar thereafter, with a larger establishment to settle into and make their home, and that one not an easy place to adapt to on its pillars rising out of the sea. Patrick had grown up there, but recognised its problems from a woman's housekeeping point of view. At least the children would delight in it all, young Pate in particular looking on that castle as his idea of heaven.

They would all cope.

PART TWO

26

With the years passing, so a new life started for Patrick and his family, new responsibilities and priorities, new problems and demands, new powers and what went with these, but new satisfactions and opportunities also, as well as their new domicile. Cope they all did, but it was a major challenge and break with the past.

The late Cospatrick had had his own ways, methods and emphases, which were not necessarily his son's. The earldom's older vassals, lairds and even traders and merchants were used to different rules and customs, and took some time in adjusting. Justiciar's duties in Lothian were more demanding than expected and took up considerable time, ill-doing seemingly on the increase. Patrick was kept busy indeed, and in consequence saw but little of Alexander that spring and summer.

It was perhaps just as well, then, that the news which came from the king was unexpected and, as far as peace for the realm was concerned, good. Alan of Galloway, returned from Ireland with his new young wife, had fallen ill, apparently fairly severely so. This resulted in a halt to his aggressive activities, towards the Isle of Man as towards others, however temporary this might prove to be. And Olaf Morsel was finding his takeover of the Hebridean kingship by no means acceptable to all up there, and in consequence was fully occupied in seeking to consolidate his position, so was in no mood for further adventures meantime. Peace of a sort prevailed, then, all along Alexander's western seaboard, thankfully, and no calls for armed men were made on the Earl of Dunbar and March.

It turned out to be, in fact, the king who came to

Dunbar, after a month or two, with Joanna, on what might be called a social visit, pleasing as it was unforeseen, staying for a couple of days, a happy occasion for all concerned, ensuring a little break for Patrick from his demanding duties, even though it proved scarcely that for Phemia, who had to provide the suitable hospitality. But it did bolster her husband's new-gained authority in his earldom and other responsibilities, and at the same time gave the monarch some first-hand insight into the problems and considerations that went with the governing of a large lordship. Unlike a kingdom to rule, an earl had no standing council of advisers and officials to aid and guide him. It all was valuable for Alexander to learn, for his better understanding of his nobles' pressures, needs and interests.

That autumn Patrick's brother William married a daughter of one of the earldom's senior vassals, Christiana de Corbet, of Corbet Tower near to Morebattle on the Kale Water, very near to the border. He fell to be allocated some extra lands to assist in supporting an enlarged establishment, and was given the quite substantial property of Fogo, near to Eccles, which would help in the supervision of the middle Merse. But this marriage did mean that William, in becoming a family man, would be less happy over his frequent trips to the Low Countries; so Patrick appointed his brother-in-law, the other William, to assist in this important trading task. He would have liked to go himself, on occasion, to improve links with Veere, Bergen and the rest, but meantime that was out of the question.

The wedding took place at the church of Morebattle, a prepend of Glasgow, strangely enough, and after attending it, Patrick and Phemia paid a visit to Roxburgh, none so far off, with a warm reception at court. Joanna still showed no signs of pregnancy, as lively as ever. She informed that her brother Henry was negotiating to wed Eleanor of Provence, a notable heiress who ought to make a worthy queen, and who would strengthen the Plantagenet interests in France. Patrick's father-in-law, Walter the Steward, was beginning to show signs of his age but was still Alexander's principal prop and stay. His daughter Christian was still at court, although less close to the king now.

Alexander was eager to have his friend made High Constable, but felt that he could hardly take the necessary steps to do so while Alan was continuing to be a sick man. If he died, of course, that would solve the problem, as it would others! Patrick was less than anxious to attain that prestigious position, which meant titular commander of the royal forces in the field, to add to his already over-many responsibilities. If some new office was designed for him, in place of the chamberlainship, he would prefer it to be fairly nominal.

He was acting the justiciar at Haddington some weeks later, in October, when a messenger from Roxburgh arrived to inform that King Henry was renewing his urgings anent the defining of the borderline between the two realms, which had remained undecided since the former abortive surveys. Patrick was one of the appointed commissioners, and while he could have done without this addition to his tasks, he was concerned in the matter, and an obvious representative since his earldom marched with the Debateable Land over quite lengthy stretches. So he had to devote some time to this renewed survey, and an unprofitable exercise it again proved to be, with little progress achieved although much heat engendered. One fairly brief stretch of hilly and empty territory was accepted, parallel with the upper Bowmont Water due south of Yetholm, but that was as far as agreement went, and it took some days to gain that. Henry would be displeased; but his own commissioners were anything but co-operative.

Another time-consuming interlude occurred in November, a very strange admixture of the celebratory and the funereal, in which Patrick was involved because of family connections, and Alexander for state reasons. The former's brother's new wife Christiana de Corbet had a sister, Alicia, who was to marry one Malcolm, nephew and heir of the Earl of Fife, one of the most senior lords of the land, indeed Coroner of the Kingdom – that was with the hereditary right to place the crown on the king's head at his coronation. The wedding took place in the church of the nunnery of North Berwick, founded by the father of this earl and near to the castle of Tantallon, of which this nephew was the keeper, North Berwick being the southern terminal of the ferry across Forth connecting the Fife earldom with its Lothian property. So it was little trouble for Patrick and Phemia to attend this ceremony, only a dozen miles from Dunbar. But in the celebrations in the castle thereafter, dire word was brought over from Fife. The Earl Malcolm had suddenly died, and the new bridegroom, his own father being dead, was now therefore eighth Earl of Fife. This totally unexpected circumstance produced inevitable and considerable upset and confusion in matters celebratory, for the feasting had to be postponed and many of the guests ferried across the firth to Dunimarle Castle in Fife, the seat of the great earldom, and the nearby Abbey of Culross, this last founded by the said earl on the site of the renowned St Serf's monastery. And, since the new earl and bridegroom would automatically become Coroner of Scotland, and his uncle it was who had crowned Alexander in 1214, the king felt bound to be present at the interment. So amidst something like chaos, many of the wedding guests had to be got across the choppy Forth to Culross, this east of Queen Margaret's Ferry and Dunfermline, quite a lengthy sail, in less than calm weather. Alexander at least would be able to cover most of his journey on horseback.

Patrick had never been to Culross, much as he had heard of it as the birthplace of St Kentigern or Mungo, who had founded Glasgow, son of the Princess Thanea from his own Traprain Law, daughter of King Loth, so Culross was a locality highly important in Scotland's story. The present abbey, built on the site of the ancient monastery, however recently constructed, was a handsome edifice. The service of burial, to be conducted by the Dean of

St Andrews, Bishop William now being old and frail, had to await the arrival of the monarch, so a strange atmosphere prevailed, a mixture of melancholy and mourning for the old earl, and of congratulations and felicitations for the new and freshly married one, and his bride, most there only anxious to get the interment over in dignity and as soon as possible.

Alexander duly arrived, with the Steward and other notables, and the eighth Earl of Fife helped to lower the seventh, his uncle, into the crypt beneath the chancel, prayers were said, and all could disperse to their own destinations, the bridal party returning to Tantallon to resume due celebrations, Patrick and Phemia with them.

Out of all this one issue developed, as far as Alexander and Patrick were concerned. For the late earl had been Keeper of the Great Seal of Scotland, this an honorary office not a hereditary one. So it fell to the crown again, and the king promptly bestowed it upon his friend, in lieu of the chamberlainship, and while they waited for the High Constable's title to become available. The recipient was appreciative, but thankful that it did not seem to carry with it any very onerous duties, the said Great Seal being kept securely locked up in Roxburgh Castle.

So it was parting again, and returns to the ferry scows.

It seemed rather odd, somehow, to return to the resuming festivities at Tantallon, and Phemia and Patrick thought that they could quite acceptably make their excuses and head home for Dunbar and the children. Brother William admitted that he would prefer to do likewise, but for Christiana's sake felt that they must put in an appearance.

The excuse Patrick made was that he was to attend court to be installed as Keeper of the Great Seal. This was true enough, although in fact Alexander had left it to his friend to decide when the visit could be made most conveniently for himself.

It was a week later that Patrick set out for Roxburgh for

this demonstration of the royal favour. He knew fairly well from his past duties as Chamberlain what the office of keeper entailed. It could be more or less a nominal title, the Chancellor of the Realm in fact mainly using the Great Seal, as distinct from the Privy Seal, for the many occasions for which royal sanction was required, such as the selling or transfer of lands from one subject to another, all lands in the kingdom in theory being under the superiority of the monarch and his seal necessary to establish his consent to the transfer. So it was in very frequent use. To spare the Chancellor, usually a senior cleric, and at present one William de Bosco, with the need to affix the seal to every royal document, the Keeper of the Seal was appointed; but in fact the constant use of it was delegated to a Clerk of the Seal, who did the actual sealing normally – all very delegatory. So Patrick's duties would consist of merely calling at the court whenever he was conveniently able to do so, and making a token gesture of examining the register of the seal's use and checking with the clerk, no onerous task.

The installation ceremony was brief and simple, the king announcing his appointment before such members of the council as were at court at the time. This happened to be the Steward, the High Justiciar himself newly installed, and the Bishop of Glasgow, sufficient for the occasion. So, save for the handing over of a document signed by Alexander and endorsed by the Privy Seal, which followed, Patrick was now Keeper of the Great Seal of Scotland, the Chancellor's approval being taken for granted.

However, there was a surprise, demonstrating the king's continuing fondness for his long-time friend. The new High Chamberlain was to be appointed, none other than Patrick's own brother-in-law William, now calling himself de Home. Alexander had found him good company on the various occasions when they had met, and decided that he would serve well in the chamberlainship, linking him still with Patrick, and living now so nearby to be readily available. William would be knighted, as was suitable.

The new Keeper of the Great Seal returned home very appreciative of the royal esteem and favour.

27

Scotland, or much of it, sighed with a sort of relief. Alan of Galloway was dead. A threat, not only to the western seaboard, had been lifted, Alexander, and indeed Patrick amongst the most unburdened; not that the latter had any desire for the High Constableship, as had been suggested, but that armed conflict with Galloway now seemed unlikely, and his part therein not required. But who would succeed Alan, his only son the illegitimate Thomas? Would it be Devorgilla, the eldest daughter, wed to the Baliol? Or one of her sisters? They all had English husbands. Would an English Lord of Galloway be acceptable, even to the Galwegians? All awaited developments and consequences.

They did not have long to wait. Thomas the Bastard announced that *he* was now Lord of Galloway, and named many of the most prominent men of the province as his supporters. To be sure he had had sufficiently long, during his father's illness, to test out attitudes and reactions; and it seemed that, by and large, the Galwegians preferred him to any of his half-sisters' English husbands.

What now? This Thomas, illegitimate as he was, had married a daughter of the slain King Reginald of Man and the Isles in his father's cause against Olaf. Was this significant now? How would the Morsel react? Questions abounded that winter and spring, and not only in Scotland.

But it was Scotland which learned first of the new Galloway regime's ambitions. Thomas, in June, led a quite major assault on Ayrshire, the Kennedy country. South Ayrshire had been more or less under the sway of Galloway, although nowise part of it, for long; but this attack went far beyond that, well into the Barr, Dailly and Girvan areas, burning and slaughtering. The Kennedys protested vigorously and appealed to the crown.

Alexander felt bound to act.

So an assembly of the forces of his lords was called for, at Moffat near where Tweed, Clyde and Annan rose, the most central and accessible meeting-place for men from all over southern Scotland. And, needless to say, the Earl of Dunbar and March had to make good his promise of large-scale aid in his liege-lord's cause. He demonstrated his loyalty by seeking to produce possibly the largest contribution to the royal army by bringing no fewer than fifteen hundred mounted men to Moffat, worried as his countess was by this development. He was glad to see, at the muster, that his force far outnumbered any other lord's total, the nearest rivals being the new Earl of Fife's and the Steward's, each around six hundred. Alexander was duly appreciative.

The strategy, presently agreed by all, was not to head for mid-Ayrshire, and a direct confrontation, but to assail Galloway itself, at its central and leading area, in the Loch Ken and River Dee vicinity. Alan had died at Threave Castle, on the Dee, his principal seat; and presumably that would be where this Thomas would be basing himself. An attack there would almost certainly bring him hastening southwards to counter it, and with the Kennedys hopefully harassing his rear. To ensure this last, the Steward, who knew this country well, with his sons-in-law the Earls of Lennox and Carrick, would take about one thousand men to aid in these tactics, so that Thomas would be caught between two forces, a major handicap. Patrick, for one, deemed this wise planning.

The intention was that the Galwegians were forced to take their retiral southwards over the long and high pass between the all-but-mountains known as the Rhinns of Kells, where the River Ken rose, and where they might be ambushed successfully. There was not a lot of choice for them if they were heading for Loch Ken, the Dee and Threave, unless they went west-about by the coastal area, which, if they were in a hurry, was not to be expected, a much longer route. The Steward's task was to make the Kennedys see the sense of this, and co-operate.

So proceeding as far as mid-Nithsdale, there was a parting of the ways, the royal array heading on west by south, the Steward's group carrying on up Nith to cross over the more modest Mennock Pass, by Sanquhar and so into southern Ayrshire by Cumnock, where they hoped to join the Kennedys.

Alexander's main force was soon into very hilly country, passing Moniaive, and thereafter following up the Dalwhat Water, swinging northwards now. No large army could move fast, and they had to camp for the night on the bank of this river below Craigdarroch Hill. Patrick was distinctly concerned about the timing, for the Steward's company would have a considerably less cross-country and hilly route to take over to the Nith's junction with the Afton Water and so down into Ayrshire. Just where in that county the enemy was operating at present they did not know, but it was all Kennedy country, and they would learn details quickly enough. So the danger was that they could assail Thomas's people too soon, and that these would turn back for home through the high hills before Alexander's host was able to reach and deploy their chosen ambush in the Rhinns area. Alexander recognised this, and agreed that their overnight halt should be a very brief one, weary as they all might be with long riding.

They were on their way by dawn, up the Dalwhat Water, and able to cross over a minor pass under Colt Hill to reach the River Ken. Up this major stream they turned, almost due north now, into really high hills, and none so far from their proposed destination.

As the twisting valley narrowed they were able to discern the traces of a large force having passed this way, but some time before, and obviously heading north, as were they, hoof-tracks, old horse-droppings and debris; so clearly Thomas's people had come this way, and the probability was that they would return by it also. But not too quickly, it was to be hoped. Would Thomas already know of this royal invasion of his Galloway? He would have his informants in the Moffat area almost certainly. The movements of armies were not to be hidden. It was to be hoped that this likewise did not bring him back southwards over-soon for their purposes.

The River Ken rose high amongst these Rhinns, a lofty area where also rose the lesser rivers of Scaur, Deugh, Afton and indeed Nith itself, all flowing in different directions. It was anticipated that the Galwegians would come up the Afton Water, cross the high pass and descend into this Ken valley. The objective was to attack them there, strung out as they must be in the ever narrowing defile, cut them up and defeat them.

There were problems, of course, for the would-be attackers, the principal one the necessity of hiding their own men up on the valley sides so that they would not be seen by the front riders of the enemy and their main force warned. Also the said slopes, although they would be steep, must not be so much so that the attackers could not descend them more or less in line and at speed. Much depended on the chosen terrain, then, as was always the way with ambushing.

Patrick, concerned over all this, volunteered to go on ahead to survey the possibilities, taking half a dozen of his own men, to be able to send back relays of messengers. Just before he set off, there was an announcement. Two messengers came after them in haste, to declare that the Earl Farquhar of Ross had arrived late from the north at Moffat, and had decided that in the circumstances his best course was to follow the Steward's force into Ayrshire to aid in that enterprise rather than try to catch up with the king's army.

Patrick's little group were able to ride up the riverside, a fairly rushing torrent now, at fully three times the speed they had been making. Their track kept rising and the valley ever narrowing. Patrick's eyes were ever busy scanning the sides in especial. Finding a suitable area to hide and charge down from was not going to be easy. There were bushes and stunted trees growing on the lower slopes, but higher was mainly bare, and incapable of hiding hundreds of men. Presumably they would have to station themselves over the crests of the ridges to be out of sight from the valley floor, using individual watchers down amongst the bushes to send up warning when and if the enemy appeared.

They were about two miles up Ken when Patrick perceived a possible site. A large tributary burn coming in on the left, the west, had carved out for itself a quite deep ravine which opened into the main defile. This was quite thickly wooded with dwarf hawthorn and whins, sufficient to hide many men. On the other eastern side they would have to wait behind its summit until they heard the ravine section making the first assault, then come over to assist. The only disadvantage here was the fact that this subsidiary burn, at its actual junction with the river, had formed a fairly wide and marshy flat, something of a water meadow, which would not help down-charging horsemen. This extended for a few hundred yards, so it would only affect a proportion of the attack on a long strung-out foe.

Patrick sent back two of his men to inform and bring on the host, and went forward himself to prospect further.

There was a fairly straight stretch after that providing no cover, but suitably narrow, to keep the Galwegians riding no more than two or three abreast.

He decided that this area would serve, if Alexander agreed.

When the king and his force arrived, all were well pleased with the prospect, and set about dividing up their men, some to enter the side ravine but most to climb the opposite slopes and hide themselves over the ridge, spreading out northwards for fully half a mile. Meantime scouts were sent forward up-river to keep watch for an enemy approach.

By this time it was midday, as they settled to wait.

No word came back to them from the scouts, as Alexander and Patrick sought to marshal their smaller party as best they could in the confined space amongst the trees and bushes. This would form an initial striking force and give the signal for the long line up on the hill opposite to start their descent. Instructions given were precise. It would be a dismounted assault for this ravine group, the horses hidden well up the burnside, this because of that marshy area in the main valley.

They waited and waited and still no warning was sent of any enemy approach. This either meant that the Bastard Thomas was still dealing with the Kennedys, the Steward and Farquhar of Ross; or else, unfortunately, he had chosen a different route homewards.

Dusk fell, and they settled down for the night, watchmen posted at various points. It could be assumed, surely, that the Galwegians would not make their journey by night.

Most of them were able to sleep undisturbed, and for longer than the night before.

Morning saw all ready, prepared. A messenger from the forward scouts came to report that these were now right up at the pass itself, between the summits of Alwhat and Blacklorg, and from which they could see northwards a fair distance into the lower country, and with as yet no sign of an army approaching. So clearly there would be much waiting yet.

Patrick took the opportunity to climb up the far side of the valley to inspect and inform the main body of their host, spread out behind the crest, these under the command of the Earls of Mar and Menteith. All seemed to be well there, although hunger appeared to be beginning to afflict the men, their pouchfuls of oatmeal run out. This was empty country and providing no cattle or sheep to fill empty bellies.

It was mid-afternoon, with Patrick returned to the king's side, before at last word was sent down from the pass. A host was indeed approaching up the Afton Water, seemingly in two sections, one only indistinctly, distantly seen, well behind the other. This could be either the Galwegian rearguard, fighting off the Kennedys and Steward attack, or just that force itself following on after the enemy.

So all were warned and readied. It would not be long now. They had judged aright, evidently. Thomas was for home, and by this route.

Their scouts arrived back, saying that the foe had now threaded the pass and were beginning the descent into the infant Ken valley. Menteith and Mar went sent information.

It made tense waiting now, so much depending on disciplined and co-ordinated action, and the terrain with major difficulties for attackers as well as defenders, spilling out of that ravine constricting to say the least.

Lying low, hidden, they eventually heard the approaching array before they could see it, the clop of hooves, the jingle of harness, the clank of steel, loud in the confines of the defile. Plans carefully made, the ambushers counted the minutes.

Patrick had convinced Alexander and the others that the best strategy was to let the first files of the foe past without interruption, then to dash out and split the column into sections, many sections it was to be hoped, and so all lacking leadership. Much would depend on the stretch of marshy ground in front. The track followed this west side of it, but some of the enemy might follow the east side, which could complicate the issue.

Peering from behind their leafage they watched the leading Galwegians trot past. How many to let go? Would Thomas himself be there, at their head? They were not sporting banners or heraldic horse-cloths to indicate leadership.

Alexander was impatient to attack, but Patrick managed to restrain him. Let about one hundred go past, he urged. There would be many more hundreds behind. Cut off at least this advance guard from the rest. Then hopefully, when these turned back to assist their comrades, seek to drive them into that marsh. There did not seem to be any using that other, eastern side. They could see no distance up the valley.

Counting, counting, at length Patrick rose, and Alexander with him. A single blast on a hunting-horn signalled the assault; and out from their cover the attackers surged, swords, battle-axes and dirks drawn, shouting their challenge.

Surprise was complete, at least. They drove through the narrow column of horsemen, only a few of the enemy actually in the line of their onset, these quickly overwhelmed, slashed at, horses rearing in fright and throwing some, others being driven into the soft ground beyond where they floundered hock-deep and worse. A proportion of the assailants, leaving these, turned right-handed, southwards, to face the files already past and now reining round and back in alarm; but most of the king's men rounded in the other direction to face the oncoming column. From on high, yelling indicated that the host up their had seen and heard, and was moving into the downhill action.

Patrick was with the smaller south-facing section. Deliberately he led them down across the track and into the marshy ground. There they sank into the moss and mire and pools up to their ankles, but not sufficiently to bog them down nor immobilise them, unlike the horses which, with their weight and shod hooves, went in much deeper, and hobbled helplessly. And in the sudden alarm and all but panic at the unexpected onslaught, those forward riders turned and came spurring back to aid their fellows and, unwisely but almost inevitably, also came plunging into the water meadow, since that is where the assailants were. And, to be sure, were promptly in trouble themselves, bogged down and plunging about in disorder, as of course was Patrick's intention. He now led his men forward, however difficult and heavy the going, to attack the troubled and disconcerted horsemen.

These would have been better to dismount, in the circumstances, and meet their foes on more equal terms; but no doubt the feeling of height in their saddles and the ability to wield swords right and left therefrom, kept them mounted. They learned, grievously, that although height could certainly assist swordplay, with attackers stooping and dodging, dirks slashing at unhappy horses' bellies, and these outnumbering them by at least four to one, the superior height was of scant advantage.

It was a disorderly and incoherent engagement, but there could be no doubt as to who won in this preliminary skirmish. Patrick, bent double and managing to avoid down-slashing swords, soon recognised amidst the clash and clamour, the shouting and the shrill neighing of injured horses, that his tactics had been successful. This forward group of the enemy was utterly routed, many jumping off their faltering mounts and more fleeing afoot than staying on to fight. In it all, he wondered whether the Bastard Thomas was one of this leading company.

As the pressure on himself, as leader, lessened, he was able to glance elsewhere around him. He saw that the north-facing struggle appeared to be going very much as his own had done, with the bog working for the King of Scots and the Galwegians in trouble. But he also saw a less satisfactory situation. The force from the high ground opposite had duly descended, somewhat raggedly as was to be expected with their horses slipping and slithering on the steep and broken slopes; but unfortunately those at this end of the line had chosen to come to assist the king's grouping, but not proceeding up on the far side of the soft ground as they should have done but to plunge directly ahead and into it. As a result these were now equally bogged down as were their foes, of no assistance to anyone.

Cursing, Patrick could only leave them to extract themselves as best they could. He marshalled his own men in some measure to go and reinforce Alexander's assault.

This proved to be as chaotic fighting in the mire and waterlogged ground as elsewhere. But it was clearly proving worse for the mounted Galwegians than for the ambushers on foot. Patrick's people's arrival indubitably helped, but this section of the battle was all but won without them.

What, then, of the rest of the lengthy line of the enemy, further up the valley? Because of the twists and turns of the defile, it was impossible to see what went on there. But surely the Menteith and Mar host would be making a greater impact than at this lower end.

Patrick managed to reach his mud-spattered liege-lord's side, and panted out his brief report and comments. Alexander, in this his first real battle, gasped less than eloquently but asserted success, at least thus far. The enemy was in dire trouble and disarray, whatever else, even though not yet wholly defeated. Once they could get round that next bend in the valley they might be able to judge how near they were to total victory.

And then there was a new and not anticipated development, heralded by wild shouting above the prevailing din, high-pitched and indeed coming from higher, and not on the other eastern side but on their own. Gazing up, they saw hundreds of men, kilted men, on foot, charging down the steep braeside north of their ravine, with broadswords high and round targes, Highlanders obviously, and making their own fearsome attack. They could only be Farquhar's Rossmen, choosing a strategy of their own. If there were more of these further up, then Thomas's people were going to be assailed on two sides, and dramatically.

The enemy, at least those in sight, were all fleeing now in disorder, such as could. And there was not much scope even for flight, with those steep valley sides thronged with eager adversaries. So it was rearwards that the would-be escapers fled, that is, into their own oncoming ranks, to the further confusion of all, these already being challenged on their flanks. It was all disaster indeed for Galloway.

Round a major bend in the valley Patrick and Alexander presently could see only bloody havoc ahead, but flight back northwards the major preoccupation other than escaping hurt and death. The day, clearly, was won. No doubt these escapers would have to face the Steward and the Kennedys further up, unless they could get out of this Ken defile.

When the royal force could be brought into some sort of order and the situation weighed up, with Earl Farquhar being congratulated on his spirited contribution, the principal question was what of Thomas the Bastard? Was he amongst the slain or wounded? Or had he escaped? None of the king's people knew him by sight. So their quest was difficult. But they had been left with a number of wounded and prisoners in their hands, and questioning these they learned from one that the Lord Thomas and his friend and adviser, the Lord Gilrod from Ireland, had been seen to ride off, back northwards, fairly early in the encounter. It was probable that they had escaped.

This was disappointing news, although there was still a possibility that they might fall into the hands of the Steward and the Kennedys. But at least this defeat should clip the Galloway wings for a while, especially when the royal army had made the advisable descent on Threave Castle and the other base areas.

That would be their next objective.

It was evening now, and they decided to encamp here, tend to the wounded, put injured horses out of their misery and make at least a gesture at burying the dead, that bog useful for this. The need for food was now serious, especially with the arrival of the Steward and the Kennedy force, so that thousands of men were there assembled in the narrow valley, congratulations general but not allaying hunger. So a hard-riding party was sent off southwards somehow to collect provisions of a sort from the nearest villages, Dalquhairn apparently the largest, which they had passed on their way up Ken. A sufficiency to feed an army, even exceedingly modestly, would be no easy task to attain, and the local folk would be less than co-operative, it was recognised. But needs must.

The provision brought back eventually was scarcely

generous for all those empty stomachs, Patrick and others, unused to warfare, learning how it came about that armies ever got the name for ravaging the countrysides they traversed. It had to be mainly slaughtered cattle and sheep, with sackfuls of oatmeal. Fortunately there was plenty of wood in their ravine to make fires for roasting the very unseasoned meat. And oatmeal, washed down with water, could help limit the pangs of hunger.

There did not seem to be any risk of a counter-attack by the Galwegians.

In the morning the move was made southwards down Ken. At least there were no problems as to where to go and how to get there. For in time the Ken would widen into a dozen-mile-long loch, and at the far south end of it, the river emerging was the Dee, strange as this might seem; and on an island in this river was Threave Castle, their main objective.

They had some forty-five miles to ride altogether, and met with no opposition, scarcely to be wondered at, with their fully seven thousand armed men. By Carlae and Strahanna they came to Dalry, the first major community of the Glenkens area, over a score of miles, where they were able to gain the food they required from the cowed and frightened folk, Alexander forbidding any unnecessary sacking and terror. Another three miles brought them to the castle of Kenmure, quite large, but proving to be abandoned, no doubt in haste. This they pillaged for more food, and then part destroyed, as warning, and moved on to the head of long Loch Ken, this sudden widening of the river, for that was all that it really was, quite extraordinary and stretching southwards for a dozen miles; although the lower half of it might equally have been called Loch Dee, for that major river came in from the west to enlarge the lake. Until this it had been only some six to eight hundred yards wide, but now it became all but double that, dotted with islets and promontories. Another six miles they rode down the east bank, by the village of Parton, and all as suddenly narrowed again, at

Glenlochan, and it became the River Dee instead of Ken, all highly unusual.

On the way the army had encountered no sort of opposition, although the land proved to be fairly populous. No doubt the word of Bastard Thomas's defeat had preceded them, the people in consequence lying low. At any rate Alexander and his leaders found nothing to demand assault on all that lengthy progress, which took them all day.

They knew enough about Threave to realise that it would be no easy target, set on an island in the wide river. Boats would be needed to assail it; and it was highly unlikely that its defenders would have left any such available for attackers.

They proceeded down the Dee for another two miles, with dusk settling on the land; and at a bend there, where a sizeable stream came in from the west, found Threave island. It was larger than they had anticipated, almost three-quarters of a mile in length, the castle, tall and stark, rising at its southern end, a lofty square keep within a courtyard, with rounded angle towers at each of its four corners. No banners flew above it this evening.

It was quickly apparent that no boats were to be had along the riverside; and even in the fading light evident that these had been taken over to the island, where they could be seen tied up, quite a rank of them, near the stronghold. Was Thomas out there in that fortalice? It was his main seat, as it had been his father's. But would he have come here? Or fled further afield? This Gilrod, his friend and alleged instigator, had come from Ireland, with men. Might they have returned there? It was less than twenty miles, after all.

The army encamped for the night facing that inaccessible hold. Alexander held a council. What was to be done? Besiege the place from here? Almost certainly, since its keepers had taken all boats over, they had assumed that they would be assailed; therefore they would have stocked up with food, and could no doubt hold out for long. And since the besiegers themselves were direly short of provisions, they it was who would be apt to suffer most.

There were suggestions that parties should be sent out, up and down the river, even back to the lochside, to try to find and bring back boats. But it was realised that it would take a long time to gather sufficient craft to carry the necessarily large force needed; and meantime Thomas, if he was indeed over there, could well have made his escape by night in one of his own boats.

It was Patrick who proposed swimming. Brought up as he had been in sea-girt Dunbar Castle, he had been a swimmer since childhood. Many others could probably swim well, including men from his own force. The island was none so far off from this bank. Swim out then, some of them, and bring back boats, this very night. There would likely be a fairly strong current, but if they started from well upstream that could be used to help them. It might take some time to get a sufficiency of the craft over, two or three crossings, but the night was young.

What if the oars had been removed from the boats? he was asked.

Patrick thought this unlikely. What point in it, over there? But if they were, three swimmers could tow a boat, with the current, even though they might have to land well downstream. Enough swimmers, then. He would lead the attempt himself.

Most of the lords were distinctly doubtful; but Alexander backed his friend, saying that it was worth a try. So Patrick went off through the camp seeking swimmers, starting with his own Dunbar and Merse men. And he met with a fair response, especially amongst the younger men, who seemed to look on all this as a challenge and a dare, not to be outdone by their fellows. He hardly had to go beyond his own people; but the word quickly spread, and volunteers arrived from other groups. Without actually counting them, he had perhaps three hundred swimmers, surely enough for his purpose.

He had them all make for the riverbank; and not only

these but large numbers of others who, weary as they all might be from long riding, did not want to miss this spectacle, much of chaff and advice forthcoming.

Not merely the rank and file came to see the start of this endeavour, the king himself foremost. Some way upstream Patrick called a halt, and began to strip off his clothing, urging silence on all. He told his swimmers to wait meantime. He would go in alone, to test the current, then return to lead the attempt.

So in he waded and quickly was out of his depth. The July water was none so cold. There was a current sure enough, quite strong but not in any way daunting. He swam for perhaps fifty yards, and felt himself being carried downstream, but was able to make headway, however slantwise. So far so good. He turned back, landing well below the waiting men, and running back up to them.

He was concerned about watchers on the island. Probably guards would confine themselves to the castle's walls, but it was possible that some might make patrols of the banks, even though they were not likely to anticipate swimmers. But the odd boat *might* have been found.

He told his volunteers that they should go a little further upstream to enter the river, to make best use of that current; they did not want to be carried past the boats. And to be careful not to splash, swimming as silently as was possible. It was not a windy night, and sounds could carry. How many boats there were lined up over there he did not know, but the more they could bring back, one way or another, the better. Then, all prepared, he waved them in after him.

It was surely one of the oddest of military actions, hundreds of naked and unarmed swimmers, in darkness, ploughing their way through the strongly running water, seeking to make no noise whether by panting, speaking to each other, or by their arm and leg movements.

They did not all swim at the same speed, but it did not take long, with the help of the current, to reach their objective. Just how many boats were moored together there Patrick was unable to count, but he guessed almost a score. Hoisting himself up into one of them, he discovered the oars duly lying therein. Probably it would be the same with the others. So far, no sign of patrols.

Taking the oars, he waited while his men followed his lead. He was calculating. How many would each boat carry? And how many men required for the assault on the castle? Therefore how many crossings? His own boat, crowded, could probably bring over twenty at a time. If the others were similar, say four hundred to each crossing. Double that would surely be sufficient. How these were to capture the stronghold was another matter. One thing was very clear: he had far more swimmers than required. But he could hardly leave the extra men here, naked and unarmed.

So he sought, by gestures, not shouts, to get them all piled into the various craft, and, almost as full as they would be coming back, they set off, in somewhat ragged order, and less than silently, with the oars to get out and dipped, deciding who should go in which boat and the like. Whether this was heard from the castle or not, he could not tell, but there was no sign of alarm or approach.

They rowed over, plenty of oarsmen at least.

The king had moved his men somewhat downstream to meet them, and these now took over the boats, Patrick having a word with Alexander. He would go to resume his clothing, and come over again with the second crossing. It was agreed that the two groups would probably be enough for any assault on the castle.

The swimmers reclad, only a few of them elected to go over again with Patrick when the all but empty boats came back. So far all had gone according to plan, they were told.

The king was waiting for his friend on the island, although some of his company had gone on to prospect the stronghold and its defences. Alexander admitted that he was at something of a loss to know what was to be done now.

Patrick, with the new arrivals, went forward then to join

the others, and to inspect. Presumably their presence must be known by now to the defenders, although there was no indication of this, nor challenge.

A circuit of the walls, in the dark, revealed no obvious means of entry, the drawbridge at the gatehouse up. All there used to castles, Patrick was not the only one to say the obvious way to scale the walls was by heaving grapnels up attached to long knotted ropes, and when these caught on projections, and held, men to climb up and over, many grapnels and ropes. Unfortunately, however, they did not have any grapnels nor ropes. The walls were fully twenty-five feet in height, and no doubt topped by parapeted walks, for guards. To get over these without ladders or the said ropes was not possible.

What, then?

Patrick thought that the only course open to them at this stage was to announce their presence. Go round to the gatehouse and declare that this was the King of Scots, in force, requiring word with Thomas of Galloway. If the answer to that was a shower of arrows or the like, then there would be nothing for it but siege. If this was prolonged, then it might be possible for some of their army to range around and seek to lay hands on ladders, even battering-rams or what could be made into such.

For want of better suggestions, this was accepted. So all moved round to the southern front of the hold, to assemble before the moat and gatehouse behind, there to have a horn blown.

This done, they received immediate answering shouts, proof that their presence had not gone unobserved. Who came thus by night to Threave, was demanded.

The Steward raised voice. "I am Walter, High Steward of this realm," he called. "Here is His Grace, Alexander, King of Scots, requiring speech with Thomas of Galloway."

"The Lord Thomas is not here," came back. "Why comes the King of Scots thus, by night?"

"His Grace does not require to give answers for his decisions to you, sirrah! He requires entry to this hold."

Silence.

The king took over. "I, Alexander, as your liege-lord, command access from Threave's keeper," he announced. "I desire no harm to any therein, so long as all here keep my peace hereafter. I have seven thousand men here waiting, so you cannot resist for long. I seek only peace in Galloway. So, open to me."

Again no response. But when that hunting-horn was blown loud and long, it did gain its own answer, in another sound, metallic clanking. It did not have to be explained to most hearing that this was the chains which supported and worked the drawbridge being unwound. The bridge was being lowered and the portcullis, its iron gate, raised.

Patrick was not the only one to sigh with relief. But was it full capitulation? Or merely indicating some sort of parleying?

They waited until the wooden timbers thudded down into place, and the moat could be spanned. No persons came out on to it.

"It looks as though entry is to be given, Alex," Patrick said. "But it might be but a device. To coax you within and then to hold you captive as price for relief from siege."

"Think you so? It could be, yes . . ."

"Send forward others. A party, to see. Not yourself. I will go with it, if need be."

"No, not you. They could hold you also, Pate. See, some of your men. A score, say."

A group of Mersemen were sent forward, swords and axes in hand, to cross that bridge and in under the gatehouse arch. All around the monarch waited tensely. For minutes there was no sound from the castle. Then a call came from the gatehouse.

"All well, all well! They submit. All is well, my lord Patrick."

Thankfully the hearers exchanged glances, nodding. A general move to the bridge and over was made.

Under the gatehouse arch they found some of the Mersemen waiting with an elderly individual whom they declared to be keeper of this hold, MacAskill by name. He bowed jerkily to them all, not knowing which was the monarch. He had little or nothing to say for himself, save that the Lord Thomas had not been at Threave for some three weeks.

Somewhat bemused by this anticlimactic situation after all their efforts, the swimming, the boating, the circuit of the walls and the question of scaling these, and now this surrender, without so much as a blow struck, Alexander could think of nothing more telling to demand than that he should be taken on a tour of inspection of the castle.

This was acceded to without demur, and they were all conducted over the premises, men with lanterns leading them, and eyed distinctly askance by guards. Patrick it was who thought of sending messengers over to Walter Comyn, Earl of Menteith, left in charge of the main force across the river, acquainting him with the position.

Threave proved to be a fine place, of strength and a variety of assets, even its own small mill, worked by a sluice from the river, as well as barracks, stabling, storehouses and an ice-house, all in the wide courtyard with its angle towers. The visitors observed that there was much provision in the stores, so it was as well that a siege had not been necessary. The tall keep was capacious and strong, the walls of great thickness, honeycombed with closets and little L-shaped corridors, some with even narrow stairways leading to upper chambers. This, the callers reminded themselves, had been the Lord Alan's headquarters, source of much trouble for the realm.

Alexander and most of his lords decided to spend what was left of the night therein, more comfortable than the encampment and with ample food and drink available. It all seemed somehow less than dramatic and appropriate, being treated like guests in this house which they had come to assail, all their great array not necessary, indeed all but now an embarrassment.

In the morning they found some of Menteith's men, searching the neighbourhood for supplies, had come across a casualty from their ambush, wounded, who had managed to make his way back to his farmery at Carlingwark and he, questioned, told them that the Lord Thomas had said, after the defeat, that he intended to flee back to Ireland, with Gilrod, but that he would be back in due course. This was what had been more or less anticipated, so probably there was no point in searching Galloway for the pair. So meantime the king's task could be considered accomplished, and successfully. A return could be made to Roxburgh and elsewhere, leaving Menteith and a proportion of the force here, to base themselves on Threave and seek to ensure that Galloway caused no further trouble.

They were packing up camp preparatory to moving when an unexpected development arose. A quite large party of men arrived on foot from the nearby community of Causewayend of Carlingwark, these all with ropes round their necks and hanging down therefrom, this a symbol of surrender and admission of guilt, in the hope presumably that the king might forgive and pardon them and theirs, a strange gesture. Some of the lords suggested that it would be a pity not to hang one or two of them, since they came so prepared; but Alexander was not that way inclined. He told them to remove their ropes and go back to tell their neighbours that their sovereign-lord was merciful and desired peace in this province of Galloway, as in all his realm. Let there be no more uprisings and revolt.

Then it was northwards and eastwards for home. Could they claim to be victorious?

28

Resounding victory or otherwise, Alexander used it to confirm his desire to appoint Patrick High Constable of Scotland, a position which in theory carried with it the responsibility for all but keeping the peace in the realm, this scarcely the recipient's ambition, with enough on his plate as it was. Phemia did not enthuse over the appointment either. Friendship with the monarch was a pleasure and a privilege, to be sure, but it could be a distinct handicap for a family man.

That summer and autumn, oddly enough, the problems of keeping the peace, although they came from Galloway, were created not by the folk there themselves but by the force left under the Earl of Menteith to keep the province in order. Earl Walter was the son of another Comyn earl, William of Buchan, and this elderly man now fell ill and was thought to be dying. So the son had to return to that great earldom in the north, to be present at his sire's last days and to ensure that the resultant change in overlordship of the great lands went smoothly and satisfactorily. He therefore had to leave the king's Galloway force under the command of sundry lieutenants. And these proved to be broken reeds, unable or unwilling to control their men who, finding themselves more or less masters of an entire province, and ill-led and undisciplined, began to misbehave on a major scale, plundering, ravaging, raping and creating mayhem. This in turn produced uprising of the injured locals, tough folk in any case, with clashes and great disorder. Alexander sent the Earl of Carrick to try to restore order, but with the offenders quite out of hand, even assaulting churchmen and their establishments, actually murdering the Prior of Tongland and his sacristan, that young man was unable to bring the situation under control.

The all but inevitable happened. Thomas the Bastard and his friend Gilrod came back from Ireland to resume possession of Galloway.

This was the position, with the king greatly concerned and declaring that he would have to take an army westwards again, and this at Christmastide, when an invitation arrived from Henry Plantagenet for his brother-in-law and sister to attend his marriage to Eleanor of Provence, this on 14th January in London. Alexander felt that he could nowise refuse to accept so important an occasion and one to emphasise the desired friendship between the two realms. So the Galloway situation would have to be left to others, in especial the High Constable. Patrick was to assemble a large army again, in the king's name, and go to put matters right in that troublesome province.

What a way to have to pass Yuletide.

The muster of the necessary forces took place at Roxburgh in the monarch's presence, just before he and Joanna set off for England, he declaring that he had every confidence in Patrick's ability to put all to rights, this almost apologetically. The Steward would accompany the royal pair south, but his son-in-law, Lennox, and the somewhat guilty-feeling Menteith, now become Earl of Buchan, could act as lieutenants. The Bishop of Galloway and Alan, Abbot of Melrose would go with them to express Holy Church's horror at the murders of its clergy, and to call down curses upon the culprits.

So an army of some five thousand rode off, in dismal chilly weather, westwards, with the High Constable in command, none any more enthusiastic than himself over the entire venture.

It took them three unpleasant days' riding, going by Tweed, Ettrick and Yarrow to Moffat, and then over to Moniaive, to reach Threave, where they found an exasperated Carrick unsuccessfully seeking to round up and punish the errant marauders, and at the same time having to watch out for attack by the returned Thomas and Gilrod. He was thankful indeed to see this army, and to be relieved of his command and responsibility.

The word was that Thomas was at Gatehouse-of-Fleet, westwards a further score of miles, near where he had landed from Ireland, and said to be gathering his own army. Patrick reckoned that dealing with this threat was his first priority, coping with the mutinous and dispersed occupation force able to wait. He was concerned to get over to this Gatehouse, across difficult country, he was informed, before any large enemy force was mustered. Fortunately some of the Tongland monks had come to tell of their ordeal to the bishop and abbot and, Tongland being about midway between Threave and Gatehouse, they offered to act as guides. So Patrick left Buchan in charge by the Dee, and with two of the monks leading, rode on through the night, slow and testing as this was in darkness, by Ringford, not far from the devastated priory, and Twynholm and the hill-track by Muiryard. With the grey, wet dawn, weary and jaded as they were, they managed to descend on the Galwegian camp by the Water of Fleet, a sleeping camp, in total surprise.

What followed could not be called a battle, the enemy unable to defend themselves in any organised fashion, indeed Thomas himself captured in his tent, unarmed, although Gilrod effected his escape. Some individuals fought bravely enough, but were overwhelmed by numbers and unpreparedness. Patrick was not particularly proud of this feat, although he was of their night-time advance through that testing country after a long day's riding.

The Bastard was a burly young man, quite good-looking save for a cast in one eye. Scowling, he kept his views on the situation to himself as he was led away under strong guard.

The Galwegians' camp provided the victors with a fair amount of food and drink, so they settled down there, with such prisoners as they had taken, for much needed rest and refreshment, guards stationed.

What to do with Thomas? Some of the lords thought that he ought to be hanged there and then for treason, thus ending any possibility of further trouble over his claims to Galloway. But Patrick would not have this. Any such decision would have to be taken by the king himself; and he doubted very much whether Alexander would so choose. They must keep the man prisoner until the royal will was known, and somewhere sufficiently secure where no attempts at rescue could be made, well away from this Galloway, possibly in Edinburgh's rock-top fortress. They would wait another day or two at Threave to see if any further uprising eventuated, with this Gilrod still unfortunately at large. Would he attempt to rescue Thomas? It seemed unlikely that at short notice he could hope to raise another force large enough to challenge the five thousand of their own array.

In the morning, then, it was back to Threave, Patrick sending out some of the local Tongland monks, as the best enquirers, to try to discover the overall situation with the Galwegians, especially, if possible, where Gilrod might be.

In the event, they did not have to wait for more than the one day at Threave, for two monks arrived there from the Fleet estuary to announce that Gilrod had in fact sailed for Ireland from Ardwell within hours of the surprise attack, a very hasty departure. So there was no one of sufficient authority to muster and lead Galloway into renewed state of war meantime, whatever the future might hold. Patrick decided that a return to Roxburgh would be in order, taking Thomas with them.

It took another three winter days for their journey; and on arrival it was to find Alexander already back there, to the surprise of all. He and his queen had returned so promptly, not only on account of the Galloway situation, but because Joanna had announced that she thought that she might be with child, and wished to be at home as soon as possible in the circumstances.

The news was, of course, of great interest and satisfaction to all at court. Scotland could be going to regain an heir to the throne before long, other than the far-out Bruce of Annandale.

As to the Bastard Thomas, Alexander would not hear of execution. Yes, he would confine the man in Edinburgh Castle meantime. And he had decided to get in touch with the three daughters of the late Lord Alan and their English husbands, the lawful inheritors of the lordship, to see whether they would agree to a joint takeover of the province, with his help if need be, on condition of promised firm support of the royal authority there.

The Steward was sent south to contact these three, Devorgilla and John de Baliol at Barnard Castle, in Durham; Helen and Roger de Quincy, Earl of Winchester, in Hampshire; and Christiana's Sir William de Fortibus, Count d'Aumale and Lord of Holderness in Yorkshire; this quite a major mission. Patrick might have been sent, but with the Galloway situation still doubtful, the Constable's presence might well be called for in Scotland.

The king was installing his own representatives to govern Galloway – Sir Thomas Randolph of Nithsdale to be justiciar and sheriff of East Galloway and Dumfriesshire, and Comyn, Earl of Buchan, based on Wigtown, in the west – when, by a strange coincidence, another death, with three sisters as heiresses, occurred, this in England. John the Scot, Earl of Huntingdon and Chester, suddenly died; and since he was in fact heir-male to the Scots throne, this presented problems, he leaving no male heir. Alexander therefore claimed the Huntingdon earldom, with its wide lands in so many English counties, as of right, leaving the Chester earldom to be divided or fought for by the sisters and their husbands. So a messenger had to be sent promptly to the Steward, still in England, to seek to sort out this matter also, while he was there, to inform King Henry as to Alexander's assumption of the Huntingdon lands.

While this situation was preoccupying much of the

monarch's mind, a still more personal one was more prominent. This was the state of the young queen's health. Joanna had thought that she was with child; but her monthly woman's cycle having restarted, this proved to be not the case. Pains however continued, with bleeding, and her lively nature was inevitably much affected. Alexander was worried, for he had grown very fond of her. Patrick and Phemia were also concerned, for Joanna had become their friend.

When eventually the Steward returned from his long and difficult mission in England, he brought tidings both good and bad. The Galloway sisters and their husbands had agreed to take over and divide the province between them, and to pay due allegiance therefor to the King of Scots. But the Huntingdon situation was less good, indeed highly unsatisfactory. Whether at the Plantagenet's instigation or otherwise, the Earl John's three sisters promptly sold all the lands of the earldom to King Henry, claiming their right to do so under English law, dividing the proceeds amongst them, while not claiming the title of earl. This, needless to say, grievously worried Alexander. Huntingdon had come to the Scots crown by the marriage of its heiress well over a century before, its *sole* heiress, to King David of pious memory. The three Scots monarchs since, Malcolm the Fourth, William the Lion and now Alexander, had paid fealty to the Kings of England for these broad lands, the holders of the actual earldom only, as it were, tenants-in-chief. The three sisters had no right to sell the lands, however much Henry may have coveted them. So here was trouble indeed. The rents and revenues in eleven English counties were one of the main sources of Alexander's personal wealth; he could not afford just to let this go. The Steward had made this point very clear to all concerned, but had not been offered any satisfaction.

Alexander, therefore, was faced with a serious dilemma. He desired to keep good relations with his brother-in-law Henry, as well as between the two kingdoms; but he needed those Huntingdon revenues. And there was now

297

no heir-male to his throne, leaving Bruce of Annandale heir-presumptive. He decided to demand a meeting with Henry to amend this situation. The Steward would go back south, but supported this time by Patrick. Also an important churchman, Bishop David de Bernham of Dunkeld. This cleric was notable in a number of ways, succeeding William de Home as High Chamberlain. He was a very able man. The Primate, old Bishop William of St Andrews, had departed this life; and his archdeacon, prior and canons at St Andrews nominated their own choice to succeed him, one Geoffrey, Precentor of Glasgow and Canon of Scone. However, Alexander wanted this de Bernham, who had founded four churches, to be Primate, and had petitioned the Pope to have him appointed. So, after this visit to the English court, Bishop David would go on to the Vatican, hopefully to be consecrated Bishop of St Andrews and Primate of the Scots Church.

It was one more errand for Patrick, which he could well have done without. But he recognised its importance for his friend, and if he could help, he must.

The three of them, with a small escort, made good time on their road, Walter the Steward, despite his years an excellent horseman, and de Bernham no hold-up. They learned that Henry was at Windsor, and so were able to avoid London, completing the long journey in four hard-riding days.

Henry received them well enough, and they met his queen, Eleanor of Provence who struck them as a quite formidable and strong-minded young woman. No actual concessions were made to the envoys, but Henry did agree to meet Alexander. He suggested at Doncaster, in one month's time, approximately halfway between them.

He asked after his sister, and was much concerned to hear of her health problems. He asked whether she was receiving all possible medical attention, and offered to send up two of his own physicians to treat her. The bishop assured that Holy Church had sufficient able leeches and chirurgeons in Scotland, who were doing all that could be done for the queen. Her brother looked doubtful, presumably regarding the Scots as somehow inferior in such matters, as in others.

The visitors did not linger long at Windsor. At least they had arranged the necessary meeting of the monarchs.

Alexander proved grateful. He informed Patrick that he had decided to initiate a new command to improve land use in the realm, having long been aware of the much terrain which went untended and unproductive in the land. The churchmen, with their lands, were better at this; but the nobility looked on the land in general as mainly suitable for hunting and hawking over. His scheme was for not only tenant-farmers and the like, but everyone who occupied even a few acres of ground to make fullest use of it, the lords and lairds to see that they did, by royal command. The best way to deal with this, he declared, was to assess the possibilities of the terrain by the number of milk cows kept thereon. Sheep normally were kept on the hills and moors, where the land was unsuitable for improvement anyway. But any man with even four cows was to clear, drain, remove stones and make fit for tillage such of his land as was capable of being ploughed and sown. And if it could not be worked by oxen, owned or borrowed, then the tenant had to do it with his own hands and muscles, in accordance with Holy Writ which said that every man, by his own wit and wisdom, must support himself and those dependent upon him. The realm should greatly benefit thereby, no?

Patrick, considering, had a somewhat guilty feeling that his own earldom might be failing in this respect. The sheep-strewn Lammermuirs were admittedly not suitable for such improvement, but in the fertile Merse there could well be quite large areas not being made use of to the full. He and his father had sought to increase prosperity by trade, but this of land development they had not tackled. He promised to see what could be done.

The time for the visit to Doncaster, in the West Riding of Yorkshire, to meet the Plantagenet duly arrived, and

Alexander took with him the trio who had been his envoys to Windsor. Bishop David de Bernham had just arrived back from Rome, consecrated as Primate. But on reaching the town it was to encounter disappointment. Henry was not there. He had sent his apologies, saying that problems of state had detained him in the south; but he had ordered Walter de Gray, Archbishop of York, John de Lacy, Earl of Lincoln and Sir William de Raleigh, Treasurer of Exeter, to represent him, with his clear instructions. Also the papal legate Otho, who could help in acting as arbiter if such was required.

This was unfortunate indeed, for these representatives, however high placed, could not act in the same way as the monarch himself, and must be limited in negotiations and unable, as it were, to bargain and concede beyond the royal instructions. Whether the Pope's representative would be of any help was doubtful.

Once discussion started it was quickly evident that no yielding up of the Huntingdon lands was being considered by Henry. He had bought them, and they were now his property. The earldom itself could remain with the Scots crown; but that was a mere title, and carried with it none of the revenues, so needful to Alexander. Henry's proposed concession was to do with the ancient Scots claim to Cumberland and Northumberland. Not that he was pre-pared to cede these to Scotland, but that he would grant to Alexander personally two hundred librates of land therein, with the rents and revenues, such lands to be selected by a commission of two Scots and two English lords or knights, with the guidance and advice of a dozen good men and true of the two counties, meeting at Carlisle and then traversing the terrain and interviewing the landholders involved, to ensure helpful co-operation. Such lands would be held by the King of Scots in fealty to the King of England.

This, of course, was a very inadequate compensation for the lost Huntingdon properties, however convenient as to situation and links with the past. Alexander said so, in no uncertain terms. But his fears that the English envoys were not in any position to bargain or trade benefits was amply proven. Not that the Scots had anything much to trade, in the circumstances. It was all something of a wasted effort and journey. The papal representative's arbitrating skills were conspicuous by their absence.

Only the one worthwhile development eventuated. There had been considerable losses to Scotland since Alan of Galloway's death by shipping being attacked in the Irish Sea by English pirates, and seemingly highborn ones, the de Maresco brothers, these presumably kin to the late Richard de Maresco, Prince-Bishop of Durham. Protests about this had fallen on deaf ears hitherto, but now Henry's envoys agreed to have a stop put to this, and some compensation paid.

That was as far as the proceedings went. Agreeing to appoint the two negotiators for the Cumberland-North-umberland survey at Carlisle, the Scots departed, less than happy. Alexander felt that he had been let down by Henry, not only on the matter of the lands and revenues but by not sending him advance notice about not being present at Doncaster. It was something of a humiliation for a monarch to have to attend in person at a delegation of subjects without their own king.

Patrick sympathised.

29

The legate Otho paid a visit to Scotland that summer to ensure that the Precentor Geoffrey, Canon of Scone, who had been denied the bishopric of St Andrews and the primacy, should be installed in his successful rival's stead as Bishop of Dunkeld, thus restoring concord in the Scottish Church. While at Roxburgh, Otho expressed concern over Queen Joanna's health. He said that King Henry was worried about this, fond of his sister, and was urging that she should come down to London to be examined by the various expert physicians and chirurgeons there, such superior, it was assumed even by the legate, to any to be found in Scotland.

Alexander was non-committal; but he was in fact seriously anxious over his young wife's state.

The negotiations for the Cumberland–Northumberland deal had reached stalemate, little progress made, disagreement over various areas and with sundry landowners seemingly unsurmountable. Patrick was sent to Carlisle to try to smooth out the difficulties, but to no good effect. The English representatives dug in their heels; and it was notable that the lands they were prepared to offer were almost always the least worthy and profitable, producing the poorest returns. And since the entire object of the exercise was to compensate in some measure for the loss of the Huntingdon revenues, this was not to be borne. In the circumstances, the age-old claims to these two counties adjacent to Scotland were not to be given up, Henry must be told.

And there were other sources of disagreement between the two realms. Not only had English piracy not ceased in the Irish Sea, but the promised compensation was not forthcoming. Also Walter, Bishop of Galloway had died, and the new Primate de Bernham was appointing one Odo, Abbot of Holywood, to the see, when the Archbishop of York objected, and consecrated Gilbert, Abbot of Glenluce and Master of Novices, this at York itself, declaring that he had the right as metropolitan so to do, from centuries-old prerogative. The legate Otho's preference for England meant that this might well prove to be supported by the Vatican. All this worried Alexander, and he decided that another meeting, in person this time, with his brother-in-law was necessary, no mere representations sufficing. He sent a letter to the Plantagenet to that effect.

He got a surprisingly prompt response to this request, and surprising in more than its celerity. For Henry proposed that they meet at York in six weeks' time to settle all difficulties; and not only themselves but their wives also. He would bring up some of his best physicians to examine his sister's condition and hopefully prescribe for her betterment.

Alexander could not but agree to this, his anxiety over Joanna's continuing ailment contributing. He would have preferred the meeting to be elsewhere than at York, with this of the Galloway bishopric to discuss, and the archbishop their host presumably; but at least with Queen Eleanor to be there, no failure to put in an appearance by Henry was likely. He sent his consent.

In the meantime, de Bernham had to postpone his installation of Abbot Odo. And Patrick and the Steward were sent to the troublesome province of Galloway to help Sir John de Baliol and his wife Devorgilla, who had arrived there from England, to take over the authority. The other two sisters and their spouses were less eager, it seemed.

It was strange to be back at Threave Castle again on a very different mission than the previous one, actually to be rowed over to the island escorted by Baliol himself, in welcome.

The Lady Devorgilla proved to be possibly the most beautiful woman that Patrick had ever seen, tall, shapely and fair, of proud bearing but amiable disposition, markedly different from her father. She made an excellent hostess, and was glad of advice as to the running of the lordship, fairly clearly not going to leave it all to her husband. She said she thought that there ought to be little opposition amongst the folk to the new authority, they having had enough of wars and fighting. Her half-brother Thomas she was sure would have learned his lesson; and she pleaded that he might be released from his imprisonment in Edinburgh Castle. She and her husband would hold him secure at Barnard Castle, the Baliol seat, if King Alexander would so agree.

They spent a week with the couple, riding around the province and appreciating its qualities, places of interest and scenery in a way that had not been possible before with military matters on their minds. They discerned no serious problems likely to face the new regime, save the question as to the division of authority should the other two sisters come to claim their share of the lordship. Devorgilla thought that there ought to be little difficulty there, believing that Helen and Margaret and their husbands, having large lands and responsibilities in England, and indeed in France, at Aumale, would be well content to leave the actual running of Galloway to her and her John, while receiving their due share of the revenues.

The visitors left Threave having made new friends.

Alexander was quite happy to release the Bastard Thomas into the assured care of the Baliols.

The journey to York with the ailing Joanna had to be much slower than usual, inevitably. With her internal bleeding she could no longer ride for any distance, so a litter slung between two horses was contrived for her. And since she required considerable attention, Phemia volunteered to go with her as lady-in-waiting, to Patrick's satisfaction. Their children were now old enough to be left for more lengthy periods, Elizabeth Mary indeed becoming quite an independent and capable youngster, more obviously so than her quiet and reserved brother Pate.

Forty miles in a day was as much as they could cover in these circumstances so that it took them five days, spending one of the nights at Barnard Castle, a fine place of considerable strength, which Alexander acceded would be a suitable house of detention for the Bastard Thomas.

They found that Henry's party had arrived at York the day before. The royal meeting proved to be quite dramatic, Henry obviously most moved to see the change in his sister. The two queens had never met before, and the somewhat masterful Eleanor quickly took charge of Joanna. It became apparent that it was largely on her initiative that the three physicians had been brought to York. Alexander was concerned that these would not practise the favoured remedy of bleeding on his wife, who was losing more than sufficient blood already; but he was assured that this was not the intention. Treatment by purges, and the application of herbal salves, lotions and ointments, with careful dieting, was the agreed appropriate programme, an ongoing process it seemed. After quite prolonged examination it was urged, with Eleanor's strong backing, that the patient should return with them to London for treatment over a period which might well demand weeks. This, needless to say, had Alexander in a quandary, and asking whether it would not be possible for the physicians, or at least one of them, to come back to Scotland with them instead? But this was negatived, Eleanor vehemently backing Henry over it all; in fact the impression given was that his queen was the moving spirit in it all.

As to the problems and difficulties that had been the root cause for this meeting, Henry proved to be, at least in word, amenable. He declared that he had dismissed his two representatives on the Carlisle commission and appointed others, with his clear instructions as to a fair and reasonable outcome of the survey, agreeing that this assessment must not be allowed to hang fire as had the borderline exercise of those years before – the which he wished to be renewed hereafter as a matter of some urgency, the present Debateable Land situation being highly unsatisfactory and leading to constant lawlessness. Did not Alexander agree?

As to the piracy, he had taken strong steps to see that this was ended and the perpetrators punished; and he had in fact brought generous compensation moneys with him to York.

The matter of the Archbishop of York's appointment to the see of Galloway was the most controversial aspect of the assembly, with the legate Otho declaring Vatican support for this. Alexander and de Bernham claimed that since none could deny that Galloway was part of Scotland and had never been attached to England, the Primate of the Scottish Church must have the right to nominate its bishops. The archbishop asserted that this area had been converted to Christianity by St Ninian from Cumberland, across the Solway Firth, and had ever since been a pendicle of the Church of England, under York. Moreover, as metropolitan, his own position was undoubtedly senior to that of the Bishop of St Andrews, as all others in Scotland, so his decision must stand. Henry himself took no part in this controversy, but with the Pope's representative backing York, the Scots were in a no-win situation, however protestingly so. They had to be content with the archbishop reminding them that it was a Scot, Gilbert, Abbot of Glenluce, whom he had appointed to the see, when he could have chosen otherwise.

Three days of this admixture of negotiations and family and health concerns, and one more treaty was signed and sealed. It was farewells, very moving ones. It was out of the question for Alexander to consider going south with his wife. He could not be away from his kingdom for weeks, it was recognised; and if this treatment was going to save her from becoming a chronic invalid, it must be given the chance so to do. But it all made it a sad and emotional parting, for, although the pair had never actually been in love, they had grown fond of each other. It was distressing for Phemia and Patrick also, these two at least by no means convinced that this advised remedy and course for their friend was necessarily so much better than any that she could have in Scotland, whatever Queen Eleanor's assertions. But Joanna herself seemed content to go along with it, and her husband accepting the situation, who were they to object?

So the parting took place, amidst much well-wishing, and the two royal trains headed off north and south.

30

One of the causes for Alexander heading back to Scotland in some haste was the unexpected news that Olaf the Morsel, King of Man, had suddenly died, leaving an only son aged only fourteen years, Harold; and the word was that Hakon of Norway had taken this youngster as it were under his wing and indeed promptly sent for him to join him at his Norse Bergen. This in itself was not ill tidings, but its effect on the Isles and West Highlands generally could be the cause of trouble. Hakon appeared to have got over the problems at home that had been preoccupying him, and this move anent young Harold of Man could well mean that he was again turning his roving eye on the Hebrides and the Highland seaboard in general, allegedly aiding the new young King of Man to establish himself, but in reality to take it all over himself as an appendage of Norway. This was bound to alarm Ranald of the Isles, also Duncan Campbell of Lochawe and Lochfyne, and they were seeking Alexander's aid.

Little as the king sought any such Highland involvement at this stage, he felt that he had to make some gesture. The difficulty up in those parts, was always the same: shipping. Scotland had no real navy; plenty of merchant ships, yes, but these were slow and heavy compared with the Norse and Islesmen's longships and birlinns; and the West Highland seaboard, with its innumerable sea lochs and literally thousands of isles and islets, was quite unsuitable for merchanters and indeed for their shipmen. And horsed armies were at an enormous disadvantage in such conditions.

So there was not very much that Alexander could do, to

effect, other than make some mere token of his concern and support. He sometimes wondered whether the Highlands and Isles were worth claiming as part of his kingdom, vast territories as they were, their clans utterly unruly and providing little or no benefit to the rest of the nation. But this was where the most ancient royal line in all Christendom had come from, and he could by no means abandon his roots.

Some demonstration by the monarch must be made, in this situation, therefore, however superficial it might be, symbolic; some sort of fleet once again assembled at Dumbarton, the Steward and Lennox inevitably involved and, of course, the High Constable. It might be sufficient to give Hakon pause, and to reassure the Islesmen and the Campbell.

The gathering of the necessary vessels took some time, and it was well into October before any start could be made. One thousand men were not difficult to muster; more could not be carried in the available ships, so no major contribution was demanded from Dunbar and the Merse.

Over a score of ships of various types and sizes looked impressive enough, flying the lion rampant and saltire banners, sailing down Clyde and up the Kyles of Bute; but none aboard esteemed the expedition as more than a token flourish, an indication that the King of Scots was concerned. So, once again, something of a holiday atmosphere prevailed, unsuitable as this might be. Up long Loch Fyne they tacked, eventually to draw in and land at Tarbert, which they knew so well, there to await Duncan Campbell. Undoubtedly he would swiftly be informed of their arrival in his waters.

They did not have long to wait. Campbell birlinns appeared at this Tarbert the very next day, with Duncan and some hundreds of his people, well pleased at the royal presence. When Alexander asked what he could usefully do, in the circumstances, it was to learn that a demonstration in force by the monarch could be valuable, without any actual fighting. The situation was peculiar, in that Ranald MacDonald of the Isles and himself, Campbell, were all but hereditary foes, the former always threatening the Campbell lands. But the greater threat from King Hakon, in the name of the boy Harold, was on a quite different level, worrying them both equally, with a possible Norse takeover of the entire seaboard. So the fact that the King of Scots was concerned and prepared to combat anything such was highly important and must be made clear to Hakon. What Duncan suggested was a sort of tour of the coastline and islands, showing the royal standard, as it were. The word would indubitably get to Norway and hopefully give him pause. With winter approaching, no Norse sea-going invasion was likely until spring, so this present excursion would serve to give the Viking due warning.

Alexander, with Patrick, the Steward and Lennox, was somewhat relieved to learn that this was all that was required of him meantime.

The proposal was that they, with the Campbell birlinns, should sail back down Loch Fyne and into the Kilbrandon Sound, and so round the Mull of Kintyre into the Sea of the Hebrides. Then up to the Isle of Islay, where Ranald had his headquarters, call on him there and enlist his co-operation if possible. Then on and circle the other major isles and probe into the major sea lochs, right to Skye, before crossing the Minch to the Outer Hebrides, this for a demonstration along those far coasts before a return south. That ought to make it very evident that the King of Scots was alert to any threat to his kingdom, also to any co-operation from Norse-held islands. It would take some time, admittedly, but unless the weather broke down unseasonably it could all make for a quite pleasant voyage, October being a fairly good month for these parts. There should be no difficulty in gaining supplies of food and drink en route from chieftains and islanders.

Alexander wondered whether all their thousand men

were necessary for this, but was assured that they would all help to convey the desired message.

So in the morning a move was made down-loch, birlinns both ahead and astern of the king's ships, Kintyre flanking them on the west, first Cowal and then mountainous Arran on the east, the holiday feeling nowise dissipated.

After fifty miles of this, they rounded the dramatic Mull of Kintyre and quickly became aware of the different conditions, the ships starting to heave and roll in the swell of the open ocean. But now that they turned to head northwards, the prevailing south-west winds helped to fill the sails without so much tacking required and speeded them on their way. They passed the comparatively modest Isle of Gigha, this without stopping.

It seemed strange, after a whole day's sailing, to put into West Loch Tarbert for the night, to end up little over a mile away from where they had started, with well over one hundred miles covered in the interim. But that was the way of things on this western seaboard. All could now stretch their legs and seek food, some even finding lodging and feminine comfort.

In the morning they could see Islay ahead of them, perhaps the strangest of the Inner Hebridean islands in that, although large, it had no mountains, and because of this had more fertile land and much greater population. Here Somerled's descendants made the seat of their great domains, however many castles and fortlets they had to the north and west. The very different Isle of Jura, with its soaring, shapely peaks known as the Paps, was nearby, and the contrast notable.

The Campbell led the fleet up the east side of Islay close to this Jura, seeking the haven of Askaig, this a convenient landing-place for a visit to the Lord of the Isles' seat. But well before they approached this harbour they were being shadowed by ever growing numbers of longships and birlinns, their coming not going unobserved nor ignored. Whether the lion rampant and saltire banners reassured the Islaymen was not to be known.

Landing at this Askaig, although a deal more impressed by the exciting prospect of neighbouring Jura, the king and his lords, with Duncan and other Campbell chiefs, leaving most of their people at the ships, commenced their walk up to Loch Finlaggan where, it seemed, they were likely to find Ranald of the Isles, nearly three miles inland. In fact they did not have to walk a full mile before they saw ahead of them a large company of men approaching, with the Galley of the Isles standard flapping above the leading ranks, bagpipes playing.

Ranald MacDonald proved to be a fine-looking man of early middle years, with a great head of tawny hair, clad in tartans. He halted to wait for the new arrivals to come to him.

"Ranald mac Donald mac Ranald mac Somerled, I, Duncan mac Gillespick mac Colin mac Duncan mac Gillespick, come to bring you, Alexander, by the Grace of God, King of Scots," the Campbell called. "His Grace honours us all by his royal presence and goodwill."

The other eyed the speaker in no very friendly fashion, but searched the other visitors' faces to discover which was the king, for Alexander wore no especial garb nor symbol of his status. The monarch stepped forward then.

"My lord of the Isles," he said, "Greetings! I have heard much of you, and wish you well."

"Sire, your servant, just!" Anything less like a servant than this man would have been hard to imagine. "What brings my lord king to Islay, at all?"

"I sent His Grace the word that we, yourself and my people, are threatened by the King of Norway who, in the name of the young ruler of Man, is said to seek to take over our domains," Duncan announced. "His Grace has come in person, with these his lords, to demonstrate his favour and to assure us of his aid."

"So-o-o!" Ranald said, after a slight pause. "Here is an occasion, just! My lord king, I, Ranald, welcome you to the Isles. As to all my islands and lands." He swept a plaided arm in a wide gesture. "Come, you!" he invited, all but commanded, and waved over to his pipers. These, half a dozen of them, promptly puffed into their blowpipes, squeezed their bean-shaped tartan bags, and after a cater-wauling of wails and groans, rallied into a fiercely rousing but tuneful march, sufficiently loud to drown any converse by those nearby. All the Islay party turned about, and with Ranald in the lead marched off back whence they had come, leaving the visitors to follow on, if so they would. Duncan Campbell shrugged, and gestured forward to the monarch, who, smiling at Patrick and the Steward, readily walked on at the tail of all the MacDonalds.

Thus they were introduced to the Isles.

They had quite a tramp of it for men more accustomed to horse-riding than to foot-walking, up a rising moorland track and past a cluster of thatch-roofed cothouses sur-rounding a stone chapel on a little mound, this with a decorated standing stone rising close by, folk here watch-ing all with interest, and waving to their chief. This, Duncan said – and he had to shout – was the village of Keills.

On they strode, the pipers at least helping to keep them pacing in a sort of marching time, Ranald never so much as glancing back to see that his sovereign was duly following on. Their road rose steadily until they reached a kind of minor pass, where the view opened widely before them, westwards, over rolling moors and grasslands and shining stretches of water, inland and sea lochs, mile upon mile, with some hills on their left. They swung off right-handed soon, and there before them lay, quite near at hand, a long and fairly narrow loch, over a mile of it, amongst fairly gentle slopes. At its north end were two islets, one of fair size, the other small, the larger occupied by a tall castle with square keep and round angle towers linked by curtain walls; the smaller also built upon, seemingly a chapel. Down to the shore they all trudged, Alexander chuckling at it all, mere appendages as the new arrivals appeared to be.

When they got to the water's edge, just opposite the

castle isle, there was no pause in the procession. Straight into the loch the pipers led them, although there were boats moored nearby. Astonished, the southern visitors hesitated about following on, but were informed by the Campbell that this was normal procedure and that there was an underwater causeway of stone only inches below the surface, which zigzagged over the two-hundred yards or so gap to the island. Necessarily strung out now, for the causeway was not wide, they were warned, perhaps unnecessarily, to watch their steps and follow exactly those in front, for the zigzags were sharp and not readily seen in the disturbance, and they could be into deep water at either side. These Islesmen apparently cared nothing for wet feet and legs, if this was the usual access to the castle. How their womenfolk looked on this process was a matter for debate; presumably they just hitched up their skirts and splashed over.

The Lowlanders, however doubtful about walking through water, could scarcely stop to remove their footgear. Led by the monarch, heads ashake, they followed on, raising their feet higher, at first, than those in front, until they perceived that this made for more splashing than steady normal walking. They heedfully watched their immediate precursors, anxious about those sudden twists and turns.

With the pipers now drawn up on the islet's bank before the gatehouse, and playing the others over, they thankfully reached dry land again. Ranald had marched right on under the gatehouse arch without pausing, and it was only when the rest of them were into the courtyard, flanked by lesser buildings against the curtain walling, that he turned and stood at the keep doorway, to welcome them all formally into his house, in hospitable flourish now, announcing that refreshment awaited them upstairs.

In the hall above, the refreshment consisted of great quantities of liquor, the strong Highland water of life, *uisge-beatha*, which the Campbell assured was excellent for countering cold, wet feet. There three women greeted them graciously, the Lady Seona and her two daughters, Marsala and Morag, all bearing themselves well and seeming nowise off-put by this invasion, nor in awe of their guests. A simple meal would be ready for them shortly, they were informed, although later, in the evening, a full repast would be presented.

It was all a new experience for Alexander, for he was treated no differently from the other guests, courteously enough as that might be. He had to remind himself that these MacDonalds looked upon themselves as *kings* of the Isles, whatever their style of lords, as the great Somerled had done, so they could see this monarch as something of an equal.

Alexander, however, far from emphasising superiority, did indicate his authority in that, much as he appreciated the kind welcome and hospitality, he could not burden his hosts with their presence for long. It was only noonday as yet, and they had a great circuit of isles and territories to cover; and he could not be away from his duties in the south for overlong. Therefore, please, some mere modest provision now, to complement the liquor, and they would be on their way back to their ships.

The ladies accepted this decision with bows; but Ranald questioned it. Did this mean that a fleet of his longships was required forthwith, he wondered, to accompany the others? The king looked at Duncan Campbell, who declared that the presence of the Lord of the Isles' ships would be advantageous, but that only a token squadron would serve well enough. Ranald waved that away imperiously, and strode off, presumably to organise a full-scale muster of the Isles fleet, or at least as many vessels as could be assembled at short notice, nothing less than that suitable for the lordship.

So, without seeing more of the Lord of the Isles meantime, the guests presently took their leave, and went splashing back across the causeway, carefully led by a guide who knew the zigs and zags, to walk down to Askaig and the ships. Duncan said that there was no need to wait for the Isles longships; these could sail and be rowed at twice the speed of the king's merchanters, and would soon catch up.

Discussing this great-grandson of Somerled, they duly reached the harbour and embarked.

They set sail again up the sound, the scenery on the east, Jura, side so much more challenging than on the west. That island was long, almost thirty miles, and but little populated seemingly. At its northern tip, the newcomers, alarmed by the roaring noise, were told that the Gulf of Corryvreckan, which separated it from the smaller isle of Scarba, held the most dangerous whirlpool in all the Hebridean Sea, grave of craft innumerable, and producing this menacing sound.

They did not have to avoid this, however, for they were heading due north for Mull before swinging east for the Firth of Lorne, this into the mainland. Here, off Scarba, Ranald's fleet caught up with them, no fewer than forty longships and birlinns, all sporting square sails with the Galley of the Isles painted on the canvas, lengthy oars sweeping, and pipers playing in almost every bow. There was to be no doubt about identities hereafter.

Off the south coast of Mull, a huge island, and mountainous, Alexander knew sufficient of his ancestors' origins to be aware that the sacred Isle of Iona was somewhere near here, and asked whether they could sail past it. Campbell, while admitting that this was somewhat out of their way, conceded that the monarch's wishes must be met, and swung the fleet, now amounting to over one hundred vessels, in a westerly direction, to round the long peninsula of the Ross of Mull, so that they could circle round the quite small island of St Columba behind, a place as lovely as it was important, the shrine of Scotland's story. They saw the abbey, near the eastern shore, and could identify Tor Abb where the missionary saint built his humble cell, and the Reilig Oran, where so many kings were buried. How many of his distant ancestors lay there? Alexander wondered.

Circling the island in a lengthy procession, those pipes still playing, they made now for the wide mouth of the Firth of Lorne. It was not intended to go far up this, which could lead right into the heart of the Highlands, and take all day, but to sail round the small but significant isle of Kerrera to make their presence known at the Oban, on the mainland, a centre of influence for a great area. Then back, and up the twenty-five miles of the Sound of Mull to the Sea of the Hebrides again.

This was all achieved, and they were able to anchor for the night in the bay below another of Ranald's many castles, Mingary, on the peninsula of Ardnamurchan, the most westerly point of all mainland Scotland. More hospitality was provided for Alexander and the leadership in the castle. The king was a little concerned that this show of strength was going to develop into a mere procession round the Lord of the Isles's strongholds.

In the morning, the view opening before them was breathtaking, all the proud display of the Inner Hebrides, seemingly to all infinity, from nearby Coll and beyond to low Tiree, known as the Garden of the Isles, then on to Muck and Eigg, the tremendous peaks of Rhum in the background, with further, much further away, the blue silhouette that was Skye, with lesser isles between, all set in the glittering sea. None from the Lowlands had ever seen nor imagined the like, and were almost beyond words in wonder, Alexander admitting to Patrick that he could scarcely believe that this was all part of his realm.

Round and amongst this plethora of islands they sailed, gazing, Ranald's own longship now doing the leading, with not only the pipers playing but gongs beating time for the steady sweep of hundreds of long oars, with panting chanting from the rowers. The king's merchant ships, and even Campbell's birlinns, seemed exceedingly dull and ordinary by comparison. Whether all this was achieving the object of the exercise, spreading the message of the King of Scots' warning to the Norsemen, was another matter.

They rounded Tiree, admired the mighty cliffs of Eigg with its single pointed Sgurr, stared at the serried peaks of Rhum, each with its peculiar halo of white cloud, so strange to see in an otherwise cloudless sky, and were told that these were nearly always there, sometimes just above the tops, more often, as now, crowning the summits themselves, why no one knew. And by evening they were making for Skye, its jagged Cuillin Mountains like the bared teeth of the largest island of all, told of the legendary Fell Hound of the druids, chief of the demons who occupied those Cuillin Mountains, who bayed at night and could brew storms most terrible. No storms on this occasion, and entering the Sound of Sleat they sailed up as far as the Castle of Knock, on its own bay, where they were well provided for and heard more of Cuchulain and the Fell Hound.

It was agreed that, on the morrow, after some navigation of the dangerous waters of this Skye, they should strike out over the Minch, some thirty miles, to Lewis of the Outer Hebrides. This lengthy chain of islands, almost one hundred miles of them, were very largely Norse-held, although Ranald claimed them as his. It was explained that, from this Lewis southwards, by Harris, North and South Uist, Benbecula, Eriskay, Barra, Vatersay and Mingulay, with many lesser isles, had long been settled by the Vikings; but most there had no wish to come under the rule of King Hakon, much preferring their own independence, sometimes paying lip-service to the Lord of the Isles, but only that and never to the King of Scots. A sail down the length of these would do no harm and possibly convince some of the Norsemen that they would be better allied to Ranald, and in theory King Alexander, than to Hakon.

In the morning, then, it was due west for them, across open sea, with the distant barrier of the Long Island, as it was called, beckoning them on. There was no suggestion that they should halt or even land there, Alexander beginning to be worried about the time he was absent from his court and responsibilities there, with so much that might be demanding his attention; they would merely show a presence, sail down from north to south the hundred miles, close enough inshore for their respective banners to be seen and noted, and then return to Islay and Kintyre.

This they did, and it proved to be a highly rewarding exercise for the southern passengers, whatever impression it made on the Outer Hebridean residents. The scenery was constantly eye-catching and colourful, however varied, from sheer craggy headlands to serene heights, from dazzling white-sand bays to dark-scarred gulfs, from gleaming waterfalls and deer-haunted corries to seal-bearing skerries, all guarded by myriads of islets. But the visitors did not have to be told that these were dangerous waters, however beautiful, and were warned of down-draughts, overfalls, tide races, and what the Norse called roosts, whirlpools, all caused by channelled winds from the wider ocean beyond and by submerged mountains and valleys of the Minch itself.

It took them all day to cover that prolonged succession of the outermost rampart of Scotland. They drew in for the night at a bay of the southernmost isle, Mingulay, where, for once, there was no castle of Ranald's to offer them provision. He had a hold at Lochmaddy, they were told, much further north, but it was seldom used.

The long sail back to Islay in the morning took them almost another entire day; and, with a blustery wind and rain, the preoccupation with scenery diminished notably. All realised that they had been very fortunate hitherto.

The royal party was able to take advantage of the Lady Seona's hospitality at Finlaggan after all, and found it more than generous, her husband now on familiar terms with Alexander and treating him like some sort of dependent relative, however proudly distant he remained towards Duncan of Lochawe. So they parted on good enough terms next forenoon, and sailed off for Kintyre. At the mull thereof they took leave of the Campbells, with mutual congratulations and thanks. Let them hope that King Hakon was, in due course, impressed and warned.

They were at Dumbarton by nightfall, and spent the evening in Lennox's hilltop fortress, all so very different from their experiences of those two weeks in the Isles.

Picking up their horses next day at the Steward's house of Renfrew, the company found it almost strange to be in the saddle again after all the time on shipboard. What would they find at Roxburgh?

They found sufficiently dire and tragic news. Alexander was a widower.

Joanna had died, despite all the physicians' efforts. She had apparently been buried by the nuns of Tarrant, in Dorsetshire; why there was not disclosed.

Scotland was without a queen. The monarch was not alone in mourning.

Patrick was thankful, on returning to Dunbar, to discover all well there. Phemia already knew of Joanna's passing, such tidings travelling fast and far, mainly by the tongues of begging monks, the friars who ranged the countries for good causes. So young a woman to die! What now?

31

Yuletide over, it was not long before Patrick was summoned to Roxburgh for a meeting. The council was now the more concerned about an heir to the throne. Scotland required a queen. Alexander should remarry. Bruce of Annandale was all very well, but there were others equally close to the royal line, and there could be disharmony, even perhaps civil war, if *he* succeeded.

The king himself was not so eager, Phemia's sister Christian ever nearby to comfort him, unwed, although now a mature woman. But he recognised that monarchs should have wives, and suitably highborn ones, and was prepared to heed his councillors' advice.

Round a table they discussed the possibilities. There seemed to be a dearth of unwed princesses who might be considered. And national policies and alliances had to be balanced with personalities. There was a majority of those present in favour of a French bride. Relations with Henry and England were reasonably good; but alliance with France was always a wise precaution, which could, at need, threaten the English from across the Channel if troubles erupted with Scotland and, of course, vice versa; a traditional concept. A Frenchwoman, then, of worthy standing.

King Louis the Ninth of France was too young to have marriageable daughters, and his sister was already wed. Buchan mentioned Sanchia, sister of Henry's queen, Eleanor of Provence; but most there thought that this would be overmuch like seeking to be all but included in the Plantagenet family, wedding a sister-in-law after a sister; unsuitable, Patrick sgreeing with this.

It was the Steward who suggested Count Ingram de

Coucy's daughter, Marie. De Coucy, one of France's greatest nobles, had married the daughter of Otto, Count of Gelderland in the Low Countries, himself a very powerful magnate, and had two daughters, one married to the Count of Guinnes, this Marie the other. A marriage to her would ally Alexander to important houses, for de Coucy himself was descended from a brother of Louis the Seventh.

All there considered that this suggestion was good, as worthy a match as was likely to be achieved. And since it was the Steward's suggestion, he it was who was delegated to go to France and see the lady, and if she seemed suitable, acceptable to be Queen of Scotland, and her father was agreeable to the proposal, then to make all necessary arrangements. Kings were seldom able to marry wives from choice of looks or personality; hence the frequency of mistresses.

Patrick, listening to the debate, was thankful that it was his father-in-law, not himself, who was selected to go on this mission. He had a sufficiency of tasks and responsibilities to see to in his two earldoms, and was anxious to see not only more of Phemia but of his growing-up family.

As it transpired, however, Alexander had an alternative duty for him presently, and an odd one. The papal legate, Otho, arrived back in Scotland with unexpected instructions from the Vatican. The late Bishop Adam of Caithness, who had been so cruelly slaughtered and burned up there eighteen years before, was now to be elevated to the status of martyr, if not quite saint. Why it had taken all this time for this decision to be made by the Pope was not explained. But it seemed to be some sort of demonstration of papal authority, which was considered to be necessary now and again, in different states and realms of Christendom; and nothing such had been carried out in Scotland for many years. So Otho was to be conducted up to far Caithness, there to perform what was necessary to transform the said dead prelate into a martyr, as it were officially. The legate seemed to assume that the king would himself accompany him thither, but Alexander had other priorities, and delegated the peculiar task to Patrick. That man thought that a churchman, a bishop or abbot, would be much more suitable a substitute; but although Richard, Prior of Melrose was indeed to escort the legate, it seemed that a high officer of state was also necessary; and Patrick had been somewhat involved in the unhappy business all those years ago.

Less than enthusiastically, then, the High Constable and Keeper of the Great Seal took on the responsibility of getting the Vatican's representative three hundred miles to the north-east tip of Scotland for this strange ceremonial. He decided to take young Pate with him as a relief from solely clerical company, and a chance for the youth, now almost a man indeed, to see something of the land without any dangers likely to be encountered. At least they would be assured of excellent hospitality on the way, all Church establishments certain to vie with each other in the entertainment of the Pope's envoy.

This indeed did eventuate, and to a degree never before experienced, by Patrick at least. Otho was no fast rider, and considered forty miles in a day more than sufficient, so that they went from one abbey, priory, monastery or hospice to another, for seven nights, being lavishly provided for at each and all. Never had Patrick eaten so much fine food and taken so little exercise to work it off. If all senior churchmen lived like this, small wonder that so many of them grew portly. The young Master of Dunbar and March wondered whether this was normal in his sire's travels. Admittedly the further north they progressed, the smaller grew the establishments, but the greater the welcoming efforts.

Otho made no very amiable travelling companion, an aloof, silent man, language difficulties not helping. Patrick was thankful to have his son at his side, and left Prior Richard to act the attendant.

North at Inverness, the seat of the earldom of Moray, they swung north-eastwards to reach Ardersier, where a ferry of scows would take them across the narrows of the Moray Firth to what was known as the Black Isle, whereon was the Chanonry, the Bishop of Ross's base, at Fortross. This was going to save them a considerable mileage, these churchmen having their own methods of journeying. The bishop conducted them further north-east still, to a second ferry across the mouth of the Cromarty Firth, at Cromarty itself, to Nigg, sparing them almost sixty miles, and on to Tain, where a third ferry took them across the Dornoch Firth, another great saving, these ferries all manned by the monks and lay brothers, to their own advantage, compared with the travelling of ordinary folk.

Dornoch, the northern terminal here, was the seat of Gilbert, Bishop of Caithness, he who had succeeded Adam, and who was ready for them, having been warned by messengers sent on ahead. He was proud to show off the splendid new cathedral which he had built since his appointment those years before, presumably with the aid of his powerful de Moravia family, near the episcopal palace, and which Otho inspected all but without comment, however fine Patrick esteemed it.

Bishop Gilbert was a strong character, as was required for this troubled diocese, more warrior perhaps than cleric, but friendly enough and less in awe of the legate than had been their other hosts. He himself was going to accompany them on northwards for the remaining ninety-five miles to Halkirk, which he had expected to cover in the one day. Otho declared otherwise, needless to say. So they had to halt for the night at Latheron, on its spectacular coast of cliffs and caves, some of these as long as a quarter of a mile they were told, but where there was only a very modest hospice, which scarcely pleased the legate.

It was inland after that for the remainder of their journey, over the typical, upland Caithness moorlands north-westwards. At Halkirk, eventually, the digging up, from under the stone-slabbed floor of the church, to intoned prayers in Latin by the legate, of the body, or what was left of it, of the departed prelate, was promptly put in

324

hand. The corpse fortunately had been well wrapped in grave-clothes and, after seventeen years, at least not smelling. The remains were then put into a litter, to be slung between two horses, and, the proceedings having taken less than an hour, with no further ado the company remounted and turned on its tracks to head back for Dornoch. It seemed a long way for all these eminent characters to have come for this.

There was no suitable overnight halting-place on the twenty-five miles return before Latheron, so Otho had to pass his longest day's riding, as part of a kind of cortège. Not that any especially solemn atmosphere prevailed, the legate's attitudes being stiffly critical rather than reverential or funereal, the others more or less leaving him to his own thoughts, Patrick and Bishop Gilbert getting on well together and questioning the worthiness of the entire proceedings. Young Pate was bored with all this slow riding.

The return to Dornoch saw rather more formal and impressive observances. A grave had been prepared before the high altar of the new cathedral in their absence, and when all was ready, with the bells from the steeple tolling ponderously, the body was carried in procession before something of a congregation, to the accompaniment of choral chanting, to be deposited in the chancel. There the legate, never one for eloquence, made a brief pronouncement, again in Latin, blessed some holy water and sprinkled this on the corpse's improved grave-clothes, now a handsome chasuble over an alb, with a crossed stole, but all body and features hidden. Then, raised hands heavenward, Otho declared something incomprehensible, presumably informing their Creator that He now had an authentic martyr in his celestial keeping. To a choral accompaniment the elevated one was lowered into the crypt-like grave, benediction pronounced – and that was that.

It seemed to Patrick a long way to have come from Rome to achieve such an end; but perhaps he was lacking in due appreciation and understanding.

325

A notable repast was then provided for all concerned in the palace. And thereat the legate sprang something of a surprise on his host, a not unpleasing one so far as his non-clerical escort was concerned. He announced that his duties at the Vatican called for a much more speedy return than had been this outward journey. He had been away overlong. A ship should be found to take him back to Rome, not all this horse-riding. Bishop Gilbert to see to it.

That prelate had to declare that Dornoch was no port for large sea-going vessels unfortunately. But Inverness was, and might be able to provide a ship. He would take the legate on a small craft from the haven here, to convey him to Inverness, and there would seek to see him installed on some merchanter, which would at least carry him some of the way to his desired destination, probably to France or the Low Countries. The likelihood of finding a ship prepared to go as far as Rome was improbable in the extreme, even for the Pope's representative. But once on the Continent there ought to be craft available for the onward voyage.

Otho seemed less than approving of this programme, but still insisted on making his departure by sea. Patrick, his son and Prior Richard, however, made up for it by their thankfulness to be able to ride on southwards at their own pace and in less exalted company. They would be home in less than half the time taken to come.

Next morning, then, they said farewell to Gilbert of Moravia. They received no thanks from Otho nor any blessing, and departed, the bishop sending one of his monks with them to ensure that they were taken across the various ferries expeditiously, saving them much riding.

They wondered what had been gained by this peculiar expedition. But Pate, Master of Dunbar, had certainly gained in experience.

32

Patrick's arrival at Dunbar thereafter presented him with reminders that all his tasks and problems did not have to be odd and far from home. One, or it could become two, had developed very near at hand.

He, like his father before him, was Justiciar of Lothian amongst his other duties and responsibilities, one which he had never enjoyed, sitting in judgment on his fellow men not being to his taste. Indeed he had thankfully continued with his uncle, Constantine, second son of the fourth earl, as deputy, as his father had done before him. Constantine was a quiet, unassuming, studious man, unwed, whom the family saw but little of although he lived none so far off, in one of their subsidiary castles, Luffness, on the shore of Aberlady Bay some ten miles west of Dunbar. Had it not been for the justiciary appointment he would have developed into something of a recluse. But he had made a good if perhaps over-merciful judge for the eastern areas of Lothian, saving his brother, and later his nephew, much time and unwelcome effort. Now an elderly man, he had fallen ill, Phemia reported. She had visited him. And unfortunately, whether as a result of his incapacity or otherwise, trouble had arisen to disturb the peace, and very local trouble, demanding authoritative action.

Luffness Castle sat at the head of the great bay of Aberlady, and had close by, as castleton and fishing-haven, the little community of Luffnaraw as it was termed locally, really Luffness Row. The fisherfolk thereof shared the open waters of the Firth of Forth, or Scotwater, with other similar groups along the shoreline, such as North Berwick, Cockenzie, Saltpans, Fisherrow and Musselburgh; but they looked upon Aberlady Bay as their own preserve. It was a most notable feature of the firth, some three miles wide at the mouth, where the Peffer Water entered the estuary, and penetrating inland for fully a mile, this enclosing a great area. What was especial about this bay was not only its size but the fact that it was very shallow, indeed drying out at low water, the long and wide sand bar at the mouth effectively serving as a barrier to the tides. So it could provide a vast spread of sand and mudflats, ideal for shellfish and oysters, also ideally attractive to flatfish, flounders and the like. These, lying just below the surface of the sand, at low water, could be speared by wading fishers, a favoured and profitable activity for the Luffnaraw folk, even the women taking a hand, or rather a foot, in this; for barefoot it was possible for the wader to feel the flatfish stirring when trod upon, and the spear jabbed down for a catch, care having to be taken not to spear the said foot itself. Recently, however, this bay area, which had always been looked upon as belonging to Luffness and Luffnaraw, had been invaded by fishers from further west, particularly Cockenzie, these claiming that all the foreshore between high and low water was public property, and that they had every right to dredge for oysters there and to spear flukies, as they called them. This had led to conflict, and unfortunately one Cockenzie man had been struck down by a couple of the locals, his catch taken from him, and sadly he had drowned in one of the saltings pools thereafter. All but war broke out between the two communities, and it became a matter for the justiciar.

So, his Uncle Constantine bedridden, Patrick himself had to officiate. Normally such courts of justice were held at Haddington, the county town; but in this instance, with the folk and the scene at the coast, Patrick decided to hold his enquiry into it at Luffness Castle itself, able to visit and consult his sick uncle at the same time. He took Pate with him, for a different kind of experience.

The castle, founded on the site of a former Pictish fortlet by the second earl a century before, was quite a major hold, very different from Dunbar, set not on any rock-top but on a low promontory at the head of the bay, and so guarded on three sides by the tides and mudflats and the Peffer Water, the remaining flank being protected by a wide water-filled artificial moat. Within this quite large area rose the high curtain walls of a square, with round angle towers at each corner and a keep near the gatehouse, this typical enough of most large castles, where Dunbar was not. It had become distinctly neglected of late years, Constantine being uninterested in defence and having no need for it, he roosting in two or three rooms, with a couple of servants, and leaving the rest more or less abandoned. The name, Luffness, had a strange genesis. A notorious Viking raider, Anlaf the Dane, had captured this Pictish fort four centuries before, and two of his party had fought each other, for some reason unknown, both being killed, one called Lofda. These had been buried beneath the fortlet flooring, and their remains were still underneath the present keep's stones, marked by little crosses – which they scarcely deserved, both being pagans. So Lofda's Ness or headland had become the name, Luffness.

Seeing his uncle in his bed, Patrick was struck by how poorly he looked, thin and halting of voice, clearly unable any more to act deputy justiciar. Younger than the late Cospatrick, he seemed older than his brother had ever appeared. He did, however, say that he had ordered the arrangements for the court hearing, the accusers and the defenders to be present there by noonday.

So presently, in the great hall of the castle, little used these days, Patrick sat on the dais platform, with Pate at his side, and representatives of the two communities there available for consultation; and the two Luffnaraw fishermen were led in by one of the Dunbar notables, another bringing in the Cockenzie accusers. It was then announced that the court was in session and justice would be done, by the justiciar, the lord Earl of Dunbar and March himself.

Patrick recognised that he had a difficult case to hear and judge. For one thing, these Luffness men were his own people and the Cockenzie ones were not. And the matter of the right to fish, dredge or spear in Aberlady Bay was by no means clear-cut. In theory all Scots foreshores between high and low watermark were in the public domain, even though usually proximity to the lands of powerful magnates was accepted as reserved for the folk thereof. But he was anxious to appear as impartial as was seemly, and to avoid trouble with his vassal, Sir Alexander de Seton, the Cockenzie laird.

He made a declaration, first of all, that although this alleged offence had been committed within his own territories, he would seek to make true and fair judgment, and impose suitable punishment if such was found to be required. Then he called upon the accusers to present their case.

It was noteworthy that this was put by the Seton Castle deputy keeper, an indication that the issue was seen as important by its owner, although the laird himself was not in court. Cockenzie was a much larger community than was Luffnaraw, to be sure; and this had its own implications for Patrick. When he required a muster of his manpower, the latter could provide perhaps a score where the former could raise one hundred.

The Seton spokesman declared that Tosh Wright, from Cockenzie, had been spearing flukies one evening in Aberlady Bay, as he had every right to do, when he was approached by the men Matt the Skate and Dod Smaill from Luffnaraw, who said that Wright was stealing their fish, and demanded his catch from him. When he refused to give up the string of flukies he had around his shoulders they grabbed it from him, and as he sought to ward them off, they struck him so sorely that he fell into the shallows. Taking his fish, they left him there without heeding his state. In the morning, Wright's body was washed up on the tide. So it became a case of bloody murder.

Patrick asked whether the accused had a spokesman, and if not what they had to say to this charge?

The man Matt himself replied. He declared that he and

his friend Dod had had no intention of killing this Cock-enzie fisher. He had no right to be spearing in their bay; others of his sort had sought to do this before, and should be taught otherwise. They had taken his ill-gotten catch, and he had lashed out at them as they did so. They had struck back and he had fallen. The water was shallow, barely up to their knees, and he had been in no danger of drowning. They had left him there, to pick himself up. The fact that his body had been found on the shore in the morning was no fault of theirs. After they left him he must have fallen into one of the deeper pools of the Peffer Water on his way to land, and drowned. They denied any fault in the matter.

This was all said somewhat haltingly, but was definite enough.

Patrick had guessed that this might well be the defence, and without actually making up his mind in advance, had considered the pros and cons of it. Had it not been for the subsequent death, it would have been a small matter which would not have merited any sort of hearing, certainly not in a justiciary court. But this side issue of foreshore rights complicated the case, and he had to be careful in his judgment of that, whatever else.

"As to this charge of murder," he declared, "I find against it. Clearly the two accused had no intention of slaying the unfortunate Wright. They struck him, yes, and he fell. In water, shallow water, it is easy to lose footing. They did not help to raise him up again, but turned away. Therefore I accept a charge of common assault. But only that. For assault, they must be punished. My decision is that they go to Cockenzie for two days in each week, for a month, to work on whatever tasks the family of the man Wright, or those dependent on him, may choose for them to do. Also to take with them, on each occasion, the same number of fresh flatfish that they stole from the man. Any assault on the pair while they are in Cockenzie would be to earn stern punishment from myself, in its turn. Is it all understood?"

Silence in court.

"As to this of the right to fish or seek shellfish on the foreshore of Aberlady Bay, or elsewhere, I agree that this is accepted under our common law. But prevailing custom is also to be considered; and it has been customary for long that only the people of Luffnaraw, Aberlady itself and Golyn, fish there. So, while others cannot be prohibited from so doing, it is my advice, rather than my ruling, that on one day each month the fishers of Cockenzie and otherwhere may come there unmolested, at times depending on the tides, to dredge and dig and spear. At other times they can visit the bay as they may wish, but not to fish. Does any contest this advising?"

Again no voice was raised.

"Very well. That, I say, is a fair judgment. It is my charge, as justiciar, that there shall be no further disharmony between the folk of this my lordship and earldom. All honest men to see that my findings are carried out, to avoid further judgment by myself. I declare this court adjourned." And he rose.

All were ushered from the hall.

Pate announced to his father that since Aberlady Bay was theirs, he did not see why other folk should be allowed to use it, even occasionally. After all, on Dunbar Common, theirs also, only Dunbar folk were permitted to pasture their beasts. He was told that that was different, that whereas such was granted, as of right, to a single community, certain rights on the foreshore around their coasts were understood to belong to the community of the realm, not just to the local people. He would have to learn these distinctions. For one day he too would be earl and justiciar.

Thereafter they made a tour of the castle to discover what state all was in, and ascertain what repairs and renewals were called for, Patrick feeling somewhat guilty that it all had been permitted to become thus neglected. He of course had other castles and houses to keep up, at Hailes, Tantallon, Gifford, Lauder, Ersildoune, Home and Ayton, all demanding his attention; but this was one of the largest and most important. His uncle was past seeing to it, so *he* must.

Then it was back to Dunbar.

It was, strangely enough, not long before another justiciary court was required in Lothian, and a greatly more important one, even though the initial cause of it all was allegedly a mere sporting challenge. There had been a knightly tournament at Haddington, and two of the combatants had been Walter Bisset, Lord of Aboyne, a notoriously difficult man, and none other than young Patrick, son of the late Thomas, Earl of Atholl, and therefore nephew of the also late Alan of Galloway. Bisset had married Ada, one more of the name, Galloway's sister, and so was the aunt of this Earl Patrick, he now settled in Atholl. Whether the challenge to joust was on account of some previous disagreement as to lands or otherwise was not clear, but the two were evidently not on good terms, uncle and nephew as they might be. At all events, in the tourney, the younger unhorsed the elder, to the latter's mortification. And that very night, the house in Haddington in which Patrick of Atholl was lodging was set on fire, and the victor died therein. However, the body had not been sufficiently consumed by fire to hide the fact that death was by strangulation, not burning nor suffocation.

Suspicion immediately fell on the Bissets – for John Bisset, Walter's son, had been seen examining the exterior of the house that evening. The young Earl Patrick unwed and leaving no heir, his earldom would come to his next of kin, his uncle and cousin, the Bissets. So both were taken into custody, and the justiciar called upon to hold trial into the matter.

Needless to say, this was as difficult a task, and as important, as ever Patrick was likely to face as a judge, an earl foully murdered and the suspects his heirs, both lords. He hastened to Roxburgh to see the king, and to suggest that since both the victim and the accused came from the north, Atholl and Mar, the justiciar north of

Forth and Clyde should handle the case. But Alexander said no. He pointed out that it was normal for trial to be held where the crime was committed. Also that in those northern areas the various parties would have friends and enemies, and these could well influence a just verdict. He declared that Patrick, however much he disliked sitting in judgment, would make the most trustworthy judge. So the Justiciar of Lothian to hold this awkward trial, and in Haddington.

The tolbooth of that town was not large, and with a sizeable company of the royal guard, reinforced by Dunbar men drafted in to keep order, the monarch himself not attending, the trial was held in the royal palace, built by William the Lion, where Alexander himself had been born, this standing on the western outskirts of the walled town. The Bissets, uncle and nephew, were brought from Lethington, not far distant, by Sir Hugo de Gifford, known as the Wizard, since with their highborn status it was considered unsuitable to lodge them in the town's tolbooth.

Patrick sat in judgment, with de Gifford on one side of him and Sir Alexander de Seton on the other as councillors. Very much aware of how many were the pitfalls possible ahead of him in this compared with the recent trial at Luffness, he recognised that the entire nation would be concerned with the outcome.

When the two accused were ushered in, they gave no impression of being captives, or in any way acting as though threatened by judgment, nodding up to the justiciar as an equal, and sitting down on a bench near the dais, not standing as was the rule.

When Patrick opened the proceedings by addressing them as Walter, Lord of Aboyne and John, Master of Aboyne, he was quickly shown the attitudes to be adopted by the pair, for Walter immediately broke in to declare that John was no longer to be addressed as Master of Aboyne but as Earl of Atholl, in right of his mother.

Patrick ignored that, and went on to declare that the said

Walter and John Bisset had been accused of the murder of Patrick, Earl of Atholl in this Haddington. Did they plead guilty or not guilty? And if the former, plead any circumstances which would lessen the offence and perhaps mitigate sentence?

Both quite casually declared not guilty, Walter adding that this so-called trial was but a farce, contrived by their enemies, particularly de Hastings, who sought the earldom of Atholl for himself, in the right of the youngest of the Lord Alan of Galloway's sisters, his mother.

Clearly these two were going to defend themselves, deeming no spokesman or representative necessary.

Patrick announced the circumstances, saying that at the tournament Walter had been unhorsed by the late Earl of Atholl, and hot words and accusations had followed. And that same night, the house in the town where the said earl was lodging had been set alight. There was no doubt that the blaze was not accidental, for evidence had been found of fire having been started in three separate places. And when the bodies of the earl and his two attendants had been recovered in the morning, while the servitors had clearly been burned to death, the body of the earl, although part burned, was found to have been strangled, the cord round the neck indeed still in place . . .

Walter Bisset interrupted to say that the Earl Patrick was a hot-blooded and arrogant young man who had many enemies. Why pick on them as the killers?

The first witness was called. This was a reputable one, Mark Letham, actually Deacon of Trades in the town. He swore on oath that he and a friend, one Gavin Struthers, had seen the Master of Aboyne going round the house that late evening, and, watching, they had noted him emerging from a low wing where the horses were stabled.

His companion, the man Struthers, then came forward to confirm the sighting.

John Bisset scornfully declared that in the dark of late evening anybody could have been taken for the fire-raiser, if such it was. Here was no true identification.

Deacon Letham asserted that there was no doubt. The Master of Aboyne had one shoulder uplifted higher than the other, as all could see. The man they saw had also. And they recognised the features. They had seen him at the tourney.

That produced the expected stir in court, since there was no hiding this shoulder peculiarity in the younger accused.

That still was no proof of fire-raising, the uncle asserted.

Patrick called another witness, a more lofty one this time, the Master of Buchan, son of the Comyn Earl of Buchan, who had been one of the contenders at the tournament. He announced that he had been close to the late Earl Patrick when he dismounted after unseating Aboyne, and had heard the master, John, angrily tell him that he had unfairly unhorsed his opponent by the trick of first attacking the horse and not the rider with his lance, and only struck him when Aboyne was half out of his saddle. The master had cried that he would pay for this, and dearly.

That, and coming from another earl's son, made a major impact on all but the two accused. Walter Bisset said that he had indeed been unfairly assailed, contrary to all tourney rules; and his nephew denied saying that it would have to be paid for.

There was nothing more in the way of evidence, for or against. Patrick was faced with the task of summing up. He declared that all the circumstances pointed to the accused, one or both, as being probably responsible for this grievous crime, his two councillors agreeing with him. The Bissets had been seen by many to be angry with the dead Atholl, one heard to make a threat, and then observed, at a late hour, prospecting the house which was to be burned. And they both had much to gain by the death of the young earl. No other likely offender's name had been suggested or seen as possible. In the circumstances, therefore, he, as justiciar, had no option but to declare the accused as guilty.

There was uproar in court, most of it anti-Bisset, but the accused and a few friends loudly protesting.

When he could gain quiet, Patrick informed that he had spoken with His Grace the King before coming here; and their liege-lord had expressed his grave concern, and said that if the verdict was guilty, then dire punishment must be enforced. But that if actual proof could not be produced, as distinct from all but assured probability, then the death penalty ought not to be announced, but a lesser punishment. His Grace suggested banishment from the realm, together with forfeiture of lands and titles. This, therefore, he, Dunbar and March, pronounced. Banishment and forfeiture. This in the name of His Grace. Let Sir Hugo de Gifford, holding the guilty pair, see that they were safe confined until their due expulsion from the kingdom.

He rose, duty done. This had been Alexander's wish, whatever the verdict. To execute a lord of parliament and a claimant to an earldom, especially connected with Galloway, would be highly injudicious, to say the least.

Patrick, leaving the court, and thankfully, hoped that this would be the end of justiciarship duties for some time. Indeed he would have liked to resign the position, but recognised that not only was it hereditary in the family but that no other obvious nominee was available. But as to this case, of course, there still remained the possibility of reaction from the Bissets and their friends, powerful in the north. Would they take all this lying down?

33

That question, as to possible reaction, was not long in being answered, and not, significantly, from northern Scotland. Of all places it came from Rome, or at least from the Pope's legate Otho, in England. How he had achieved it was not explained, but he had obtained a sentence of excommunication from the Vatican against the murderers of Patrick, Earl of Atholl, these other than the unjustly accused Bissets; and this sentence was to be proclaimed from all churches in the kingdom, by His Holiness's command – an ironic touch indeed, proclaiming the Bissets' own innocence, and a mockery of the King of Scots and his justiciar. That Otho was no lover of Scotland.

And that was only the beginning of it, as it transpired. The Bissets, whether through Otho's good offices or otherwise, gained access to King Henry; and the word of their intrigues and vengeance against the Scots crown began to reach Alexander. Walter was telling Henry that through his queen's Coucy and Guinnes connections, the King of Scots was negotiating a firm military alliance with Louis of France against England, with specific targets set for both nations, the Scots to regain Cumberland and Northumberland, and France to regain the dukedom of Aquitaine. Not only this, but that Alexander was using the Galloway connection with Ireland to plan a takeover of the English-held provinces there. And, they had heard, the Plantagenet was being sufficiently gulled by all this to grant Bisset the manor of Lowdham in Nottinghamshire until he should regain his lands in Scotland, and meantime also a pension. So much for royal clemency towards murderers.

When they learned, further, that Henry had instructed

all authorities and magnates in Yorkshire, Lancashire, Cumberland and Northumberland to deny all passage to and from Scotland by any soever, the king sent for Patrick to form one of a deputation to go to inform Henry that the Bissets were lying, and that no hostile plans were intended against England. The other two envoys were to be the Steward and Bishop de Bernham, the Primate. The trouble was, of course, that this of barring all passage through northern England was going to complicate, possibly prevent, the journey. There was nothing for it, then, but to go by sea. Patrick was to visit Berwick and arrange that one of the vessels in trade with the Netherlands should take them to the Thames, en route.

It so happened that Bishop de Bernham was staying at Dunbar Castle when these instructions arrived. An extraordinary prelate, he was quite the most enterprising and mission-conscious Primate the realm had had for long, establishing and dedicating new churches all over the land, too many to enumerate, and convincing landholders to pay for and support them and their priests. In Patrick's earldom of Dunbar and the Merse he had founded Bara and Yester, Pencaitland, Gullane, Aldhame, Channelkirk, Gordon, Greenlaw, Polwarth and Chirnside, and now at brother William's Fogo. At the astonishment of others, his declaration was that if St Columba could do it amongst the heathen Picts, then he could at least seek to emulate amongst Christian folk.

This of the mission to England seemed to appeal to him as but another challenge. Patrick was duly enheartened thereby. The bishop would have to return to St Andrews first, to make arrangements for his absence, but ought to be available for the journey in, say, ten days, by which time Walter the Steward should be on hand also. Meanwhile Patrick would go down to Berwick-upon-Tweed to seek out a suitable ship for their voyage.

Two weeks later, then, the three emissaries set sail southwards in a vessel laden with Lammermuir wool, salted mutton and fish, and smelling strongly thereof, for the three-hundred-mile voyage, less than noble berths necessarily provided for such lofty passengers but no complaints made. The wind mainly against them, they took a day longer than hoped for on the way, but since they were by no means expected, this was not of importance.

Turning eventually into the Thames estuary, they wondered as to their reception at London Tower, in the circumstances.

However, it was the Earl of Pembroke, the Marshal, whom they encountered there, the king himself being at his favoured Windsor. They were received frostily enough, but there was no barring of their onward way westwards, indeed they were provided with an escort of the royal guard, and the necessary horses, although that was perhaps an indication of hostility rather than of helpfulness.

At any rate they reached Windsor Castle without any actual trouble, however uncommunicative their escort, and there were ushered into the presence of Queen Eleanor, with her baby son, Edward by name. She knew Patrick and the Steward, of course, but not the bishop. Although something of a masterful woman, she showed no actual enmity to the envoys. She informed that her husband was out hawking but would be back shortly. She also mentioned that the legate Otho had returned to Rome. The Bissets were not spoken of.

When Henry Plantagenet returned, he was obviously embarrassed at the visitors' presence. After all, he had had quite pleasant relations with two of them, and clearly he had heard about de Bernham and his very positive ministry. To treat them as enemies now, and in front of his queen, would have been as awkward as it was unseemly. The envoys remarked on the fine little boy he had gained as heir to his throne. They did not refer to Alexander's new queen, Marie de Coucy, who was now pregnant, in case this seemed to imply criticism of the late Joanna as having failed to produce the desired offspring.

When the young Edward started to bawl, and his mother led him from the chamber, it was de Bernham who led off as, in theory the most senior, Primate of the Scottish Church.

"Sire," he said, "we have come from His Grace Alexander to acquaint Your Majesty with his entire goodwill towards your royal self and your realm. He is much concerned that you have been led to feel estranged towards him and his kingdom by . . . miscreants and liars, not to mention murderers!" That was straight talking. "We must convince your Majesty that the spleen of guilty men must not be allowed to endanger the harmony and peace of two sister nations."

Patrick wondered whether the King of England had ever been spoken to quite like that before.

Henry indeed blinked. "I, I must judge the issue for myself, Sir Priest!" he said.

"Undoubtedly, Sire. But from knowledge, not from the hatred of resentful evil-doers. We have come to inform you of the truth. We do so not only in the name of Alexander of Scotland but of Almighty God in His heaven. God's concerns are love, order, beauty and truth. Here is truth, as I await God's judgment!"

Unused to such authoritative representations, the king looked at Patrick and the Steward almost anxious for their more normal address to a monarch.

"Our liege-lord Alexander, Majesty, would have us leave you in no doubt as to his kind regard for your royal self," Patrick put in. "And the falsity of allegations otherwise. He has no plans for any especial pact with King Louis of France, as he understands that you have been wrongly informed. Nor any designs on Ireland. He has accepted your grant of lands in Cumberland as adequate. What other false word Walter Bisset has given Your Majesty we know not. But all such is to your own hurt as well as to King Alexander's."

"His Grace is much troubled," the Steward added. "The two realms must remain on good terms. That, next

341

to the good governance of his own kingdom, is his principal concern."

Henry took a pace or two from them, and then turned back. "The legate deemed it otherwise," he said.

"Then this legate is an unworthy emissary of His Holiness," the bishop declared. "He has been less than helpful in Scotland. I will send word to Pope Gregory to that effect. I have already given instructions that his sentence of excommunication on the murderers of the young Earl of Atholl, ordered to be read in our churches, should have the names of Walter and John Bisset added thereto."

Henry eyed this very forthright cleric all but warily.

"We urge that Your Majesty withdraws your favour from these Bissets," the Steward went on. "Now that you know the truth."

"If it *is* the truth!" the Plantagenet said.

"Does Your Highness prefer the word of convinced murderers to that of your fellow monarch and his envoys?" de Bernham demanded. "And I will remind you that *I* speak also in the name of Holy Church."

Duly impressed or otherwise, Henry turned away. "I will give commands for your due entertainment," he observed, which committed him to nothing.

It was normal for others, however worthy, to bow out of the presence of any monarch; but de Bernham was not finished with Henry yet.

"Sire, you will, we hope, also give orders that your halting of passage through your northern counties to Scotland be lifted, since so we return to His Grace."

This was, of course, the test, the touchstone as to the success or failure of their visit. The king paused, and then nodded curtly.

"I shall so command," he said. And not waiting for any of the usual bowing and backing from the royal presence, he strode for the door and out.

The trio looked at each other, eyebrows raised.

"My lord Bishop, you make a telling ambassador!"

Patrick declared. "I swear that you have put him at a loss."

"So long as we gain what we came for," the other said. "And he does not think better of it – or worse! And more than this of permitting passage."

A personage of the royal household arrived presently to conduct them to a wing of the great round-towered castle, where accommodation was provided for them. They dined there, alone, well catered for. But they did not see anything more of the king or his wife that night.

In the morning, the envoys wondering what was to be their next step, it was Queen Eleanor who came to them. She announced that her husband was gone on business unspecified; but that he had taken due note of what they had to say, and sent his good wishes to King Alexander. Horses would be provided for them, and a fair escort to ensure their untroubled journey back to Scotland. She bade them a reasonably civil farewell.

This time they indeed bowed out from the royal presence. It looked as though the Plantagenet was not for risking any further audience with the Primate of the Scots Church. But the signs were, hopefully, that their mission had been successful.

They did not linger at Windsor.

A satisfactory return home without incident followed, certainly no problems as to passage. Their escort did not leave them until the border itself, almost within sight of Roxburgh. There Alexander was glad to see them, and grateful for what their embassage appeared to have achieved.

It was some two weeks later that word arrived, of all people from Devorgilla of Galloway and her John Baliol, declaring that the Bissets had been sent to Ireland by Henry, another sort of banishment, and their pension and the Nottinghamshire manor withdrawn from them. It looked to be as near to an apology and acceptance as a King of England could allow himself to make, with dignity.

Sighs of relief resounded throughout Scotland.

Whether that sentence of excommunication could now be forgotten was uncertain, but the Primate decided that it could be ignored meantime. He had already written to Pope Gregory.

34

Relief and more than relief was the prevailing reaction, when, in September, Queen Marie was brought to bed of a son, to be named Alexander also, and Scotland at last had a direct heir to the throne. Whether Bruce of Annandale also rejoiced was another matter. But prayers of thankfulness were offered in all churches, instead of papal excommunications, bonfires blazed on hill-tops and castle beacons, and there was dancing in the streets. The Scots, with their clannish and patriarchial background and society, tended to look upon their monarchy as almost familial rather than regally masterful, as was more general.

In all the celebrations, Alexander, in his gratitude, made some new appointments. The High Justiciarship of the Realm, become vacant, he bestowed on Walter the Steward. Bishop de Bernham, already Primate, could not be raised higher, but was made President of the Council. But Patrick's plea was to be relieved of the office of Justiciar of Lothian, a role which he had never enjoyed. This was granted. He was given the merely honorary title of High Seneschal; and Sir William de Lindsay, son of Sir David of Crawford, was made justiciar instead. Relief therefor, at Dunbar Castle. Being Seneschal demanded little or nothing of him.

Patrick did, however, have to see quite a lot of this Sir William de Lindsay in the months which followed, for, coming from Lanarkshire, he knew little of Lothian and had to be acquainted with his duties and introduced to local magnates, as well as found a residence. He was given the small tower-house of Nether Sydserff, none so far from Dunbar. Actually, a far-out relation of the Steward, and therefore Phemia, he proved to be a personable and effective character, unmarried, who had caught the king's attention.

Phemia liked him, and he became quite a frequent visitor at Dunbar. And not only himself, for he often had his nephew staying with him, a son of his elder brother, Sir David de Lindsay of Crawford, another David. This very good-looking young man made a noticeable impact on daughter Elizabeth. With her brother Pate recently come of full age, the Cospatrick family was reaching the stage of branching out.

Another concern for Patrick was that his brother William, at Home, was in poor health and becoming unable to continue with his tasks anent the Low Countries. This was serious, for the trade there had become of ever growing importance to the earldom, the wool, salted mutton and fish and quarried stone producing the greater part of its income now rather than rents and the like. So it was decided that Pate should take over his uncle's responsibilities there, as a useful step towards one day becoming earl himself. Patrick would take him to Veere and Bergen op Zoom in the spring, and introduce him to the conditions, the traders and personalities there.

Now that Phemia no longer had children to rear, she announced that she had always wished to see more of the world, and would like to accompany husband and son on their journey, which nowise displeased Patrick.

So, come April 1242, leaving Elizabeth in charge at Dunbar Castle, the trio had one of the Berwick ships come up for them, and set sail for Veere, the king declaring that he wished that he could have come with them, for he too had never been out of Scotland and England.

The weather favourable, they made better time than on the previous voyage to the Thames, and landed on Walcheron Island in half a day's time less than it had taken to reach London.

Phemia thereafter was much taken with all that she saw, the tall, narrow, brightly painted and shuttered houses of

346

brick, even the streets cobbled in red brick, the numerous churches and busy markets, the canals and waterways, the windmills and vast level views. Also the folk themselves, sturdy, independent but friendly. Pate was taken to meet the wool-brokers, the merchants, see the sorting-sheds, the spinning and weaving mills, and meet the burgomaster, the craftsmen's guilds and the barge-owners and skippers, impressed by the businesslike effectiveness of all, and the evident wealth generated, perceiving the importance of it all to Dunbar, indeed to Scotland. He had realised that the large numbers of Flemings, as they were called, at Berwick, Eyemouth and elsewhere represented great commercial interests over here; but quite the scale of it all, and the trade links with the other kingdoms and duchies, not only of the Low Countries but of France, even Venice and the Empire, he had not understood.

After a week at Veere, they set off, by barge and waterways, for Bergen op Zoom, which had become the main destination for the import of the stone and gravel which was so much needed in these stoneless lands, the trade which Patrick had developed so that it now represented a major source of his and his people's wealth.

There was less to see here of especial interest, but they did pay a visit to Bruges, quite a journey but a very worthwhile one, of some seventy miles by boat and canal. It was a magnificent city with its mighty dom-kerke or cathedral, the spire of which was higher than any building they had ever seen, an individual free-standing belfry almost as high the Chapel of the Sacred Blood, the palaces, the wide market-places, the parks and gardens, of this the central mart of the Hanseatic League, and the greatest centre of commerce in all the world. Phemia was all but overwhelmed, but charmed also. Why did they not have places like this in Scotland?

Despite all this interesting visiting and viewing, the Cospatricks could not be unaware of an air of tension of a sort prevailing, little as this seemed apt for these Low Countries people. It was the echoes of trouble at Rome, they learned, indeed chaos, and at the Vatican. Pope Gregory had died the previous August, and his successor, Celestine, had only lasted for three months when he too had died. Meanwhile the papal throne was vacant, and great was the rivalry and intrigues of the various contenders and their supporters, actual fighting taking place, hatred rather than Christian love. And, of course, lacking a Pontiff, the ultimate rule over Christendom was suspended, with results far outwith matters of worship.

The visitors could not be unconcerned as to what effect all this might have on their own country. That Otho, for instance? Would they get a new legate or nuncia?

The trio could not linger overlong in these parts, however enjoyable their visit, with so many responsibilities awaiting Patrick in Scotland, for he was still High Constable, Keeper of the Great Seal and Seneschal, as well as having the two earldoms to rule. So it was back to Veere and, finding a ship, Pate declaring that he thought that he now knew approximately what was required of him here.

They did not have long to wait for a vessel, and this at least with a cargo of cloth, tapestries, spun goods and pantiles, so that the smells were less off-putting than on the outward voyage.

Their return to Dunbar was to learn of a catalogue of deaths, although they had been gone less than five weeks. And some were direly close. The elderly Walter the Steward had suddenly gone to still higher things. Patrick's sister-in-law Christiana Corbet, wife of brother William, had died. His uncle Constantine had also passed away, at Luffness. William de Fortibus, husband of the third of the Galloway sisters, had departed this life. And the Bishop of Argyll, who had been helpful to Alexander over the Isles situation, had drowned at sea.

The Cospatricks were all but dazed by these tidings. Not only Phemia was overwhelmed by the sudden passing of her father; Patrick had become very fond of him over the years of working together, admiring him greatly. Scotland was going to miss its High Steward indeed; and although he would be succeeded in the hereditary office by his son Alexander, he was a retiring and silent man with, as yet, little interest in affairs of state, who based himself on the Isle of Bute, where he had married Jean MacRory, daughter of its lord.

As to Christiana, his sister-in-law, Patrick had never felt close to her; but his brother William, a sick man, was going to miss her sorely. They had a small son, and the situation at Home Castle was going to be not only sad but very difficult. Constantine's death at Luffness was a different matter. Old, and a recluse, few were greatly going to miss him; but it did mean that Patrick was going to have to think about what was to be done about that castle and property.

The passing of William de Fortibus of Holderness, without an heir, meant that the Galloway situation would be simplified, leaving the Lady Devorgilla and her Baliol husband supreme there, for the second sister, the Countess of Winchester, took no interest in the lordship, nor did her husband. The king had considerable respect for Devorgilla, a reliable and able woman, so this demise presented no problems for the realm. And the Bishop of Argyll, although a loss, would be replaced by de Bernham with some suitable nominee.

In all this of gloom and mourning, there was however one more cheerful and hopefully promising development. Daughter Elizabeth announced that she and David de Lindsay had plighted their troth, much in love with each other, and now sought her father's agreement for them to marry. Happy enough about this, Patrick saw it as an answer to the situation at Luffness. He would have to provide a dowery for Elizabeth, and this would serve very well. Let the young couple see to the rehabilitation of that property.

The family went to condole with the Lady Beatrix and her daughter Christian at Renfrew, and pay their respects at the grave of Walter.

It had been a strange homecoming.

35

It was not long before Patrick was summoned for a further duty by his liege-lord. A request, almost an order, had arrived from Henry Plantagenet to meet him at Newcastle for a suitable reaffirmation of good relations between the kingdoms, with all outstanding issues to be resolved. He, Henry, would bring worthy guarantors for the accord, and he trusted that Alexander would do likewise. He suggested four prelates and twenty-four barons on each side. A safe-conduct was included for the Scots party to pass through Northumberland – this a gesture which Alexander looked upon as almost an insult.

However the meeting, an opportunity hopefully to solve differences, was not to be refused. The company assembled at Roxburgh. Patrick took Pate along with him, for, Master of Dunbar and March, he could serve as one of the required barons, and gain some experience of such state affairs. De Bernham had brought the Bishops of Glasgow, Dunkeld, Brechin and Dunblane. The new Steward had been ordered to attend; and the Earls of Lennox, Carrick and Menteith joined, with their baronial vassals. Patrick found his but little-known brother-in-law less than interesting company.

Since Newcastle was a port and could be reached by sea, Patrick had thought that perhaps they could counter the safe-conduct slight by taking ship; but the numbers involved in the end precluded this, many of the barons proudly having brought their ample trains. So it proved to be a great array which set out in early August for the meeting, all but a host. Henry himself was responsible for this, in demanding so many guarantors for any treaty.

It was just under one hundred miles to Newcastle, going by Tweed, Till and so to Wooler, which they reached for the first night; thereafter crossing Breamish, Aln and Coquet to the Tyne – and requiring no production of safe-conducts on the way.

At the walled town, they were the first to arrive. They camped at the riverbank outside it, Alexander setting up a handsome pavilion under the lion rampant standard. To while away the waiting, they held tourneys, archery contests and racing, watched from a distance by the Newcastle citizenry.

When, next day, Henry duly arrived, he brought with him an even larger and more splendid legion than Alexander had done, practically an army indeed, with the Earls of Pembroke, Hertford, Gloucester, Oxford, Winchester and Lincoln. All looked as though prepared for battle, although this was probably only a warning demonstration that Henry wanted his way at this meeting. The Scots did not take it too seriously, for the word was that the Welsh were rising in rebellion, and the Plantagenet would not wish to become embroiled in hostilities in the north while this danger threatened in the west.

The English army settled down some four hundred yards from the Scots encampment, with much stir and banner-waving and horn-blowing. Alexander and his advisers stood waiting and watching, but were certainly not going to make the first move, as though approaching Henry submissively.

It was the Archbishop of York, now elderly, who eventually made the first move. With a group of lords, spiritual and temporal, he came in dignified fashion to announce to the King of Scots that His Majesty of England had come thus far to speak with him and to seek an answer to sundry questions, in the hope of fullest accord between the two realms. Was His Grace so minded?

Alexander declared that he was, otherwise he would not be at Newcastle this day. Tell King Henry so.

The metropolitan then said that His Majesty suggested

that he, the archbishop, should conduct the King of Scots, and such as he wished to have with him, to the castle which gave the city its name, for converse and discussion, leaving their separate companies where they were meantime.

Alexander acceded to this, and with his bishops, earls and barons followed the prelate's party to the towering fortress, built by the Conqueror's son William Rufus and enlarged by Henry the Second.

Here, in the lofty hall, with its dais platform, minstrels' gallery and tapestry-hung walls, they had to wait again for Henry, who clearly was determined that *he* should not do the waiting. But at least there was a sufficiency of wines for the visitors.

When the Plantagenet arrived, with Pembroke and the others, he was warily civil, seemingly less sure of himself than he had sounded in his messages and letters. He allowed the archbishop to initiate the discussion.

"His Majesty wishes Your Grace to know that he has withdrawn his favour from Walter and John Bisset of Aboyne. He has sent them to Ireland, in the care of the Earl of Tyrconnel, who has affirmed his loyal duty to His Majesty, and his readiness to defend the English-held provinces and territories of that land with all armed strength."

Alexander glanced at Patrick and de Bernham. This strange opening was both something of a conciliatory gesture and also a threat. The Bissets were all but banished; but the Irish powers controlled by England were to be readied to move to Henry's aid if required. It was none so far across the Irish Sea to Scotland.

The King of Scots inclined his head, not commenting.

"Also the young King Harold of Man, new returned from Norway, has undertaken to keep King Henry's peace," the metropolitan went on. "And brought King Hakon's word that *his* Norse Irish power will also be of support in this."

So the threat was amplified. In the event of trouble with Scotland, Man and both the English and Norse strength in Ireland would be active in Henry's cause.

"It is *my* wish also that peace and amity be maintained with Ireland. Also Norway and Man," Alexander said levelly. But it was Henry he addressed, not the archbishop.

The Plantagenet stroked his chin. "That is well," he agreed. "Likewise, my desire is that peace may be maintained with King Louis of France."

So there it was. The Scots alliance with France was being seen as the danger to England, and was to be negatived.

This curious series of observations and desires, in avoiding any actual statement of the reason behind this meeting of the monarchs, nevertheless made the strains between the two nations clear. The Auld Alliance between France and Scotland: that was at the root of it.

De Bernham spoke. And he addressed the archbishop, as was suitable, not King Henry. "Scotland's friendship with France is of long standing, but by no means warlike," he asserted. "Save, indeed, towards the infidel! Even now we are in contact with King Louis over his proposed crusade to the Holy Land. With which king and Church agree and would take part."

That was shrewd. For since King Richard Lion Heart's day, the late King John's brother, England had been lukewarm about the crusading issue, Henry, like his father, showing little interest in it, despite papal pressure. Here was a subject to put the other side on the defensive, while it not seeming altogether irrelevant.

The metropolitan coughed. "The crusading matter is being considered," he said. "But while the Vatican is in the process of appointing a new Pontiff, the question is suspended." That was probably the best that he could do.

Patrick joined in. "King Louis is determined to go on with it, despite problems at Rome," he asserted. "He should be supported by all good men. And the Scots are with him in this, as in much else. War against the Saracens, not against fellow Christians."

Alexander backed him in this, advisedly, which forced Henry to make comment.

353

"I have spoken on this with the legate Otho," he conceded. "But who knows what is to be, now? Matters nearer to home demand our heed."

"If His Majesty fears the attentions of France, Sire, then should he not be glad of King Louis's concern with crusading? Or so I would judge." That was Patrick again, addressing Alexander.

Henry frowned, obviously wishing to be done with this awkward subject. "My concern here is this of our two realms. I am well content that you assure me of your goodwill on the matters which we have spoken of. There is also this of Cumberland and Northumberland. You accepted, before, that the lands I offered you then would content you. I take it that you do not resile on that? That is well. But it would be of advantage to both kingdoms if this vexed matter of the borderline was to be settled once and for all between us. Another commission to see to that, then?"

"*Your* representatives have been less than prepared to give as well as take in that," Alexander declared.

"I will appoint others and instruct them well. So-o-o!" The Plantagenet drew himself up. "Here, then, is my proposal for the ensuring of our mutual accord and good understanding. I say that we should show our decision and contentment in this by making contract for a marriage, in due course, between your infant son Alexander of Rothesay and my young daughter Margaret. How say you?"

There were moments of silence. Here was a totally unexpected proposal, and one on which Alexander's advisers could scarcely voice an opinion. Infants both, to be pledges, warranties, for the peace of two kingdoms. Was this to be considered?

Patrick for one wondered as to the rights of it, bairns as it were bartered, all but sold before they could even speak? But such a contract could surely be revoked, annulled? And in this case, with the female the English one, it could not be a way of perhaps seeking to gain the Scots throne by marriage.

Was Alexander thinking along similar lines? He was looking thoughtful indeed.

Henry added, pointing. "*You* married my sister. Right that your son could wed my daughter."

"They are so young! But perhaps such intention could be considered, yes. Scarce a contract, but an intention."

"So be it. My clerks will write the necessary words for a treaty which we will sign and seal. Establishing this of Ireland, Man and Norway. Also of the French peace. Of Cumberland and Northumberland. And of the borderline to be settled. Is it agreed?" He did not mention crusading. "Our witnesses will add their seals."

There was feasting that night, but in separate quarters for the two delegations, on the grounds that there were over-many for one, but fairly clearly because Henry did not wish to have to act host to Alexander and seem in too close relationship at this stage. Not that this distressed the Scots.

In the morning, in the castle again, there was quite a ceremony of signing and sealing, no fewer than fifty-six seals, over and above the royal ones, to be attached to the parchments by the various guarantors.

The parting thereafter was formal rather than affable. But at least peace had been re-established and relationships restored after a fashion. Long might they last.

36

Such relationships were not long in being tested, even if actual peace was not endangered thereby, for this of defining the borderline, one of the terms of the treaty, was to be promptly put in hand. Once again Patrick was involved, with the Earl of Lennox and David de Bernham, who was ever more having to take over the role which the late Walter the Steward had filled. Alexander felt that such lofty negotiators were advisable, to help counter any English obstructive tactics, it being unlikely that Henry would appoint the like. He also decided that they should change their starting-point of the survey from the East March, which had proved so difficult, to the West. So, in late September, the trio and their escort set out for Dumfries and the Solway, not entirely hopefully. The Lord Robert Bruce of Annandale, displaced heir to the throne, would join them as local representative and adviser.

That big man, less than welcoming, joined them at Dumfries, and warned that it was going to be no easy task, not only the English likely to be awkward but the folk on the ground, the Marchmen also. These, on both sides, cherished the undefined area of the Debateable Land as advantageous, with their own laws and customs and freedom from authority other than their own swords and lances. In some sections hereabouts the undefined area could be as wide as ten miles. Fixing any line through this was likely to be a problem indeed, and as difficult for the English commissioners as for themselves, almost certainly. And anyway, the mosstroopers were unlikely to heed anything such, so that the exercise would become little more than a formality.

Thus prepared, they headed on south-westwards for Gretna, near where Esk and Sark and Liddel and Eden joined salt water, the appointed meeting-place. There they found the English delegation awaiting them, new come from Carlisle. These, from the first, looked on Bruce with ill-disguised suspicion, however superficially civil they were to the others. They proved to be led by the Bishop of Carlisle himself, the other two being Wharton of Nateby and Musgrave of Musgrave and Kielder. Probably they had heard that the Scots group included none other than the Primate, and so must be matched by a prominent churchman.

A preliminary discussion as to procedure revealed that the English were no more confident about the Debateable Land situation than were their opposite numbers. Clearly they looked upon Bruce as all but a Marchman himself, and therefore committed to wrecking tactics in advance. They agreed that it was unlikely that the wretched moss-troopers would take any heed of a line established by them anyway, at least for the first thirty miles or so. But King Henry had insisted that such should be delineated, and marked by cairns of stones – even though the Marchmen would probably demolish these thereafter.

In these circumstances the commissioners started off without any major or mutual opposition, accepting that the River Sark, a lesser stream than the Esk, should for the first few miles form the borderline, the boundary its centre, this heading almost due north from Gretna. This was well enough, uncontroversial, for some three miles, to where a tributary, the Black Sark, came in from the west, and its junction with the main stream formed a great marshy area known as the Solway Moss, land of no value to anyone. East of this was the common grazings of the village of Longtown, and since that community had always been accepted as part of Cumberland, no questions arose as to the border here. Northwards of this the Sark ran through better land, on both sides; and here they were not long in perceiving that their presence was not going unnoticed. Horsemen were to be seen watching them from heights and eminences on both sides. News travelled fast in the Borderland. With their escorts they were unlikely to be interfered with by the Marchmen, but the hostility was not to be doubted.

It was agreed that the Sark, still coming from north-wards, should be accepted as the boundary for another four miles, whatever the mosstroopers thought of it all. But thereafter there was question. At a small towerhouse and hamlet called Crawsknowe, Bruce pointed out that this was Armstrong property, and that their land, along with other Armstrong holdings, extended eastwards for some miles, clearly Scottish. Musgrave said that they had Armstrongs on the English side also, and that the line could not be defined by the names of the occupiers. Further north there were Grahams on both sides, the same applying elsewhere. This could not be denied. However, it was conceded by the Englishmen that this Armstrong land, as far as the River Esk, some four miles, should be Scottish. But after that, English, Armstrongs or not.

At the greater River Esk it did not take long for dispute to arise. The Liddel Water joined Esk hereabouts, and while upper Liddesdale was most certainly in Scotland, the lower section, from Riddings to Kershopefoot, was English.

This claim was ridiculous, it was asserted. Canonbie was a Scots town, and its common land extended eastwards to the Liddel. Rowanburn, further north-east, had a priory, which de Bernham declared was under the authority of the Bishop of Galloway. The Bishop of Carlisle could not deny this. And nearby Whitlawside was Johnstone property, Scots again.

This stretch was contested, apart from Rowanburn, and their escorts were told not to erect any of their stone cairns for some eight miles. All this survey had used up the September day, and de Bernham emphasised his authority by insisting that all the company should go to spend the night in Rowanburn Priory, in fair comfort and at the monks' expense.

358

That evening the Scots discussed the situation. So far things had gone none so badly. But according to Bruce the real test lay just ahead where, entering the high hills, the Kershope Burn came in from the right.

Armstrongs and Elliots here looked upon a great tract of uplands to the east as their country, the Blinkbonny Heights and beyond to the Larriston Fells, well east of Liddesdale; indeed Armstrong of Mangerton and Elliot of Larriston looked upon themselves as all but chiefs of their names, and certainly would consider it an insult to be called Englishmen. Yet the English were known to assert that the border should continue up to the Liddel Water. Here would be the clash.

And so it proved, next day, when they came to Kershopefoot, and the Scots began to cross the ford of the Liddel to follow up this tributary. Prompt was the outcry. Why go up there? was the demand. That led into England. Hold to the Liddel.

Scarcely an argument took place, for with two bishops and two earls and a former heir to the throne present, as well as chiefs of names, such would have been highly unsuitable. But the two sides were vehement enough in their claims, and impasse was quickly reached, Musgrave particularly obdurate. It seemed that some of *his* land was none so far off, at Kielder and Bewshaugh, on the headwaters of the River Tyne. None would deny that this was in England.

Patrick it was who challenged him. "If you, sir, are so close, then you must know well Elliot of Larriston. Do you claim him to be in England?"

"That rogue! Do *you* claim him as a Scot, my lord? I would judge you well quit of him! Whatever he calls himself, Larriston Fells are in England."

"Not only would Elliot dispute that. *I* do!" Bruce declared.

"Since our friend Musgrave lives there, he ought to know," the Carlisle bishop put in.

De Bernham spoke up. "Should we not go to see this

Elliot, then? Two neighbours, my friends. Hear both, and judge."

The English group could scarcely refuse this reasonable suggestion. Without enthusiasm they forded the Liddel and proceeded up the Kershope Burn and into the hills. All the time they knew that they were being watched by the local Marchmen.

For almost ten upland miles they rode, north by east, the steeps of the Larriston Fells beckoning them on. At a place called Hobb's Flow, on Bruce's guidance, they left this stream to climb over a small pass through a shoulder of the fells. They came down through it to the Liddel Water again, to renewed English assertion that this should be the border.

A short distance up this and they were met by quite a company of mosstroopers, not just watchers these, and all armed to the teeth. Their leader, a hatchet-faced man, elderly but sitting his horse proudly, hailed them.

"I am Larriston," he announced. "Who rides Larriston land lacking my permission? I see Bruce of Annandale there. But who else?"

"There are the Earls of Dunbar and March and of Lennox, Elliot. Also the Primate of the Church. And, and English representatives. We survey the border-line."

"Ha! You do? Our folk have been watching you at it these two days. You, Bruce, should know better than this. The border is well to the east of this." And he pointed over the Larriston Fells.

"So we have told our English companions, Elliot. But . . . they differ!"

"Then they are in error. Like most Englishmen!"

"Not so, Elliot. I say that the border is at the Liddel. I am Musgrave of Musgrave and of Kielder."

"You are? Then you should know better! Think you that *I* would live in England?"

"Then you should move across Liddel, man!"

"Those are *my* fells, Englishman! Think you to take

them from me?" He whipped out a sword and held it high. "Try it!"

Behind him men growled like angry dogs.

De Bernham intervened. "The Kings of Scotland and England seek to establish the true borderline, my friend. We are their commissioners. Where say you the border runs?"

"There is no line, as you should know," he was told. "We have our own lands here, as Musgrave, even he, knows well. Where we ride at will, sirs. At *our* will!"

"We know of the Debateable Lands, yes, Elliot. But there must be a border somewhere, no? Where Scotland ends and England begins. Where is it, hereabouts? You should know."

"Ask Musgrave. He should also."

"He says the Liddel Water."

"Then he is a fool as well as a liar! It lies along the foots of the Kielder Fells."

Wharton snorted. "Marchmen!" he scoffed.

"I will take you there, if you wish," Elliot said.

The Scots eyed each other, even if the English did not.

"I think it unnecessary, sir," Patrick said. "We know that there are these hills between the Liddel and the Kershope Waters. We have just come through them. And between here and Kielder Fells, many miles. Can we not agree on some line midway? East of these Larriston Fells but west of the Bewshaugh and Kielder ones?"

"No!" That was Wharton, Musgrave supporting with a shake of the head. "The Liddel."

"Here is no worthy attitude," de Bernham declared. "There must be give as well as take in these matters."

Bruce added, "We all know that north and east of here it is all Scots: Armstrongs, Olivers, Laidlaws country, as well as Elliots. No question that Riccarton and Wauchope and Hermitage are *not* in England. So how does the line reach there, from this Kielder on the Tyne?"

The only answer was from the Bishop of Carlisle. "Strike north to Liddesdale, my lords, through the Foul-mire Heights. Empty land, till we reach the Liddel. That should not be difficult to plot. Liddel we insist upon."

Lennox, who had spoken but little in all this, shook his head. "We waste our time," he asserted now, strongly. "If you insist on what we can never accept, there is deadlock. Further talk and survey useless."

"I fear that is so," de Bernham agreed.

The Englishmen remained silent, but clearly unrelenting.

"Then naught for it but to return to King Alexander and report," Patrick said. "Report that we have achieved only the establishing of the borderline from Gretna up to Kershopefoot. Less than twenty-five miles? Further than that, failure. He, the King Henry also, will be much aggrieved."

"Less so than if we had given away much of his English ground," Musgrave asserted.

"Give away!" Elliot, listening and grinning, hooted. "No man can give away what he does not possess! And seek you to *take* what you claim, and you will learn that quickly enough!" And he pointed his drawn sword directly at Musgrave, and wheeled his horse around so abruptly that it pawed the air, and rode off. His men, shouting scornfully, followed after him.

That seemed to be the signal for more than these Marchmen to depart. Patrick glanced at de Bernham, who nodded.

"We will leave you, then, my lord Bishop and your friends," he said. "From here, riding up Liddesdale, we will be into the Middle March in thirty miles. And be with King Alexander, at Roxburgh, before dark. And leave you to inform King Henry in your own good time."

None thought to improve on that suggestion, and they parted there without more ado and with only stiff formality, the two bishops alone making gestures of respect.

The Scots set off at once, north-eastwards, although Bruce went westwards for his own Annandale. Patrick, for one, after the experiences he had had in that East March survey, little surprised at this outcome.

37

Alexander was, of course, disappointed over the failure of this third attempt at border-defining, but not unduly so, for it had been at Henry's suggestion rather than his own. The actual line was not so vitally important in the circumstances that prevailed along that stretch of the land. And anyway, he was somewhat preoccupied with other matters. He had been invited to attend a wedding, and at all places at Oslo, in Norway, this at the suggestion of King Hakon and young Harold of Man. Hakon had given his daughter Cecilia to marry Harold, a notable indication – and as notable that Alexander had been invited to it. Not that he could spare the time for the travel involved, with so much on his mind at home; but the asking was important. It looked as though Man and Norway were now anxious to be at peace with Scotland. And this would be a great boon as far as the Hebrides and the Islesmen were concerned, and the Argyll situation. So de Bernham was to go as representative, Patrick also, if he wished; but that man asked to be excused, also with all too much to be attended to at home, his Merse earldom in especial demanding much oversight.

There was other news also. A new Pope had at last been elected, the Cardinal Fieschi, taking the style of Innocent the Fourth, and amongst other actions had appointed Otho to be Bishop of Porto, this a distinct demotion for a legate, and to the acclaim of Scotland. Who the new legate would be remained to be seen, but it was hoped that he would be kinder. However, less welcome tidings from the Vatican were that this Innocent had appointed a canon of Florence, one Andrew, to be Abbot of Dunfermline, an extraordinary development which puzzled all the Scots Church. It so happened that the Primate had already nominated a new abbot there. De Bernham, a man of independent mind if ever there was one, objected to the Pope and Innocent declared himself as displeased.

So the problems of border-defining were meantime not forgotten, but left in abeyance until they heard of the Plantagenet's reactions.

And then came further news, and this dire indeed. The bridal couple, returning from Norway, had both drowned, their vessel wrecked in a storm off Orkney. The Bishop of Norway had died with them. Fortunately Bishop de Bernham had been on another ship, further south, and had missed the worst of the storm.

This was grievous in more than the sadness of it all, for the heir to Man was Harold's young brother, Reginald or Ranald, a mere boy. And in the turbulent and warring situation in the Hebrides a child monarch was a recipe for trouble. Alexander feared the worst, and with reason.

De Bernham, who while attending the Norway wedding had been instructed to use the new friendly attitude towards Scotland to try to have the ridiculous situation righted whereby the long Kintyre peninsula was claimed by Norway after King Magnus Barelegs's famous boat-trip over the mile of land between West and East Loch Tarbert. Hakon had only said that he would consider this; but in the new situation resulting from Harold's death, and Hebridean troubles all but certain, the fear was that this folly would not be righted. Not only was Kintyre a seventy-mile-long stretch of Scotland, but it was the closest part of the mainland to Ireland, and so significant strategically. On Alexander's orders de Bernham had offered a substantial sum in silver as inducement, Hakon always being known to be in debt to the Hanseatic League, but this did not clinch the matter. So the situation gave cause for worry. That myriad of long sea lochs penetrating deep into the heart of the mainland could endanger so much of the rest of the kingdom.

The news seemed to be consistently bad. Of all things, Louis the Ninth of France, preparing for his great crusading venture to the Holy Land, fell ill, indeed sank into a trance, out of which it was feared that he would not recover. So concerned was all Christendom about this – save perhaps for the Plantagenet – that the Pope himself hastened to Lyons where Louis lay, to lead prayers for the monarch's recovery and the success of his crusade thereafter, even promising sainthood in the event of their prayers being answered. All churches throughout the kingdoms to join in these supplications.

Whether as a result to all the praying or otherwise, Louis did regain consciousness and began to make a good recovery, vowing to go ahead with his great venture. And Innocent ordered, in gratitude, substantial contributions to be ingathered by every bishop in every land, all magnates to assist or face spiritual penalties. Rejoicing became somewhat more muted.

Meantime Patrick was dealing with the many issues inevitably coming before the ruler of two great earldoms, Pate even more of a help, a young man he and Phemia were proud of. Brother William lingered on, no happy recovery there at Home, and something of a problem. But at Luffness, Elizabeth and her husband David de Lindsay were doing well, repairing and restoring, even building new extensions, dredging the moat and improving the surroundings, and establishing good relations with the Luffnaraw denizens. This young Lindsay was proving an asset to the family.

The news reached Scotland shortly thereafter. Louis of France, despite his recent and alarming illness, had set out on his crusading venture, and was calling on all noble and knightly men who professed the faith of Christ Jesus either to follow him to his rallying-point at Cyprus, or to send their representatives and manpower, in order to expel the infidels who had taken over the Holy Land. God had restored himself to health from near death for this purpose, and all should rally to the godly cause. Pope Innocent further added his urgings to all Christian kings and governors to see that they were fully represented on this endeavour by their highest and best, with fullest contributions in money and shipping to carry the crusading host; not only this, but he required true and detailed reports from all realms as to their efforts in this most important and necessary demonstration of Christian faith and unity.

There had been crusading before, of course, five of them, all less than successful, including Richard Lion Heart's effort; but this of St Louis, as he was already being called, was different, a vastly more general and unified campaign.

Alexander of Scotland called a council.

Before it met, he had a word with Patrick. "My good friend," he said, "this demand from the Vatican places such as myself in a dilemma. If the King of France can go crusading, others could do so. Some may. Richard of England did, and died for it, leaving chaos in his kingdom. Some may say that *I* should do so, follow Louis's lead. But I have only a six-year-old son as heir, a child. And with this of Hakon and the Isles challenging me, I cannot consider leaving an infant in the rule of my kingdom. So I must be represented by others! At this meeting of the council I will have to make my position clear. Yet give a lead. How say you, Pate?"

"You are suggesting that *I* go, Alex?"

"I do not wish to prevail on you. But all know that you are close to me. As well as High Constable of Scotland, bearing our sword of state. You could be seen by all as my personal representative, as none other would. How think you of it?"

Patrick took his time to answer that. "I have two earldoms to look to. And you may need me in this of the Hebrides and Argyll . . ."

"I know it. But even Hakon may be considering this appeal, like other monarchs. And you have your son, whom you say is proving able, worthy, now he is a man."

"You wish me to do this, Alex?"

The other shook his head. "I do not know, rightly. I need you here. And would ever have you by me. But none would serve to lead Scotland's host in this so well as yourself. And it need not be for so long . . ."

"Aye, how long? How long would I be gone? That is the question. Weeks? Months? Even years, perhaps? These Saracens are no feeble foe, as they have shown. Fierce warriors . . ."

"No, no. I would say no lengthy stay. A presence. If the warfare is prolonged, then you would have to come home. Others sent to take your place. This, I judge, would apply to all realms. Louis himself will not wish to be away from France overlong. Kingdoms cannot be left without their leaders for long. After a spell, you would return and be replaced."

Nodding, Patrick could not make refusal. Perhaps he should feel honoured? Perhaps he should be eager to go, a knight for Christ? Take the Cross, as it was said. But . . . leaving Phemia! And he might never come back . . .

"Very well," he said thickly.

Alexander it was who shook head again, as though regretting what had been so decided.

At the council meeting thereafter he announced that the Earl of Dunbar and March, High Constable, would lead a Scottish army in the cause of Christ, under King Louis. He asked for volunteers.

There was no evident surge of enthusiasm. The Holy Land was a long way off, and thought of by most as all but a mythical place, the Jews thereof as little concern of theirs, none so much better than these Saracens. Even the prelates present were scarcely eager, the Primate himself merely observing that the Pope was strong on the matter, as they all knew. Some of the lords said that they would send vassals and contingents, and the clerics that they had already remitted moneys; but only young David de Hastings, the new Earl of Atholl, and Neil, Earl of Carrick, Phemia's sister Margaret's husband, promised to go themselves.

There was much to be discussed other than personal involvement, numbers of men to be provided, shipping to be assembled, provisioning and the like. After the meeting was over, the three earls concerned, with the monarch, got down to details.

Cyprus, where Louis was making his base, with allegedly fifteen thousand men, involved a lengthy voyage, and in ocean-going ships. Best to assemble at Dumbarton, then. So Patrick's own vessels, from Dunbar, Eyemouth and Berwick, would have to sail right round Scotland to reach the Clyde estuary. Others from Leith, the Fife ports, Dundee and Aberdeen also, much organising necessary, apart from all the mustering of manpower. They talked and planned for long.

Next day, home to Dunbar. Phemia had to be told. Patrick did as best he could, well aware of what the news would mean to her.

"Lass," he said, "I am to be off on another of my journeys. This time not to the West March, nor to England, nor even to the Low Countries. Further afield. I am to take the Cross, as they say! To join this crusade of Louis of France. Alexander would have it so. I, I fear that I will be gone for some time."

Eyes widening, she stared at him. "The crusade!" she whispered. "*You!*"

"I did not wish it, my dear. I did not. But he, the king, would have it so. He cannot go himself, with only a child to leave to keep his kingdom. I at least have Pate. He wants me, as Constable and his friend, to lead the Scots force. All the nations have to join in this. Send their thousands. It is not my wish, even though perhaps it should be, in Christ's cause. But I have no choice."

"Patrick! Go to war! Against the heathen Saracens! Oh, my heart, must you? Have you not done sufficient for Alexander without this?"

"I bear his sword of state. Someone must carry it to the Holy Land, it seems. But it may not be for overlong, lass. I can come back after a while. Even though it is not all over.

Another go to take my place. Your sister Margaret's Neil of Carrick is going. Also the new Atholl. And a large host."

Phemia drew herself up and went to the window to gaze out at the waves, silent.

He went to her, to take her in his arms. "Be not so troubled, my dearest," he besought her. "I will take good care of myself, never fear! And come back to you. A month or two . . ."

She turned, gripping him tightly, drawing a deep breath. "If you must, so be it. But . . ." She left the rest unsaid.

They spoke, then, of other things, what must be done in preparation, the shipping, what was required of Pate and herself while he was gone, the Home situation, and more, talk to lessen the impact, to ease acceptance if that was possible.

But that night, in bed, she clung to him and wept quietly.

38

It took a full month to launch the Scots expedition at Dumbarton, Phemia and Pate and David de Lindsay sailing with Patrick round the north of Scotland to see him off. A fleet of about twenty ships had been assembled to carry the fifteen hundred men who formed the Scottish contribution, sufficient, even if fewer than Alexander would have wished.

There was a surprise when the king himself arrived to wish them farewell, a notable gesture. He knighted two or three of the lairdly ones involved, and while he was at it, also David de Lindsay, to give him more authority to act as lieutenant to Pate the Master while Patrick was gone.

The two younger earls were already there, waiting, with their contingents.

The eventual parting there at the quayside was less grievous than it might have been, surrounded by others as Patrick and Phemia were, and talk general if incoherent. Holding each other all but at arm's length, husband and wife gazed into each other's eyes, for moments that were timeless, and said it all without words. Then an almost abrupt kiss, and a turning away.

But, after a pace or two, the man came back, to say, in a strangely positive, certain voice, "I am yours. Always. And always will be. Here and hereafter. Know it, as I do."

She raised a hand to touch his cheek. That was all. But it was enough.

Alexander said, "I will see to her, Pate," as he clasped his friend's arm.

Patrick punched his son on the shoulder, and strode on up the gangplank to his ship's deck.

Of course, casting off, sail-raising and edging out amongst the other vessels took time thereafter; but the bustle and shouting of it all served temporarily to overcome the ache of it, for one man at least. The quayside began to recede.

Patrick had left part of himself thereon.

The *St Ebba* led the way down Clyde.

Not only Patrick, no doubt, was glad of the talk thereafter, of how far they had to go, how long it would take, the route, the lands they would pass, and the like. None of their shipmasters had ever been further than the north of Spain, some fifteen hundred miles, it was reckoned. But that would be well under halfway to their destination, Cyprus, they calculated. The Middle Sea was unknown to all, save by reputation, said to be hazardous and some two thousand and more miles long, and littered with isles, great and small, Cyprus near the far end.

With the continuing south-westerly winds, progress was not fast. It seemed strange, not only to Patrick, to be sailing down past Galloway and the Isle of Man without any warlike intentions. They passed close to the Isle of Anglesey off North Wales and crossed the great Cardigan Bay, all eyeing the Pembroke coast with interest, where King Henry's chief adviser took his title. Then on past the tip of Cape Cornwall, at St Just, steering well clear of the Isles of Scilly beyond, and so out into the open ocean.

They had already sailed almost four hundred miles, and with the contrary winds, had taken three days and nights to do so.

They glimpsed no sign of France thereafter, passing well to the west to make for the north-west tip of Spain, at Corunna, and so down the lengthy coast of Portugal, having avoided the notoriously dangerous Bay of Biscay. Portugal was ever at war with neighbouring Castile, Queen Blanche thereof, Louis's mother, left to rule France while he was gone.

At last, nine days after leaving Clyde, they rounded the great Cape of St Vincent, to turn south-eastwards to cross the Gulf of Cadiz, the hot wind behind them now, and speed improved, to make for the narrow mouth of the Middle Sea, between the headlands of Marroqui of Spain and Almina of Tangier, this last in the Africa of the enemy Muslims, a landmark indeed.

Into that strange land-locked sea they sailed, the wind now suddenly dropped save for unexpected and occasional gusts with their own dangers, the heat become a concern for the travellers, crews as well as passengers. None had ever been in these waters before, and with the unpredictable winds and with islands to look out for as well as the possibility of attacks by Muslim ships, the Scots skippers were more than uneasy. However, after a day of it, they were joined by a small fleet from Seville, a province of Spain from which the occupying infidels had only recently been driven out, and which was now gallantly supporting the crusade. So, sailing along behind this, the Scots were spared much anxiety.

Three days were spent before they reached the Balearic Isles of Majorca and Minorca, now well out of sight of the African shores. And still on eastwards for another two hundred and fifty miles, to the huge, mountainous island of Sardinia, none so much smaller than Ireland. Sicily lay ahead, with the Muslim peninsula of Cape Bon of Tunisia just in sight. So far, although they had seen individual low-built ships, presumably enemy craft, there had been no fleets, no challenges. One more large island, Crete, had to be passed before reaching Cyprus apparently.

Well before they arrived at their eventual destination, they were sailing amongst groups of shipping, some larger fleets than their own, all heading eastwards, and flying the banners of kingdoms, principalities and dukedoms. Louis was going to have no lack of support.

Cyprus proved to be extensive, the third largest island of the Middle Sea, lengthy between two mountain ranges, reaching eastwards for about one hundred and forty miles, although only a third of that in width. There were, it seemed, many ports; but Famagusta at the eastern end was the principal one, where Louis had established his head-quarters and where they had been instructed to proceed.

Along a varied coastline of cliffs and bays and sandy beaches they sailed, and they found Famagusta Bay, although large, so full of ships that there was no room for the Scots and Seville fleets. They had to go on further eastwards still, finally to cast anchor. The village of Salamis here was small, and no place to house hundreds of men, so all would have to sleep in their cramped quarters aboard the vessels, however much they might stretch their legs walking during the day.

And walking it had to be. The assembled hosts, all come by sea, were without horses. How this was going to affect their forthcoming assault on the Saracens remained to be seen; but the knightly fighters, used to mounted warfare, were bound to find it a major handicap.

Next day, then, Patrick and the two other earls had to walk to Famagusta, to report the Scots arrival to King Louis, very feeble-seeming as this struck them. But at the great port they found that Louis was not there presently, but north at Nicosia, the capital of the island, where the so-called King of Jerusalem had his seat. Richard Lion Heart had captured Cyprus from the Saracens and installed the Lusignan family there, whom the first crusade had made titular monarchs of the Holy City.

Nicosia was apparently a score of miles from Famagusta westwards, inland, so that it was no place to walk to; presumably Louis must have *some* horses. So he would have to do without word of the latest arrivals for his host meantime. His brother, Prince Robert of Artois, remained at the port however, and to him Patrick made his report. It seemed that Louis had brought his queen with him, as well as two brothers. From the prince they learned that the host now numbered about thirty-five thousand, a goodly force to confront the infidel. When the assault would commence they were not told.

They returned to Salamis. With all their crusading mouths to be fed, they realised that provisions would be scarce, however fertile were some parts of the island. They would have to set their men to sea-fishing.

It was almost a week before they were summoned to Famagusta, to meet Louis. He proved to be a handsome and very approachable man in his mid-thirties. He welcomed the Scots cordially, thanked them for their support and said that he had heard only good of their King Alexander. He declared that his intention was, within the next few days, to assail the Egyptian coast and seek to take the fortress of Damietta. Lacking horses, his strategy was to be siegery, and so to have the Saracens come to *them*, not go challenging them on their own ground, and to force them to fight afoot also. If Damietta fell, they would besiege other fortresses, Cairo, Acre to the east and Tunis to the west, their great fleet of ships their notable asset. The food situation for the host was becoming a problem on this island, so a move soon, without waiting for further reinforcements to arrive. Let the infidel's lands feed them!

The sooner the better as far as the Scots were concerned. Meanwhile they could help in the construction of siege-machinery, battering-rams, ballista, mangonels, catapults, slings, and the making of rope-ladders, attached to ships' anchors as grapnels. That was better than idle waiting.

So at last the great venture commenced, no fewer than one hundred and fifty ships carrying the thousands of men and all the arms and siege-equipment setting sail south by west for Egypt and the mouth of the Nile, where stood the fortress of Damietta guarding the river which was the principal trade route for so much of North Africa. It was none so far off, by Middle Sea standards, less than three hundred miles. They would time it to approach under cover of darkness, if possible.

Local shipmen guiding them, they were told that Damietta lay some nine miles from the sea, on the right bank of the main mouth of the Nile, in a wide delta area which contained other lesser outlets of the river, making a difficult approach, with a wide sand bar all but closing all at low tide. Only the one approach was possible, therefore, for sea-going vessels; and the deep channel being fairly narrow, ships would have to enter it singly, in line, all of which would demand careful planning. The nine miles from salt water could not be negotiated in darkness, and this meant that total surprise of the fortress was impossible. However, the flats of the delta were empty mud and sand, and unoccupied by man or beast. But if the guards at the fort were watchful, they would have ample warning of the approach of a long line of ships.

Louis and his lieutenants had to take all this into consideration. Problems there were, but also certain advantages in that the fortress, being part surrounded by the river, could be challenged from the ships as well as from land; and any enemy attempts at support or reinforcement would be very difficult.

Then there was the question of numbers. To besiege a stronghold, and with ships taking part, how many men would be needed? Certainly not thirty-five thousand. If a large army of Saracens came to try to relieve the fortress, then many more would be required. But still such a total? Cairo was the main seat of the Sultan Salih-Ayyab of Egypt, and none so far off. But other important bases of the infidel were as far west as Tunis and east at Acre in Palestine. If detachments of the crusading host were to be sent thither they could well have the effect of preventing aid coming to the sultan at Damietta and Cairo. So, say, ten thousand each to those two outlying areas, still leaving fifteen thousand for the Nile siege? Sufficient, surely?

This was agreed. Prince Robert of Artois, then, would take one force westwards to Tunis, and his brother, John of Joinville, one east to Acre.

The dividing up of the fleet and manpower in the darkness off the Egyptian coast was inevitably somewhat chaotic, ships being detached more or less at random, rather like a shepherd and dogs might split up a flock of sheep. It was not until much later that Patrick discovered that David of Atholl had gone off to Tunis with some part of the Scots fleet, leaving himself and Neil of Carrick with Louis's main section.

By first light they were heading into the river-mouth, at half-tide, with mudflats stretching far on either side. It was exciting to think that this was Africa, all but a different world, the heat, even at this hour, certainly confirming it. The land ahead appeared to be mainly flat, with no cliffs and prominences. Patrick had been expecting to see the Damietta fortress distant on a rock-top, or at least on hills, but nothing such showed.

The ships were in single file now, and the Scots ones well down the line, all proceeding slowly, for there was little wind, and the river flowing fairly strongly against them. At length they came in sight of their destination, and found the fortress very different from those to which most of them were used, not standing high but lying between two wide moats fed from the Nile, its tall yellow walls, of seemingly octagon shape, rising massively, but no central keep or angle towers. Beyond this lay a township, with wharves and quays and storehouses, the trading port of Damietta. The river made a great semicircle round the fort.

The crusaders were faced with problems. The ships were not going to be able to get close to those walls, as had been hoped. Not only that, but there was no room for all the seventy or so vessels to line up nearby on the river. There was nothing for it but that most of them should land their men and then go on to moor at the quays of the port, which meant that a sizeable company of men must be left aboard to ensure that they were not attacked and taken over by the townsfolk, this after unloading the siege-machinery.

Patrick, landing with most of his men, was summoned to a council by King Louis. They could see heads above the parapets of the fort. They were being watched, but so far no obvious action being taken.

Louis discussed this situation with the leadership. Somehow they must get the siege-engines across those wide moats. Rafts were required, and while ferrying these they would be under attack by arrows from the walling. Somehow rafts must be constructed, using any wood available, this some of the supports of the engines themselves, ships' boats, boarding, anything that would float. Also portable overhead shelters would be required, to protect the rafters from arrows. All this would, of course, take time, and allow the Saracens to muster forces to come and aid the besieged. So meantime a major proportion of their manpower must go to form a defensive ring round the town to counter any such attack developing from inland.

Patrick and his Scots were amongst those allocated for this duty. They marched off, with more than half the host, along the curving riverside and through the town with its strange flat-roofed buildings, from which the inhabitants stared at them askance. But no actual assault developed. Beyond the town, at a wide bend in the river, they took up their positions in a great arc, this under the command of another of Louis's brothers, newly arrived from France, Charles of Anjou.

The array settled down, facing south and east, the river at their backs and this, lacking bridging, providing ample security at their rear. Cairo, the sultan's capital, lay due south about one hundred miles, and presumably it was from there that attack might be expected. They encamped, and under Prince Charles's orders, began to dig trenches and ditches before them, as defensive measures.

For his part, Patrick, like others, used to mobile and horsed warfare, found all this unsatisfactory, irritating, boring, just to sit there waiting. And when, almost certainly, the Saracen hosts arrived, they would be horsed and with the advantage, these ditches and thrown-up ramparts far from unsurmountable. It made a poor prospect, and hardly what they had come all this way to face, inactive.

As two days and nights passed, and three, the discontent grew, and not only amongst the Scots. Presumably those back at the fortress would be less disenchanted, they at least having positive action in view, not that raft-building would be very inspiring work; but with siegery to look forward to, perhaps already begun.

Patrick had to admit to himself that he was not used to being comparatively unimportant in this campaigning, under the command of others. Always he had been a leader, not the led; he here had princes, dukes and the like in control, and his position was minor. This, together with the inactivity, had a negative effect on him, although he told himself that it should not.

On the fourth day of it, however, tidings from Louis changed all. The fortress had fallen, the siege brief but successful. The battering-rams, catapults and mangonels, once in position, had been very effective against the soft local sandstone walling, and great gaps had been made, through which the attackers could gain entrance without having to use those grapnels and rope-ladders. The defenders proved to have been comparatively few, and although they had fought well, had been vastly outnumbered and quickly put down. So it was victory, at least initially so, Louis's strategy vindicated.

Satisfaction high, Louis declared his intentions now. They would sail on up Nile heading for Cairo itself, the sultan's seat. Salih Ayyab was said to be sickening, and this might well favour their cause. The objective was to capture Cairo and as many other Egyptian cities and towns as was possible, and thereafter barter these for the Holy Land cities further east taken and occupied by the Saracens: Damascus, Haifa, Jaffa, Tyre and Sidon; indeed Jerusalem itself, the principal target. The first successful steps had been taken in this ambitious project.

So, leaving a small garrison to hold the captured fort, the army re-embarked, to sail their ships up the great river, known to be navigable for many hundreds of miles, spirits high, Cairo ahead, a mile of strung-out vessels.

Progress was slow against the strong current, with winds fitful. It was reckoned that fifty miles in a day would be as much as they could expect to cover.

In the event, fifty miles was to prove as far as they did

cover, and not only for that first day. For just before the fall of darkness, sudden in these parts, they saw ahead of them a major community, no village this like many they had passed. And as they neared it, they realised that this was a fortified city within high walls. None of Louis's people knew what this might be; but clearly it was something that they could not just sail past and leave behind them. Like Damietta, it used a major bend in the Nile for its protection; but it was very much larger. Another siege, then? So soon?

The fleet drew in, to anchor a couple of miles from the city, and one of their smaller craft was sent forward to prospect, dark as it quickly became, while Louis held another council.

The question was, seal this city off by leaving, say, a couple of thousand men to surround it, and the rest go on for Cairo? Or all assail it now? They had already left some of their force back at Damietta to hold it as garrison; if they left more here, their numbers would be the less for their main objective, the sultan's capital; and who knew what other strengths they might come across on this river on their way thither, requiring to be dealt with also. They could not go on reducing their array. Attack here, then, in the morning.

Their scouting vessel returned presently, to inform that this was no modest challenge ahead, a fortress indeed with mighty battlements, even the harbour area protected by buttressed walls and a gatehouse. They would be able to get some of their ships close to sections of the walling there, unlike Damietta, but they might only be able to win access to the port area, which itself could be protected by further defences. They had all but run down a belated fishing-boat and had captured its two-man crew, and these, although their language was not to be understood, had declared that the city was called Al Mansurah.

This information, despite its serious implications, did not alter their proposed tactics, however much it might delay them. They could not leave this place behind them unassailed.

That hot night they all underwent a new experience, mists of a choking sort rising from the river and its marshy surroundings, with clouds of biting insects. Such had not troubled them at Damietta, which was presumably spared it by the salty water and sea air. But now they were deep inland, with deserts none so far off beyond these marshes, they imagined; and this night-time misery could be normal, a trial indeed, reminding the Scots of the lesser plague of midges of a summer evening at home. How did the folk of this Al Mansurah put up with it? Perhaps they grew immune in time, or had some means of countering it.

It did not make for a restful night.

Daylight at least gave them all relief from this infliction. The fleet hoisted sail and moved up to the city. They saw that here also moats had been dug to prevent access by ships to the main walling; but not, of course, at the harbour approaches. Here the defences rose directly out of the river itself; how this contrived, they knew not.

There was an arched entrance to the port area, under a sort of gatehouse, from which a massive iron barrier had been dropped to prevent entry, not unlike that at Patrick's Dunbar Castle, although on a much larger scale. So no ingress there. But right and left of this stretched some hundreds of yards of the defensive walling, to which they could get their vessels close. So here they could attempt some battering attack from the ships, while men were disembarking further, to march round the landward side of the city to complete its encirclement. Patrick had feared that he and his would again be chosen for this dull, waiting duty, but fortunately not; they would be part of the assailing force here.

As the ships closed in, all were left in no doubt that their presence was awaited, however unwelcome. Showers of arrows began to reach them from the walling parapet, and, close-packed, men fell. But they had manufactured those shelters for protecting the rafts at Damietta, made of sailcloth and planking, held up on poles, and these did serve their purpose fairly well; that is, until fire-arrows were substituted, and these, oil-soaked cloth attached, were not long in setting fire to the canopy. And not only that but the ships' rigging and furled sails, even the decking, a dire development demanding much activity from the waiting men, at considerable danger to themselves, with ordinary arrows continuing to come over amongst them. Men sought to cover themselves with anything that came to hand, over and above their padded defensive doublets of leather, Hitherto discarded on account of the heat, like their steel helmets. Those with knightly armour, of course, suffered least.

Under these conditions, battering at walling from the vessels' sides was difficult to effect and maintain, hard as it was to position the rams, although the catapults could operate well enough. The task was at least made less difficult by the sandstone of the barrier, once again, so much softer than the stone and rock with which they were familiar at home, this very vulnerable to the steel-tipped snouts of the heavy rams. Once a hole was made in the facing, thick as the walling was, it could be pecked and dug at until a cavity was driven through, and this then enlarged to offer access for men to scramble through. A sufficiency of these, and entry could be attempted, men carrying the rope-ladders with them, required at the other side.

All this would have to be synchronised, so that the defenders were spread out, dispersed as far as possible. Those up on the parapet-walk would find it difficult to reach the attackers, but men waiting below would be in a good position to assail them as they came down the ladders. So the entire attack had to be further complicated by, at the same time, tossing up grapnels and their knotted ropes to hook on to the crenellations and allow other men to climb up, there to confront the arrow-shooters and distract them from seeking to assail the comrades who were making the gaps in the walling. These climbers also to seek to hurl down missiles on enemy at the wall-foots, to prevent them slaying the descenders.

Patrick was amongst those who chose to climb the ropes,

heavy work in his chain-mail and steel helmet, and with a mace to clutch, sword meantime at side, the knots on the rope making it possible, but only just. At least they could not be effectively shot at with arrows while so engaged. Other climbers were encouraging each other with shouts.

He made it to the parapet more slowly than some because of his armour, and climbed over on to the wall-walk, to the clash of steel, the archers now being engaged by his colleagues. Because these were bowmen, the enemy were less quick with their swords, and were being dealt with fairly effectively, especially those leaning over the inner parapet and concerned with what was going on below. Patrick saw one such opposite him, seeking to train his crossbow at a steep angle to shoot at the attackers entering through the gaps, and he had the satisfaction of striking the aimer at the back of his neck with his mace and seeing him topple over and fall the forty or so feet amongst the chaos of assailants and defenders down there: the first blow he had struck so far in this campaign.

Elsewhere others were similarly engaged, the attackers having the advantage, the bowmen tending to be preoccupied with what was going on behind them as well as in front. With many more coming up the ropes from the ships, it was not long before the parapet-walk was cleared of the enemy, and Patrick was able to shout down to the vessels urging no more climbers. Then, those up on the wall head were able to draw up the ropes, carry them over to the other side and drop them down, hooking the grapnels securely. The descent began, to join in the fighting below.

By the time Patrick was down amongst it, the defenders, such as were able, were already retiring along piers and quays towards the city. The attackers waited for a sizeable company to assemble through those holes in the walling, before themselves moving in some sort of order after the enemy.

The harbour area was by no means full of vessels. But this was not what was occupying Patrick's attention. It was the fact that ahead of them another line of high walling screened off the port from the city proper, and into the two great gateways in this the discomfited enemy were streaming. So, more battering work to be needed, for no doubt there would be the iron portcullises lowered here also to bar undesired entry.

Sure enough, before the newcomers were halfway there, they heard the clanging of the great gates being dropped down, further access denied.

Patrick turned back to see to the raising of that outer portcullis which they had managed to bypass, to allow their ships to enter this harbour, or some of them. So far, so good. But this second barrier might take as much overcoming as the first.

In the event it took more, for it quickly became evident that these inner walls were higher and stronger that the port's ones, and moreover were more heavily manned. Arrows began to come over in showers from them, and the would-be attackers drew back out of range, to wait.

Presently the first ship came in slowly, with Louis and his leaders aboard, to survey the scene, congratulate the attackers thus far, and to plan the next stage, Patrick receiving his share of the plaudits. Conferring thereafter, they saw that the one advantage here was that the siege-machinery could be landed from ships on to the quayside and so reach the wall-foots readily and effectively. But those arrows. Clearly there were more archers here, many more, and once within range of these, getting the rams and catapults against those walls was going to be a bloody business indeed. More shelters would have to be constructed, and less inflammable ones. Solid wood, if possible, would be best, however heavy to bear up. At least there were these enemy vessels, mainly fishing-boats, but some larger, to break up and use. But that would take time, much time.

Was there any chance of a sally out against them from the city? Probably not while the enemy could sit secure within those walls. But they must be prepared for such.

A strange situation developed then, the attackers keeping well out of arrow range, and busy, more ships and men being brought in from the river. The local vessels were boarded, all deserted by their crews, and brought to positions where they could be all but demolished, their lighter timbers used to build the so necessary shelters, no easy task without proper tools and only ropes and twine available for joining and tying up.

Evening came, and although some of the work could go on in darkness, the mist and insect misery recommenced, to cursing. Some of the crusaders were already swollen severely with bites, and with not a few complaining of dizziness and nausea, undoubtedly from the bites. So much for fighting in Christ's cause. Most men elected to spend the night either in the ships' cabins or under sailcloth, which helped in some measure to restrict the onslaught of the urgent flies.

Patrick was amongst the many who knew dizziness, with swollen skin, next morning, King Louis also, and indeed Prince Robert of Artois a sick man.

The slow and lengthy task of shelter-building from broken-up boats went on that day, and by mid-afternoon it was reckoned that sufficient had been constructed to cover the handling and pushing forward of the rams and mangonels. A start was made, no great numbers of men necessary for this, the remainder standing back. Promptly the arrows came, fire as well as the other sort. The watchers were glad to see that the shelters seemed to be effective, some smouldering going on but no actual catching alight of the timbering.

The machinery reached the stonework, and the battering commenced.

More shelters were required, of course, for the attacking force to reach the walling, but not until worthwhile gaps had been created; so all kept out of range. The defenders had now started to drop bundles of oil-soaked flaming cloth from the parapet down upon the shelters over the rams, and these did have more effect on the wood, for they burned for longer; but still the battering was able to go on.

The hole-digging seemed to take a long time, and meantime the mass of the force could only stand idly. It made a very strange sort of warfare, so different from anything even the most seasoned fighters were used to. Some of them, to be sure, were still making more shelters.

At last, the signal was given. There were sufficient gaps large enough to offer entry. Advance, then.

The arrow hail resumed, but the canopies, heavy as they were to carry on their poles, were very effective, and there were few casualties. Patrick had organised a larger rope-climbing party, and these spread themselves along the walling with their grapnels. The blazing cloths were now a major menace; but it was difficult for the hurlers thereof to drop them accurately on individuals directly below without themselves becoming targets for the cru-saders' own archers. Grapnels of course could be un-hooked and cast down, with their ropes and climbers, and some attackers fell thus; but with all the arrow-shoot-ing and the cloth-kindling and carrying, the enemy could not use all the defensive measures to the full, especially with a proportion of them concerned with seeking to drop more flares on the mob below who were passing through those gaps.

Patrick, self-appointed leader of this parapet assault, came to near disaster himself when a spell of dizziness came over him when halfway up his own rope and he all but fell, having to hang there, tightly clutching one of the knots, until his head cleared sufficiently to carry on up. These strange attacks could be affecting others also, he recognised.

Up on the walkway, he found no enemy to assail personally, all being dealt with. So he decided to move along to the right, ordering others to do the same to the left, realising that this walling would extend all the way round the city, and others of the enemy could be coming from unassailed parts to the aid of the fellows hereabouts.

Once past the harbour area, however, he found no opposition positioned, and guessed that the manpower of Al Mansurah was probably fully stretched for ground-level defence. So he returned, and helped in the transferring of the ropes and the descent thereafter to the turmoil below.

He and his were scarcely needed there, however, for the enemy were already beginning to retire all the way along the line towards the nearby city streets. Louis and his lords were restraining their people from pushing on after the retreating foe. The attack on the town itself must be conducted in a disciplined and orderly fashion, as far as was possible, if utter confusion was not to arise, and control be maintained. Messages were sent back to inform the other section of the army presently blockading the landward side of the city that entry had been won, and for them to make assaults on the walls there to help draw off such of the defensive force as might be possible.

The sudden darkness of these parts, with its mists and flies, was about to descend on all when, as fully marshalled as might be, leaving only a modest guard on the ships in the harbour, Louis led his host on into the town, with strict instructions as to keeping in touch, not penetrating far up side streets and alleyways, order and control the key.

They met with only occasional and unco-ordinated attack, easily dealt with, the governor of the city evidently having lost any unified command. With darkness and mist taking over, and no lights showing now, it proved to be a most curious sort of victory, if such it could be called. They had won entry to the city, but had they won the city? Until daylight they could not be sure.

The leadership having reached the furthest eastern walling, and opened the gates there without any serious opposition, the besiegers at the side could come in to join them, or some of them, a sufficiency being left beyond in case of any assault from the land. There was no point in seeking to penetrate, infiltrate and take over the maze and network of narrow, twisting lanes, yards and passages of this warren of a town in these circumstances, with all their strange, secret housing, where the city folk were lying low. Nothing for it but to wait until daylight to assess the situation, meantime remaining watchful, ready. There could be little sleep for the occupiers. They must just congregate in the few open spaces, market-places, mosque-yards and the like, inside the mosques for some indeed, to escape the flies. Some fires could be lit, from purloined furniture, in the hope that the flames and smoke might dispel some of the insects.

A grim and wakeful night was passed, but without attack other than from the winged enemy. Most there envied their comrades left to guard the ships.

In the morning it was possible to make a more intensive but still far from thorough inspection of the city, the folk in the main still keeping within their houses. A circuit of the walling revealed two lesser gates, both standing open, out of which presumably some of the defending enemy had made their escape in darkness, possibly whoever had been in command.

What next, then? With much of this sickness prevalent amongst the crusading force, Louis himself far from well, it was felt that any onward advance towards Cairo was scarcely advisable meantime. Rest and feeding for their men was essential. They would remain at Al Mansurah for a day, at least. Many went seeking food and drink, the wounded were attended to, and most were thankful to sleep.

It was mid-afternoon when the alarm sounded. Messengers came hastening from the landward units to announce that a large host, horsed, was approaching from the east.

This news had its very positive effect on all. If this was the sultan's army, coming from Cairo or wherever, then what was to be their best tactic? Mounted, they would be much advantaged over the crusaders. Get back to the ships, then? But would they have time to get all out of the city and aboard, and then on to the Nile? Not if the enemy was approaching fast. All within the walls, then, and the gates closed, those two posterns as well as the main entrances.

Patrick, for one, doubted the wisdom of this. To shut themselves up in this city they would become the besieged instead of the besiegers. Better to get their people out somehow into the ships in the harbour and out on the river. The horsed enemy would have difficulty in stopping that, at least at this stage. They might be able to summon up boats from further up-Nile, but that would take time.

Louis, however, decided that they should remain where they were, secure, until the situation became clearer.

So, the crusaders found themselves manning those parapet-walks on the wallheads, organising their defence, all along the landward side, crossbows and arrows gathered, and cloth and oil sought to set alight if and when necessary. It was all an extraordinary reversal of roles.

The enemy approach was certainly alarming to behold. How many thousands of horsemen were coming into view was hard to estimate, for they came on in groups of varying sizes, and spread over a great area of empty level land east of the Nile; but it was a vast host, and more ever appearing, out of the distant dust-clouds raised by so many horses over a dry land. What could those thousands do? The horses would be of no help to them in assailing these high walls, but only if it came to hand-to-hand fighting. For all their numbers, the Saracens would be faced with the same problems as had confronted Louis's army. Would they have any siege-engines? Probably not, but they could construct such, no doubt, in time. Time, that was the essence of it all, this also for the likely collecting of boats which could in the end wipe out the advantage the crusaders had in their ships.

This recognition, the time factor, became ever more clearly the concern of Louis's leaders. To remain besieged in this walled city was a sure recipe for disaster, time-wise as in other respects. The population would much outnumber them and would gradually whittle away their strength. The food situation, already serious, would become dire. And in enemy country the besiegers would no doubt grow and grow in numbers. And also growing was the sickness produced by these climate conditions.

They must get away, out to their ships, and back to salt water, quickly. Not complete retiral, with a return to the Middle Sea and Cyprus – that would be a sorry end to their great enterprise. But at least to Damietta, the fortress not the town. That smaller strength they could probably hold, within its moats, where the horsemen would be further disadvantaged. And there send for their two detachments, at Tunis and Acre, this doubling their strength again, and being able to challenge the Saracens effectively.

It was decided to effect their withdrawal to the ships that very night, difficult as this would be in the conditions prevailing.

In the darkness, mists and flies, unpleasant it was but no formidable task to marshal their coughing men and march out through the two gates to the harbour area, hoping that the enemy meantime would not start assailing the landward walls and gain undefended entry behind them. Getting their numbers on to the ships took time, amidst some inevitable confusion; but still without attack from the rear. Then the overcrowded vessels to be edged out through the port gate, to join their other craft waiting at the river, and a redistribution of the men to the various ships, all less than simple in the gloom, and with the injured and sick to take along. Inevitably not all Patrick's Scots got on to the same ships.

Then, with little in the way of wind to fill their sails, it was off northwards, in line, for Damietta.

That fifty miles, in these conditions, took them until noon next day. Their approach could not go unnoticed from the town, of course, and sailing past it to the fortress they could see men hurriedly leaving the latter, townsfolk no doubt who had entered it but had no desire to become involved in another siege.

In the event, disembarking their force, they had no

difficulty in gaining access to the stronghold, for although the portcullises had been lowered again, the walls were not manned. They found the place deserted.

It was now just a matter of settling in, manning the defences, and sending out foraging parties, on both sides of the river, to try to collect a sufficiency of food. Fortunately there were a number of small delta communities where armed men could appropriate the mutton, goat's meat, poultry and meal so greatly needed. Ships were sent off east and west to summon back those detachments.

After all their activities it was now a matter of waiting for developments. And hoping that the sickness, which was being called the plague, did not further smite them, for here near the sea they were spared the mists and insects of the inland areas.

Patrick, himself far from fit, was glad of the rest, like so many others, King Louis himself included. Only four days they had, with fair quantities of food arriving, before the expected opposition materialised, and that of course before the reinforcements from Tunis and Acre could possibly reach them. The Saracens' horsed host loomed up from the south seemingly in vaster numbers than ever. It was to be siege again. Their ships were sent down-river to escape any possible attempts at boarding and taking over, until their forces from east and west arrived. The fortress was put into a state of twenty-four-hour defence.

It was not long before they were totally surrounded, with the enemy host establishing itself in encampment beyond the moats, as though for prolonged stay. This aspect of the situation did not greatly worry the defenders, for the longer they camped there, hoping to starve out the besieged, the greater opportunity for the crusading allies to arrive in their ships, and a joint assault could be mounted, from river and fortress, to seek to rout the dispersed enemy.

But that was not to be. That same night, the Saracens' attempt to take the stronghold began, considerably after darkness had fallen, and in unexpected fashion. Fires began to appear from all around the walling, so evidently the enemy had managed to cross the moats, probably by pontoon bridges made up of fishing-boats, these fires large and blazing brightly, lighting up the night. But it was not for light that these fires were lit. From them presently came flaring missiles hurled into the air, presumably from catapults, these to soar high over the walling and to fall in to the buildings behind. Not just small flares attached to fire-arrows these, but probably large bundles of cloth or blanketing, oil-soaked again, which would continue to blaze for long, hundreds of them. These Egyptians were evidently great fire-raisers. And these tactics were eminently successful, for very quickly the dry wooden roofings of the fortress were ablaze, the entire night becoming a sort of red and smoke-filled hell on earth, and the Damietta fort an inferno. And still the fusilade of fire continued, many of the missiles now aimed to fall on the parapet walls themselves, affecting the defenders there. What havoc they were creating amongst the men on the ground within, Patrick, himself up on the walk, could only guess at.

The enemy seemed to have an unlimited supply of whatever their fire-ball projectiles were made of, and of oil, for they kept on coming. The screams of burned men rang out all around, with individuals to be seen in the lurid glare running about on the walk beating at flaming hair and clothing.

Patrick realised that fire-arrows were coming up also, this when one such ripped the upturned collar of the padded leather jerkin he wore beneath his shirt of chain-mail. Another inch or so to the right and it would have been the end of him. But even so the blazing arrow set fire to such hair as hung below his helmet. Dropping his mace and dirk, he sought to beat out the burning tresses, scarcely aware of the pain.

He did manage to quell the small conflagration which the left side of his head had seemed to become; but the steel of his helmet had become fiercely hot with the blaze, although the arrow itself had fallen away. He tore off the morion, which was increasing his dizziness and pain, and cast it from him. Then, head in a swim, he stooped to pick up his weapons. But in his staggering, he had moved some way from them. Still bent and griping, he suddenly realised, somewhat dazed as he was, that it was not mace or dirk which was there before his searching, unsteady gaze, but feet, feet in some sort of sandals under a flowing robe.

Gasping, he straightened up, to stare, but not for long, although perhaps his stare went far indeed. Far, and continued even after he fell to the flagstones of the walk, his bare head cleft through with a Muslim sword. He was seeing right back beyond the red glare to a bright, gleaming, golden light from which Phemia's loving, tender smile came to him, so welcoming, so understanding, so much his for ever and ever. Phemia . . . !

Cospatrick, sixth Earl of Dunbar and first of March, went to join his forebears, and there to wait for Phemia.

EPILOGUE

Damietta fell to the Saracens, and the sick King Louis was captured, along with thousands of others, this before the contingents of his force from Tunis and Acre could arrive. In a battle at the former, David, Earl of Atholl, had fallen. But Louis, ransomed by the new sultan for an enormous sum, survived, to lead another crusade twenty years later, equally unsuccessful, on which he himself died of the plague.

Back in Scotland, King Alexander was not long in following his friend Patrick to a better realm. He led an expedition to the Highland West that same year of 1249 when he heard that Hakon of Norway had appointed Ewan, Lord of Argyll, grandson of Somerled, to be King of Man and the Hebrides in place of the drowned Harold, and this Ewan was accepting Hakon as his overlord, rejecting Alexander as sovereign over Argyll and all the mainland territory. Queen Marie had sought to dissuade her husband from going on this expedition, for he had been suffering bouts of sickness; but he went, with Alan Dorward acting as High Constable in Patrick's place. The king died of a fever on the small isle of Kerrera, off Oban. His seven-year-old son became Alexander the Third, King of Scots, with an angry Hakon of Norway threatening trouble.